COUNT ME OUT

By Russell James in Foul Play Press

COUNT ME OUT

Russell James

A Foul Play Press Book

W. W. Norton & Company
New York   London

For my wife Jill,
with thanks for everything.

Copyright © 1996 by Russell James
First published in 1996 by Serpent's Tail
4 Blackstock Mews, London N4
First American edition 1997
First published by Foul Play Press, a division of
W. W. Norton & Company, New York

For information about permission to reproduce selections
from this book, write to Permissions,
W. W. Norton & Company, Inc., 500 Fifth Avenue,
New York, NY 10110

A complete catalogue record for this book can be obtained
from the British Library on request.

Library of Congress Cataloging-in-Publication Data
James, Russell.
        Count me out / Russell James.—1st American ed.
        p.   cm.
        ISBN 0-88150-384-3
        I. Title.
        PR6060.A473C6   1997
        823'.914—dc21   96-40475
                                        CIP

W. W. Norton & Company, Inc.
500 Fifth Avenue, New York, NY 10110
http://web.wwnorton.com

W. W. Norton & Company Ltd.
10 Coptic Street, London WC1A 1PU

1 2 3 4 5 6 7 8 9 0

BOOK ONE

ONE

In the the cooling darkened room the only visible part of her body was a naked shoulder—round, hard and smooth as a baby's kneecap. Across the pillow the girl's brown hair lay like a stole. Her warm tangled bed held the scent of sweat and body fluids mingled with perfume, and when Jet moved beside her she hardly stirred. He could smell guttered candle and unfinished wine.

For several seconds he stared dully at the wall. When he twisted to look at the girl a second time, the room began to spin around his head. He closed his eyes but it continued whirling. Inside his cranium his brain slurped like loose porridge in a bowl. He placed his hands beside his forehead.

The girl shifted. He looked at her sheet of tangled hair and wondered who she was. Whether it might matter. He watched his left hand—someone's hand—yes, it was his— drift towards her head to lift the hair away from her face. A faint memory came seeping back. The girl mumbled, looked for a moment as if she might open her eyes, but she couldn't make it. He dropped her hair.

As the motion of the room slowed to match his dead-ened pulse, Jet tried to think. He didn't often behave like this. Not often. Hardly ever. When was the last time he had wakened in the night with a pretty stranger by his side? When—*what was the time*?

As he fumbled beside the bed, the girl grumbled behind

his back. He couldn't find his watch. Was it on the floor? Tumbling off the mattress, his knee bumped against the floor, making her complain again. He found the lamp and switched it on.

She became more vocal, sat up in bed, and raised one hand to shield her eyes from the glare. Jet looked at her breasts, but they did not identify her. He stooped to peep below her hand. 'Trying to find my watch.'

'Want to time yourself?'

She cautiously removed her hand. He said, 'You look good.'

They examined each other blankly. She saw Jet's naked muscular frame, his tousled black hair and lazy smile, and decided there were worse things a girl could discover beside her bed. She said, 'Um, now you've woken me up—'

'Seen my watch?'

As if that would interest her. He stood up carefully and tottered through to the other room. He had an attractive bum but seemed obsessed about the time.

'Jesus Christ!'

That sounded bad, she thought.

'One o'clock.'

It was bad.

'Listen, I'm sorry, but um . . .'

'You have to go.'

She had one final consoling glimpse of him—bollock naked was the phrase—clutching a bundle of clothes to his chest and smiling apologetically as if he meant it. Then he said, 'I'm sorry. I have to get home to Stella.'

One o'clock in the morning, his brother Scott is awake as well. Two hours' sleep but fully alert. It keeps happening to him now. He lies in bed, eyes staring, mind racing, trying not to move in case he disturbs Claire. When they were first married, Scott had enjoyed talking with her in the night—about the way she had transformed their rented flat, and then, two years later, about how she was working miracles in their new house. They spent evenings and weekends decorating. When they had covered every surface, Claire embroidered cushion covers, made patchwork quilts, bought trinkety ornaments to stand on shelves. She had been particular about it, but not obsessed. Scott found it comforting—even flattering—to have her fuss about him, build a nest. Then he lost the job. He had been a manager at Fords in Dagenham, had stayed with them six years—till the redundancies. Fords was almost the only job he had had. Just as Claire wanted a tidy house, Scott Heywood wanted a tidy life.

After his dismissal, Scott spent eight weeks on the dole. He chased every job, bought every paper, wrote a string of letters without reply. The first interview he got, he accepted the post they offered because he had already decided to turn nothing down. That evening he sat with Claire to persuade her that, the way things were, he was lucky to get any job—even as a driver for a security firm. For the next year, Claire encouraged him to keep applying for better jobs. He doesn't bother to do that any more, though Claire thinks he does.

Now he visits the local library every week. When Claire asks where he finds time to read all those books, whether he skims through or doesn't finish them, he smiles and describes the stories, wondering why he is not affected by lack of sleep. Some nights he stays out of bed three hours, has some tea, half reads a book, and then returns to doze beside her till the alarm. She never knows.

Tonight Scott eases himself gently out of bed, into the familiar slippers and dressing gown, then slips out through the bedroom door. He creeps downstairs and she does not stir.

But little Tommy is also awake. Like his father a few

minutes before, the boy lies staring in the dark, absorbing the velvet silence of the house. Unlike his father he has stayed in bed, lying on his back. When Tommy wakes late at night, he likes to rest in the peaceful darkness, watching the pattern of streetlights on his ceiling. There is a little chink between his curtains, and whenever a car passes, a ray of night-time yellow arcs above his head like the beam of a distant searchlight. Tommy has learnt that the sound of an approaching car becomes different as it moves away. He doesn't know why. He has also learnt that when the streets are silent the footsteps of someone passing can sound uncannily loud, and that when occasionally he hears drunken laughter or frightening shouts, he should always get up and peep through his curtains so he can reassure himself that what sounds terrifying is just ordinary people rolling home.

Never lie still and wonder. Always get up and look.

By the time Jet arrives home it is almost two o'clock. He lets himself in at the street door, walks up two flights of stairs. The flat where he and Stella live—two rooms, kitchen, bathroom—is small, untidy and in poor repair. When he unlocks its shabby door from the landing he catches the smell of the supper they ate earlier. In the flat's only living room, a small table lamp is aglow. Stella doesn't like the dark. Jet tiptoes across the thin carpet towards the bedroom, whose door is not fully closed. He pushes it open wider to peer inside.

The little girl sits up and says, 'Hello, Daddy. I'm awake.'

'You can sleep now, Stella. I've come home.'

TWO

Gottfleisch was so fat they practically had to lift him into the station wagon. He looked as if he had been inflated with an airpump. He was so distended that you could imagine him tied to a hauser, floating two hundred feet above a fast food restaurant as an advertisement. When you saw his face, though, you stopped laughing.

Small eyes in a fat face, raisins in a pudding, wads of flesh that shrank the eyes till they were like little buttons concentrating the light to fire it at you like a laser: Gottfleisch had such eyes. He also had wet fleshy lips and looked as if he had never in his life needed to shave. Although he weighed about twenty stone he moved lightly on his feet. If he saw a ten-pound note blowing down the road he could run twenty yards to snatch at it. Ten yards anyway.

He had bought the Renault Espace because it was one of the few cars he could fit into—though he still needed the middle seats taken out and the back ones modified to take his bulk. Gottfleisch only ever rode in the rear. Trying to squeeze him behind a steering wheel did not bear thinking about.

On this particular day—it was a Wednesday—he was being driven by Cliff Lyons. Cliff wore his straight dark hair in a kind of crew cut. He had become used to short hair when last inside and had resolved to keep it that way. Sitting beside him was little Ticky.

Gottfleisch was crooning directions like an unctuous

tour guide: 'He will cross from Cornhill into Leadenhall on his way to Aldgate. I'll show you the route across Tower Bridge.'

'I've lived here all my life.'

'And still a driver,' Gottfleisch purred. 'There's the sign.'

Lyons knew better than to argue back. As the Espace crossed with the traffic over Tower Bridge, Gottfleisch said, 'Go straight on to the Old Kent Road.'

Cliff Lyons sighed.

Gottfleisch said, 'At this point he will call "journey point Charlie". Have you checked your watch?'

Lyons had, but no longer felt like speaking.

'Ticky, dear boy, how long did you calculate for the rest of the journey?'

'Four minutes.'

All three glanced at their wristwatches. Ticky said, 'It depends on traffic, sir.'

'Good boy.'

The Espace crawled south along Tower Bridge Road. Cliff wondered if Gottfleisch would give Ticky another peppermint. The little runt had finished those he had been given, and the sweet minty smell was now extinguished by his bad breath.

As they joined the Old Kent Road, Gottfleisch said, 'Journey point Delta.'

Ticky wriggled in his seat, releasing a whiff of body odour, and explained: 'He doesn't call "Freddy" till he's down at New Cross. Except you'll have him by then.'

Cliff cleared his throat. 'Sure he won't be followed?'

'Dead sure.'

'How come?'

'Woody told me. He'd have to know.'

Cliff eased out to overtake a bus. 'All down to Woody.'

Gottfleisch said, 'They trust Woody. That's why they let him drive alone.'

'Safer with two.'

'But cheaper with one,' Gottfleisch said. 'They have to earn a profit. And it isn't safer when two can easily plot together. We're nearly there.'

'Couldn't he turn off here to Peckham? It's quieter.'

'He has to stay on route as long as possible.'

They passed St James's Road on the left. 'One of these,' Ticky said. 'That's the one.'

The little side roads led nowhere, each of them either turning or terminating at the gas works. As Cliff squeezed the Espace between parked cars he complained, 'I'm supposed to get a lorry through this gap?'

Gottfleisch told him he would have plenty of time to practise. Ticky nodded. 'That's the yard.'

'Gate's shut.'

'It won't be.'

'Drive straight past,' ordered Gottfleisch. 'We don't want to attract attention.'

'We ain't doing the job till next week.'

'Then you have several days to become acquainted with the neighbourhood. Yes, Ticky, quite right; just below four minutes.'

Cliff watched the yard gate in his mirror, and as he manoeuvred the large car through the narrow road he muttered, 'Bloody lorry's a lot bigger than this.'

'You can come early and lay out parking cones.'

Ticky said, 'You'll have all morning.'

'Thanks a bunch.'

Cliff waited to rejoin traffic in the Old Kent Road.

Gottfleisch said, 'In the morning, you can park the lorry in the yard, then clear yourself an exit. Have a leisurely lunch. Go back and wait.'

'Just like that?'

'What could be simpler, my dear boy?'

THREE

Scott Heywood squinted at his bowl of cornflakes. How many were there in a bowl—a hundred? Say five days a week, to allow for days he couldn't face them: five hundred flakes. Fifty weeks a year, excluding holidays— twenty-five thousand cornflakes every year. Which meant that since marrying Claire—and only since then, because he didn't eat cornflakes much before—just since marrying Claire, he must have eaten two hundred thousand of the things. Actually, when he came to think about it, two hundred thousand didn't seem a lot: if he'd had a pound for every cornflake he would still not be rich. Not really. Comfortable, but not rich enough to retire. Though if he invested two hundred thousand pounds at eight per cent a year, he'd have—

'Scott! You've hardly touched your breakfast.'

She had a freshly ironed apron over her day dress, so clean and immaculate she looked like an actress in a situation comedy. Nowadays it was as if Claire took her role models from advertisements. She had become one of those bright and brittle paragons of domestic cleanliness; she sprayed lacquers on the furniture, scrubbed her kitchen with abrasive soap, sluiced surfaces with a jollop which killed every household germ.

A cornflake fluttered from his mouth. 'I was thinking.'

'Thinking!'

Tommy asked, 'What about?'

Scott blinked twice, as if he had only just woken up. 'Where we should go on holiday. What d'you think?'

His son looked blank. Claire clucked her tongue.

'That's all I was thinking.'

Claire picked a breadcrumb from the tablecloth. 'Assuming we could afford a holiday.'

'Of course we can.'

Claire smiled sadly. 'We could go to Norfolk.'

'I meant abroad. Where d'you fancy?'

'We can't afford abroad. We can't even afford Norfolk unless we stay with Brenda . . .'

Claire removed another crumb from the tablecloth.

Scott said, 'Sometimes it's cheaper to go abroad.'

'Not as cheap as Brenda's.'

'The later you book the cheaper it is—last minute bar-gains. Walk into a travel agent's and ask, "What's on for Saturday?" You know.'

'I'm not going *this* Saturday!'

'Any Saturday, when we're ready. Just ask them what they've got.'

He nodded encouragingly, but she shook her head: 'I prefer to know where I am. It takes time to pack and sort the house out. Anyway, it's term-time, and Tommy's at school.'

Scott grinned at his son. 'You wouldn't mind skipping a week, would you?'

Claire said, 'Miss a week's school? He'd never catch up.'

'Come on, Claire, he's only six.'

Tommy frowned, wondering whether six was a good thing to be or not.

'We can't afford abroad. But if you like, I'll ring Brenda on Sunday.'

Scott studied her. 'Just suppose we did go abroad, where'd you like to go?'

'Tommy, eat that up.—That reminds me, talking of foreign holidays . . .' She eyed him curiously.

'Yes?'

'Have you moved your passport?'

Scott's hand strayed towards his spoon. 'Passport?'

'Yes, it should be in the drawer with the serviettes, in my papers file.'

'Ah.' Scott filled his mouth with cornflakes.

'I was changing the perfumed lining paper and I peeped inside. My papers file should have been underneath my bank file, but when I moved the cutlery canteen—'

'I wanted to check the date,' Scott said. 'The renewal date.'

'But it's not due.'

'No.'

'I would know if our passports had expired. They're both due on the same date.'

Spoons clinked. Tommy continued to watch his parents, but since the quarrel appeared to have died at birth he resumed eating. Claire said, 'Moving things like that when there's no need. They'll get lost.'

Scott seemed uninterested.

'I'd have known if they were due.'

He nodded, ploughing through the rest of his soggy cereal.

'Not that we're going anywhere.'

'No.'

'Far too hot and the weather's terrible. We could have gone at Easter in the school holidays, but it's too late to book.'

'Well—'

'You know it is, darling. Anyway, England's best. I don't want to go somewhere common.'

'Common?'

'Abroad is common. England is civilised. Norfolk is.'

Scott tried a rueful smile on Tommy but the boy only stared at him. Sometimes Tommy sat so still at table that Scott wondered if he ate at all. Yet the food disappeared. In fact, usually by the end of the meal Tommy's plate looked so clean that it looked as if it had already been washed up. But nothing from the Heywood table escaped the dishwasher; everything from the table was scalded clean.

Tommy's bowl was empty. He said, 'I'd like to go to the Hudson River.'

They both stared at him. Scott asked, 'On holiday?'

'Of course.'

'Where's the Hudson River?'

'North America.'

Claire laughed. 'Oh, Tommy, that's much too far. We could never afford it.'

Scott asked, 'Why there?'

'There's holidays where you go on a boat and watch the whales. If you're good, they let you touch one. I'd like that.'

'Whales!' scoffed Claire. 'Whatever next?'

Ticky knew his breath smelled. He was standing at the sink in the corner of his bed-sit, pulling faces in the mirror. He stretched his mouth wide, moved his bottom jaw from right to left, peered into the pink cavity. His false teeth were out. When Ticky had first begun working for Mr Gottfleisch he assumed—like everybody else—that his putrid breath was caused by his blackened teeth. They were anachronistic, those stumps of teeth, the kind seen only in photographs of slum children in the war. Pantomime witches and pirates had teeth like that.

Quite early in his employment, Gottfleisch offered to have the teeth replaced. The offer was not out of charac-ter: Gottfleisch paid his employees a salary and ran a healthcare scheme for when they took sick. But he was not a philanthropist—he seldom employed a married man, for example, because he would have to support the wife if the man was jailed. Gottfleisch honoured his agreements, expected others to do the same. Insisted on it.

When Gottfleisch made the offer Ticky did not immediately accept; his teeth might be rotten but they were a part of him. Take them out? That seemed pretty drastic. Besides, he was uncomfortable with the concept of false teeth—they might fall out when he was on a job. Seriously, he explained to Gottfleisch, he could be running from the Bill, say, scrambling to get away, they'd come unstuck. Clatter on the ground. If the cops got their hands on those ivories, they could be as good as fingerprints, leading the law straight back to him. Anyway, how would the existing ones be taken out, he continued nervously— a punch on the jaw? Dental hospital, Gottfleisch had said. But Ticky was terrified of dentists. He had had several teeth removed already, and each one had caused him pain. His seemed to be rooted in more tenaciously than other people's teeth—corroded, maybe, stuck to the jaw. Even sitting in a dentist's chair was an ordeal—the man would jab at him, prick, be hasty with his drills. Maybe it was Ticky's stench—the dentist wanted the job over quickly, so he snatched at what he did. Another anachronism: spitting blood afterwards into a basin.

Eventually Gottfleisch said it was a condition of Ticky's employment, and he'd hear no argument. He explained that having the whole set removed would be no more uncomfortable (that was his word for painful) than pulling out only one—*less* painful, because Ticky would be anaesthetised.

Ticky gave in, said he saw the logic of it. On the fateful day, no one knew the internal battles he went through. He wanted his Ma to hold his hand—and almost patched up their quarrel so she could come. Almost. But in the end, Ticky gathered what little there was of himself together and had a cab drop him at the door. Didn't trust himself to walk there.

For two weeks Ticky was all gums, all soft and tender. He thought his face was changing shape. Then he went back for the permanent set, and was immediately over-joyed; he could not believe how handsome he now looked.—Well, maybe not handsome, he thought, but better, anyway. He viewed his cutters in the mirror, pulled faces at himself, and became convinced that he could smile at people—a full white toothy cheese. Grinning at people felt tremendous, so he did it all the time: walked right up and leered straight in their face. It was several days before he learnt that his breath smelled as before.

But that was a minor inconvenience, Ticky felt. People cracked on about his breath, but they were only teasing, that was all. What was important to Ticky was that since the refit he looked like an ordinary person, which was great. Women would be attracted to him now.

Over the next few months he found no increase in the number of women who *were* smitten by his looks. He didn't care. He looked better, felt better, and although the breath problem had not blown away he was grateful to Gottfleisch for what he'd done. Ticky consoled himself with the thought that, in truth, women only weighed a real man down. The best of them—that wasn't many, but a few—looked great in magazines or on the screen, but in real life had less appeal. Real women had blemishes, just like him. Usually they had too much flesh. They were taller than him—often heavier as well. And real-life women never behaved as they did in films.—Obviously they wouldn't perform the tricks they did in porno films, but even in straight films women smiled, wore sexy clothes, were not overweight. Not like real women.

Though it occurred to Ticky now, as he gazed in the mirror and ran his finger along his gums, that women in porno films actually *were* like women in real life: imperfect. Most of those so-called actresses in the porno flicks were foreign dikey pieces with blemishes, imperfect shapes, and disgusting private parts. Cameramen seemed obsessed with their vaginas, lingering on them close up. Who did they imagine wanted to stare at their over-worked half-shaven slits? Who gave a toss for them?

Little Ticky, what he liked, what he thought most men liked but would not admit, were young girls with skinny bodies and healthy eyes. Innocent and virginal, smooth-skinned like girls at school. Cheeky. Sweet and trusting.

By the time they married, women were past it.

He had misted the little mirror, so he rubbed it clean. In doing so, he caught a whiff of something—his own bad breath? No, it couldn't be—he was getting a complex about that. Anyway, Ticky decided, plucking his false teeth from the cup of Steradent, the older you get, the smellier, and that's a fact. Ticky hated growing old. Why couldn't he have stayed a kid?

The important thing, Cliff Lyons decided, was to get the timing right. So next morning he went back to the yard in the side street off the Old Kent Road. He wanted to see what kind of things might be happening at this time of day, what he might have to contend with. Damn little access roads stuffed with old parked cars: Gottfleisch was right—he should take traffic cones to clear a space. One thing working in his favour was that, throughout the whole business, he could take his time. The morning to get organised, and then, even after the job was done, several minutes before Force Five began to get anxious. There could be ten minutes—certainly eight—before the alarm. Another five before the cops arrived.

Ten to fifteen minutes. Inside five he would be out of the yard, on to the main road, heading south. Before the cops arrived in SE1 he should be in Lewisham.

Cliff paused outside the gates. Locked. Yard empty. But next week he would have the keys—he had considered bringing them today but didn't want to linger, didn't want to be a familiar face around the yard. He didn't want to draw anyone's attention to the yard at all. Even on Monday, this yard should be just one of a hundred places where the snatch could have been carried out.

It was a quiet spot, naturally—out of use, overlooked by blank windowless walls and deserted buildings. Someone ought to knock those buildings down, build something useful, he thought. As it was, the whole area was an invitation to vandals, was asking for trouble. Walking away, Cliff brooded on the fact that there was only one combined entrance and exit. A cul-de-sac allowed no options: one way in and one way out. On Monday, it could be just his luck for some prat of a truck driver to park his own lorry in the side road, or for some stupid accident to block his route. Murphy's Law. Cliff was more concerned about getting out than all the rest of it: the actual job was simple, it seemed to him.

He ran his hand across his crew-cut and jutted out his chin. This would be the big one, without a doubt—and if all he had to worry about was that there might be a vehicle badly parked, he couldn't grumble. If necessary, he could put his truck behind and *shove* it along the road, eliminate the bastard. Cliff grinned. No, on Monday he would act legitimately. What he liked about this number was that if everything went to plan, no one would know quite how it had happened: he could hear the radio now— a baffling disappearance, they'd say, another cargo vanished in the Bermondsey Triangle.

Cliff nodded, optimistic again. Come Monday, he'd

make sure no sucker got in the way—no lorries, no workmen, no kids. If someone did, Cliff would deal with them, whoever they were. He was up to that. Christ, he couldn't call Gottfleisch on the radio and say sorry, something's up, how about we try another day?

Next Monday would be the only chance they had.

FOUR

Friday lunchtime, Scott Heywood went to the Old Red Spot. The pub was a tube stop from the depot, but that meant that it should be too far for his colleagues to happen into. He didn't want his colleagues. He didn't want anyone to witness this assignation. He had a raincoat over his uniform—that same thin pointless raincoat that Claire made him take every day to hide the uniform when he came home.

The Old Red Spot was fairly crowded. It worried Scott, and he said so.

'All the better,' Ticky said. 'The more there are, the less they notice you. Having a drink?'

'Forbidden. You know, driving.'

'Sticklers, are they, for the rules?'

'You bet.'

'Well, not much longer. How d'you feel?'

'OK.'

'Not nervous?'

'About meeting *you*?'

'About next Monday.'

'This is worse.'

Ticky grinned at him, showing his teeth. Scott looked away and caught a glimpse of himself in an overhead mirror. The raincoat looked ridiculous. Glancing round the pub, Scott saw that he was not the only one in an outdoor coat—though everyone else had theirs undone.

Perhaps he should do the same. His driver's uniform was not conspicuous, after all. Even the yellow and black Force Five symbol would not stand out. He would be invisible, another worker, the kind who spent his lunchtimes in a pub.

He undid the top button of the raincoat but left it on.

Ticky had taken the envelope from his pocket and put it on the table. He had done so casually, putting the envelope down as if it was of no interest to him. It didn't *look* interesting; like anything else in Ticky's possession the pack had a scruffy look—a corner bent, a slight stain, perhaps a thumb-print, some kind of smudge.

Ticky was talking, leaving the pack alone so that it would become part of the furniture, unimportant, something one of them might remember to pick up.

'They got you a nice one. I will say that.'

'Don't want to talk about it in here.'

'Everyone's rabbiting nineteen to the dozen. No one's interested in us. We could discuss the job, they wouldn't know it.'

'But we won't.'

'Take a tip, Woody, from one who knows. Never go skulking in lonely places—you draw attention. Either stay indoors or choose the busiest place you know. Besides, if you ever do want one, you'll find there are no really lonely places—not round here.'

'Thanks for the advice. I'm going now.'

'Hold on, hold on, you've only just arrived. You see, doing that does draw attention. People say, oh, he's in and out—what did he come here for? Sit around and take your time.' He smiled at Scott as if encouraging him to make conversation, but it didn't work. Ticky said, 'Yes, he's done you a nice one, like I say. I was quite impressed.'

'Have you been fingering it?'

'I washed my hands.'

Scott picked up the packet and slipped it into the inside pocket of his raincoat. He said, 'If *you're* happy it must be OK.'

'Oh, I'm no expert. I've *got* a passport, but I only used it once—went to Spain but I didn't like it. You been abroad?'

'Yeah.'

'So that's your second passport. Well, I like the name. Henry Scott. Nice. If anyone says, "Hello, Scott" you won't be caught out. I think that's neat.'

'My idea.'

'Got your flight booked?'

'Of course.'

'Where to?'

'Ah, ha.'

'Does Gottfleisch know?'

'He arranged the passport.'

'Yes, but does he know which flight?'

'Doesn't need to.'

Ticky nodded, watching him appraisingly. 'He doesn't like things being kept from him.'

Scott grinned wryly. 'No.'

'So where *are* you going?'

'Back to the depot.' Scott leant across the table. 'See you Monday.'

The whiff of Ticky's breath caught him before he rose, and the smell clung to his nostrils till he reached the door. But once outside in the weak English sunlight he sighed with relief. He had been oddly apprehensive about this meeting, as if it had been one of the riskier parts of the plan—which it wasn't, of course. It was just an ordinary chat in a pub.

As he walked among lunchtime strollers to the tube station Scott felt the slight weight of the passport in his raincoat pocket. He was safer now. On Monday this would take him out of the country. Monday's outbound flight might be the only time he used it—though he would carry his proper passport as well in the hope that, once abroad, he might be able to quietly resume his true identity. It felt—what?—sophisticated to have two names.

Attention to detail was a legacy from his training in management—thorough planning, being well prepared. He now had the passport, the flight booked, and on Monday all he had to do was to carry out the snatch, hit the airport, and disappear.

As he entered the station, Scott regretted his wife's lack of enthusiasm for foreign travel—she was almost racist about it at times. No, that wasn't fair: she was equally reluctant to go anywhere: other places were never clean enough, never home. Well, on Monday, that house-proud, stick-at-home Claire would get a shake-up, would find her life turned upside down. It might bring her back to life again. She might not like what was going to happen but she'd understand in the end.

Then he remembered his son Tommy, who had said that he wanted to stroke a whale. Scott chuckled in the street. Not yet, old son, he whispered, not just yet.

In Gottfleisch's sitting room, Ticky sat alone, listening to his stomach rumbling. It was six o'clock and he had not had his tea. Being in this room was a novelty—normally Ticky didn't make it beyond the office, on the right inside the front door. But today Gottfleisch had ushered him into this room, shown him to the couch and had left him there. Perhaps he had gone to fetch some tea. Or more likely was in his office on a private call.

Ticky peered over his shoulder to check he really was alone, before he stood and stretched. Doing so might stop his stomach gurgling. The room was full of pictures and antique furniture—dark heavy stuff which smelled of linseed oil. There were a few knick-knacks, but nothing

you'd want to stuff into your pocket while the boss was
gone. If you felt foolish. The curtains on Gottfleisch's
window were red and sumptuous, looking as if they'd
once hung in an Arab's tent. Maybe they had. The lamp
was an ornate chandelier, and Ticky noticed that there
was a fresh junction point in the ceiling, as if the lamp
hadn't hung there long. He thought the carpets dis-
appointing: shabby and worn in places, none of them
lying straight. They'd be old and priceless. Ticky grinned.

He lowered himself on to the gigantic cushions of his
boss's settee. But it was too luxurious for comfort: if he
wanted to keep his feet on the floor Ticky had to perch
on the edge of the squab, and if he wriggled further back
to lean against the upright, he was so far in from the
edge that his feet stuck out like a child's rag doll. Having
squirmed into place he did not shift. He sat enveloped in
settee, fingers drumming on the cushion fabric. Across
the other side of the upholstered arm stood a high-shine
coffee table, bearing a single art magazine. Ticky decided
that if Gottfleisch ever did arrive with that drink, he had
better use the magazine as a coaster, because the coffee
table looked as fragile as glass, while the magazine looked
dull.

Ticky turned to peer across his shoulder again but
couldn't see above the sofa back. But he knew he was
alone: this was not a room anyone could creep into. It
had huge double doors which probably were not in the
house originally: they were ballroom doors—the kind a
butler should fling open and announce your name. Ticky
wondered whether Gottfleisch had had them installed
especially, had had the entrance widened to allow him to
waltz through without touching the sides.

Secure in the knowledge that no one could see him,
Ticky reached in his inside pocket for an envelope and
dropped it in his lap. He chuckled. When he had met

Woody earlier he had had both envelopes with him, and it amused him to think what would have happened if he had mixed them up. Woody would have panicked when he found out—he might have imagined himself at the airport, opening the envelope to pull out his passport . . .

Quite a thought.

Ticky picked up his own different envelope, lifted the flap, paused another moment, then he shook out the photographs from inside. First he slid them apart for a quick glimpse at the whole set, then he closed the pack. Foreign kids, by the look. The boy in the first had tight curly hair and the kind of face they used to paint on cherubim. He wasn't doing much—but that was because this little angel was in a special class: he had a haunting beauty which meant that he only had to be captured nude; they didn't have to do things to him. A kid like that must be worth a fortune, so they weren't going to waste him on some punk hired for the photo session. This boy would be kept apart and reared by hand. Probably the picture was an advertisement—it was certainly not a porno shot: they were saying, 'Here he is, the little sweetheart. Are you in the market to make a bid?'

Ticky wasn't, but he could enjoy the snap. The funny thing was that a shot like this, nothing happening, would hold a privileged place in his collection. The boy's beauty set his imagination free. The other shots, below this one, were more conventional stuff: boys and girls with adults using them. Something unusual about this particular set was that there were four shots of women with young boys. Rarities, in a way. Naturally, there was the usual fodder—oral sex and buggery, human chains—but Ticky liked the four-shot mini-series on initiation: the young lads, what eight or nine? being educated—first-hand, as you might say—by grown women. Were they meant to be elder sisters or the boys' mothers? Ticky grinned. Well, that was your fantasy—the story you invented for the pictures. The truth was that these were just models brought together for the shoot—girls on the game, youngsters . . . Nice idea, though. Ticky was not usually turned on by naked women, but in these pictures the women were important because they were the ones who had brought on the boys' erections. Which was especially nice. In too many photographs of young boys the kids were plainly not aroused and drooped like runner beans. Here they were little bean poles.

Apart from the four 'Johnny stands up for Mummy' shots, the pack included the usual studies of boys with men. In these, none of the men were drooping, but were standing and ramming home. The boys seemed resigned to it, were visibly not turned on. It spoilt the effect for Ticky; he liked to see a youngster's hard-on: it was beautiful, a work of art. So he skipped the man and boy shots and returned to the four of mother and son.

Ticky sat glowing on the sofa, legs flat out, the little pile of photographs in his lap, and he let himself forget about Mr Gottfleisch. The soft luxury of the enormous sofa lulled him into a waking dream. He ran his thumb across the surface of his photographs, touched the flesh beneath the shine. Look at the little girls, taking their lessons—Christ, stretched so wide you'd think they would crack. This one here, face down on the table, a look on her face as if she really loved it—was that an act? Not necessarily. Ticky maintained that it wasn't true kids did not enjoy sex: they did if you introduced it right. When he remembered his own childhood, he sometimes thought that sex was the only good thing about it. Yeah, all kids were the same: think of the way they touched themselves, girls *and* boys. Ticky wondered how it felt to be a girl, to have it inside you, to squeeze and . . . Ticky frowned. Strange, not to have a dingle of your own: he could not imagine that. Being a man, he knew how it felt to do it *to* someone, but not how it was to have it done to him. He had tried a few tricks, but never that. Perhaps no one fancied him. He chuckled bitterly. He was glad to be a man.

One thing in particular that he could remember about his boyhood was the sheer wonder of childish ejaculation, that magic thrill. As a boy he'd jerk off as fast as possible and when the thrill hit, he would be *zinging* his foreskin up and down—would feel the tingle right through his body, every part. Nothing like that since. Nowadays the thrill ran deeper—it seemed more necessary and brought relief, but it no longer produced that electric joy.

He studied the kids there in the photographs: did they experience the same ecstatic thrill? No, this was just a job for them. They were paid—at least, he assumed they were—but did they enjoy it? With little girls, you could never tell: they might be loving it, or it could hurt like hell. But with little boys you could see when they were on. Perhaps that was why he preferred male photos— though he was not homosexual, he told himself, he didn't fancy men. Little boys were different: fancying them didn't make him queer. Boys had smooth skins and pretty faces and lean straight bodies and apple bums—hardly different to little girls. Just easier to chat up. More responsive. More daring. But in this last photograph, there was a little girl, what was she, six years old? Such a sweet one, smooth little body.—Christ she was adoring it—look at that smile. Ticky peered at the picture, trying to see if the man really was inside her, but he couldn't tell. Sometimes they faked these shots, and when Ticky stared at this one, stared *into* it, held it to the light . . . No, this was real, it had to be; look at her face. Pert little darling, tight as a bottle of raspberryade—yeah, Ticky was normal, he was sure of that. It was femininity that appealed to him. He was not queer.

Ticky shook his head and slid the photos into their envelope, then slipped the pack away in his inside pocket. They had cost but they were worth it. Ticky exhaled. Picking up the art magazine from the side table, he fanned his face. He began glancing through the pages, so that when Gottfleisch finally did come in he would think that Ticky had been reading it.

What was in this magazine? Classical statues, historic art. Boring. But as Ticky flicked through the frozen life studies, the perfect nymphs and rippling athletes, he began to pause. These statues of cream-skinned women, they might wear robes but he could see right through. If these had not been photographs and he could have touched one of the actual statues he would be able to feel her nipples—just there, he would feel them hard. Yes, he would be able to run his hands anywhere he liked on her, and she'd never move, she'd let him stroke her. A perfect woman, you might say.

He heard Gottfleisch approaching along the hall.

Ticky sat with his legs extended on the cushion and the magazine across his lap. He wondered whether Gottfleisch had left it there deliberately, whether he'd known that the pictures were more than art. You never could tell, he decided. Gottfleisch was a devious bugger, as Ticky knew.

FIVE

Early Sunday evening, Scott carried a cardboard box downstairs. Claire was hoovering the hall. Over the noise of the vacuum cleaner she asked what he was doing.

'Tidying up.'

'You?'

'Some rubbish to throw out.'

He knew that Claire would not object to that.

'I don't know where it comes from,' she said.

Scott had closed the flap on the box so that she could not see inside. He was moving a few possessions out to the car—not too many, it would look suspicious. A few special things. In his mind was the question that he supposed everybody asked themselves sometimes: if you had to escape your burning house, what would you grab? There was nothing Scott really wanted, nothing he could imagine seriously missing later. Records and books were replaceable, and clothes were clothes. He did have a couple of favourite shirts; he would wear one of them tomorrow and keep the other in the box. He had packed the sweater he had bought last holiday, and a particularly comfortable pair of slacks. There was also a second pair of shoes, though again, he could buy shoes any time. All his clothes could be replaced. So he had packed no other clothes—except underwear and socks to last three days. He would be wearing his warm anorak, and he'd leave his raincoat at home.

What else?

He had packed a photograph—Claire and Tommy in the back garden, both smiling, Claire looking nice. He hadn't been sure whether to bring it, but somehow it had seemed right: to go without a souvenir might seem callous in forthcoming days. Though to whom? No one would judge him. No one would know. Except Claire perhaps, as she sorted through his things. It would be a puzzle for her: whether to throw his things away or to hold on to them in case he came back. All his things would remain here lifeless. He had sifted through but in the end had decided to leave almost everything behind. Tomorrow he should behave as on any normal day.

It was revelatory, really, making Scott realise that if the house ever *had* burnt down and he had not been able to rescue anything from inside, he would have suffered no serious loss. In fact, he and Claire could have used the insurance money to start again—to start, not to replace their previous life, but to start anew. Would she have done that? No. Well, for him this was a once in a lifetime opportunity—a visit from the fairy godmother, saying, 'I grant you, Scott Heywood, just one wish, so use it well.'

He would. He would reinvent his future.

He could not reinvent his past. People talked about reliving one's life, but if he *could* have relived his life—knowing what he knew now—how much of it would he have changed? Scott shrugged. Such a thing would not be possible: he could not change one selected part. To shift a single piece within the tangle would cause every other piece to move. Each changed event would change one beside it, each would change the next—just as a single change in the way that a pack of cards was shuffled would alter the outcome of the game. In a game of patience one tiny cheat, one shuffle, one readjustment to the cards could make a whole blocked game come out.

Scott carried his cardboard box through to the garage. It was something a man could wish for—a chance to cheat. An opportunity to start again. Who wouldn't want a crack at that?

Monday morning in the gymnasium, Jet Heywood came to life. Moving easily inside his tracksuit, light on his toes, thumping the punch bag. The canvas tube stood fixed like a sack of oats, juddering at each hit. Jet's shoulders ached. He felt as loose and shapeless as the tracksuit, inside which he ran with sweat. Black hair flicked across his face.

'Hit it harder.'

He ignored the voice.

'Make him feel your punches.'

The same advice he had heard for years. When you're tired, don't show it—come close, make each punch count.

'Thump it. Knock him down.'

The jarring pain along his arms. He leant towards the bag.

'Keep your arms up. Go for his head.'

Jet pulled his arms higher and tried to ignore the pain.

'Now the knock-out.—Now! Before the bell.'

Jet managed two last prods which made no impression. He stepped back awkwardly, arms down, gasping like a steam train.

'You know how to punch.'

Still panting heavily, Jet blinked at the blond man beside him.

'But you're out of condition.'

The man was an inch taller than Jet. 'Floyd Carter,' he said. 'I run this place.'

'Thought I recognised you.'

'Professional?'

'Used to be.'

Jet was still panting.

'It shows. Cruiserweight?'

'Middle.'

'You look heavier.'

Jet's breath returned, and he grinned at Floyd. When Jet was younger, this man had been famous in their area—light heavyweight, a championship contender, a local name that people knew.

Jet said, 'I started *junior* middleweight and had to move up. But not a cruiserweight—Christ.' Cruiserweights are over one hundred and sixty pounds.

'You better weigh yourself and check. Let me help you get the gloves off.'

As Floyd untied his laces, Jet said, 'I'm still inside the weight limit, don't you worry. But I'm past it now.'

'I can see that.'

'Thanks.'

'Just kidding. You in training?'

'Looking for a job.'

Floyd handed back Jet's gloves. 'Wish I could help, but I'm sorry—I have a line of ex-pros chasing for work. I could stretch that line three times round the ring.'

Jet collected his towel. 'This is the kind of job we all want—indoors and warm.'

'You got something lined up?'

'Yeah, outdoors and cold.'

Floyd chuckled. 'That's OK for summer. So tell me, what could you offer a gym—physiotherapy? Fitness counselling? Recommend a diet?'

Jet grinned. 'I can teach kids how to box.'

'No,' Floyd said, his voice level and even. 'Get yourself back in shape, take a course in something a modern gym can use, then come back and talk about it.'

'Is that an offer?'

Floyd shrugged. 'You'd have to take your turn. I'm approached by ex-boxers, ex-footballers, ex-athletes, failed medics, unhappy PE teachers, you name it. They all have *something* to offer.'

'And I don't?'

'Convince me.'

Jet nodded and turned away. Aware of Floyd watching him, he asked, 'How did *you* get the gym?'

'Hard work.'

'I can work.'

'Ten years' hard work.'

They gave each other the kind of appraising look boxers give when they touch gloves. 'Ten years,' Jet said as he headed for the shower.

'Don't give up so easily. Sometimes you have to go the fifteen rounds.'

'Well, this is my break time.'

'Come back fighting.'

Scott Heywood, uniformed, eased the van from Cornhill into Leadenhall as if acting out the commentary which Gottfleisch had given Ticky and Cliff a few days before. He followed the traffic into Aldgate, as Gottfleisch had said that he would. Then he flipped the radio and said, 'Woody here. F.O.B.'

'Read you, Woody,' she replied. 'Keep in contact. Over.'

'Over and out.'

Scott was behaving normally, calling base at each defined point, driving steadily.

Moving into line for Tower Bridge, he had time to check the mirror and assess each crawling car behind. Nothing abnormal. Tugging at his stomach was the unreasonable fear that some bastard could muscle in. Not today, please, not today. The weather was pleasant, sun shining, streets not busy for this hour.

'Woody again. Journey point Bertie. Over.'

'Nothing abnormal? Over.'

'Just perfick, Ma. I'll call back. Over.'

'Roger, Woody. Over and out.'

Scott imagined her in the office—sergeant Collinson, talking up her job. Ex-army, an example to them all. Built like a brick guard-house. By this time, his van was motoring sweetly across Tower Bridge as the sun flickered between its gaudy metal stanchions. Ex-sergeant Collinson would be in her office, out of the fine sunshine, tracing each of her drivers on the map. Like a military command centre—and why not? Collinson had spent fifteen years dedicated to the army, to what end? Out on her ear. Maybe she was a dike. In the army you couldn't be a dike and you couldn't get pregnant, so what was a girl to do? Leave quietly. Since she was now in this mundane desk job, why shouldn't she try to build her part? She had set military standards for the radio, had rearranged the office to face the map, and you could bet she still dreamt about the army.

Scott wondered if Ms Collinson knew what was in the back of his van today. He couldn't tell: she was such a stickler for procedure, everything was handled in a standard way. Even when a van came back unloaded she would not let them vary her call routine—it would be a lack of discipline; it would encourage slackness; it might help the enemy or some goddam thing. But nothing in Collinson's manner today suggested that she thought this anything other than a normal trip. Scott chuckled to himself. Perhaps it was normal to her. And she'd approve of his not telling her: greater security, no need to know. Force Five was proud of its security.

'Journey point Charlie. Over.'

'Roger and out.' Trim and crisp, like the talking clock.

The van had left Tower Bridge. Chunky Collinson would have moved the next pin on her map, the sun would shine, traffic would flow, his journey would continue to schedule. Along Tower Bridge Road south were no obstructions. Scott checked his mirror and saw nothing curious. His van with the Force Five logo emblazoned on its side would attract no interest: in these commercial parts of town, security vans were commonplace. At that very moment, heading towards him was one from Securicor. Around this area, Scott thought, you couldn't drive two minutes without seeing some company's armoured van: Securicor, Churchill, Shield, Group 4, Force Five. Who knew which carried what? Only the drivers.

What Mr Gottfleisch had known was which of the companies had the contract. But because he hadn't known which vehicle, he needed an inside employee. At the time it had seemed no more than blind chance when Scott bumped into him again—except that no one bumped into an elephant by chance. Gottfleisch had materialised one evening in Scott's local, which, though a surprise, was not extraordinary. They knew each other by sight because Gottfleisch had been associated with his brother Jet when he was in the fight game.

'Journey point Delta. Over.'

'Roger and out.'

Scott was waiting to join the Old Kent Road. Yes, when Jet was a rising boxer he had become linked with Gottfleisch—one of those rollers who attended regularly, attracted to brawn, muscle and sweat. For a while Gottfleisch had subbed Jet as a possibility. Jet had joked about it—asked Scott what kind of possibility he thought the fat man had meant? But it didn't last. Jet's was a short-lived promise: his career had flared then fizzled out, and Gottfleisch seemed content to write it off as a speculation which did not mature. Until now. It was curious, when Scott thought about it, that although it was his brother that Gottfleisch had invested in, it was finally he himself who had become entangled. He had been entangled for six months now, ever since that evening in the pub.—The astonishing sight of the man in the Red Monkey, his white shirt wide as a mainsail, his enormous blue jacket, his rope and compass silk tie. Gottfleisch had sat precariously on a wooden chair, had beamed expansively at Scott, had talked of life and opportunity, had reminisced about dear old Jet. Had shook his head sadly, eyes twinkling. Had tut-tutted, reminding Scott of how he had previously helped his big brother. Had leapt from his chair, surprisingly agile, not waiting for an answer, and had then, like a huge corpulent snowman, rolled straight from the pub out into the street without acknowledging the minder who hovered in a dark suit by the door.

When Gottfleisch left, the pub behind him was quivering. Men hid their eyes when they glanced at Scott.

At their second meeting, Gottfleisch made his proposal. One of Force Five's contracts was to carry old notes from a central clearing bank to the Bank of England incineration plant. Scott immediately saw what was coming—had protested at first, said security was tight, and that crime did not pay. Gottfleisch surprised him by agreeing on both counts: security *was* tight, but which was the firm that handled it? Said that a life of crime did *not* pay—an admirable precept, as he put it—leading inevitably to the conclusion that if one *had* to commit a crime, one should do so only once, for a reward sufficiently large to guarantee that one would not have to do so again. It was sensible business practice. Gottfleisch nodded like a banker. How would Scott react to a reward of half a million pounds? In old notes.

'Journey point Echo. Over.'

'Roger and out.'

Scott was fully alert. As he approached the side road leading off the prescribed route he checked his mirror again, saw nothing odd. His indicator clicked stridently when he slowed to turn. Cased in the rear of an ordinary security van on an ordinary road in the middle of an ordinary day, should be around two million pounds, intended for destruction but due for reprieve.

The sun shone brightly. He eased his van into the side road. Two million pounds, half a million to be his share. Five hundred thousand pounds: a sufficiently large reward, as Gottfleisch called it. Scott left the side road for the alley, at the end of which stood a yard with open gates.

Within, the high buildings eliminated the sun. Tucked around to the left, out of sight, was a large empty truck, back open, ramp down. Beside the ramp, Cliff Lyons was waiting. He waved Scott on. Cliff wanted to hurry him, but Scott sat patiently in his seat, engine idling, his van in the shade.

Cliff started irritably towards him but Scott held up his hand. When Cliff opened his mouth, Scott shushed him. He was watching the second hand on his watch. Cliff Lyons took a breath, but Scott said, 'Journey point Freddie. Over.'

'Roger and out,' replied La Collinson. Now she would move her marker to New Cross Gate, journey point Freddie on Scott Heywood's trip.

He eased forwards slowly, up the heavy ramp into the enclosed space of the large lorry, then cut the engine. Silence was sudden. Light was gloomy. When Scott opened his door it moved barely two feet before it wedged against the side panel. He climbed out. Cliff had climbed in to join him in the back of the big truck, and was yanking a chain to hoist the tailgate vertical. Scott took the other side and bolted it in place. He stared out above the tailgate into the dead and empty yard.

He asked, 'Are you going to drive?'

'OK.'

'Better get on with it.'

'OK.'

Mildly puzzled, Scott turned round, and saw the gun held in Cliff's hand. Cliff grinned as he stepped forward. 'But you ain't coming. Bye, bye.'

SIX

As the gun fired—the sudden distant crack of a backfiring vehicle—Jet Heywood was in the shower. Long hair clung to his face like black seaweed and white lather dribbled down his body like foam. Had there been one of those men present who liked to linger around men's showers, he would have lingered now to view Jet's body, though Jet himself felt he was out of shape—too much soft fleshy sheen across his muscles. But he had till the weekend to get fit.

Just now he was thinking about Floyd Carter. During his career, Floyd had fought almost to the top, and presumably since leaving the ring had been sensible with his money. He seemed comfortable. He had the smartest gym in Deptford and no doubt a peaceful family life. Wouldn't know what it was like to face real problems.

When the hot water cut out, Jet pressed the button for a second shot. This was luxury, all right. He stood with his head back, water splattering his face, soap streaming from his body to leave him clean. A fight career was about fifteen years, which was . . . one fifth of his life. Not much. By that reckoning, Jet was two fifths through, still had more than half his life to go, so it was as good a time as any to work out how he meant to live the rest. His thoughts returned to Floyd. The man must have left the ring fifteen years ago, and since then had built this business. Unlike Jet, he had planned, had used his boxing experience to help create a professional gym. He didn't restrict the place to boxers, of course—he'd let in anyone, if they paid.

Jet stepped from the shower, reached for his towel, began to dry himself vigorously. A clean warm changing room, working lockers, uncracked tiles. Out in the gym itself, Floyd employed that dumb brother of his on easy jobs like sweeping floors. A family business—nothing spectacular or ambitious, but it kept them comfortable. An easy life.

Jet unlocked his locker and removed his clothes. No point sneering at 'the comfortable life', it was a damn sight better than either of the Heywood families had. Once they had both had prospects: his brother Scott had been in management but was now a driver, while Jet himself was . . . or had been . . . No, he was not even a has-been. Jet had never been anything.

He pulled on his clothes as if they were items of prison uniform. Shabby and shapeless, they symbolised his life. He had to change them. He had to change his life.

Once his head had emerged from the sweater, Jet shook out his long damp hair. Yes, it was time for a change, time to stop drifting, get back in shape. Time to stop brooding about Angie and to accept that she was no longer here. Her face flashed before him, clear as a photograph: her blonde hair flying, her mouth wide and laughing—

No. He would not think of her. He'd concentrate on now, today, and on the tomorrows that lay ahead of him—that three fifths of his life. As he left the changing room he shivered slightly. He must keep this mood. He could control his life; it was not shaped from outside—and the first tiny step in a new direction had been to quit the Cash & Carry. It marked the change.

Outside the gym, a sunny afternoon, Jet relished his uplifted mood. It wasn't simply the invigorating shower, the exercise, the talk with Floyd—he felt as fresh and sparkling as that bright blue sky above. Maybe Floyd's attitude had rubbed off on him; maybe he had been touched with Floyd's success. In the run-down street, Jet laughed aloud. If Floyd and his dumb brother could run the finest gym in Deptford, he must talk to his own brother about what *they* could do themselves.

Probably the last person to rise from his lunch that day—and by three o'clock even the most leisurely business account restaurants were closing their doors—was the gargantuan Gottfleisch, napkin in hand. La Ristorante Veneziana would always stay open for Gottfleisch, even when, as today, he dined quietly and alone. His simple meal comprised sopa coada (pigeon soup) followed by a light plateful of coda di rospo Santa Barbara (monkfish surrounded by carrots and peppers). He had foregone desert (it was the last week of Lent) but had permitted himself a morsel of montasio and biscuits. The whole meal had been properly accompanied with a carafe of Prosecco, though because of Lent, Gottfleisch spurned a digestivo. As he stood up to stroll through the empty restaurant, Gottfleisch was wondering which cuisine was the more pleasant to linger over—French with its creamy sauces, or Italian with its elegance. French was more filling: even Gottfleisch could rise replete from a well-laden French table, but Italian had more variety, more zest. What would be supreme, he decided, was a French main course—since Italian main courses were often quite plain—with Italian antipastos and their outrageously elaborate deserts. He was pleased that today he had eschewed desert.

The waiter handed him the telephone and silently withdrew. As he prodded the number, Gottfleisch watched the waiter walk away, swaying as he moved like a bulrush in a stream. Gottfleisch had watched him on and off for two hours, and had chatted between courses. Though he had little need to establish an alibi it gave him an excuse to pop out for lunch.

Ticky answered nervously. Gottfleisch purred, 'My dear boy.'

'Oh, hello, sir. I was hoping you were Cliff.'

'He hasn't phoned?'

'Not yet.'

'What?' Gottfleisch sucked his teeth. 'You kept the line clear?' He studied his wristwatch.

'Yes, sir. There must have been a hold-up on the road.'

'Quite. Very droll.'

'I meant—perhaps he's trying to call us now.'

'Possibly. Did you monitor their phone calls?'

'Yes, sir.'

'How long ago was Freddie?'

'Twenty minutes. Thereabouts.'

'And he hasn't phoned yet? I'll be back immediately.'

'Yes, sir. But it's probably the traffic.'

Gottfleisch replaced the phone, face pensive. Traffic seemed unlikely. As he strode from the restaurant the fine meal was quite forgotten and the waiters noticed that he did not say goodbye.

Jet Heywood bit into an apple—freshly picked from a market stall—and turned the corner into Deptford Broadway. Behind him, street traders called their wares, shoppers swirled, and because in the brightly sunlit market any radios were tuned to music stations, Jet never heard the news flash:

'Reports are coming in of a bullion robbery in southeast London. Details are scarce, but it is believed that an armed security van carrying more than a million pounds' worth of gold bullion was abducted as it made its journey from a central clearing bank to an unnamed site south of the city. A police spokesman said a few moments ago that the van literally disappeared from the London streets. The armed vehicle, its driver and the bullion itself vanished into thin air. Police are treating the case as suspicious. We go over now to our crime correspondent, Martin Busby.'

From which one could deduce that there were no reporters on the spot—wherever the spot was supposed to be. Gottfleisch glared at his reflection in the bathroom mirror while squeezing toothpaste on to his brush. Furiously, he began to scrub.

What the hell was going on? Why no phone call? Why did the unimaginative cretins at the BBC think the van was carrying bullion instead of cash? Bullion? Gottfleisch spat in the sink. No wonder the police were 'baffled'. Had he been double crossed? By Cliff Lyons? Gottfleisch shook his head. He prided himself on his ability to judge character. Lyons couldn't pull a double cross—he was unskilled, unintelligent and well paid. It would be incredible for that worm to turn. There must be another explanation. Gottfleisch spat more toothpaste into the sink. Then, as a dog might shake a rat, he swilled peppermint water around his mouth, spat out a final time and stamped downstairs.

Halfway down: 'Anything new?'

Ticky poked his head into the hall. 'No, the BBC—'

'Force Five, you insect.'

'Oh, no, they . . .'

'What?'

As Gottfleisch approached along the hall Ticky backed away from him into the lounge. 'Force Five has stopped using that frequency, sir.'

'Completely?' Gottfleisch surged like a tank through the double door.

'Well, yes, sir, after they'd called him several times—'

'All right, all right.'

Ticky gestured glumly at the CB receiver, black and modern on the antique table, hissing like a frying pan. 'I can't find their new wavelength.'

'Lyons has made a run for it—*hasn't he*? He has wasted Heywood and absconded with the van. *Hasn't he*?'

Gottfleisch felt mildly sick. He lumbered towards a side table and scooped some peanuts from a china bowl. Ticky asked, 'No chance that—um—Cliff and Woody might have worked this together?'

Gottfleisch stopped chomping. On his palette was a dry tickle of peanut oil. 'Together?' He felt sicker.

'It might have been . . . easier.'

Gottfleisch shook his head, paused, glanced at Ticky again and frowned. To assuage the churning in his stomach he grabbed another handful of peanuts and began eating them in pairs. After a few seconds he made up his mind. 'No, Lyons did this alone. He had no need to involve Heywood. He did exactly what I told him—to a point. He parked the lorry in the yard, waited for Heywood, let the poor fool drive the van inside—then shot him. As instructed.'

Ticky nodded gravely.

Gottfleisch continued. 'But instead of driving the lorry down to Haywards Heath . . .' Gottfleisch turned to Ticky, finally acknowledging his need for help: 'He took it *where*, Ticky, where?'

Ticky shook his head. Gottfleisch nodded vacantly, like a benevolent uncle. Without his apparently being aware of it, his hand moved towards the china bowl for another ounce of peanuts. But he didn't eat them. When he spoke, it was quietly, as if alone.

'It doesn't seem in character for him to have pulled this by himself—though I could be wrong. Perhaps he and Heywood did work as a team.'

He licked salt from a large peanut. 'We can't sit here waiting.'

'An update to our earlier story: the armed security van missing in south London was carrying banknotes, not gold bullion as reported before. The van is white, and carries the logo 'Force Five Security' on both sides. A spokeswoman for the company confirmed that the vehicle last made contact with Force Five in the New Cross area shortly before half past two this afternoon. There was nothing untoward about that call. The spokeswoman went on to say that the driver was an experienced and long-standing member of their staff. Police have made no further comment at this stage, but we will be staying with the story and will bring you more details as they come in.'

Though the radio was switched on in the Royal Albert it wasn't loud enough for Jet to hear. He came out of the pub into spring sunlight, the warm taste of whisky on his tongue. The bright blue weather began to be disturbed by a cold wind from the north—healthy, but not a breeze to stand about in.

Jet padded along the pavement like a dog let off the chain, gratefully inhaling the afternoon's crisp air. The shower, the walk, the whisky, all combined to restore what he had taken out of himself in the gym. He might not be back yet to ring fitness—he didn't need to be—and he might carry a few extra pounds (cruiserweight, said Floyd!) but he felt good. He was amazed that a single session could have had such an effect. And, of course, now that he had quit the nine to five he could use the gym every day—well, every day this week.

Jet glanced at the splendid sky. Brilliantly clear, clumps of cloud skudding in the high winds: he and the weather were in harmony. This was the kind of day to grab hold of and carry away, hard against his chest where he could savour it.

He was free.

Ticky watched Gottfleisch on the phone. As the big man's powerful fingers stabbed the numbers, Ticky felt proud to be there with him. Gottfleisch had allowed him to stay around—like a friend, someone to trust.

'Vinnie? You haven't lost him, have you? Good, but if it's just you and Craig, you had better *both* carry a gun. It won't be easy to take Ray Lyons.'

Ticky jerked his head. *Ray* Lyons? Gottfleisch was talking: 'I think *three* of you would be more advisable. Yes, but don't blow it, Vinnie. You knew it might come to this.'

He put the phone down. Ticky coughed delicately. 'You did mean *Ray* Lyons, sir?'

Gottfleisch threw his head back, revealing his magnificent triple chin. 'Cliff's brother. Know him?'

'Well, yes, of course.'

'Insurance.' Gottfleisch noticed the blank expression on Ticky's face. 'I never thought Cliff would have the balls.' He smiled. 'But I always guard against contingencies.'

Ticky nodded as intelligently as he could.

'And as you rightly pointed out, Heywood may be in it with him. Perhaps you'd pop round to collect his wife?'

Ticky seemed momentarily stunned. 'His wife?'

'An easy little number for you. I don't think you'll need a gun!'

Ticky swallowed. 'Bring her over here?'

'We may need her. So do it quickly, before the police get hold of her.'

Ticky took two steps, then paused. 'She won't be at home, sir.'

'Why not?'

'Half past three. Fetching the kid from school.'

'There's no *time* to waste on that!'

'Well, if I get over there . . .' Ticky grinned, rising to the task. 'I could bring the pair of them, if you like. Kiddies can be most persuasive.'

'More persuasive than a wife?'

Ticky smiled. 'Much more. The boy would . . . Oh, yes.' Ticky could not stop smiling. He seemed so sure.

'I don't know.'

'Believe me, sir.' Ticky placed his fist upon his chest. 'A little boy . . . gets you right here.'

Gottfleisch studied his little minion. 'All right. Do it. No, I can't believe Heywood is involved in this.'

'You can't trust no one, sir.'

'How true. Take them both, then, shall we?'

'Yes, sir, lets.'

'In the armoured van robbery in south east London, the banks now put their loss in excess of two million pounds. All the money was in old notes due for incineration this afternoon. It is believed that although the numbers of individual banknotes cannot be identified, the notes themselves were marked with a special ink to ensure that they can no longer be used. Throughout south London a major police hunt is under way, and the police are following several leads. The missing van, white, with a Force Five logo on both sides, is distinctive and unlikely to have been driven far. Searches are therefore concentrating on garages and off-street parking sites in the New Cross area. Within the last few minutes the driver of the missing van has been named as Scott Wayne Heywood, from Lewisham. The police have emphasised that for the present it cannot be known for certain whether Mr Heywood was party to the theft or was its victim. But at this stage there is no evidence of anybody else having been involved.'

By the time Scott's name went on the air, his wife was waiting outside school in cold sunshine. Somewhere more middle class than Ladywell, somewhere suburban, would have had more mothers waiting in cars who might have had the radio on. But few drove to school in Ladywell—traffic was thick, there was nowhere to park, and few local families owned a second car. So there was no excited housewife to lean eagerly from her car window and call, 'Mrs Heywood, something dreadful on the news—you didn't know?'

She stood at the railings, slightly apart. Maybe one in four might stand alone. While other mums chattered in little gaggles, one in four stood isolated, locked in a schedule of dull drudgery—get up, make breakfast, take the kid to school; stay indoors except for shopping; fetch the kid in the afternoon; make tea, listen to its troubles, face another evening indoors alone. A woman like that might spend six hours without saying a word. Her tongue would ache from lack of use, would seem swollen in her mouth. She would develop undiagnosable illnesses with vague symptoms and frequent gloom. If she saw the doctor she would find herself hampered by the very thing that she complained of—she couldn't talk about it, she could not explain, she had lost the habit of communication.

But now for all of them, the chatterers and the still, out poured the shrieking children like a shoal of fish poured from a net—hair streaming, clothes tangled, a riot of disorderly limbs. They shouted, laughed and ran in circles. They thronged through the small cast-iron gate. Claire leant against the railings to allow the first flood to pass, and she nodded to little Stella as she saw her walk by. The girl glanced up briefly, smiled and said, 'Hello'. Claire nodded a second time, but didn't speak. Watching her eight-year-old niece set off alone down the milling street, Claire's face set in disapproval—but she turned away, looked across the playground. Tommy wandered across wrapped in thought. She drifted towards the gate, and when the boy came out they walked silently down the street, hand in hand.

Ticky's scruffy green Fiat Panda was the kind of car other drivers avoided. It relished scrapes. It had reached that nadir of dirt and dented bodywork where the next stage was to fall apart.

When he parked in their little avenue he saw kids fresh out of school and thought, she must be home by now. Four o'clock. The house stood in the sun, nothing to show whether she was inside. The area had just enough petty respectability to sport Neighbourhood Watch stickers, so he slipped out of the car and made himself walk steadily towards their house in what he hoped was a demonstrably unfurtive fashion. If he'd been wearing a tie he would have straightened it. He rang the bell.

He couldn't hear anything so he rang again.

Damn.

Ticky dithered on the doorstep, then retraced his steps. He didn't want to be found waiting when they arrived, so he climbed back inside the car. The bloody woman should be home by now. Maybe that pretty boy of hers had enticed her to buy some sweets. Ticky smiled at the thought of it. Kids—always wheedling for something.

He sat smiling in his filthy car, he and it dual affronts

to the neighbourhood. The window was two inches down and the spring-like air wafted across his face. Glowering at their door, Ticky did not notice a white car pass from behind. It only burst into his consciousness when it slowed and braked at the Heywood door. Ticky stopped smiling. To be within a hundred yards of police brought him out in hives. When the officers climbed from their Ford he shrank in his seat. Should he get out? If they turned and saw him in the Fiat they might come over and ask why. But if he left the car, where would he go? Best thing was to sit tight and keep an eye on them. Only if they noticed him would he emerge.

The two cops rang on Woody's bell—one male, one female, a family call. They turned to face across the street. Ticky didn't move. While the police glanced up and down the street, Ticky continued to wonder whether to drive away. Would that be wise—under the gaze of the waiting plod, his old Fiat slips guiltily by? They would notice that.

Where the hell was Woody's wife? By this time Ticky was slumped so low in his sagging front seat he was barely visible. Only his scalp and eyes peeped above the dash, like a crocodile submerged in swamp.

Minutes ticked slowly by. Ticky's stomach began to rumble as he realised that he and the police would have to sit and wait.

Sometimes, when Stella walked home from school, she detoured through the old Ladywell cemetery, where the long grass seemed always to be wet and where blackened trees mourned the dead. Stella would walk among the graves, looking for a tombstone she had not noticed before. Often they revealed nothing, just a name and date, with perhaps a meaningless epitaph from the stonemason's book—though some of those little poems, Stella felt, had been composed by the grieving survivor.

> 'It is a loved one that has fled
> And left me here to weep.
> But all the tears that I can shed
> Cannot wake him from his sleep.'

Stella liked the way that so many of these old tablets talked of sleep rather than death. Grief was here; respect for a life that had 'passed away', but there was no reference to the rotting corpse beneath the ground. To Stella, this made the graveyard a sweetly sorrowful place. She had no horror of it. More than once she had asked herself whether she could walk between these graves deep in the night, alone. She could do it, except for the dark. She was certain—well, fairly sure—that she didn't believe in ghosts, and even if one did appear, she knew it would not harm her. Ghosts didn't frighten Stella, only the dark itself.

Of course, at night-time the graveyard was locked. There were notices all along the railings that read, 'These Premises Are Protected By Crime Prevention Guards Ltd. 24–hour Control.' It puzzled Stella. What could be stolen from a graveyard? She had asked her father about it— asked if the guards were to stop burglars coming in to steal the gravestones. But he, of course, had said no, they were to stop the ghosts from breaking out.

She was standing where she had stood several times before, beside a small white stone, still bright after more than a century of London weather. Stella suspected that the story told on the stone was unfinished—as if the mason had run out of room or had not been paid to chisel more. On another day she had even walked around the grave, her ankles dampened by uncut grass, to check that there was nothing written on the other side. The carved side read:

> 'In Loving Memory of
> Alfred Arthur Sutton
> Who Departed this Life, October 11th, 1892
> Aged 20 years.
> I have finished my Railway Career
> I am safe in the arms of Jesus.'

What was the meaning of those last two lines? Presumably the man's parents had chosen them—or perhaps his wife. Stella wasn't sure at what age people had married in those distant days, and twenty seemed old enough to her. But the words, she felt, were a parent's choice. Had he really worked on the railway, or were those lines just part of the flowery way people spoke back then? Twenty years old. Perhaps—and this, in fact, was what Stella had decided—perhaps he had been killed at work, had been run over by a train, had had the mangled remains of his broken body boxed up and buried here.

Stella walked behind the grave and set off in a fresh direction. On each visit she liked to find one new and interesting headstone. As she meandered towards a corner of the cemetery by Ivy Road, the wet grass stroked her lower shins, and each time that she knelt to peer at a half-obscured tablet, cold fingers of damp greenery crept inside her cotton skirt to touch her thigh.

She paused beside a grey rectangular headstone which had toppled over. To read its dirt-filled wording Stella had to kneel on the grave itself.

> 'In Loving Memory of
> Martha Stevens,
> Who sweetly fell asleep on August 30th, 1890,
> Aged 2 months.

An angel took my flower away,
But I will not repine,
For Jesus in His bosom wears
The flower that once was mine.'

Stella stood up slowly and looked around the deserted graveyard. Here was a special one indeed, and she wished she had someone to share it with. Just two months old. The sweet little baby had been properly buried just as if it had been grown up. Whenever she found a child's grave—and there were plenty in Ladywell cemetery— Stella was always struck by the way that their short lives had been so solidly commemorated. Two months old. This was what Stella considered a proper headstone—more than a century old—it had lain in the grass all that time to mark the passing of a little girl who only survived two months.

Stella wondered if she should try to stand the stone upright, but she knew that even if she could, she would disturb horrid worms, beetles and scuttling woodlice. Exposing those nasty creatures would be like opening the grave itself and finding that it teemed with maggots. Stella backed away. That image was the dreadful side of death—decomposition and decay. She preferred the sad melancholy of ancient verses. Even the old-fashioned names had a fleeting beauty: Martha Stevens, Alfred Arthur Sutton. She pictured her own name carved into stone: Stella Heywood. But it seemed so ordinary, so unromantic, not fit to last a hundred years.

As she walked between the overgrown graves she felt warmed by the discovery of this special one. Perhaps she would bring flowers to Martha Stevens—to show the little baby she was not forgotten. Was she looking down? Did a dead person know when you looked at their grave? Perhaps Martha's mummy and daddy also knew that after all these years a little girl thought of their child. Perhaps they also were buried here.

At the exit gate, Stella paused to look back across the quiet dappled plots. There were so many: she might not find Martha's parents, but she would revisit the little girl's grave. She tried to remember Martha's rhyme— something about a flower worn in Jesus's bosom. Stella smiled. It was a lovely picture. No one had told her that Jesus had a bosom.

Claire Heywood, holding Tommy's hand, turned into the wishfully named street called Hilly Fields. The boy trailed behind her like a dog on a short lead. Mother and son were each occupied with their thoughts, aware of each other only as part of their surroundings, a neutral undemanding element which needed no more acknow- ledgement than the loose contact of an inert hand. Nei- ther reacted to the presence of a white police car outside their door, nor to the scruffy green Fiat parked among cleaner cars across the street. They didn't see the small balding head inside, which turned to watch them walking by. Nor, for a moment or two, did they notice the large policeman who climbed quietly from his own more impressive car to wait for them beside their house.

SEVEN

Gottfleisch stared at little Ticky with the impassive stare of an elephant seal on a rock.

Ticky said, 'Maybe they've gone by now. I could go back.'

'She's under surveillance.'

'In case Woody tries to contact her?'

Gottfleisch was not in the mood for conversation. 'Or until she follows him.'

The phone rang. Gottfleisch grabbed the receiver and gave his name. Ticky watched his face lighten. 'Very good, Vinnie. Nothing broken? Bring him here.'

He put the phone down and inhaled deeply, still unsmiling, but with the serious expression of a man who had just sampled a fine wine. 'Ray Lyons,' he said.

Ticky looked impressed. 'Ray wasn't in it with Cliff?'

'No, everything points to Cliff being on his own. Foolish boy.'

'You don't think Woody was in it with him, sir?'

'I don't know.' Gottfleisch sighed with irritation. 'I did help him with that passport. One cannot be omniscient.'

Ticky nodded guardedly.

Gottfleisch said, 'Heywood was most insistent about that passport. He wanted to be absolutely certain he'd have a quick exit—which he had, of course, though he didn't need a passport.'

Ticky smiled dutifully. 'That was the trouble though, sir, wasn't it?'

'Hm?'

'Once Cliff killed Woody he was sitting pretty—a van full of money, another sucker to take the blame.'

'I can't believe it, Ticky.'

'He had a week to think about it, see? That was the problem. A week is a long time to think about two million quid.'

Gottfleisch nodded. 'I'd have paid him fifty thousand.'

'Yes, but you told Woody you'd pay *him*. Cliff knew that. And fifty thou' is not two million.'

Gottfleisch smiled thinly. 'Perhaps I'm too trusting of my fellow man. I trusted Heywood. I encouraged his elaborate passport scheme—it was hardly difficult—and of course, I promised him half a million pounds in cash. Over-egged it a bit, perhaps—half a million. That would buy anyone's loyalty, wouldn't you say?'

'It would certainly buy mine.'

'I should hope so. As a student of human relationships, Ticky, tell me, how well did Woody get along with his wife?'

'Oh.' Ticky scratched between the remaining hairs on his head. 'Nothing special.'

'Might he have been tempted to walk out on her?'

'For two million? I'd walk out on anyone.'

At their upstairs flat, Stella collected her towel and crossed the landing to their shared bathroom. It was fairly clean. Jet had taught her to clean it when she had finished and to help him scrub it at weekends, since no one else ever came to do it. The other two families who shared with them left things damp, with smears of soap around the basin. What Stella disliked most was that after Mr Henderson had had a shave he left specks of stubble around the sink, and until every speck had been cleaned away, Stella could not to bear to wash her face.

One tiny dot of shaven hair floating in the water was like an insect waiting to bite.

In the Heywoods' two-room flat a small table and chairs stood by the window. A fridge and food cupboard leant against the wall. Stella poured herself a glass of orange juice and helped herself to biscuits from the tin. She opened her books, sniffed at the questions, then began writing on a clean page. Typical homework—no connection with anything they'd learnt today; it was something the teacher should have taught them but had not got round to. She was halfway through when she heard a board creak out on the landing. Mr Henderson? No. When the door to their flat swung open, Stella thought, that's funny, Daddy's not due for another hour.

Gottfleisch sighed heavily, as if out of breath. He hated public telephones. But at least the Greenwich ones were normally working, and in these modern booths the excess of fresh air blew away the smells. There was no alternative to a public phone. The police could trace your number the moment you rang them.

No alternative, then.

If Scott Heywood was in this with Cliff, he'd presumably follow his original plan and be out of the country straight away on his false passport. Cliff Lyons could leave without need of a false passport. Whoever had crossed him, that was what they'd do. So Gottfleisch had two alternatives: either to make this telephone call, or to dash down to Gatwick airport and confront whichever of them checked in. Hardly practicable.

Gottfleisch paused inside the booth. For a while he had considered using Ticky to make the phone call— a different voice—and had brought him along while he thought it through. Now he looked down at the little man, grinning in the cold. Hardly practicable.

Gottfleisch lifted the receiver with distaste, as if it were someone else's sausage left on the shelf. 'Duty officer, if you please.' Gottfleisch held the receiver away from his cheek. 'Good day to you. Some information about the armoured van robbery this afternoon. Yes, Force Five. The driver, Scott Heywood, recently took out a passport in the name of Henry Scott. Don't interrupt. Henry Scott. But more importantly, Heywood has recently been associated with an undesirable type by the name of Lyons, Cliff Lyons, yes, L-Y-O-N-S, Lyons, who has a record, by the way. He is your man. Put it on the radio.'

He replaced the phone. He looked like a man who had performed a painful duty. 'I feel strangely purged,' he confessed to Ticky. 'But I think that covers everything.'

Stella remained seated by her homework. From the table by the window she acknowledged her father with surprise. 'I thought you were working?'

Jet grinned. 'Not any more, sweetheart. I jacked it in.'

She frowned—not at his words, but at the telltale smell he had brought in with him. 'You've been drinking.'

'I haven't—'

'You pong.'

'I have not "been drinking". I had a drink.'

She raised a spinster's eyebrow.

He said, 'One drink—no, it was two.'

'Losing count?'

'Listen—' He pointed his finger, but then he grinned. 'I've done with drinking.'

She continued to stare.

'Over and done.'

Stella accepted his words. 'Cup of tea?'

'Yes—no, not tea.'

'You *have* been drinking. Coffee?'

'I'll have some water.'

'See?'

He gave her a lazy late afternoon smile. 'For an eight-year-old girl you don't half nag.'

'Eight and a half.'

He pulled a face. 'A half! That's nearly nine.'

She laid down her pen. 'You've jacked in your job?'

'I couldn't hump boxes week after week. How'd you like to get out of here?'

'We're moving?'

'Maybe.'

'Another job?'

'In a way.'

Stella stood up carefully. 'Are we going far?'

'Well, we'll have to leave the flat.'

'Why?' She had come close now, and Jet held her gently.

'The new job will mean travelling,' he said.

'But there *is* a job?'

'Uh-huh. I have to sort out the details.'

Stella rested her head against her father's chest. His clothes smelt of pub beer and cigarettes. 'I don't mind leaving.'

He stroked her hair. 'You don't want to stay in a dump like this.'

She jerked her head back. 'We'll be together, Dad? You're not going on your own?'

He smiled, but before he could answer, there was a knock at the door. Squeezing her arms, he said, 'We'll always be together.'

When he opened the door, there were two policemen in uniform: 'Mr Heywood?'

He nodded.

'Can we come in?'

It was another hour before the latest twist hit the national news:

'The police have just revealed that Mr Scott Wayne Heywood, driver of an armoured van which disappeared this afternoon in the Lewisham area, recently acquired a false passport in the name of Henry Scott. The name has been passed to ports, airports and emigration authorities, though, a few minutes ago, in announcing this development, a police spokesman emphasised that they are keeping an open mind on the case so far. They stress that it is not clear whether the driver took the money himself or was captured with it. Nevertheless, non-police sources agree that the second passport is an unexpected development, and must raise questions about the driver's innocence. When the van disappeared around half past two this afternoon it was estimated to have been carrying at least two million pounds in old banknotes. We go now to our crime correspondent, Martin Busby.'

There was no mention of Cliff Lyons.

—Whose brother Ray was strapped into a wooden chair in the basement of a house in Greenwich. Ray Lyons was a large, mean-looking man whose black hair had been wet-combed flat from his marble forehead. His thick dark eyebrows clung to his brow like furze to a precipice, and his angry eyes smouldered like hot cinders. They looked as if he had washed them once and they had shrunk.

He sat belted into the chair, hands tied by cord beneath the seat. His captors, Craig and Vinnie, stalked the floor around him, out of range of his untied feet. The way the blond Craig held the Mauser in his fist—awkwardly, as if it was someone's wallet he had filched—made Lyons furious with himself: a bloody amateur, probably never fired outside a range. And Vinnie Dirkin, his red hair crew-cut American style, his face a blotched assembly of old spare parts—Ray should have known that anyone who partnered Dirkin had to be a nerd. Everyone knew that Dirkin was bad news—a born loser, jinxed, walking disaster. Tough enough, yet he always seemed to come off worst—the sort of punk you slapped him in the face, he stepped backwards, tripped over his ankle, fell, cracked his head against a wall. The punk had a misshapen ear, sewn back after some affray, yet he wore a crew cut, kept the ear exposed. And it was these two had got him strapped in a basement—Jesus! Two punks he wouldn't trust to steal a car.

Ray eyed the blond kid as he edged closer, still clutching the Mauser like he didn't know what to do with it. Had they been lucky! They had jumped him half asleep, feet up, can open, watching TV. Had crept into the room just as the gee-gees rounded the straight, commentator screaming his teeth out, and they'd put the gun against his head. Said to come along.

Ray watched the kid. Pretty soon, when this game was over, he was going to stretch that boy along the floor, walk on him, maybe dislocate his shoulder, then ask him who had given them his key. Ray was confident now that this game *would* be over; they had only brought him here to be pumped. Some business about his brother. Couldn't be much. It began to sink in on Ray that the Mauser must be as useless as it looked: the kid wouldn't be allowed to use it. They wanted answers.

His chair scraped as he turned to Vinnie, lounging against the wall. 'You got my brother here?'

Vinnie shrugged.

Ray leant forward, clambering to his feet, despite being tied in his chair. 'I asked you a question—'

'Sit down!' Craig yelled.

'Fuck off.' Bent as a lobster crawling from its shell, Ray lurched for Vinnie—who nipped aside. Craig yelled again. Ray charged at Vinnie. Dirkin dodged as Craig came in behind. Ray checked, lunged backward, felt the chair-leg catch Craig's trunk. He thrust again, twisted, tried to stay on his feet, but felt Craig grappling with the chair. Ray swung it, came round fast, was suddenly face to face with Craig. Or face to chest, since he was bent double by the chair. As Craig's fist crashed towards his head, Ray kicked up between his legs. But from his stooped position he couldn't make it. He and Craig both lost their balance, and as Ray fell back he twisted to avoid falling on the chair.

He still fell badly. The wooden chair refused to break. Ray slithered across the floor, trying to catch Craig before he rose, but with his hands beneath the chair he could not move quickly enough. Craig scrambled up, skipped away, darted back to punch Ray's head.

Ray launched straight at him. But now Dirkin had joined the fray—had hold of the chair, was heaving from behind. Ray let himself be pulled. This time when he hit the floor, the unfortunate Dirkin was beneath him, almost impaled, could have been stuck to the floor like a moth to a board. A chair-leg splintered. Struggling to his feet, Ray pulled his hand past where the leg had been—but because his body was strapped in, because his hands were roped together, he found himself still attached to the wooden chair. The hell with this. He rushed at Craig, saw him raise the Mauser, saw him step aside because he could not fire.

The door crashed open. No one moved. Framed in the doorway was little Ticky, like the weather man in a cuckoo clock. Ray started forward. But behind Ticky the space filled with a colossal presence: Gottfleisch, bleak-faced, fresh laundered and in command.

'We've met, of course,' declared the fat man.

Craig said, 'He tried to escape, but we—'

'Enough.' Gottfleisch moved a hand. 'That was an old chair, I presume?'

No one answered. They all breathed heavily.

Gottfleisch continued. 'You understand why we brought you, Lyons? Where's your brother?'

Ray stared at him. He had thought Cliff was working for Gottfleisch—what had he done?

'You heard the question?'

'I heard.' Ray saw no point in silence. 'I don't know where he is.'

Gottfleisch's expression did not change. Ray said, 'I'm supposed to talk, tied in this chair?'

Gottfleisch stared at him. After several seconds, Ray lumbered to the bare brick wall, stood sideways on to it, then suddenly twisted and crashed the chair against the wall. Another leg fell off. Ray suspected that to break the back away from the seat could be painful, but he had no choice. Again he smashed against the wall. Nothing happened. Though his back was afire, the damn kitchen chair would not break apart. Ray prepared to smash again but Gottfleisch said, 'That's enough, you'll disturb the bricks. Vinnie, dear boy, set Lyons free.'

Everyone paused. As Vinnie edged across to Ray he seemed to wince with remembered pain. Ray didn't move. He waited.

Gottfleisch stepped fully into the room. 'Don't raise your hopes, Lyons. Despite that little tantrum of yours, you won't leave till you have told me what I want to know.'

Ray nodded. He could talk to Gottfleisch, who was a man he could respect. Vinnie fumbled behind him, untying the belt till the chair fell away. Ray Lyons stretched. His hands were still roped together but it felt good to stand erect.

Gottfleisch said, 'That rope's too slack.'

The little gnome who stood beside Gottfleisch grinned, fumbled in his jacket pocket, brought out a pair of handcuffs. Gottfleisch turned to him and smiled for the first time since he had appeared.

'You do collect the most extraordinary things.—No, don't tell me, I'd rather not know.'

Jet stood with his back to the room, staring out of the window as if there were something outside that might be interesting. He heard a policeman come out of the bedroom.

'Nothing.'

The black cop sniffed. 'If I'd just stolen two million pounds, that isn't where I would hide it.'

Jet flinched at the words 'two million': it was the first time they'd said how much. He turned to find the cops watching him expectantly. He felt dull, disinclined to speak. Beside him at the table Stella sat doodling in her exercise book.

'So where is he?' asked the white cop.

Jet didn't reply. Stella said, 'I hope you've left my room tidy.'

Jet reached down and touched her shoulder.

'Is that what you teach your daughter—to cheek policemen?' The cop glanced around the room. 'So you're short of money, right?'

'Who isn't?'

The policeman leered. 'Not your brother, right? Not any more. How much you hoping for?'

The white one joined in: 'Mr Heywood, you know the second passport your brother acquired?'

No reaction.

'You know: "Henry Scott"—it was on the news.'

Still no reaction.

'It wasn't you who phoned us about it?'

Pause.

'Was it?'

The black cop laughed. 'Hey, I forgot that. Was that you?'

Jet looked at him. They held the silence.

'Your brother didn't pull this on his own, did he?'

'I wouldn't know.'

'He must have talked to you?'

'No.'

'Surely you talk to your own brother? When was the last time you saw him?'

'Yesterday.'

The cops glanced at each other, then the white one said to Jet, 'If he's hidden the van, d'you think that we won't find it? Or he can use that second passport? Or he can show his face? Believe me, by this time tomorrow, the whole thing will be over.'

'So why are you here?'

The white one smiled. 'Perhaps this was just a mistake—you know, a sudden madness? Carrying all that money, he suddenly realises what's in the back, and drives away? By now, of course, he's in deep water.'

His companion continued this softer line. 'If he gave himself up now, that'd make a hell of a difference.'

'Much lighter sentence.'

'Don't you want to help him? I mean, the man's busted anyway, but you could . . . do what a brother should.'

'That's right, Mr Heywood. It's what I'd want *my* brother to do for me.'

Jet shook his head. 'Are you rehearsing for a TV series? Look, I don't believe my brother did this—he's too straight.'

'Could have been an impulse.'

'Where d'you think he'd hide?'

'He was hijacked.'

The black cop came close. 'Oh, come *on*! Are you going to help, or do we take you down the station?'

'Am I under arrest?'

'Helping with enquiries.'

Jet sighed. 'If I come down the station, who'll look after my daughter?'

No one replied. The black one said he'd call the station and as he strolled to the far side of the room he unclipped his mobile from his belt. They watched him identify himself, then: 'We've interviewed the suspect's brother. Says he doesn't know anything. Shall we bring him in?'

He held the phone to his ear, and they saw his expression change. 'Oh, right. Can I reveal that?'

He carefully reclipped the mobile to his belt, as if it was important that it hung at the regulation angle. As he came across the room he seemed to be deciding what to say. He didn't look at the white cop but kept his gaze on Jet. He came so close that he could have held Jet in his arms.

'I'm afraid they found the van. It had been burnt out. Your brother's body was found inside.'

So far, the news had not been relayed to Claire Heywood's house, where the front room reeked of uncleaned uniforms. The policeman and woman seemed to fill the room, and Claire felt invaded. They kept asking questions, standing in front of her at either side, so that she was not able to look at both of them at once. She wanted to sit, but it didn't seem correct somehow to lounge in an armchair while being interrogated by police. Besides, if she left them standing they would loom over her. And she wouldn't invite them to sit—their bulky uniforms, dusty with street dirt, touching her upholstery—

'What? I'm sorry, I didn't catch that.'

'I asked what time your husband normally comes home?'

'Oh, I—' For some silly reason Claire glanced at her watch. 'Around six, but it varies. It rather depends on what duties he has to perform.'

'Duties?'

'Yes, he's—he's not a nine to five worker, you know. Sometimes he has to see an important job through.'

'Make a late delivery?'

She closed her eyes briefly. 'Some of my husband's clients can be very demanding.'

Claire realised that she would have to sit down. She wondered if they would allow her to bring in a kitchen chair: it might look out of place but at least it would have a straight back.

'Were you expecting him at his normal time tonight? He didn't say anything?'

'No. Can I—'

'Yes?'

She glanced at Tommy in his armchair—the only person sitting.

'Can I sit down?'

'It's your house.'

It didn't seem like it. Claire hesitated between the too-enveloping armchair and the spacious sofa, but she chose

the chair. To choose the sofa might encourage the policeman to sit there too, like an insurance salesman trying
to ingratiate himself.

'Where do you think he's gone, Mrs Heywood?'

The soft comforting armchair made her realise how
much she had been containing herself. She closed her
eyes and tried to relax. Her shoulders were hunched into
her neck, and as she forced them down she heard the
man repeating, 'Where d'you think he's gone?'

Gone. The word struck hollowly like a funereal bell.
She had a sudden vision of Scott driving an open sports
car, his arm draped round a girl's shoulder, her blonde
hair blowing freely in the breeze, their faces in the sun.

'Is there some favourite spot you go on holiday?'

The policeman's face appeared in front of her. Something about its brutish masculinity typified the callous-
ness of men—they way they always set the rules, did
what they chose, dragged women along.

Or left them behind.

'Mrs Heywood—'

She burst into tears. In a single moment the tension
in her body had disappeared, as if she had held her breath
too long and had now released it.

'Oh Christ,' the policeman said. As Claire wept into
her hankie she didn't see his glance to the policewoman.
Already, Tommy was out of his chair, had grabbed his
mother's arm, was glaring up. 'Leave my Mummy alone.'
His six-year-old treble sounded severe.

'Yeah.' The policeman gestured to his companion to do
the feminine compassion bit, but she came hesitantly.
When she touched the boy he shrugged her off. She rested
her hands on him.

The man said, 'I'm sorry, Mrs Heywood, but I have to
ask these questions. Do you know of any travel plans your
husband might have made? You know—the passport?'

Through her tears she remained obedient. 'He hasn't mentioned any to me.'

Her answer made Tommy frown, but no one noticed. The big cop decided to plough through her grief: 'Mrs Heywood, do you think . . . is there any chance he's gone off with someone else?'

She sobbed the louder. Tommy shouted, 'Go away! You're horrible!'

He told the woman, 'You'll have to take the boy away.'

When the policewoman tightened her grip, Tommy tightened his own upon his mother. 'No! I'm not leaving my Mum.'

As the woman tried to free his fingers, Claire said, 'Go with her to the kitchen, Tommy. You'll be all right.'

'They're hurting you.'

'No.'

'She's hurting *me*!'

Claire could not bear the fuss; it was so undignified. 'Please go along with her, darling. Mummy will be fine.'

'I *won't*.'

'Please, darling. They only want to talk.'

'No.'

'It's grown-up stuff.'

Though he looked affronted, Tommy released his hold. When the policewoman tried to take his hand, he wriggled free and marched to the door. 'I'll be in the kitchen. Call if you want me.'

The woman followed. But before she reached the door, the man signalled above Claire's head, pointing upstairs, moving his fingers to his lips to indicate that she should check there silently. The woman withdrew. He watched Claire dry her tears.

'I know it's painful, Mrs Heywood, but we all want to help your husband.'

She shivered. 'How?'

'We think he got into this by mistake. Perhaps you could try to think where he might be hiding.'

'I don't know.'

'You do want to help him, don't you?'

She looked up at the policeman angrily. To her own surprise she said, 'He can burn in hell.'

NINE

In the morning before he got up, Jet listened to the radio news in case it might have changed, but it hadn't: the burnt-out van, ignited with its own petrol, the charred remains of the driver's body, all the money carried off. It surprised Jet that they could be so certain: paper would have burnt, disappeared away. But the police insisted that the money had gone. Maybe Forensics could tell, by sifting embers, raking ash. Maybe they knew what kind of residue was left by paper. Maybe they had opened the black oven that had been a van, let the heat out, then poked inside. Empty. Or maybe there had been no need for Forensics—any idiot could have guessed that the money would have been removed. No one would hijack an armoured van, set light to it, shoot the driver—only to let the money go up in flames. That was the other news, of course: they had shot the driver.

In an odd way, Jet was relieved—Scott hadn't suffered in the fire. They hadn't locked him in the cabin and let him die there, trapped in flames. Presumably the men had thought there was little point trying to make it look an accident—sad death of a driver, cargo up in smoke. Who would buy that? No, instead, they had behaved clinically—seized the van, driven somewhere quiet, taken the money, destroyed the evidence. Scott was part of the evidence. Maybe when they had stopped him in the south London street they had not worn masks, and afterwards were afraid he would identify them. Around Bermondsey, people were used to pretty extraordinary street fashion, but men in masks, well, they'd stand out.

Perhaps Scott had known them. Indeed, yesterday, for the first few hours, everybody wanted to suggest that he had been involved. The police acted as if convinced of it. That story about the second passport, as if Scott had planned it all along . . . Jet shook his head. Last night, when he had told the police he did not believe it, it had been the truth: not his brother, not old Scott. Too damn straight.

Jet was out of bed now, was fixing cereal for Stella. She had heard the news. Breakfast for the Heywoods was silent, indigestible, and neither of them made any attempt to speak. They turned the radio off. Once or twice they touched each other's hand, tried a half-smile, a little nod. Then he walked the child to school.

The shabby green Fiat Panda stood unnoticed at the kerb. At this time of morning the little street was tight with as much traffic as it ever saw. In the fifty-yard stretch by the school railings, the few cars dropping off their children jostled for position like cattle in a pen, shouldering into gaps, vacating them, pumping exhaust fumes into the air. They were old, well-travelled second cars—where the husband had the better, or where this was the only car they had. They had the look of second cars. Ladywell was a poor district—not tenemented and hard, but under-nourished and scraping by. Most kids came to school on foot.

Ticky's Panda blended well. City dirt had muted its vivid green until the car had taken on the same greyness as its surroundings. Behind the wheel, its tiny driver perched like a ventriloquist's dummy, and his bright eyes, like the dummy's, seemed painted glass.

Once he had spotted the Heywoods, Ticky sat upright. Jet wore a comfortable old tracksuit, and the way his unfashionably long dark hair bobbed in the breeze reminded Ticky of an athlete from the old Eastern Europe. Little Stella had her dad's dark hair, and her almond face looked sad and thoughtful, as if she was brooding about her uncle. Ticky watched for people's reactions in the street—yes, he could spot them. Other parents turned to watch the Heywoods as they passed. Jet seemed unaware but Ticky, focusing on Stella, saw her dark eyes flicker from side to side. Until now, she might have distanced herself from the tragedy, but among her schoolmates she would become involved. When Jet left her at the gates he stooped to kiss her, but she turned self-consciously and walked away. Halfway across the playground she turned to see if he was still there, and he waved to her, just once.

From the front seat of his car, Ticky continued watching. Jet strode away. Parents melted from his path. In the playground, slowly hovering children closed in on Stella like encircling gulls. Ticky opened his car door and jumped out. Beside the railings, he ambled, hands in pockets, like a dawdling parent.

'They was always thieves.' A woman's voice, and Ticky stopped.

'You can't say that—he was respectable.'

'My arse. His wife's a stuck-up cow.'

'I feel sorry for her.'

'You can't trust drivers. Think of minicabs.'

'But he's dead.'

'What about that passport? There's no smoke.'

Ticky peered through the school railings. Stella was almost invisible to him now, but as far as he could make out, the kids around her were not taunting, but were agog to hear her story. Their little faces were alert. Ticky thought them sweet.

'We won't see *her* again.'

'His missis?'

'You mark my words.'

Ticky glanced across his shoulder at the two women close behind. The know-all had her arms folded.

'They'll look after her, you'll see.'

'Who will?'

'His gang—if they get away with it.'

Ticky concentrated on the playground.

'Don't be daft—they murdered him. You don't know what you're on about.'

'We'll see.'

'His poor wife. I bet it's ages before the funeral. Them post-mortem people always hang on to the body.'

'Want to get it right. Make sure they find everything.'

'They found that bullet in him.'

'Lucky it didn't melt.'

'What they can do!'

'I told you about that minicab I took to Hammersmith?'

'Hammersmith—what for?'

'When I found that packet of you-knows in the back?'

'Oh yes. Had they been used?'

'No! The driver seen me in his mirror. They're mine, he says, they're mine.—What, in the back seat of your car, I says, not likely. Where else? he says. I said, they fell out of someone's handbag. Finder's keepers, I'll have them now.'

'You could have tossed him for it.'

'Oh, you minx!'

When the large woman stepped back laughing, she collided with Ticky against the railings. 'Sorry, son,' she said, clutching his arms. 'Shouldn't you be in school?' Then she saw his face, his thinning hair. 'Oh sorry, love.'

Staring up at the two huge women, Ticky felt like a kid caught with a cigarette. 'That's all right,' he muttered, scurrying away. But before he was out of earshot he heard, 'Could've used a bath.'

Ticky marched beyond the railings to the corner of the street. By the time he turned, the women were strolling away. Everyone, in fact, was drifting homewards. Cars were gone. Ticky wandered slowly back beside the railings, peeping inside to watch the children assembling in untidy lines. They looked so innocent, so fresh. Ticky wasn't fooled: he knew that behind their beguiling faces, kids were more devious than they looked. Dirty little buggers, most of them. Little characters already formed. This playground, like any other, had fat boys who would never be thin, little know-alls, little runts. And they wouldn't change. They'd be the same when adults. The tough kids, the studious, the also-rans. Look at the pretty ones—the way they preened. Look at that tall boy, born to lead. Look at the smarmy, I'm a good boy, just you touch me and I'll scream—the dangerous type. Look at the lonely ones, who would not tell.

Among the lines of fidgeting children, Ticky located the sombre Stella with her gypsy hair. She looked lonely. The bars of the iron railing were rough and rusty against his face, and he stepped back and walked away. A teacher called class numbers. At the end of the railings, Ticky took a final glance. As they trooped into school, the lines of obedient children bobbed like flowers in the April sun.

In the house of mourning, curtains had been closed and electric lights glowed against the day. Claire, gaunt and thin, sat in an armchair with a tray of untouched breakfast beside her on a side table. Young Tommy sat at her knee. A tired-looking policewoman held Claire's wrist with all the enthusiasm of a student nurse taking a pulse.

Jet asked if he and Claire could be alone.

'Can't do any harm.'

As she left, the policewoman patted Claire's lifeless hand and said, 'See you later, dear,' as if Claire cared. Jet waited till they had gone.

Tommy said, 'Hello, uncle Jet.'

'Hi. You OK?'

Tommy nodded, but he didn't smile. Claire said, 'This is dreadful.'

'I know.'

'Did Scott ... give you ...'

'He didn't tell me anything.'

Claire let out a sigh. 'They still think he was involved in it.'

Jet paused. 'Because of the passport?'

She frowned. 'How d'you know about that?'

'It was on the news.'

She paled, and he put his hand gently on her shoulder. She said, 'I can't listen to it.'

'You shouldn't try. Don't you want that breakfast?'

She shook her head. 'How about you, Tommy?'

'I had some orange juice.'

'Didn't you eat anything?'

'No.'

After a moment, Jet crossed to the curtains and tried to peer through a gap without disturbing them. 'Can't the cops shift those reporters?'

No one replied. Jet left the curtains and sat down in the other armchair. 'Has anyone else come?'

She shook her head.

'I'll have to see Dad.'

Calmly, Claire said, 'A few days ago, Scott was fiddling with our passports. He asked where we'd like to go.' Her voice trembled on the final word.

'Did you tell the police?'

'What's the point? Scott is . . . dead. It doesn't matter now.'

'Well . . .'

'Scott was going to send for us, I'm sure.' She gazed at him, dry-eyed. 'That's why he asked about our passports.'

Jet licked his lips. 'Where did you tell him you'd like to go?'

'Nowhere. I didn't take the hint.'

'Did *he* suggest somewhere?'

'I don't think so.' Claire glanced down at her son. 'Of course, he couldn't . . . be more explicit at the time. He had to make sure he arrived there safely, and that no one would know where he had gone, and . . .' Her voice petered out.

'Then he'd send for you?'

'Yes.'

They fell silent again, till little Tommy looked up at Jet and said, 'He'd tell *you*.'

'But he didn't.'

'He could have phoned you from his hideout.'

Jet smiled sadly. The boy continued. 'I bet his plan was—'

'Shut up, darling, there's a dear.' Claire's eyes were closed, and her face was drawn. 'Let Mummy have a little hush.'

Ray Lyons lay in a foetal position on the concrete floor, a gag taped across his mouth. His left wrist was handcuffed to his left ankle, as was his right wrist to the other. He felt things could have been worse: he and Brick Mulloney had once trussed a punk like this while they transported him in a van. But Ray had done it properly—crossing the punk's arms to restrict movement: right wrist to left ankle and vice versa. Painful. When he and Brick had rolled the punk out of the van and unclipped him, they found that the punk couldn't stand, couldn't even straighten on the ground. Said his back had gone. Eventually Ray and Brick had heaved on him from each end and had forced his body straight. The punk had screamed more about that than later, when they had Doc Martined him. What had amused Brick most about it—he just could not stop laughing—was that when they first pulled and released the punk, he immediately refolded like a spring. Like a weak spring, he didn't curl quite as tightly as before—just almost. Brick liked the game—wanted to keep stretching and releasing to see how far the punk would bounce back. But Ray said it was better to kick his head.

Today, though, Gottfleisch's boys were playing gentle—after they tied him they just dropped him on the floor. Ray, if he'd wanted to hold someone, he'd have put the boot in, softened him up. But it seemed that these south London punks didn't know why they'd taken him—some wrangle with his brother, that dickhead Cliff. They didn't know how to question—went through the motions, that was all. Dirkin had hardly touched him—because, presumably, he was afraid of what might happen after Ray was released. Which was comforting—because it meant he *would* be released. In fact, the only bruises Ray had incurred so far had come from the blond kid, Craig. Ray Lyons sniffed. Life was too short to waste on fretting about stuff like that. He would save his anger for when he could use it.

Jet said, 'Let the servants get it.'

When the doorbell rang the Heywoods made no attempt to answer it but like a pre-war middle-class family in their parlour, stayed where they were. They heard someone trundle down the hallway to the door. Heard him talk to whoever had called. Heard the door close, and whoever was out there come inside. More muttering in the hall. They waited.

Somebody knocked on the living room door.

Jet called, 'Come in!'

The new man was older, tall and gangling, wearing tweedy plain clothes in the vain hope that one day someone somewhere might not recognise him as a cop.

'Oh, Mrs Heywood? Good morning.' He glanced at Jet. 'And you, sir.'

They watched him. At Claire's feet, Tommy slipped his thumb into his mouth.

'I have some news for you about your husband. I—er—naturally, we would wish to inform you before releasing it more widely.'

The policewoman appeared. She came straight through the doorway and floated towards Claire.

'Yes, I suppose that in a way, this may seem like good news, but . . . Well, we've done the autopsy, Mrs Heywood, and—er—it appears that the body in the armoured van was—um—not your husband.'

Tommy looked at Jet and smiled.

TEN

At that moment, Ray Lyons was half asleep. When he heard the key squeak he rolled over, first on his front, then into a kneeling position, which was how they found him: Craig and Vinnie, followed by Gottfleisch. The three men marched over and stopped before him as if they had rehearsed the move.

Gottfleisch said, 'Take the gag out.'

It was his blond fag who did it, Ray noticed—Vinnie trying to keep his sheet clean, just in case. Craig reached forward and ripped the sticky tape from Ray's mouth. Then he hesitated. Ray had drawn the bung of the gag into his mouth so that it was tucked behind his strong teeth, which lay bared.

'Open up.'

Ray did so. Staring coldly at Craig, he opened his teeth about a finger's width apart. The bung was jammed behind his sharp teeth, and he was daring Craig to stuff his finger inside to pull it out. While Craig hesitated, Ray slowly closed his teeth, grated the edges together, then opened them again.

'Use this,' said Gottfleisch, producing a nail-file from his jacket pocket. The blond kid poked the curled end into Ray's mouth and extracted the bung. It came awkwardly, and while Craig fiddled to get it, Ray did not move. He knelt before the three men, arms pulled tight behind his back as if waiting for communion. He looked angry. He sustained an air of cold stillness as if it were he who threatened them.

Gottfleisch took back his nail-file. 'This is the last time we shall talk.'

His two supposed musclemen moved closer to stand one either side of Ray.

Gottfleisch said, 'Tell me where your brother is.' He left the sentence in mid-air, as if there might be some consequence he had left unsaid. Ray stared back silently, and Gottfleisch tilted his head to show that he expected an answer.

They continued to watch each other. Gottfleisch hissed, 'Where is he?'

'Want me to make something up?'

A glint of light flashed on Gottfleisch's nail-file. 'I am not a patient man, Lyons. Did your brother tell you what he was doing for me?'

'No.'

Gottfleisch sighed. 'Then I'll tell you, as a special favour. After that, you will help me find him.' He leant forward, placing the point of the nail-file on Ray's cheek. 'If you don't, I shall gouge out your eye.' He held the pause, then asked softly, 'Understand?'

'Yeah.' Since the nail-file stayed where it was, Ray chose not to nod.

'Yesterday an armoured van disappeared, containing two million pounds.'

There was a slight reaction in Ray's eyes, a slight stiffening in his posture, which suggested to Gottfleisch that Ray had not expected this to be what they talked about. That was unfortunate: perhaps Ray would not be able to help, after all. Gottfleisch removed the nail-file from beneath Ray's eye.

'After your brother intercepted the van, he should have delivered it to me. But he didn't.'

'I heard about it.'

'From him?'

'From the telly. It was on the news, wasn't it? They found the van.'

'But no money.'

'Well, the van was burnt out,' Ray said.

'And the driver had been shot.'

'Not by Cliff. You can't lay that on him.'

'Of course I can. It's what I instructed him to do.'

Ray was silent. He watched Gottfleisch. Vinnie and Craig waited at Ray's shoulders like a pair of unused cushions. Gottfleisch said, 'Now, you will be aware that what I have told you makes you dangerous to me.' He pointed the nail-file. 'Where would Cliff go?'

Ray shrugged.

Gottfleisch narrowed his tiny eyes. 'I advise you to think very carefully. Who does Cliff know? Where would he hide? Don't waste my time.'

Having held his kneeling position for so long, Ray's knees were beginning to hurt. He shifted his weight back on his heels. 'The first thing he'd do . . . is he'd call me. But he didn't.'

'Why not?'

Ray shrugged.

'Who else might he have called?'

'Two million quid—why should he call someone?' Ray asked wryly. 'Cliff don't have a girlfriend. No one special.'

'Another gang?'

Ray frowned. 'Who else was involved in this?'

Gottfleisch did not respond.

'Just Cliff and the driver? He shoots the driver and is on his own?'

'Correct.'

'With two million quid?'

'Yes.'

'Don't seem very clever.'

Gottfleisch was about to reply when suddenly the basement door burst open and little Ticky came rushing in. 'Mr Gottfleisch! Can I have a word?'

'Later.'

'It should be now, sir.' He held his place in the doorway. 'Only take a moment, sir.'

Gottfleisch hesitated, then came. He closed the basement door. Outside in the carpeted hallway, Ticky repeated the latest news from the radio. Gottfleisch asked, 'Have they named him?'

'No, but the thing is that the stiff ain't Woody—that's all they said.'

'Then who the hell—'

'Well, presumably . . .' Ticky shrugged.

'I see. There's no chance that anybody else could have muscled in?'

'Seems unlikely, sir, doesn't it? And if someone else *had* jumped 'em, well, there'd have been *two* bodies in the van.'

'So, presumably, as you say—'

'It must be Cliff Lyons.'

Gottfleisch nodded. 'So Scott *Heywood* is the naughty boy.'

ELEVEN

Three times the grey Cavalier circled the block. In a restricted parking area on the main road it waited five minutes then cruised past again. No one. No police. No press. No one on to this particular angle yet. Finally, the two men shortened the block and drove straight to the house. They got out. Vinnie knocked at the door. Doing so started dogs barking somewhere inside, and they heard a man quieten them. The door opened on a chain. Through a six-inch gap appeared an old man's unshaven face. He stared at them suspiciously. His dogs whined.

'Mr Heywood?'

'What?'

'I'm a friend of your son.'

'He ain't here.'

'I've got a message from him.'

'Scott or Jet?'

'Scott. It's about this trouble he's in.'

'What?'

'Trouble.'

'No thanks.'

'He asked us to call.'

'Scott did?'

'Can we come in?'

'You better go to *his* house.'

'He said come here.'

Out of Arthur's sight, Vinnie waved Craig to go round

the back. 'Scott said he'd told you about us. Is he back yet?'

Craig disappeared. He slipped round the side of the end-terrace house, into the yard. When he tried the back door it was locked. Craig removed his right shoe and with one smack of the heel broke a small pane of glass. He was about to put his hand through when the door jolted and an alsatian's head appeared. It barked at him, snout damp in the air. It kept barking. Another dog growled. The two animals thumped against the door, loosening tiny shards of glass from where Craig had broken the pane. He put his shoe on and ran from the yard.

At the front he found the old man still at the door. Vinnie was saying, 'That was seven and six, you know, in old money.' God knows what they were talking about.

'Box of matches?'

'No word of a lie. I still got it.'

'I can't stand here rabbiting.'

'We'll just wait in the hall. It's freezing out here.'

'I've got to see to me dogs.'

'They'll fetch the neighbours out, all that yapping.'

'Sod the neighbours.—'Ere! You've got your foot in.'

'Come on.'

'All right, all right. Lemme open the door.' While Arthur fumbled with the chain, the dogs racketed behind. Vinnie asked conversationally, 'Got them all tied up?'

The chain fell. Arthur was saying, 'Hang on,' as they heard the bolt scrape.

It was only as the door creaked open that Craig realised what would happen. He ran for the car. Vinnie was too slow. The gangling carrot-top was taking a step forward, grinning inanely, as Arthur's dogs burst free. They flattened him. When he hit the concrete a huge alsatian pounced on his chest. Saliva dripped on Vinnie's face. He tried to push the dog away but it bit into his arm and would not let go. Vinnie screamed.

Because the second dog had paused to tear Vinnie's trousers, Craig gained a decent start. With the hound loping after him he hurled himself into the Cavalier and slammed the door. The dog barked fiercely and drooled against the glass. Its claws scratched the window.

Meanwhile, Arthur was dragging the first dog from the terrified Dirkin. 'Come on, Beauty, that's right. Come on, Beauty, you silly bitch.'

Though the alsatian was still roaring at Dirkin like a lion deprived of meat, though it shook its head and clawed his clothes, it nevertheless did allow its frail old master to drag it away. But it was still growling menacingly. Vinnie lay like a spilt bag of groceries. His arm felt broken and he did not dare move.

Then, as he began gingerly to sit up, he saw the second dog bounding back his way, and he flinched. He whimpered. But the dog cantered past him to old Heywood's feet. Vinnie pushed himself upright. He had reached the stage where he hardly noticed what was going on around him—the two dogs slavering by their master; the grey Cavalier with Craig locked inside; the old woman on the pavement, shouting, 'You horrible old man! Those dogs ought to be destroyed.'

Vinnie began to cry.

At the junior school gates, the crowd was never the same: some mothers came daily, others dipped in and out, and on most days there would be at least one new or rare face—a father deputised, a grandmother, someone unexplained. Missing today was Claire Heywood, but whispering regulars noted that although *she* hadn't come, her brother-in-law had. One or two nodded to him, but nobody spoke. They also ignored the new face—the tough-looking black woman who kept to herself—single mother, bet your life.

The moment Stella appeared, Jet knew she'd had a bad day. She had her head up, walking stiffly, a tight smile on her face as if she was being called out at Assembly in front of the school. While others ran in groups across the playground, Stella walked on her own. Two or three kids called 'Good-bye' but their words rang false; loud and distinct, only spoken for effect. When she reached Jet he tried to hug her, but she held herself apart.

'Carry your bag?'

'I'm all right.'

As they walked beside the railings she slipped her hand into his. It was easier this way—one hand in her father's, one hand carrying the bag.

Jet said, 'We could go through the park.'

'Let's go straight home.'

Jet squeezed her hand. He paraded his daughter like a new girlfriend past watching eyes. But there was one person who seemed not to be watching them at all: the tough-looking black woman who was now trailing behind. She had no child with her.

Approaching the corner, Jet said, 'Through the park is quickest.'

'No, this way.—Some of my friends play in the park.'

She led him to Ladywell cemetery, past the gate-house, on to the small neglected chapel beside the drive. It was locked, and some of its windows were broken. Beyond the chapel, branching off, was a narrow unmade path. Here, secluded from prying eyes, Stella stopped, deposited her bag carefully on the ground as if it were a suitcase on a railway platform, then flung her arms around her father and burst into tears. He pulled her against him, cupping her head in one large hand. Her black hair, tied for school, had started coming loose.

Her schoolfriends had jeered at her—had asked her why she came to school, why she hadn't stayed away like Tommy, why she wasn't in hiding or making plans to escape with her famous uncle. Was she on for a share of his two million? Who was the body in the van?

Jet said, 'It isn't uncle Scott.'

'I know. We heard the news at lunchtime.' She had buried her face in his clothes.

'Let's sit down.'

Jet collected her bag and led her to a lonely seat among the graves. He took her on to his lap and began to tidy her hair.

'You'll make a mess of it.'

'It's a mess already.'

'You'll make it worse.'

She tried to grin at him through her tears, raising her hands to untie the clips. 'Men!'

Jet chuckled, wiped her face, then licked his thumb to clean the smears that lay below her eyes. She squirmed as if he was tickling her. 'Stop it, Dad, you'll make it wetter.'

Fifty yards away across the graves, the plain clothes black policewoman watched Scott kiss his daughter lightly on the lips and pull her closer to him. The woman knelt beside a headstone so she would not appear too conspicuous. The noise of light traffic from Ivy Road was just loud enough to make it hard to hear what they said, but it would be a mistake for her to draw any nearer. Kneeling at the graveside, she wondered why they had come to this place—whether to meet someone, or to be alone. The graveyard seemed a peculiar place to choose. The little girl remained on his lap, and he began fiddling with her clothes.

'You've lost a button on this shirt.'

'I know.'

He frowned at her, their faces so close that they almost touched. 'You've not been fighting?'

'Only once. Anyway, *you* do fighting for a job.'

'Used to. Were they picking on you today?'

'Just a bit. They're jealous.'

'What about?'

'When they heard he wasn't dead. They thought I'd lied to them.'

'Did they say that?'

'Sort of. They said uncle Scott would be caught and put in prison for years and years. But they're still jealous.'

'Better stay away from school tomorrow. Maybe the next day as well.'

'You said we'd be going away.'

Jet smiled. 'You don't really have to go back there at all.'

She leant back to study his face. 'What, never?'

He placed a finger on her cheek and kissed her forehead. 'Let's go home. I bought apricot cake for tea.'

She clambered from his knee and waited as he stood up. She let him carry her bag as they walked along the path.

'I don't have to go back to school?'

'Nope.'

She was silent till they reached the chapel. '*When* are we going away?'

'Soon. I'm seeing Joe Hake tonight.'

'Oh.' Her shoulders drooped. 'Not him again. I thought you'd done with that.'

'Well, if we want to get away—'

'I thought you meant somewhere exciting.'

'That's exciting.'

'Yes, but—'

'What?'

'I thought you meant . . . with uncle Scott.'

He snorted. They were now on the main drive out of the cemetery, approaching the gate into the street. 'No, I'm sorry, Stella. Whichever way this pans out, we won't be going anywhere with uncle Scott.'

As they reached the gates, she asked, 'Are you sad about him?'

'Not as much as when I thought he was dead.'

'Is that why you're going back to Joe Hake?'

'No, I need the money.'

Behind them, the plain clothes policewoman, who didn't look like a single mother now, watched them pass through the gateway into the broad and open street. She kept some distance behind as she followed them home.

As he opened the door for Gottfleisch, Ticky grinned. Across the room, Ray Lyons lay trussed and oven-ready, his black hair loose and matted where the gel had hardened. Each wrist was handcuffed to an ankle. In the sudden light he blinked and scowled.

'No doubt you're hungry,' Gottfleisch said. 'Time for tea.' He glanced at his watch. 'Five o'clock.—Just after. We waited for the headlines.'

Lyons wriggled upright against the wall, saying nothing.

'Which hand do you eat with?' asked Gottfleisch. 'Or won't you even tell me that?'

Ticky had the key clenched in his fist, and as he approached the prisoner he raised it like a sweetie for a child—but he kept clear of Ray's restrained feet. 'Roll over, please.'

Ray leant to the left. Crouching beside him to unlock the cuff, Ticky murmured, 'We put the kettle on. There's bread and jam and a big cream cake, and if you want something cooked—'

Ray grabbed him by the throat. Ticky choked, his eyes

bulging, but even as he clawed at Ray's tightening fingers he had the presence of mind to throw the keys across the floor.

'Let him go, Lyons,' snapped Gottfleisch.

'Gimme the key.'

With Ray's free hand gripped around his throat, Ticky swung hard at his face. Lyons flinched, watched Ticky's face changing colour, then dragged him closer and butted with his head. He aimed for the nose but Ticky ducked, took it on the forehead. Ray would have butted again but Gottfleisch intervened. Ramming an elegant shoe into Ray's ribs, he grabbed his oily hair and slammed Ray's skull against the wall. Ray tried to swing a punch but Gottfleisch caught it. Twenty stone of the fat man's weight was concentrated through the leather shoe thrust against Ray's rib cage. Gottfleisch heaved harder on his hair—stretching him—then stepped back.

Ray found himself free—but powerless. Ticky rolled away. Ray was left on the floor, left hand cuffed to heel, Gottfleisch standing over him.

Gottfleisch said, 'You stupid man.'

Ticky turned away, not wanting Lyons to see him feeling nauseous.

'We were about to feed you and let you go.'

'Get stuffed.'

Gottfleisch watched impassively while Lyons arranged himself more comfortably, kneeling on his handcuffed left knee like a boxer at the count.

'The curious thing is,' Gottfleisch continued, 'that we wanted to offer you our sympathy. It seems that your brother Cliff may have . . . been in an accident.'

Ray didn't speak. He just breathed heavily.

'The police will need someone to identify the body, and they will presumably look to you—next of kin, etcetera.'

'Bastard.'

'I'm as distraught as you.'

'Who did it?'

Gottfleisch paused. 'Perhaps we might help each other to discover that?'

'Fuck off.'

'You don't have many options.'

'My brother . . .'

'The body may not be his.'

'You know it is.'

'I suspect so, but I'd prefer to be certain.'

'You want me to identify him?'

'I knew you had a glimmer of intelligence. Yes, if you wouldn't mind.'

'The cops are looking for me. You gotta let me go.'

'I don't have to do anything of the sort. If you disappeared, Ray, the police would assume you were the brains behind Cliff's unfortunate scheme. That scenario is rather tempting.' He studied Ray, letting the thought sink in. 'Cliff dead, you missing.—But is Cliff dead? That's the question. I'm sure we'd both like to know. Why don't you squat here and ponder the wisdom of co-operation? Ticky and I will prepare a fresh pot of tea.'

While the kettle boiled, Gottfleisch, in an untypically considerate moment, wiped the gash on Ticky's brow and applied a clean sticking plaster. Smoothing it in place, he said, 'A whole day wasted.'

Ticky kept his eyes closed as he savoured the soothing fingers on his face. Gottfleisch continued, 'Woody missing, the police nowhere. We have snatched the wrong man.' He left his hands on Ticky's shoulders. 'And at this very moment, half the British population is scouring the countryside for a hidden cache of old ten-pound notes. But no one has found a thing.'

'They wouldn't say if they had.'

When Gottfleisch moved away, Ticky opened his eyes. 'Can't we do nothing to force the game, sir?'

'Suggestions welcomed.'

'Well, we've already got Ray Lyons—perhaps we need one of the Heywoods.'

Gottfleisch was rummaging in the fridge for a cream bun. 'We've been through that. Woody was prepared to walk out on his family, so why should he return?'

'There's his kid—the little boy.'

A tiny blob of cream appeared on Gottfleisch's nose. 'Forget it. D'you know what disturbs me, Ticky—what really burns me up? Scott Heywood is an amateur but may get away with this.'

'You reckon he did it?'

'Who else? Though he may be in league with someone.'

'Excuse me, sir.' Ticky took a piece of kitchen paper and wiped the cream from his master's face. 'He'll feel different now.'

Gottfleisch moved away, 'In what way?'

'Well, look at it from Woody's point of view. It was all right when he was planning it: something to look forward to, a lovely dream. And when he was *doing* it, there was the excitement, all on edge. That was good too. But now's the let-down. He's sitting there with all that money, can't show his face, the whole of his life stretched out in front of him. And he realises he'll have to spend all his life in hiding—never see his family again, nor his friends. Always on the run. He'll be feeling lonely, after just twenty-four hours.'

'Twenty-seven.'

'This is the second night on his own. And I bet he really is on his own—some lonely hotel room—no gorgeous women, no fancy meals, no sitting back and laughing at us. He starts wondering why he done it.'

'Perhaps.'

'He wants to talk to someone—like his wife.'

'He can't.'

'But he'd like to, sir—that's the point. He's feeling sorry for what he did.'

'Too fanciful, dear boy.' Gottfleisch ate a fairy cake, one gulp.

'Maybe. But there he is—sitting in that hotel room with two million quid he can't spend, and he thinks, my old woman could use some of that. A hundred grand—two hundred maybe—he could buy off his guilt.'

'You empathise, I see.'

'Then he hears she's been snatched—well, that really cuts him up. He wants to do something.'

Gottfleisch rested his weight against the sink unit while he regarded his protégé. 'A student of human nature.'

'Only guilt, sir. That's what I know.' Ticky grinned. 'Anyway, Woody hears his kid will be hurt unless we get the money back. The little lad. His pride and joy.'

'Don't get excited, Ticky. How do you suggest that Woody hears of this—should we write him a letter—place an advertisement in the newspapers? Do you really imagine we can kidnap his family? They're under permanent police guard and don't leave the house.'

'That won't last long.'

'I am far from convinced that Woody is behind this, or even alive. At any moment now I expect the police to announce the discovery of his body. Then where will we be?—Cliff and Woody both dead, the money still missing.'

'Another gang, sir?'

'It only needed one unguarded word.'

Gottfleisch's benign smile disappeared like water down a plug-hole. Suddenly he thumped the cupboard door. 'Two million pounds, Ticky! There must be *something* we can do.'

TWELVE

The swoop came at ten o'clock next morning. An anonymous grey Fiesta pulled up outside the house and two people leapt out. The man was tall, morose, in a shabby suit, and his once red hair had greyed until it looked like coconut matting faded in the sun. The woman was burly, forty, and wore sensible shoes.

When Hoach opened the door they swept past toward the stairs.

'You the landlord?'

'Yes, and who—'

'Which one is it?'

'I don't—'

'Family Heywood.'

'Oh—'

'At the top?'

As they pounded up the stairs Hoach trailed half a flight behind. He was a portly man with wispy hair, about fifty, though no longer counting.

'This it?'

'Just a mo.' Hoach was on the final flight of stairs. 'That's the one.'

They knocked.

The landlord dropped back to the half landing. 'I don't think—'

When they knocked again, the reverberations made other doors shiver in sympathy.

'Are they asleep?'

'I don't think so.'

'Mr Heywood! Are you in there?'

For a moment, silence throbbed. They thumped again. Mr Hoach, fearful of damage to his door, and now certain no one was in, shuffled up the remaining flight of stairs. 'I've got a key.'

The woman said, 'Hand it here,' but the coconut man intervened: 'The landlord has the legal right.'

She bristled but stood back. Hoach fumbled with the key, couldn't fit it in the lock, and by the time it opened he glistened with sweat.

The woman strode past. Hoach might have preferred to wait outside, but felt himself gently pushed inside the flat. The man said, 'Like you to witness what we find.'

'What a mess,' she said, opening a drawer.

'Miss Pyson! We really don't have the—'

'I beg your pardon, Mr Creel?'

He winced as she flicked through the contents of the drawer. 'Miss Pyson, may I remind you of the procedure?'

Miss Pyson inhaled as she slammed the drawer back into place. Creel said, 'Thank you. Now, Mr Hoach. Serious case. Little girl registered as at risk. Mother gone, father inadequate. Today she didn't go to school.'

Hoach shook his head. 'Kids often miss out on school.'

'We need to see her,' said Miss Pyson.

'Why?'

'Can't tell you that.' She flashed a short chilling smile. 'Can't discuss our cases. You know the girl?'

'Well, I see her.'

'You live here?'

'Of course. I—'

'Does she ever come into your flat?'

'No—'

'But you do see her?'

Hoach frowned. He didn't see why he should be called to account. 'The girl lives in the house. Of course I see her. What's this about?'

'How does she behave with her father?'

Hoach realised where this was leading but decided not to be drawn. 'I'm not answering questions, Miss um . . . Yes. In fact, as owner of this property, I think I may have to ask you both to leave. No one's here, see?'

Miss Pyson stared at him, immovable as the furniture. Her colleague said, 'Understand your feelings, Hoach. But can I breathe a word in confidence? This little girl, you see— well. Miss Pyson and I may seem to be coming on a bit strong, as it were, but we have seen some pretty tragic cases. We only have the child's interests at heart. That's why we have to ask these . . . embarrassing questions.'

'Embarrassing?'

'You know the kind of thing: have you seen any signs of . . .' He nodded.

'Abuse?'

'Yes?'

'No.'

Creel tried again: 'Does the little girl seem afraid of him—withdrawn? Have you ever seen or heard anything which you thought a little odd?'

'Can't say so.'

'Not even little, inconsequential things?'

'Nope.'

Miss Pyson asked, 'Is Heywood a good father, would you say?'

'Well, yes, generally . . .'

'Except?'

Hoach shrugged vaguely. 'Well, he isn't here all the time.'

'Is somebody else here? Does she have visitors?'

'No. I mean he . . . sometimes leaves her on her own.'

'Ah.' She gleamed. 'At night?'

Hoach looked uncomfortable. 'Well, daytimes, mainly. He works.'

'But sometimes Mr Heywood does leave the child at night?'

'In the evening, yes. Occasionally.'

'How late?'

'Oh, I don't know.'

'After midnight?'

'No. Not usually.'

'But sometimes?'

'I don't know.' They waited. 'Perhaps.'

He could see them mentally completing a form. Suddenly tired, Hoach wandered to the door. 'You'd better stay, then, if you want.'

'Thank you.'

'Mr Hoach,' called Miss Pyson. 'Could you confirm that this flat accommodates just the two of them?'

'Of course.' He hesitated at the door.

She smiled. 'Is there a bathroom?'

'Oh, sorry, d'you want to . . .? It's across the hall.'

'That's not what I mean. Is it shared?'

He nodded.

'And just one bedroom?'

'Yes, they have it through there, see? This is their lounge cum kitchenette.'

'Thank you, Mr Hoach.'

When he had finally shuffled out of earshot, Miss Pyson said, 'One bedroom.'

'It can be difficult to find a two-bedroom flat.'

Miss Pyson stretched her muscular neck. 'A girl needs her privacy.'

She walked across to the bedroom door, peeped inside, then turned with triumph in her eyes.

'One bed.'

Ray Lyons arrived back around lunchtime. Unshaven since the day before, his black hair slicked down but loose around the collar, he looked like a gypsy in a stolen suit. He scowled at Gottfleisch. 'What you were saying earlier,' he began, 'about we could help each other.'

'Co-operation,' Gottfleisch purred.

'What's in that?'

Ray shuffled his feet on the Turkish carpet, uncomfortable among antique furniture. He felt like an item on display.

'Was it your brother?' Gottfleisch tried to look solicitous.

'The hell do I know?'

'Ah.' The large man's face hid his irritation. Perhaps Lyons felt upset: calling at a mortuary to identify the charred remains must have been distressing, even to him.

'You did see the body?'

'What was left of it.'

'Mhm?' Gottfleisch breathed politely, like a host at a dinner party making small talk with his first guest. 'Badly burnt?'

'Yeah. That mortuary gave me the chills. When I seen bodies before, they've been where they dropped, you know? Somewhere natural. That place, they've been brought in, mucked about with . . .'

Gottfleisch nodded encouragingly, the solicitous host.

'The body was waiting on a table, under a sheet . . .' Ray looked hard at Gottfleisch and held his eyes. 'I mean, that is dead, you know? That's really dead.'

'You saw it?'

'Yeah. It was a lump of meat.'

Gottfleisch's stomach rumbled.

'I couldn't recognise it.'

Ray stared at the floor. He moved his foot and ruckled the carpet. 'They'd done his dental records. Christ knows how.'

'Oh, they'll have a computer bank. Trace the dentist that Cliff was registered with, ask for his file—'

'They'd have had to root about to find the teeth. His head was roasted meat. Well done.' Ray grinned mirthlessly. A black joke to hide his pain.

'Any possessions that you could identify?'

Ray answered slowly, his thoughts elsewhere. 'No. They reckoned he was wearing uniform. They had a belt that hadn't burned. And they showed me a boot—or part of it.' Ray looked up. 'That'd be the other feller's, right?'

'Heywood?'

'Yeah. Cops thought it was *his* body at first. Must've been the teeth that said it wasn't. So.' Ray rubbed his hands. Gottfleisch looked blank. 'There's a lesson for you: if you don't want a body identified, knock out its teeth.' Ray stared at the empty fireplace.

'Did the police suggest that Heywood dressed the um . . . your brother in his uniform?'

Lyons stared at him, eyes black as coal. 'They didn't say.' He was rubbing his shoe again on the Turkish carpet. Gottfleisch winced. 'They think Cliff and Heywood worked the blag together and . . .'

'They said that?'

'I could tell. Where's Heywood?'

'I wish I knew.'

Ray Lyons studied him. 'He's got the money?'

'I assume.'

'Well, he didn't burn it.—That was on the news.'

'The police will be guarding Heywood's house, of course.'

'Yeah, they want him. Like you do. Like I do.'

Gottfleisch smiled as the conversation turned his way. 'You'll want revenge, of course, Ray, not the money. But if you do track him down, you'd be entitled to your brother's share. That's only right.'

'How much?'

'Oh, quite substantial. Your brother stood to make a hundred thousand pounds. Just fancy that.'

'Out of two million?'

'He was only a small player, Ray.'

'What was Heywood's share?'

'The same.'

'I want his share too. I get him, he won't be needing it.'

Gottfleisch looked offended. 'I understand your grief, Ray, but it does seem to have coloured your way of looking at this. Two hundred thousand pounds!'

'You was paying that out already.'

'I have considerable expenses, Ray.—My business partners, setting this up ... And laundering money, as I'm sure you know, reduces its value to less than half. If I gave you two hundred thousand ...' Gottfleisch pretended to calculate on his fat fingers. 'Goodness! I'd have hardly a penny left.'

'Two hundred grand.'

'You're a hard man, Ray. All right. But only if you find him—and the missing money, of course.'

'Right.'

'Remember, Ray, this money is hot. Don't imagine you could run away with the lot and spend it.'

'Nervous?'

'All my life I have been too trusting. What I am offering you, Ray, is two hundred thousand pounds in *clean* money—cash, bank account, whatever you like. Swiss, Cayman Islands, I can arrange it. You need never work again. But you aren't interested in the money, Ray, I understand that. You want revenge.'

'Two hundred thousand is only ten per cent.'

Gottfleisch approached him, beaming. 'Oh, two million is a newspaper fantasy! Banks exaggerate for their insurance claim. You'll do very well. Think what you could do with so much money.'

'It ain't enough.'

'Ray.'

'Four hundred.'

'My goodness!' Gottfleisch laughed. 'You would ruin me.' He was warming to Ray Lyons now. He loved to bargain. He had offered Cliff and Scott over half a million—notionally, because Scott would not have drawn his share—so he still had a little left to play with. And Ray would only be paid if he found the money.

'I'll tell you what, dear boy. Deliver all the money intact, and I'll raise your fee to—pause a moment, Ray, think what you could do with this—to a cool quarter of a million.'

'No.'

'That's two hundred and fifty thousand pounds—a fortune.'

'Four hundred.'

Gottfleisch tutted.

Ray said, 'Split the difference: three hundred grand.'

Gottfleisch grimaced. 'You are seriously asking for three hundred thousand pounds?'

'Right.'

'I see. You want to split the difference?'

'That's what I—'

'So if we split your three hundred and my two fifty, that's two seventy-five. Two hundred and seventy-five thousand pounds.'

'No, I said—'

'That's agreed then, Ray. You've forced me up to two hundred and seventy-five thousand—in absolutely clean, unimpeachable new banknotes. You'll be set for life.'

Ray exhaled. 'All right.'

Gottfleisch took in a lungful of sweet air. Money was so much more binding than ties of blood.

THIRTEEN

When Jet and Stella came home, it was early evening. They had been playing tourist in the West End—the palace, St James' Park, Westminster, Trafalgar Square. Jet had decided that since they were leaving soon they should do the town one final time. Seeing the sights cost little money and their lunch—a café in Brewer Street market—was also cheap. They spent their afternoon in a Leicester Square cinema and came out into the bustle of West End crowds—foreign tourists, milling teenagers, office workers going home. On the bus, Jet and Stella sat upstairs, looking from the window at a panorama of passing lives, detached from those below as in the cinema where what they had seen had not been real. It didn't touch. It didn't hurt.

Their flat seemed familiarly dingy. Creel and Pyson had left mid-morning, and the furniture was undisturbed. Yet there was a chill about the place. It no longer seemed like home.

'Fish and chips?' Jet suggested. 'Out or in?'

'I'm exhausted.'

'It'll make the room smell.'

'But it's nice.'

'Put the kettle on while I'm out.'

'Don't be long.'

If Jet had waited another five minutes—if he'd stopped

to make the tea—Ray would have confronted him in the flat. He had driven over, Craig and Vinnie in the back, Vinnie only along to point Jet out. Craig kept making snide remarks about Vinnie's arm being in the sling, like: 'Hey Vinnie, d'you think that dog still wants a bone?' and 'How'll you get out of your shirt tonight—get a woman to pull it off?' But Ray told him to shut his yap.

'That's Heywood,' Vinnie said. 'Over there. He did some boxing, remember, so he can be useful.'

But Ray had gone. Craig slipped out the far side, walking quickly to catch him up, leaving Vinnie to clamber out alone. With one arm, even the simplest things were awkward.

April sun had sunk beneath the rooftops and the light had become steely. No one else was in the street. Ray blocked Jet's path. 'I want a word with you.'

Jet paused. Hearing Craig approach behind him, he turned his back against the wall. He saw another one, wearing a sling.

'Where's your brother?'

Jet shook his head.

'Don't fuck with me. Where is he?'

Jet waited. Lyons kept his hand in his pocket as if he might have a weapon there. Vinnie's sling might hide something too. Ray nodded to the hovering Craig and said, 'He's yours, then.'

Craig twitched as if he meant business, but he was one step out of range. Jet moved. His left flicked misleadingly, and his right fist crashed across. Craig ducked, arm raised to shield the blow, but it smashed against his face. He tumbled. Even as Jet was turning, Ray's cosh came for his head. Jet swung away from it, but then as he surged forward, Ray whipped backhanded across his face. Jet dodged but it caught him on the arm—the sudden monstrous ache dragging it down. He jabbed a left—

connected—saw Ray's head jolt away. He pulled back to jab again.

Which left his right side unprotected. Ray swung the cosh and caught him across the ear. The same arcing movement took the cosh above Jet's head. Ray thumped it down. The cosh crashed against Jet's skull and laid him out.

When Ray dropped easily to one knee, cosh raised to strike again, Vinnie said, 'He's gone. Don't kill the bastard.'

Ray hesitated. Vinnie said, 'We're supposed to talk to him.'

Lyons glared at the two men as they stood in front of him. 'Get the fucking car.'

During the journey, Jet vomited on the carpet, and though they kept the windows open the reek of it filled the interior. Craig and Vinnie were in the rear, right on top of it, as it were, and had nowhere clean to put their feet, so they rested them on his body. Craig kicked him a few times but by the end of the journey, Jet was regaining consciousness, so Craig stopped. He and Vinnie sat in the dark, their feet on Jet, wondering if he really was half unconscious, whether he would make a sudden grab for them, and what they should do if he did.

Ray stopped the car and said, 'This'll do.'

Vinnie peered from the car window. To one side of the road, the Thames lay grey and sullen in the twilight, and immediately beside them on the other side lay the enclosed water of an old dock, prettified, landscaped but deserted. It was separated from the river by an iron swing bridge, painted red, constructed from huge industrial girders that seemed out of place. It was like an over-ambitious metal sculpture commissioned by a quango, though it was the only piece of original docklands on the site.

When the men hauled Jet from the car he seemed unable to stand up. Craig and Ray took one arm each and dragged him down some steps to the gravel path beside the dock. At this lower level, evening twilight had turned to gloom. Ray said, 'Time for a chat.'

He took Jet beneath the arms and heaved him on to a black metal park bench overlooking the water. 'Don't he look comfortable,' Ray sneered, and he slapped his face.

Jet slumped sideways, tried to right himself, but folded forwards across his lap. Ray yanked him upright.

'Your brother—where's he gone?'

Jet's eyes were open, trying to focus. Ray leant closer. 'See that water? If you don't talk, sunshine, that's where they'll find you. So where is he?'

Jet mumbled. Ray punched him. On the iron bench, proffered by the seat back, Jet was an ideal height for Ray to smack him round the head. Jet raised his left arm weakly; his right arm would not work.

'Too fucking easy.' Ray hit him again.

When Jet slid sideways, Craig moved to pull him straight, saying, 'Not such a tough guy, after all.'

'Shut up.'

Craig muttered, 'He's fading out again.'

Ray grabbed Jet's shoulders and shook him. 'Wake up! You hear me?'

Slowly, Jet opened his eyes. Suddenly, he kicked upwards between Ray's legs. But he was too weak; Ray caught his foot between his thighs, grinned, and punched him in the mouth. 'Oh, I'm glad you did that, Heywood. I thought you was all done.'

He thumped three more blows to Jet's head. There was no resistance, just a moan of pain.

'Piss around and I'll take your head off. You're gonna tell me where he is.'

Jet stared at him, seemed to think about it, then vomited down his front. Ray stepped back. 'Oh, that's disgusting.'

In the dark well of the enclosed dock, the three men stood with their backs to the water, staring at what could have been a drunken derelict on the seat. His face and shirt were streaked with blood. He was barely conscious.

Ray said, 'I think I'll do the bastard.'

He studied his helpless victim like a gardener deciding where to prune, but as he moved forward Vinnie warned, 'Hit him again and he'll be a goner.'

'So?'

'We'll get nothing out of him.'

'He's got nothing to tell.'

'You got to give him a chance to speak.'

Ray snarled, 'A chance? He had a better chance than my brother.'

Vinnie gulped. In a curious way, he was pleased that his arm was unusable, in a sling.

Ray said, 'His fucking brother killed my brother.' Jet had fallen sideways. 'Oh, get up!'

Ray heaved him vertical, but Jet was unconscious. When Ray punched him he toppled sideways to the ground.

'Shame.' Ray gazed moodily at the body and kicked it in the side. He took his cosh from his pocket and smacked it lightly against his palm. 'One more for luck, eh? Make certain. Before we bung him in the water.'

'The cops'll know you done it,' Vinnie said.

'Fuck off.' Ray knelt beside Jet's head.

'If his brother killed your brother, and then if he's killed as well . . . I mean, it's obvious, isn't it?'

'His brother . . .' Ray shook his head. 'I can't leave it.'

'They'll know.'

Ray smiled up at him. 'You'll be my alibi.'

'Oh, no.' Vinnie began to back away. 'I was never here. I never saw you.'

'Don't give me aggravation.' Ray turned to Craig. 'How about you?'

It was growing darker by the minute. Craig said, 'I reckon we should keep looking for his brother. That's where the money is.'

Ray glanced aside. They couldn't tell if he had understood the point about the money, but he turned back to the inert body and rubbed the cosh above its ear. 'Feels quite soft. Surprising.'

He took Jet's head in his left hand and lifted it from the gravel. Then he tapped around the skull as if checking for a change of sound. 'See down the middle? That's where it joins. Smack a baby there—even with a pencil—and it cracks open like an egg.' He laid his cosh along the line.

After several cold seconds Ray stood up. He glowered down at the body, kicked it, and then asked, 'Suppose we chucked him in the water and he drowned naturally, what d'you think?'

Areas of the city where street lamps do not shine are pitilessly dark. In the night sky, stars seem subdued by the city's light, yet that same suffused glow does not penetrate into alleyways, yards and cavities. In these black tomb-like places the sounds are deadened. There is none of London's normal background drone, and the surging sound of a passing car has an unexpected clarity; first a rustling in the air, a rising note, then a momentary climax and sudden fall. The air lies still.

In these well-like cavities the night-cold air between buildings seems to gain extra weight, to hang motionless, to be a darker colour, more opaque. On Surrey Water by the Thames a chill wind cuts beneath the red bascule bridge and runs like flood water across the ground.

He has been staring at the sky, but he does not blink. He lies awkwardly on his back, so motionless that any passing nocturnal creature might never notice him. On his right shoe, pointing upwards from the gravel, crawls a snail, its tiny horns quivering in the night, its trail of slime glistening in the dark.

Another car goes by. The noise disappears. Because the man has made no move, an urban fox which every night visits the dustbins of Hithe Point Estate slinks closer. It detects a ripe rancid smell which it finds attractive, and a smell of blood. The fox crouches, snout on paws, a single body-length away. In absolute silence, the fox eases itself across the gravel, its bushy tail lifted an inch above the ground, its nostrils trembling. Neither fox nor man has blinked. Approaching from the side, the fox sniffs at a caked mess upon his front, then tentatively licks at it. Emboldened, the fox places its paw on his inert chest and leans towards the encrusted face, from which the blood smell arises strongest. While its wet tongue licks the crust away, the sweet salty taste encourages the beast's saliva, tempts its mouth to gape, causes its vulpine teeth to drip and its panting breath to wake the man. Who emits a noise. Whose body jolts. Whose arm ineffectually crunches gravel—and the fox is gone. At the massive iron bridge the fox disappears without looking back. It could be lurking beneath the girders. The man doesn't know. Perhaps the animal did not exist. The man only knows that his whole body burns with pain. He wonders where he is. He wonders what strange dream can have awakened him to find a fox staring in his face.

It is after midnight but she is not asleep. She wears a thin nightdress and socks, and because of the cold she has her dressing gown tied tight. Though it isn't really cold. Since eight o'clock she has had the fire on, but though the room is warm and fuggy, Stella walks around it with her hands clasped beneath her arms to keep them warm. She prefers to walk. Whenever she sits in a chair too long her body tenses and she has to prowl around to relax. It is as if walking in the room makes up for not walking in the streets, for not searching everywhere outside until she finds him.

She should have gone out hours ago when he did not come back. She knows where the chip shop is, and if she had gone there then she could have asked if they had seen him. But he told her not to go out. At first, when he did not return, she thought the people in the shop might have set a new batch to fry, which could easily take ten minutes. Or perhaps he'd popped into a pub, which could take half an hour. But when a whole hour had passed and Daddy still had not come home, it had become too late to ask the chip shop if they had seen him: either he had been an hour ago or he'd never arrived. They'd think her odd. And if he had slipped into a pub beforehand, then he might even now be in the shop, and if she was outside searching they could miss each other as he came back. And Daddy says she must never ever go out after dark.

Has he forgotten her? She can not believe it. Though there was a time after Mummy went when he did sometimes stay out too late. He would go to the pub, get in with friends, and be out too long. Stella hated those days, but Daddy doesn't do it any more. He has told her that she means more to him than Mummy ever did.

Something must have happened. Stella pictures him in an ambulance, or lying in hospital, unconscious. Perhaps at this very moment some doctors are looking at each other and asking, has he got a family? They might never know. She hates to stay here in the flat, but Daddy has insisted that she does. Should she go down to Mr Hoach? He could phone the police—though that might get Daddy in trouble for leaving her on her own.

Stella does not know what to do. Outside is dark. So are the stairs and landing. Here in the flat she can keep lights on in both rooms and watch the television.

By ten o'clock Stella knows that something dreadful must have happened and that she must go downstairs to Mr Hoach. It seems awfully late. Creeping out to the unlit landing she can hear nothing from downstairs. Perhaps he is out. Or in bed asleep. Stella doesn't like to knock on Hoach's door.

That is when she does it. Stella decides that she will watch the rest of the news and if Daddy is still not home by the end of the programme she will go down to Mr Hoach. She sits huddled in Daddy's armchair, wrapped in her dressing gown. She watches the screen, and falls asleep.

When Stella awoke, it was in front of some awful programme with people talking, and for a while she thought it was the news until she saw how late it was. Stella paced around in front of the set. The room lights glared at her. She knew she must go downstairs but she felt guilty for falling asleep. A clear voice inside her head told her that she should not wait there in the room, she should be outside in the streets looking for her Dad.

She heard a creak on the floor outside.

All evening she had feared the worse. She had pictured her father terribly dead, had imagined his killers on the stairs outside, had heard sinister shufflings in shadowy corners—but only now did Stella scream. Just once. As the door opened she held her breath. She rammed her fist against her mouth. But when the door swung fully open and she saw Daddy framed against the dark—wild, bloody and slightly swaying—she dropped her hand and hurled herself across the room.

Jet reeled. His child was clutching at his waist and rocking him where he stood. He tried to come inside the room but she was pulling at him, dragging him back to the darkened landing, crying, 'Daddy' and 'You're filthy' and 'You're bleeding' and 'Come to the bathroom' and he let her lead him back across the outer hall. But when she switched on the bathroom light he cowered from it, shielding his eyes from the cruel blaze. 'The dark,' he mumbled. 'Make it dark.'

She switched it off. In the cool darkness she went to the basin and turned on the tap. Jet lumbered after her. He felt for the edge of the bath tub and sat down heavily, slumping forward so that his battered head tumbled towards the china sink. But she caught him and cradled his face against her dressing gown as they waited for the water to run warm. In the smudged charcoal light they could barely see each other. Water splashed and gurgled. She put in the plug.

'Will you be able to wash yourself? Can I help?'

She used a sponge to dab his face and he sat with his eyes closed, as warm water tricked like tears through all the grime. Stella was becoming accustomed to the soft grey light, and although she saw his many wounds she would not cry.

'I can't get the blood off,' she said. 'Not unless I rub.'

Jet took the sponge and sat with it held against his head, tepid water trickling down his forearm, plopping like raindrops into the basin. Trickling water and his laboured breathing were the only sounds in all the world.

He was leaning heavily against her and she said, 'Wake up.'

He opened his eyes and peered at her through the

heavy darkness. She whispered, 'What happened?' but he shook his head, then frowned and closed his eyes.

Stella began undoing the buttons to his sodden shirt. Though he muttered, she carried on. She unpeeled the shirt from him and tossed it in the bath. Then she re-wet the sponge and dabbed at his dirty body. A cut on his face had begun to bleed, but she wouldn't risk a plaster—it looked too tender.

'Can you stand up? Lean on me.'

There was one frightening moment on their way back when he suddenly lurched against the door jamb, but she steered him into the flat and closed the door. She gave him a momentary hug, then led him to the bedroom and sat him down. When he sighed it was as if all the breath had left his body. She removed his shoes.

'Get into bed. Go on.'

As he crawled beneath the duvet on her little single bed he seemed to have already fallen asleep. He sighed once but did not move. He began to snore. Sitting beside him, Stella stroked his hair. Delicately, she tried to ease his head into a more comfortable position but he shuddered and shifted, then lay still. Stella frowned, then bent close to him to be sure that he was still breathing. The smell was terrible. She kissed his cheek.

After a while she went into the living room to turn off the lamp. The only illumination now came from her bedroom—the little lamp that Daddy had bought to shine through the nights. Familiar shadows filled high corners of the room, and their old wardrobe, as it always did, stood bulky and menacing in the dark. At the bedside she knelt, checked his breath again, then sat beside him and looked around. She wondered what to do next. Across the hall, her father's ruined shirt lay in the bath tub; she ought to rinse the blood off and leave it to soak. But it was so very late. If she got up early she could do it then.

Stella wrapped part of the duvet around her toes. Daddy's shirt didn't matter. She would sit at his side all night like a nurse. As the minutes ticked slowly past, Stella realised that she was hungry. She had had no supper. She wondered if Daddy had ever bought those fish and chips—if they were lying discarded, cold, still wrapped in paper, being sniffed at by passing cats. Had an animal eaten her supper?

To think of it made her feel guilty: as if her supper was important! Stella peered through the feeble light to where Daddy slept, mouth open, his black hair matted with dried sticky blood. What had happened to him? In the silent room she felt her eyelids growing heavy. Stella shivered in the cold. Carefully she lifted the duvet and crept beside him in her bed.

FOURTEEN

Though Ray Lyons had heard the term, he had never attended a breakfast meeting before. High-powered businessmen were keen on them, he'd heard, but there was little call for them in Dalston. He was not impressed. Ticky was holding a teacup delicately in his hand and trying not to slurp, but Ray stood beside the table like a waiter after closing, wanting to clear away. He stared at Gottfleisch and thought about the money. Two hundred and seventy-five thousand. Call it three hundred. Christ, why not call it two million?

They were in the fat man's conservatory, and the man had a fan-heater blowing round his feet. The trestle card-table in front of him bore a substantial breakfast of healthy foods—Swiss muesli, dates and cream, compote of apricots and prunes, black rye bread with Austrian cheese. Gottfleisch had invited his guests to partake but they did not seem enthusiastic—Ticky had munched an apple, Ray had gone without. As far as Ray was concerned, Gottfleisch ought to eat a more conventional breakfast: sausages, bacon, things like that. Not this European rubbish. Ray would have eaten toast and marmalade, but the black bread did not look toastable and he wasn't going to eat it as it was. Gottfleisch had invited him to sit on a folding canvas chair but because it looked like pretend-safari junk he chose to stand. Ticky sat though, bouncing around in his chair because his feet couldn't touch the floor, while Gottfleisch lounged on a white painted iron bench softened with cushions—an ornate rococo thing with fat bow legs that had either been designed that way or had buckled from Gottfleisch's weight.

Ray stared at a lush plumbago, and wondered if it was an ivy. Two million pounds. Behind him, Ticky continued his apple and prattled. 'He set us up, sir, didn't he?' Munch. 'Now he's laughing at us.' Gulp. 'Thinks we can't get at him.' Bite. 'Thinks he's smart.'

Ticky paused to swallow the pieces crammed in his mouth. 'We've got to get at him where it hurts, that's what I think.'

He paused expectantly, and Ray, still turned away from them perusing tendrils of the plumbago, pictured the little runt perched in the chair with apple juice running down his chin.

'Pass the coffee pot, dear boy.'

Ray wondered why Gottfleisch put up with him. He acted like a colonial civil servant in some old movie—Ticky his houseboy, his little slave.

'What I say, sir, is we should smoke him out.'

'Mm, you mentioned that.'

Maybe Gottfleisch *flaunted* the little toad, like those South American women who wore a live beetle as a brooch.

'If we snatched his son, then Woody would have to show himself.'

'Why?'

Ticky spluttered over his apple. Resignedly, Ray turned.

'It wouldn't be natural, sir, to abandon him.'

'Natural?'

'Well, we could do anything to the boy.'

Gottfleisch smiled, and Ticky looked away. Ray said, 'I'll leave you two to dream something up.'

'Leave us, Ray? You haven't told me about last night.'

'Ask Vinnie or your little blond friend.'

Gottfleisch took a napkin and patted his lips. 'You're fond of violence, aren't you?'

'I can hand it out.'

'You nearly killed him, from what I hear.'

'I should have.'

'Did I ever tell you that I used to watch Jet Heywood box?'

'What, the one last night? Lovely mover, was he?'

Gottfleisch studied him. 'I want to find his brother.'

Ray smiled. 'So do I, old son.'

And he left.

Gottfleisch watched as Ticky cleared the breakfast things.

Ticky coughed. 'Are you happy to use Ray Lyons, sir?'

'My boy?'

'He's nasty.'

'Not quite our type?'

Ticky was piling their few plates. 'I know you don't think much of my idea, sir, but I can tell you the school that Woody's kid goes to.'

'He'll be watched.'

'Not for long.'

'Children, Ticky . . . so emotive. Wouldn't it be wiser to aim for his wife?'

'Oh no, sir. He walked out on her.'

'And on his son.'

'That's not right, sir—by your leave. He walked out on his old woman, not his little boy. I bet he misses him already.'

'Ticky, Ticky.'

'Think about it, sir. Woody's in that lonely room, thinking he'll never see his kid again. But he says, no, of course I will, when this blows over. Then he hears the boy's been snatched. He hears what we might do to him. Well, suddenly, that money seems like a pile of shit—'

'Ticky, I'm trying to digest my breakfast.'

'Sorry, sir. Well, the cash will be like . . . lavatory paper, won't it? Worthless. He can't spend it. He can't lead a life of luxury on money that could save his kiddy's life. It'd be like he had killed the boy himself.'

Gottfleisch shook his head. 'Kidnapping, Ticky. *Killing* the boy. We couldn't do that.'

Alone in the glass conservatory they held each other's gaze. The fan-heater hummed. Ticky said, 'It's the only way we'll find Woody.'

Gottfleisch glanced at the remaining food but decided he was no longer hungry. He sighed. What he valued in Ticky was that the man was loyal—would do whatever Gottfleisch said and would not question it. Ticky had his weaknesses, of course, but was a faithful servant. A rare quality.

'Assuming—just assuming, my dear boy, for the sake of argument, as it were—that we did manage to take the boy, how would Woody learn of this?'

'It'd be in the newspapers.'

'But how would he know who *had* the boy? We can't telephone him.'

'Newspapers, sir. We leak the story and he reads about it. "Driver's Old Gang Snatches His Child. Gang won't release the boy till they get the money." That sort of thing. We don't give our names, of course—'

'I'd prefer the BBC. Papers take too long.'

'As you like. Anyway, it'd be like placing an advertisement. Everyone hears it, but only Woody can win the prize.'

Gottfleisch eased the table away to enable himself to stand up. 'No, no. A bright idea, but far too fanciful.'

'I don't think so, sir, with respect. We can keep Lyons out there looking for him, if you like, but, well . . .'

'Keep our options open? I hear what you say.'

Though it was broad daylight, the knock at the door reverberated as loudly as in the dead of night. At the little table, Stella stood up from her cornflakes. She had hardly started across the room before the door swung open.

'You must be Stella,' the woman said. They were sliding through the door.

The child ran to the landlord who had led them in. 'Mr Hoach—'

'Don't be afraid,' the woman said.

'Make them go away.'

'I—'

'Is Mr Hoach a friend of yours?' Miss Pyson's glittering gaze flicked towards the man.

'I'm just the landlord. I must be going.'

But Stella clutched at his sleeve. 'Please—'

Hoach tugged at Stella's fingers and the ginger-haired man asked, 'Is your father here?'

Hoach pulled himself away and scuttled for the door. 'You'll be all right.'

'Please, Mr Hoach—'

Creel said, 'We're not going to harm you, for goodness sake. Now, Stella, I see that you're not in school again. Why not?'

Miss Pyson closed the door on the fleeing landlord. 'Tell me, Stella, do you like Mr Hoach?'

Stella stared at her.

'Or are you afraid of him?'

Stella shook her head.

Creel asked, 'Who else lives here in this house?'

Stella licked her lips, then said, 'You shouldn't be here.'

'Now, young lady,' Miss Pyson boomed. 'Does your father know you're not at school?'

'Where *is* your father?'

Stella hesitated. 'He's asleep.'

Creel looked quickly about him. 'You mean, he's here?'

'Ssh!' hissed Miss Pyson. Bending towards the child, she whispered, 'So Daddy hasn't gone to work?'

'No, he's . . . No.'

Pyson showed her teeth. 'And where is your father now?' She cocked her head. 'In there?'

Stella nodded.

'Well, my dear, we wouldn't want to wake him, would we? But let's make sure he's still asleep.'

Stella reached out too late to stop her, but she and Creel were already stalking to the bedroom door. Stella glanced toward the landing, but she couldn't run away and leave Daddy here. Pyson peeped inside the bedroom, then turned to Creel. 'You see?'

Softly, she reclosed the door. Stella, mesmerised, watched them approach her, not realising that the expression on their faces was meant to convey sympathy. Pyson whispered, 'Has Daddy just come home?'

'No, he—'

'Let's sit down.'

Stella was feeling strangely weak, and allowed herself to be led across to the small dining table. While she and Pyson sat by the window, Creel squatted beside them on the floor. He said, 'Daddy's still asleep, I see,' and smiled at her encouragingly.

Stella nodded.

'Though *you're* up and about.'

'Do you want to speak to my Daddy?'

'In a minute. Rather talk to you.'

Stella didn't like the sound of that. 'I could wake him.'

'Wouldn't he be cross?'

'I'll get him.'

But as she made to leave the table, Miss Pyson covered her hand with her own. 'Not just yet, my dear. Do you like this little flat?'

'It's all right.'

'Lived here long?'

'For a bit.'

'And whereabouts do *you* sleep, my dear?'

'In that room.'

'Is Daddy in your bed?'

'Yes, he . . .'

'He what, my dear?'

'He . . .' Stella decided not to speak.

'Did Daddy sleep in your bed all night?'

Stella nodded.

'And did you sleep with him—in the same bed?'

'Yes.' She saw them staring at her again. 'I had to look after him.'

They waited. Stella waited. Creel asked, 'Like a little Mummy?' She did not reply.

To encourage her, Pyson nodded and even smiled. 'Of course, you don't have a Mummy now, do you? Just you and Daddy, isn't that right?'

Stella frowned. She felt uncomfortable.

'Do you think it's nice—in bed with Daddy?'

Stella was becoming visibly distressed. Creel muttered, 'Not here.'

'The Centre?'

'Would be best.' He smiled bleakly at the little girl. 'Now, Stella, let's pop down to our office. It isn't far.'

'No.'

Pyson said, 'You're supposed to be in school, Stella. You don't want to get into trouble.'

'I've . . . I don't . . . Daddy said I don't have to go there any more.'

Pyson stood up. 'Daddies are not always right, my dear. Now come along.'

'I want—' Stella cowered from her outstretched hand.

Creel said, 'Take the child downstairs, and I'll do the necessary with the father. See you in the car.'

Stella looked quickly around the room as Miss Pyson murmured, 'You'll be all right, Stella. Don't worry.' Her hand closed around Stella's wrist.

Creel said, 'Be safe with us.'

'No.'

Pyson had her in her grip. She asked Creel, 'Will you wake him?'

'I think I'll leave a note.'

Stella screamed. Creel snapped, 'Quick—get her out.'

'Come along, my dear.'

Pyson began to pull her from the table—but Stella grabbed a mug of tea and dashed it in her face.

'You little—'

Stella rushed across the room. 'Daddy! Daddy!'

'Stop her!'

They chased her into the bedroom, pausing briefly inside the door. 'Smells like a brewery,' Pyson said. Stella was beating the shape beneath the duvet. 'I'll get her out. You hold the father.'

'Daddy!' Stella's hands clawed at his body.

Miss Pyson wrapped her arms around the child. 'Come along, my dear.'

The duvet started sliding from the bed. The man beneath it tried to sit up.

'Still drunk,' Miss Pyson snapped.

Jet cleared his throat.

'Daddy—help!'

Pyson backed with the struggling child towards the bedroom door. 'Hold on to him!'

As Pyson tried to pull her from the room, Stella grabbed the doorjamb. Creel moved towards the bed. Jet slid into a sitting position, tried to stand, but fell to his knees. Stella released the doorjamb. Miss Pyson staggered a moment, and the girl pulled herself away and ran back to the bed. Creel could not stop her. She clutched at Jet as he tried to rise.

Pyson called, 'Pull her away!'

Creel hesitated.

'He's drunk. I'll do it.' Like a great white shark, Miss Pyson nosed towards the kneeling man. But he had Stella in his grasp and she was clinging to him. With the flat of his hand he pushed Pyson away.

'He hit me! Oh, *you* deal with him.'

'Look at his face.'

'*Deal* with him, Creel!'

'But look, Miss Pyson, look at him.'

She flinched, first at Creel's extraordinary reaction, then at sight of the man. His face was swollen, bruised and cut. Cradling his daughter to his chest, he knelt on the floor swaying as if to an unheard lament. Creel moved, and Stella cried, 'Please don't hurt my Daddy!'

Something was wrong. Jet was trying to speak. Creel asked pointlessly, 'Are you all right?'

Jet mumbled something which sounded like Go Away.

'In a drunken brawl,' decided Pyson.

Jet made another attempt to stand, but he could only slump upon the bed. Creel asked, 'What happened?' and Stella, clinging to her father, said, 'He's been beaten up.'

'Because he was drunk,' insisted Miss Pyson.

Stella said, 'He was mugged.'

'Let me deal with this,' Creel said. He frowned at Jet, then knelt beside him. 'Don't worry, Mr Heywood. Look at me.' He peered into Jet's eyes. 'Watch my finger. Keep your eyes on it.'

Pyson waited, and when Creel stood up she asked, 'Concussed?'

'I should imagine.' He turned to Stella. 'Mugged, you say?'

'Well, he went out to get our supper, and . . .'

'He'll have to see a doctor.'

Jet muttered, 'I'm all right.'

'Mr Heywood—'

'Who are you?'

They did not answer. He said, 'Get out.' Jet seemed to be trying to focus on the blooded pillow. 'Christ, Stella, look at your bed. Am I bleeding?'

He touched his head, and when he brought his hand away there was scarlet on his fingers.

Pyson asked, 'Mr Heywood, do you remember what happened?'

'What?'

'Last night. You were attacked.'

Jet lifted the pillow and gazed at it as if he had never seen a pillow before. 'Did I sleep here?'

Miss Pyson became alert. 'You can't remember?'

There was silence. Stella tried to prompt him. 'I put you to bed.'

Creel frowned. 'Is this your bedroom, Mr Heywood?'

Jet did not reply. Stella said, 'No. Daddy sleeps out there.'

'Where?'

'On the sofa. It makes into a bed. Only . . . It's stiff, and last night I couldn't . . .'

Miss Pyson knelt beside them with a disarming smile from which Stella recoiled. 'Has Daddy slept in your bed before—on other nights?'

'No. His bed's out there.'

Jet made a choking sound. When Creel moved closer Jet waved him away. Creel asked, 'Who's your doctor?' but Jet was trying to stand. They watched him stagger to his feet.

'The man doesn't need a doctor,' Pyson announced. 'He needs the hospital. Come along, young man.'

Stella grabbed Jet's hand. 'I'm staying with Daddy.'

'It's all right, Stella,' Miss Pyson said. 'We have lots of room in the car.'

'Police seem no nearer a solution in the "Drive Away Millions" affair. Scotland Yard sources confirm that they are actively investigating the possibility that the dead man, Clifford Henry Lyons, was an accomplice of the missing driver, Scott Heywood. The pathologist's reports state that Lyons—found in the burnt-out van—died as a result of shooting, and not from burns inflicted from the blaze.—Martin Busby, presumably this is now a murder hunt as well?'

'Oh, certainly a murder hunt, Michael. Quite clearly, Lyons was shot dead *before* his body was dumped in the fire—and that makes it murder.'

'Is there any firm evidence that Lyons himself was involved in the robbery?'

'We must be careful here. Police have said that, according to information received, Lyons was an accomplice. But they can't confirm it.'

'Information received?'

'They're not revealing anything about that. What they *are* saying is that a massive international search is under way for Scott Heywood.'

'The police are reasonably convinced, then, that it was the driver, Heywood, who stole the money?'

'They haven't said that either. We must remember that Scott Heywood was a man of unblemished record. His

family is still living in the same house, and seems to be
in a state of genuine shock. Naturally they are under
police protection.'

'But there is no sign of Heywood himself?'

'Nor of the money. He and the two million pounds have
simply vanished into thin air.'

Stella, cold and waif-like, huddled over her plastic cup of
orange juice, an old magazine on her knee. From time to
time a passing nurse would pause beside her but Stella
always said that she was waiting. They grew used to her,
stopped approaching, forgot about the pale child sitting
alone. Creel and Pyson had left—the formidable woman
softened by the obvious damage sustained by Heywood,
and softened further perhaps by the fact that her earlier
assumptions now appeared to have been hasty, possibly
false. Stella turned a page of her magazine. She looked
up, studied the nurses again, and wondered whether she
should ask one outright about her father. In the continual
bustle, the climate of purpose, with the passing adults
sure of their tasks, it would be easy to be lulled. Waiting
for him here was not the same as it had been last night,
when she had waited and waited and he had not returned.
It was different here. She knew where he was. He had
become part of this huge health machine, a component
in the process, passed from inspection table to sick bay,
safe in the system like a parcel in the post. Yet as the
long morning crept by, as other outpatients opened their
bags of sandwiches, Stella found that her worries were
growing worse. Daddy was so obviously ill. When they
had arrived at the hospital he had seemed hardly able to
walk; his battered face had looked terrible. Now he had
vanished inside the hospital. Stella imagined the laby-
rinth of corridors, the stark wards, the harshly lit operat-
ing theatre where her father might be lying on a hard

rubber bed. If he died, who would come and tell her? Would anyone remember that when the dead man had arrived, he had been with his daughter? Who still waited. Who, as the hours passed, would become part of the furniture, forgotten and alone.

She jumped up. Hobbling towards her was an old man, head bandaged, face puffed and bruised. The way the old man walked was as if he leant on an invisible stick. She threw her arms round him. He said, 'I didn't know if you'd still be here.' He sounded tired.

Stella did not know what to say. 'Of course I am.'

'I thought they might have ... taken you.'

'Oh, *they* went ages ago.'

'Did they?' He remained standing. Despite the bandage he did not look as frail as when they had arrived. He smelled of soap and disinfectant.

She asked, 'Are you in a ward?'

'No, I'm ... I'm all right.'

'Don't they want you for observation or something?'

He smiled faintly. 'I think they've observed enough of me.'

'Can we go home?'

Hoach met them on the stairs. He had been hovering in his room, peeping from the window, assuming that eventually they would come back. He popped out on to the landing like a jack-in-the-box on a weak spring, and he positioned himself in their path.

'I don't want trouble here.'

'That's good.'

'This is a respectable house.'

Jet waited. Hoach said, 'You know, this kind of thing . . .'

Jet raised an eyebrow. It hurt.

'I mean, Social Services. People will think I'm running one of their doss houses.'

'That's finished now. The Social Services won't come again.'

'I don't know.'

The Heywoods gazed drowsily at him. He continued: 'And just look at you. Been in a fight?'

'It's not Dad's fault!'

Jet touched her. Hoach said, 'People will talk.'

'What'll they say?'

Hoach had not yet associated his tenant with the other Heywood in the news. 'It brings down the tone, people fighting. You're not Irish? If we have any more of these incidents . . .'

'Yes, yes.'

'I mean, if the Social Services have to come round again . . . And your girl should be out at school.'

'Can we go up now?'

Hoach stood aside to let them pass. When the Heywoods reached the next landing he heard the girl say, 'It's not fair, what Mr Hoach said.' But Hoach snorted to himself: not fair, young madam! Her father brawling, the Social Services calling round.—And he knew why they'd come: a pretty little girl, living alone with her no-good father. It wasn't right. Skipping school. And why was *he* here in the daytime, both of them wandering round? Bet your life he'd lost his job—there'd be rent problems soon.

Social Services was only part of it—there were those other men who had called earlier. Nasty types, they had seemed. Mean and low class. One had his arm in a sling—could have been in the same wretched fight as Heywood. Perhaps they were the sort of villains Heywood was going to associate with, his new friends, the sort who thought they would be able to come round any time. Hoach would not have that. His was a respectable house. He straightened his tie. He might have felt easier in his mind if he had known that, upstairs in their flat, Jet and Stella had started packing their few things.

BOOK TWO

—

FIFTEEN

He had bought a wind-up clock from Woolworth's because here, they were not connected to the electric mains. Late at night, the rusty tick of the metal clock was the loudest noise inside the caravan. Wind could whistle at the window, occasional night-sounds might be heard outside, but within the semi-darkness its throaty tock was like the heartbeat of a living organism. It seemed to bind the interior shadows into a warm protective embrace. Walls came closer, corners disappeared, and the single night-light glowed like the last embers of a dying fire.

In her bunk-bed Stella stirred. She glanced at her father in his own berth across the narrow space and found that he was watching her. They both smiled. The dim light deepened their brown eyes, made the individual strands of their hair melt into common blackness around their faces. That murky light seemed to draw everything together; Jet seemed softer, younger, while she seemed older than her eight short years. Gazing at him in his bed a single arm's length away she felt that this was how he must have looked before she was born—the young husband, her father to be. In the week since they had left the flat his bandage had been removed and the bruises on his face had disappeared. He had recovered, yet it seemed to Stella that he was more gentle with her than before, as if that fearful beating had broken something inside.

Sometimes, Stella believed that the caravan held a kind of magic, spreading a benign radiance to their days. To her, its snug interior did not seem cramped—simply convenient and intimate. Whatever she wanted was within reach—just as now, at this moment, she had only to stretch out her hand to touch her father. Everything she wanted. All through the day the magic stayed with her. When Jet was out she did simple housework; when that was done she was free. Every night he slept across the way from her, and in the darkest hours she could watch him sleep. He watched her too. Someimes, as now, she would turn to find him looking at her, his eyes glowing across the gap.

He said, 'You should be asleep.'

'I can lie in.'

'You're a night owl.'

'Mhm.' She turned on to her back. 'This is the wonderfullest time. Every minute seems to last for ages. Nothing's waiting to be done.'

'No pressure. You don't mind the dark?'

'You're here. And we've got the lamp.'

They lay listening to the clock. From outside there was no sound. After a while, Stells whispered, 'Are you still awake?'

'I am now.'

'Don't be eggy. Why don't we go out and get some air?'

'Not again.'

'Come on.'

'You're a vampire! It's cold out there.'

'It isn't.'

Stella slid out of bed, found her dressing gown and put it on. She stood over him and touched his face. 'It wasn't cold last night.'

'It rained.'

'Drizzle. It wasn't cold.'

'I'm asleep.'

'Oh, come on, Dad.' She tilted her head. 'I'll go on my own.'

'You won't.' He erupted slowly from the bed, the blanket trickling like lava down his sides. She was at the door. 'Like a little puppy dog,' he grumbled. 'Put your wellies on.'

While she wriggled into her well-used red rubber boots, Jet pulled a pair of trousers over his pyjamas and found a sweater. 'Will you be warm enough?'

'I told you, it isn't cold.'

'Maybe not in here.'

Hand in hand, Jet and Stella wander through the empty fairground. All the lights have been turned off, trailers are shuttered for the night, stalls and rides loom in the dark. He and she leave their caravan and the line of wagons alongside the site and walk on to the pitch. They move between silent sidestalls to reach the long rail of the Dodgems. Towards one end of the wooden floor, empty cars huddle like sheep, their masts like drunken flagpoles into the nets. Around the Dodgems, the other stalls—joints and hoop-las, shooting galleries, arcades and whisks—are all long closed. Each of the main pathways has coir matting laid on the ground, but the mud oozes through as they walk along.

Beyond the Dodgems—open, vulnerable—the Helter-Skelter is closed as securely as a Martello tower. Then comes the Octopus, its folded tentacles frail in the dark, its tub chairs gleaming in the moonlight. Without a word, Jet and Stella continue through the side-stuff toward the motionless Big Wheel. Towering above the fairground day and night, the Wheel always seems so permanent, and to Stella, who once watched it happen, it seems unbelievable that this vast solid frame can be erected in hours and dismantled in less when the fair travels on. Stars twinkle like fairy lights between its spokes.

'It's great when the crowd has gone,' she declares solemnly. 'Magic.'

'But dark. You're still not frightened?'

'No, this isn't scary dark.'

From beneath someone's trailer, a dog growls softly. Perhaps it has recognised them. She says, 'In London I was scared, but I'm not here.'

'What about in the caravan when I'm working?'

'I don't stay in much on my own.'

This is because she helps around the stalls. Every fairground kid stays up late. Every stall can use more help.

'I've got lots of friends here.'

'Hope they keep an eye on you.'

'Of course they do.' She takes his hand. 'Like I keep an eye on *you*.' Jet chuckles. 'Well, the doctor said you must take it easy. You cracked your skull.'

'Not exactly—'

'He said—'

'Concussion. That's not as bad.'

Stella sniffs. 'I'll still keep an eye on you.'

They pause by the Waltzer, its gilded lettering cold in the dark.

'And it's dangerous, what you do.'

'You're a real old nag.'

'Like a wife?'

They are both silent as they walk on, each remembering her missing mother. The cold mud squelches beneath their boots, and as they return to the waiting caravan Stella clings more tightly to her father's arm.

In the afternoon, as day crowds mill about the fairground, Jet doesn't have much to do. But for Stella, working on Duke's coconut concession, afternoon is the busiest time—young kids out with their parents give the stall constant trade. The children try to win a prize, then Duke shows them how it's done. On the stall, instead of coconuts, Duke uses shaky pyramids of old tin cans. To win a prize the punters have to knock them all off the trestle. It looks easy, yet people find that somehow there always seems to be one last battered tin that will not fall. Stella's job is to pile the cans back up again while Duke draws in more customers. He offers his set of wooden balls like a bargain no one should refuse, his thin trustworthy face screwed up in sympathy, his kind eyes welcoming the next in line, like the uncle you wish you'd had.

Jet is alone inside the boxing booth. This will be his first season after a two-year absence, and the first time he has not come to fight. Age is catching up with him, but in any case, Joe Hake has told him that he can't afford more than two fighters and he had hired two before Jet signed on. Which, since Jet has recently had his head cracked open, is probably just as well. Although Jet played down the severity of his injury, Joe has never been easy to fool.

He climbs into the empty ring. For the first time, he is employed only as a canvas-man; to help erect the structure, then sweep up and look after it through the week. He also looks after the boxing kit—polishing gloves, brushing boots, washing blood stains from vests and trunks. Every morning Jet puts gumshields in the jar to sterilise, hangs jockstraps on a line to air. He refills water bottles, cleans out the rosin tray, checks the bottle of massage oil.

At the moment he is padding around the canvas-covered platform, brushing vigorously with a stiff broom. Rosin and dust hang in the air. He likes to begin in the centre of the ring, sweeping the fine grey dirt outwards to the ground. Then he sweeps again, the fine dirt floating above the canvas and resettling when he has moved on. He has to sweep it twice, sometimes three times, but Jet feels towards the ring as to an ancient relative—he will respect it, talk to it, keep it from becoming scruffy and forlorn.

Three years ago, of course, returning in such a humble fashion would have hurt his pride, but now his only regret is that he earns less money. Apart from that, a canvas-man's life is free and satisfying—outside conventional society, travelling with the fair. Even his working hours are a kind of bonus, giving freedom at the best times of day: a couple of hours cleaning in the daytime, then the main shift before going to bed.

Jet collects the ladders so he can check the lights.

Travelling life is familiar to him, although Stella has not experienced it before. In the old days, when Angie was still with them, Jet worked the fairs alone—which added to their problems. In those earlier summers on the road, Angie would materialise unexpectedly throughout the season, when she felt like it, he supposed. Which she did less frequently as time went by. Obviously it was no basis for a marriage.

Now he has brought his family with him—or the part of it that matters. His work is menial, and until his head is better he cannot box—and he will soon be too old to box at all. But none of that matters. All that does matter is that he has Stella, and that he and she stay together in careless freedom.

There is freedom also for Claire Heywood, now that the press reporters have decamped. She can walk out of her front door without being accosted—although she does still check from her upstairs window before leaving home. For two days there has been no mention on the news—no revelations, no rumours, no further comment. For the first few days after Scott disappeared, Claire had approaches from national papers, from an agency, from cajoling voices that she ignored. She was offered money but would not take it. One telephone pest suggested that the reason she wasn't tempted by his money was that her husband was sitting on two million, but she put down the phone. Laying herself open to the newspapers would be worse than posing for topless photographs.

Photographs.

Some have appeared, blurred and grainy, after her brief emergences into daylight, her face shielded from the unkind flash. And a clear picture of Scott has been issued by the police. Last week, when the heat was at its greatest, papers asked for photos inside her house. They tried sneak shots through the windows. Journalists wouldn't understand that she doesn't want their money; the very mention of it makes her sick. All Claire wants is to hear something from her husband. Sometimes she fantasises about what she will say to him—long conversations inside her head, harangues almost. With each day that passes, the shock is becoming more bearable, but the pain of losing him, of having him suddenly eliminated from her life, remains acute. Each night she sleeps alone and feels the cold. She assumes that her feelings in this period must be something like those after losing a limb: first the shock and agony, then as the healing process begins, a dawning capacity to reorganise, to rebalance and carry on. Life does go on.

The health visitor has told her that it is bad for Tommy to stay out of school. Claire, ever obedient to official advice, has taken the boy back to the cheerful company of his little friends. That's how the health visitor expressed it: his little friends who will make him cheerful. So now Claire herself spends days alone, no longer badgered by reporters, but equally no longer greeted by her own friends. It's not that they shun her deliberately; perhaps they're waiting for her to make the first move, as they would wait for a bereaved widow. Perhaps. Because it is like that: she has been bereaved.

The house seems silent. She isn't sure why it seems so different now; after all, until this dreadful business, her days were often spent this way—Scott at work, Tommy at school. Nowadays, she doesn't even play the radio. It isn't company any more.

The familiar drone of the vacuum cleaner creates a cocoon in which she walks free, in which all outside sounds have been obliterated. Housework fully occupies her mind, as she exercises well-practised skills. But no more visitors; they trampled her carpets, opened cupboards and rummaged through drawers. It was like being present at a burglary in one's own house—helpless, unable to intervene. She didn't even have the right to protest. Most of all, Claire cannot forget that awful day when the police brought their hideous search warrant. On that day she confined herself to the kitchen, made pots of tea, and for once, just for once on that shameful day, Claire Heywood offered nothing to her visitors, did not acknowledge them, made them realise that they were unwelcome invaders in her home.

He did not belong there, although he had the right. As a resident of Lewisham—or as anyone, come to that, who paid admission—little Ticky was entitled to use public swimming baths if they were open. Weekday mornings after half past nine the pool was mainly used by school children learning how to swim. They came in parties, shrieking off the bus, loosely supervised by PE teachers, two to a class. Ticky had found that if he arrived about 9.15 he could be in the changing room, dressed in trunks, as the first school groups arrived. Ticky preferred to be already changed—didn't like to peel off his grubby underpants in front of little boys; didn't want to rub shoulders with them, one might say, since he and they were of a similar size. There the boys would be, whipping off their uniforms, just as Ticky folded away his clothes. All around him would be thin angular bodies, elbows cocked, knees bending as their pants came down. Ticky would busy himself at his locker, would repack it, maybe blow his nose, and out of the corner of his eye he would peep at the tiny penises and smooth behinds. He was very careful. Rule One was not to catch any young lad's eye—the littler terrors would see right through him like a shot. Rule Two was he did not hang around. Ticky reckoned he had down to a T how long he could linger in the changing room before attracting attention to himself. And the other way of avoiding notice was to vary the timing of his visits, changing days and the hour of day. Ticky had the whole schedule pretty much off by heart. Sessions with infants he avoided—wonderfully sweet little things, so pretty, but much too young. Teenagers he skipped, because they frightened him—even Thursday afternoons, with the teenage girls; Christ, they were the most terrifying of all. Some were overweight like fat old women, some had no sexuality at all, but perhaps a quarter were the sort men fantasised about: see them wet in the pool in their slippery costumes, and most men would be back in the changing room buttering their cob. But to Ticky these girls were frightening—healthy *women* was what they were. If Ticky encountered a full-grown teenager threshing through the water he moved out of the way. And to see one of those girls glancing scornfully at his puny frame made him shrivel smaller. He would sink beneath the cooling water or slink back to the changing room.

Junior school was Ticky's preference, like today. He was moving from the company of semi-naked nine-year-olds, through the exit shower into the pool. He didn't need to hang around the changing rooms as if little *boys* turned him on. He liked to play with them but he was not gay. No, he was as hetero as the next man, maybe more. Christ—Ticky grinned as he strutted beside the swimming pool—he had a more active sex life than most men.

In the pool were less than twenty people—the usual few oldies ploughing through a weekly constitutional before the kids came and spoiled their fun—plus half a dozen miscellaneous: the out of work, the shift workers, and men here for other reasons. No one would ask.

Ticky might have jumped straight in, but there were too many people today, someone might be watching, so he climbed warily down the steps. Not too cold. Once he was in to his waist, he jumped out from the wall and began to swim away. He had an ungainly, almost desperate doggy-paddle style that, though moderately fast, caused a lot of spray. By the time he had reached the deep end, gaggles of kids were ranged around their teachers along the side, ready to jump in. Ticky clung to the rail and eyed them. Some of the girls in their one-piece costumes were like little mannequins—rounded hips, gently swelling thighs, the first suggestion of budding breasts. This was the age that Ticky loved, innocent perfection.—Ticky corrected himself: not innocent, oh no, no, no. Behind those unblemished faces could be the most amazingly dirty minds—curious, furtive, yearning for experience.

Ticky wasn't indiscriminate. Half the kids here he would never look at, and half the others were like uncracked seeds. Only a quarter at most showed that grain of knowledge: Ticky imagined their little fingers groping between their thighs as they discovered themselves. Lucky ones might have a little friend who'd join in their sensual game: Doctors and Nurses, Mums and Dads, Statues, Operations—any one of those wonderful feelie games Ticky longed to play. Even with these more aware children Ticky remained particular: kids had to look right, to have a kind of knowing innocence, an elfin beauty to stop his breath and leave him half-paralysed with desire.

Today was lifesaving practice, Ticky's favourite. All around the pool, boys and girls divided into pairs and jumped into the water to practise simple exercises. Already some were swimming on their backs, one supporting the other, little tummies pushed out, legs kicking vigorously in the water. Ticky plunged from the rail and swam determinedly among them, carving clumsily between the children like a frog among the goldfish. Several times he brushed against one, several times he stroked a young child's side. In one delightful moment his hand cupped a blonde girl's bottom, but he swam straight past her, eyes fixed to the front, as if he hadn't realised. He threshed through water churned by children's legs. Choppy waves splashed against his face. Cool ripples soothed his skin. When he reached the far end, a young girl in a wet black costume was pushing herself from the pool, her delicate biceps straining, her hard rounded bottom perched like shining mussel shells on the edge. As she paused for breath, streams of clean water ran from her thighs. Inches away from Ticky's face the child's tight backside was cut by a single crease, the underflesh of her bottom showing pink and new. In the round channel between her spotless thighs the stretched material of her costume was clinging tight. The child heaved herself from the pool. Ticky remained in the choppy water, his flustered face buried against the rail. He did not dare to turn around because he knew that at that moment the material of his own costume was stretched as well. He waited, holding the vision in his thoughts. He was not ready to move.

Not yet.

SIXTEEN

Good and evil, black and white, that was how it looked: the young black man, tall, lean, muscled around his shoulders, a pitiless gaze; his white opponent, big, comfortable, beer-bellied—a man you could imagine on the farm loading hay, working out of doors, built like an amiable cart-horse. And he moved like one. He trotted from his corner, shook his head, pawed at the black man, then got hit. The pro boxer was sticking long jabs in his florid face. Blood spurted immediately, shockingly soon, as if the pro had thrown paint. The injured cart-horse raised his gloves, charged forward. The pro clipped him as he lumbered by. Contemptuous flicks drove the man on to the ropes and when he tried to protect himself it did not work. Desperately barging forward, using his weight to struggle free, he saw the hovering boxer and swung a massive, hedge-clearing blow, but it missed by a yard and left him stumbling. The pro chopped his head. As the cart-horse turned he almost whinnied. He flicked gobs of blood through the floodlit air. The boxer circled, just outside his range. This time, when the man stumbled forward the pro parried and jabbed his face. Horse raised his guard but was thumped in the ribs. He dropped his gloves and took one on the cheek. When he raised his arms again, the black boxer stooped slightly as if to peer at delicate work, then rammed three piston blows into his guts. Horse was crumbling. His mouth fell open, and for a moment it looked as if he had something urgent he wanted to say. But there was no time. Half a second, maybe, as the pro leant back. A tenth of a second as his blow came in. Then the white man's feet had left the floor and he found himself sprawling among the ropes. He was not unconscious, but as he flailed in the tangled ropes his short fight had ended. The pro did not follow through. In a real contest he would have, but tonight he let Joe intervene. Only when Joe Hake had moved between them did the rangy black man pretend to go for his opponent. But he allowed Joe to hold him off. The crowd booed lustily; someone threw an apple. But by now Joe was lifting the bleary white man, was supporting him, was displaying him to the crowd. He reached down from the ring to take the mike from Jet. 'And we stop the contest to prevent further injury. Thank you, thank you.' The crowd booed.

'Thank you for your kind appreciation.' They booed again. Jet climbed in with a sopping sponge.

'A first round victory for Lucky Lee Leonard!' Nobody cheered.

'And let's hear a shout for the gallant loser. Come on, gents, give the lad a cheer.' Mixed boos and cheers. Joe raised the Horse's begloved hoof, while Jet mopped his red face. 'He's your local challenger—a brave fighter, gents, he done his best. He's a local lad. Show the boy you're proud of him!'

He did not look proud. The defeated cart-horse stood staring at the ground, blood and water dripping from his face. He trembled slightly as Jet led him away.

'The sport of kings there, ladies and gentlemen. The noble art.' Joe's amplified voice was directed more at passers-by outside than the crowd inside his tent. 'You've seen an excellent fight here—two brave lads and a technical knock-out. We all enjoyed it. And we have more tonight—more live boxing inside this very tent. But first, good people, before you go, please show your appreciation for our gallant challenger. You can see 'is 'at now passing among you. Yes, there it is, the poor boy's 'at. Didn't win a prize, so it's up to you. Does the boy leave here empty-handed?'

Most of the crowd were edging for the exit.

'Give your boy some con-sol-ation. He done you proud—a brave and plucky fight—so dig your hands deep in your pockets, bring out your change and put it in his cap.'

At the narrow exit stood another boxer clad in towelling robe and hood, wielding the collection cap like a heavy handgun, as if they had to buy a ticket to get outside.

'He was a brave boy, gents, a brave local boy. So give your lad his bus fare home. That's the spirit. I see pound coins falling in his hat—pound coins, ladies and gents, for the brave British boy. Don't let him down.'

Out in the trailer the brave boy's nose was no longer bleeding. As he shuffled into shirt and sweater, Lee Leonard reassured him: 'No, you did all right. Really made me work.'

Jet added, 'Your mates wouldn't have dared come up.'

'And you've got a punch,' Lee asserted, though he had not been hit. The cart-horse seemed surprised to find that outside the ring the lean and lethal Leonard seemed OK. Wrapped in a huge cream dressing gown, Leonard shambled beside him as if they were fellow patients at the hospital. 'Think any of your mates will want to have a go?'

'Not now.'

The boxers laughed. Lee wrapped an arm round the big man's shoulder. 'Hey, you're all right. You OK now?'

The man said he was. It had been a confusing night: spurred on because his friends thought him no mean fighter, entering a public ring, losing badly—what he would remember was not the pain but more the strangeness of it all. A sturdy west country man, a farm worker who had seen blacks in town but had rarely talked to one, he had found himself tonight in a ring, making contact—real painful contact—yet here was the black man putting his arm round him, grinning in his ear, just like anyone. He had a Midlands accent.

The trailer door swung open. The hooded white boxer stepped inside, waved a vague acknowledging hand as he dropped a heavy cap on the table. 'Not so bad.'

He began sorting the coins into three roughly equal piles. Lee reached across and flicked back his hood. 'You should take your hat off when you come indoors. Didn't your mummy tell you?'

The boxer snarled, 'Piss off.' He was smaller than Lee, in his middle twenties, white, shaven-headed, with a nose that had been flattened into his face until it seemed no further damage could be done to it.

Jet nudged the cart-horse. 'Here comes the good bit.'

The man was innocent. 'How come?'

'You get to share the hat. Collection for the fight.'

'Oh.' The man looked with some interest at the scattered coins. 'Half each?'

Lee Leonard chuckled, his Midland accent stronger now. 'No, not quite half. It goes three ways—you, me and the boss. He talks up the crowd for you. How much is there, Tel?'

Terry shrugged. 'I just make the piles. You count it.— Here.' He pushed one towards the cart-horse. 'I usually get ten per cent of that—'cos I hold the hat out.'

'Oh, right.'

'But Lee cut in. 'He's kidding you, man. That's all yours.'

'Oh, right.' He glanced between Lee and Terry. 'Well, thanks.'

As the challenger pocketed his money Joe Hake came in. 'All done? Let's take a look.' He took Horse's head in his hands and peered into his eyes. 'No harm done?'

'Well—'

'Good. Your mates are waiting—they'll be proud of you. Anyone says anything, tell 'em next time I call, they got to stick up their hands, come and have a go.' He winked. 'There's another show in twenty minutes. You tell 'em that. Say I need a volunteer.' Joe laughed. 'Away you go, son.' He led him to the door. 'You'll feel different now— you were a man tonight.' As he pushed him through the door, Joe clapped him on the shoulder. He paused to watch him leave, then turned to his boxers. 'Jesus sake, Lee, you wanna kill the boy?'

'I didn't—'

'First bleedin' round! He never touched you. Next time, Lee, drag it out like I keep telling you, ease up, give the punters their money's worth.'

'He was a big man, Joe.'

'So is a cow, but you only milk it. I don't like these first round knock-outs.'

'Man weighed two stone more than me.'

'So what?'

'Come on, Joe. Anyone who gets in that ring fancies himself a fighter—he probably has a scrap every Saturday night. When a man carries that much weight I want to take the sting out before he starts.'

'Sting! Listen, Lee.' Joe seemed mollified. 'It's early season and you're new to the game. These punters out there, they're amateurs, in a different league. Terry, you tell him.'

'He'll learn.'

Joe showed him the fish-eye. 'Thank you, Mr Sykes. Very helpful.' He turned to Jet. 'Take the boy in hand.'

Joe had been a middleweight, but was heavier now. He

was a burly, bustling man, middle fifties with grey-red hair, grey moustache, grey bushy eyebrows and tired blue eyes. He had been running booths for twenty years. 'What was in the hat?'

Terry pushed a pile across and Joe swept it from the table into his moneybag. 'The boy get his share?'

'Yup.'

'It's only right, 'cos his friends will ask.'

The crowd thought the hat was only for the challenger, but life wasn't like that. 'We'll wait ten minutes,' Joe said. 'You can have a nice rest.'

Jet still found it odd not to be up on the platform. His evening tasks now were to collect entrance money and to second the bouts, but during the pre-fight whip-up he mingled with the crowd outside, watching Joe and the two fighters go through their stuff. Joe did the spiel while Lee and Terry bobbed at his side. They wore robes over their boxing kit, so only their gloves and boots were visible. With Terry, even his head was wrapped inside his hood. While Joe drummed up the crowd, Lee and Terry jogged menacingly, did a little shadow boxing, glared down at the spectators. They had to strike a balance between looking tough enough to excite the crowd, yet vulnerable enough to tempt a challenger. Joe said it came down to giving the punters alternatives: on the one hand, a big man, because the crowd loved their heavyweights; on the other, someone lighter—a middle or even junior middleweight—who looked easier to beat. Until recently, Joe had toured three fighters, and as he once said to Jet, you'd expect sports to pick the man in the middle, the safe compromise, but bruisers in the crowd usually chose the heavyweight—because they *had* to, they felt, with their reputation—while anyone else took the smallest. As if he'd be easy. Which he never was. Joe believed the smaller the meaner. He and Jet could both remember that season when they had brought the little bantamweight, that mean Scottish punk, living proof. He'd have three fights a night—often giving a stone away, which was a lot at bantamweight—and he'd cut his opponents' faces so badly that by the time they'd finished they looked as if they'd been scrubbed with a cheese grater. The man delighted in it. He was serving five years now. Joe maintained that when a punter picked a heavyweight, he might walk away afterwards feeling stunned, but he'd recover within the hour. No after-effects. Big men had less to prove.

'Where's your little girl tonight?'

Jet turned. On the sidestall behind him, opposite the boxing booth, was a 'Catch Your Lucky Rabbit' fishing game. The girl who worked it had auburn hair.

'She's working for Duke.'

'Does he need her evenings?'

'He's running two stalls.'

'Hello, handsome.' She switched to a punter before Joe could resume with the microphone. 'Win a cuddly toy for your pretty girlfriend. A box of chocolates. Catch a Lucky Rabbit and make your dreams come true. Genuine gypsy magic—it lasts all night.'

She was grinning at the dithering couple. The look in her eyes suggested that gypsy magic was about to start. 'Just dangle your rod and see what you win. You know how to dangle your rod, I bet.' The lad hesitated. 'Every rabbit wins a prize.' The showgirl smiled at his plump girlfriend. 'What would you like, love—a cuddly teddy or a box of chocolates?'

'I dunno. I bet the chocolates have gone off.'

'Fresh today, love. Make him have a go. He looks clever with his hands.'

She was finishing her pitch as Joe Hake started.

Starkly lit by the string of coloured bulbs above him, Joe
paraded his boxers like a pair of slavegirls—Lee Leonard,
robe untied, jogging on the spot, loose-limbed, hands
down; Terry Sykes, snuggled inside his hood, jabbing the
cold night air.

'Live boxing here before your eyes. Live boxing tonight.
Real fights, inside this tent. Yes, sir, when I say real
boxing I mean you can try it yourself. Who will be first
to volunteer? How about you, sir? Win fifty pound. Fifty
pound is what I say, yes, fifty pound. Put my boy down,
win fifty pound.—Can you hear me, gents? Fifty pound if
you knock him out. And that's not all. Because—listen
carefully now—I'm generous—if you don't knock him out,
you can still win. Yes, sir, anyone can win! It's very simple,
a child could do it. Just last three rounds with either of
my two 'andsome boxers and you will win ten lovely quid.
I said ten pound. You don't have to knock him down. No.
You don't have to win the fight. No. You don't even have
to *hit* him! No. Ten pound, that's what I said, ten pounds.
Am I mad? I think I am. Because tonight—yes, tonight—
I am offering ten pound—this ten pound here; see it
fluttering in my fingers—ten pounds to stay three rounds.
But why stop there? Fancy your chances? Can you knock
my lad down? Fifty pound, that's what I'm offering, fifty
pound. Am I mad? I think I am. So, are we ready, gents?
Who'll volunteer? Don't hold back now, don't be shy. I'll
take the first man to raise his hand. Here you are, gents,
fifty notes. Who wants them? Raise your hand.'

Jet heard the boy stir behind him, heard his girlfriend:
'Yes, well done!'

Jet turned, surprised, but the boy was grinning broadly,
a plastic rabbit on the end of his rod. 'I want a teddy
bear,' declared his girlfriend.

'Fifty pound! Do I have a taker?'

'We'll have the teddy bear, please, Miss.'

'Just a minute, love. Let's have a look at your bottom.'

'Fifty pound, gents. Stick up your hands.'

'How d'you mean, my bottom?'

The showgirl flicked the rabbit upside down. 'Well done, sir. You've won a lovely little troll.'

'Do what?'

'Whichever rabbit you catch, its prize is written on its bottom. Look, a lovely troll.'

'I want a teddy.'

'Try another go.'

'Am I mad, gents? I think I am. Fifty pounds—I am throwing it away.'

'A teddy—'

'Every rabbit wins a prize, sir. Have another go.'

'Come on!'

'You look lucky tonight. Have another dangle.'

'Fifty pounds and no one wants it? Surely, gentlemen, you're not all wimps? Are there no strong lads here? Ain't there anyone knows how to fight?'

Jet could see a group of lads trying to encourage their leader.

'Three short rounds under Queensberry rules. No one gets hurt. Don't worry if you've got no kit—we supply it free. Proper gloves, proper boots, proper everything—all on the house. Free. So come on lads, let's be having you. Where's the brave young man knows how to fight?'

The two at the rabbit stall walked away. The auburn girl asked, 'Aren't you a fighter too?'

'Used to be.'

'You can't be too old?'

'Old enough to know better.'

She grinned. 'What's your name?'

'Jet.'

'I'm Collette.'

Joe Hake roared, 'There's our next contender! A big

hand, ladies and gentlemen, for a brave local boy. You
are local, aren't you, boy? Yes, that's the way. Right, my
lovely lords, ladies and gentlemen, tonight's middleweight contest is between this brave local boy coming up
on stage and the Dagenham Destroyer, Terry Sykes. The
contest will take place inside this stadium.'

'I've got to go,' Jet said.

'See you again.'

'Step right inside for your ringside seat. It's a genuine
live middleweight contest for a fifty-pound purse. Walk
straight through the door, ladies and gentlemen, for a
splendid exhibition of the sport of kings.'

When Jet glanced up at the boxing platform, Terry
Sykes was ignoring the local challenger. The bullet-
headed boxer had pushed back the hood of his robe and
was glaring down at Jet. That was when the name 'Collette' rang a bell. Terry had mentioned her. As Jet nipped
inside to collect the punters' money he tried to remember
what it was that Terry had said.

SEVENTEEN

The six-mile run took them along grassy clifftops from Bude to Combe Valley, where they turned for home. The grass was new, wet and springy, and whenever they looked down from the cliffs they saw the whole of the three-mile beach lost under the sea. The full swelling tide lapped at high water line, its white breakers rolling lazily round black Devon rocks. Gulls and cormorants were diving. Salt breeze whipped their faces.

The three men, sweatered and tracksuited, ran the return half at a loping pace. The damp morning and high tide kept trippers away, and for much of the run they could have been in a private park. There were isolated houses, the odd caravan, farm settlements with sheep. Jet ran with the two boxers because he enjoyed it and wanted to get fit. Every day now, he was growing fitter, though by the end of each run his head would begin to throb. He took aspirins and lost weight. Running with the boxers helped him become reconciled to touring as a canvas-man, anonymous, nothing more. Up here on the cliffs the wet air and bright daylight washed city dirt away. He felt that if he could take out his blood and examine it, he would find that it shone a brighter red. He gulped sea air.

'Beats Brixham,' said Lee.

'Brixton?'

'Brix*ham*—where we go next. South Devon. Had a holiday there once.'

'Bloody Babbacombe,' said Terry. 'There's a place—fucking farms, all too small.'

'Sounds hilly,' said Lee.

Jet was unsure of their schedule. 'We doing Ilfracombe this year?'

'Good beach,' declared Terry. 'But too much roadwork and lots of cars.'

'I like Paignton,' Jet said. 'Long flat beach.'

'Cracking women,' said Terry.

Lee asked, 'Where's Paignton?'

'Near Torquay.'

'You could write a guidebook.'

'I done this for two years now,' Terry said.

Jet added, 'I was working with Joe earlier.'

'Well, you're older, ain't yer?' Terry laughed.

Jet felt old. He could do the running, but too much talking ruined his breath control.

Terry added, 'You'll be leaving soon. Your millionaire brother.'

Lee asked, 'Millionaire?'

'You must've heard about his brother?'

'No.'

Jet kept silent. Terry laughed. 'Not a secret, is it, Jet?'

'Not now.'

'You can trust your old mate Tel.'

They both waited till Lee picked it up. 'Guilty secret, Jet?'

'Private joke.'

'Make me laugh.'

No one tried. Lee elbowed Jet. 'Mr Moneybags, how many years you been on the fairs?'

'Skipped the last two. Before that, a year on, one year off, then two together.'

'Why'd you stop?'

'Because you do.'

Terry spat as he ran. 'Well, I like it,' he said. 'Though the money's crap.'

Lee said, 'I'll only do this season.'

They had passed Northcott Mouth, and the town of Bude was back in sight.

'Be grateful,' Terry said. 'It's work, and that's the point.'

'Not my kind of work.'

Terry jeered. 'Ah, we was all full of dreams at your age. Race you back.'

He moved ahead as he always did: Terry liked to come first. They watched him storm ahead, elbows bent, knees pounding, determined not to be caught. Terry was twenty-six and by now must have known that his career was heading nowhere; he would not be champion; he was stuck on the hall and fair circuit. This was all there was.

'Road Runner,' said Lee.

Jet smiled back. But as they ran into Bude his head began to throb as usual. Nothing else was aching, and he was grateful for that.

Inside the warm caravan, condensation shrouds the two small windows while a radio plays. The table is laid for breakfast. Bacon waits beneath the grill. Stella has made both the beds and now crawls with brush and dustpan, singing with the radio. She has a small voice but pure. Wearing blue jeans and untidy hair, in a rough chunky-knit pullover almost big enough for her father, she is happy and light-headed. Preparing breakfast, keeping their living space tidy, Stella is as radiant as a happily wed young mother. Travelling with the fair, close to her father, is all she needs.

Strips of bacon on toast fingers, fresh-grilled kidneys with beads of blood, beefsteak tomatoes seared to blackness, flat-cap mushrooms, potato croquettes, two small cutlets of English lamb—no eggs or sausages to spoil the balance of his breakfast—thick granary bread spread with Welsh butter, a pot of marmalade at the side, a glass of orange juice and cup of tea (just one sugar—he is cutting down) form the centrepiece to Gottfleisch's meal.

He sits with a white napkin tucked into his collar, blue cufflinks in his shirt. On his face is a slight frown while he listens to the news. He has heard the headlines and now, halfway through the rest, he already knows there won't be a word that he wants to hear. He is hardly listening, though there might be a tiny snippet slipped in near the end. It is always possible. Each day brings a fresh crop of topical stories, obliterating what was there before. Yesterday's news. The Drive Away Millions affair has been a one-week wonder—not even that, perhaps five days—little more than a buzz of envious reportage speculating on the audacity of the crime: man sits in van; bank gives him money; man drives away; man disappears.

Now, Gottfleisch and reporters hope to find the driver who saw his chance. The other man—the one shot and left in the blazing van—is not important; he has left the game. Reporters have been intrigued by the driver's motive: did he always mean to commit the crime, or was it just an impulse? Was his second passport significant or coincidence? What about his wife? This last question interests Gottfleisch also—might Heywood contact her? But the real question, the one which intrigues everybody—Gottfleisch, reporters and about forty million of the public—is where the money is now. No one seems to have the answer, not the hint of an idea. Heywood may have smuggled it abroad, though it would not have been easy with all the fuss. In fact, the only reason to think that Scott might be abroad is that the police are adamant he is not.

Reporters have short attention spans. Conditioned by the media that they work for, they zap from latest this to latest that: fresh disasters, threats and scandals, juvenile crime. Gottfleisch knows that although neither the police nor journalists have formally dropped the case, they have already stopped concentrating on it. They know that as succeeding days drift by, it becomes increasingly unlikely that the money will be found. Some kind of explanation may eventually emerge—or perhaps the whole affair will become one of those unexplained forgotten mysteries. Two million pounds is not such an enormous sum; it can leak back into circulation unnoticed, like a glass of water poured into a bath.

Gottfleisch picks up a final finger of cold toast and wipes it through the sweet juices of grilled tomato on his plate. If others have lost interest, that is their choice. If they pay less attention to Scott's family, that should eventually become apparent to the man himself. He may try to contact them. Indeed, these next few days should be an interesting period—perhaps a rewarding one—to observe his family's behaviour. If they plan to wait a while before joining him, that should show. Gottfleisch wipes his mouth. Yes, the family is the key. They must be closely watched.

Gottfleisch sips his tea and studies the cutlet bones on his plate. There is nothing left now; all picked clean. Fat is starting to congeal. He stands up and tosses his napkin carelessly on to the table. It is time to act.

EIGHTEEN

At lunchtime a pall of peace lay across the fairground. Two hours to opening. By this time, everyone was out of bed, day had begun, but there was still a slow, coming-to-terms feel about the place, like Sunday morning in the world outside. Stella wandered among close-packed caravans and trailers. In the fair itself, bathed in weak April sunshine, they were taking off the covers, removing battens and testing the electrics. Generators hummed. Stella heard her name called by a large florid woman with grey-brown hair, who carried two zinc buckets heavy with water. Across the woman's face cut a huge smile like a slash in a brown crusty roll.

'My little dove, you had your breakfast?'

'Yes, I cooked it all myself.'

'That's the way, my dove. Don't your Daddy cook?'

'Usually.'

'Come to my place and have some tea.'

'Can I carry a bucket?'

'They're too heavy for you, love. Little girls mustn't strain themselves.'

Doris Diamonte was a widow. Working fairs all her life, it seemed natural that now her husband was dead she continued on her own. She ran the Haunted House—a little shabby now—which Stella had no desire to go inside. The House occupied the whole of a long trailer, had board extensions for entrance and exit, and a tiny

balcony above the ground floor. Between sites, Doris
towed the trailer behind the large wagon which served
as her living quarters—and she could manoeuvre the
double vehicle through Devon lanes more efficiently than
most tourists could handle cars.

'Here we are, my dove.'

Though Stella liked her own small caravan, she was
fascinated by the Diamonte wagon. Cut-glass mirrors
made the interior huge. Gilded lights glowed like candles
on pine-clad walls, twinkling on mounted china and crys-
tal glass. Along one wall stood a divan, festooned with
cushions. On the highly polished table was a small candelabra—a real silver candelabra, which Stella thought
wonderful—and at the end of the wagon was a gas fire
in mock brick surround.

'You won't want sugar, my little dove?'

'No, thanks.'

'My Marianne always had four lumps. Mind, she was
a big girl.' Doris laughed as she handed Stella her cup
of tea. The fingers of each hand were encrusted with
flamboyant rings.

'Is Marianne your daughter?'

'The only one. But she married outside the business.'
Doris gave Stella an appraising glance. 'Of course, you're
not used to fairground life.'

'My Dad is.'

'But he never brought you with him before. Not travellers, you Heywoods.'

'I'll learn.'

'Happen you will.' Doris smiled lazily at the little town
girl. 'But you might miss your little brick house.'

'We didn't have one—we had a flat.'

'Oh! Them's horrid things. People on top of you, people
down below—it's like living in a sandwich. Want another
biscuit?'

'No, thanks.'

'My Marianne would eat half the packet. Yes, when she married outside, she broke her dada's heart. Perhaps it's why he died, poor pet.' Doris smiled wistfully. 'Ah no, mustn't lay that on my Marianne.'

'Do you still see her?'

'Not a lot.' Doris's smile grew tighter. 'She don't come visiting while I'm on the road. But *you* love your dada, don't you, my dove?'

'Of course.'

'And you wouldn't leave him? No, of course not.—Oh, here's our Merlin. Isn't he a darlin'?'

Stella leant back in her chair and warily eyed the large black cat. Sleek, independent, an experienced traveller, Merlin looked anything but a domestic pet. It lapped its milk from a Worcester saucer.

Doris asked, 'You like helping on the coconuts, then?'

'I don't do much. It isn't difficult.'

'Ah, but it needs two people. My Haunted House, see, it don't need ride-boys. I just takes the money and let punters wander about on their own.' She sighed, which seemed to Stella an odd reaction, then said, 'We got an hour before people come. Want a look inside?'

'Oh no, no thanks.'

'You doesn't be frightened of the Haunted House? Little thing like you shouldn't be afraid!'

'I don't like the dark.'

'Who'd want to harm *you*, my little dove?'

'Am I mad, gents? I think I am. Fifty pounds here, can you see it? I hold up my hand, I feel the wind—no, not in me belly, darling, between me fingers—I feel the wind rippling through these be-eautiful ten-pound notes and I could lose 'em. Yes, I could. All this money could blow away and I would not care. No, I wouldn't. Because I am prepared to *give* away this money, gents, to any brave lad who can knock my man out. Fifty pound. But are you man enough? Ah! That's the question, as the Dutchman said. All right, my lads, here's how you can earn a *tenner* instead—ten pound! All you have to do is stay on your feet for three short rounds. There's nothing to it. Any takers? What—can't no one fight? I do not believe it, I really don't. I've been to Bude before, and it's famous for fighters—famous, I said. So, who's the champ, who's the local hero? Who wants to make his name today?'

They were not buying. The crowd of thirty people were happy to watch, to hear what he'd say, but none came forward. Joe wrapped it up: 'It's getting cold, gents, and we're going in. Yes, these are delicate flowers I'm showing here—they don't like your seaside weather. Complained, they did—said, Joe, we're cold! I'll take 'em indoors! Only fifteen minutes, mind, while they warm their toesies. Would you credit it? I think not. They're both pushovers for a good strong boy. So while we're away, gents, put your heads together. You've fifteen minutes to find a local hard man. Give him my challenge—fifty pounds if he scores a knock-out, ten pounds to stay on his feet. And listen—'cos I am talking to *you* now! If you don't fancy your chance with one of my champions, I will also invite keen young amateurs to step into the ring and fight each other. Yes, each other, that's what I said. Look at the bloke who's standing next to you. Fancy your luck with *him*? Three rounds, each just a tiny minute and a half, local lads against local lads—winner takes a fiver. Who's game for that? You are? Then be back in this spot in fifteen minutes. Remember, Bude's reputation is at stake—the pride of Devon. You don't want us fairground folk moving through Devon saying "They can't fight in Bude", do you? Of course you don't. Fifteen minutes, gents, and we'll be back.'

The trailer which served as changing room and general rest area smelt of massage oil and liniment. It was equipped with a cold sink, a large medicine box, and several changes of kit. On the physio table running along the centre Lee Leonard lay stripped to his trunks while Jet gave him a loosening massage. Joe hovered at Lee's head, gazing gloomily along his dark lithe body. Terry sat on a stool frowning at a newspaper. His shaven head was inside its usual towelling cowl. He asked, 'Night off, then, is it?'

'No chance.'

'They ain't interested.'

'They like to watch,' Joe said, 'but they won't come forward. Bleedin' wimps. Still, we got to do something.— Jet, if they don't come forward next time, how's about you act as gee?'

'No.'

'You mean "no choice", son. We got to do something.'

'I told you—'

'Yeah, I know, your head. I'll tell you what, we'll let you win. Let the crowd see someone earning fifty pound.'

'I'm not boxing.'

Joe laid a fatherly hand on his arm. 'Who said you were? We'll just earn a spot of gate money, and with luck you'll get a good 'at.'

'The state of my head, I'd need a helmet.'

'Hear that, Terry? Keep away from 'is 'ead.'

'Right.'

'No.'

'Jet, my son, there's a crowd out there wants to pay its money—but we've got no one among 'em who wants to fight. Listen—*are* you listening? Right. In a minute, we'll go out on the platform and I'll do me best to drum up a stick. Honest. But if no one shows, you put up your hand. Now, you're bigger than Terry, so when you come up, I'll ask if you want Terry or Lee. You choose Terry, and I'll grumble, but we'll go inside. Then, in the second round you flatten the boy.—No, shut up, Terry. All right, Jet? Fifty pound. The crowd's delighted, word gets round, we have a lovely evening.'

'No.'

'Jesus, Jet, how long you been in the business?'

'The doctor said—'

'Doctors, Christ, what do they know? Listen, you may not have to do it anyway—we might get a stick to show. But if it does come up, you both wear practice gloves, and he doesn't go anywhere near your head.—Right, Terry? Christ, it's only a game. No one gets hurt.'

'Joe—'

Had his way. When Jet stepped into the ring his nervousness was replaced by *déjà vu*. The whole ritual of putting on his kit, of bandaging fingers, of lacing gloves, of having grease applied to his face, of clambering through the ropes into the ring, of blinking beneath the glare, of hearing a crowd of strangers raising its voice to cheer, of feeling their intensity, of knowing that here on this bright-lit stage he and his opponent were the hot focus of their gaze—all this flooded over him in the ring like the barrage of white light suspended above.

They touched gloves, leather on leather. Terry held his eye. Joe muttered words they did not hear. Jet, having 'volunteered' from the crowd, was supposed to be the big local boy who might have enough weight to wear Terry down. He and Terry would mix it from the outset, Jet would take a tumble—just a standing count to alarm the crowd—and he would seem outclassed when the first round ended. In the second, he would catch Terry early, harry him round the ring, put him down inside the time. It was a conventional enough routine, but it should entertain the crowd, and would allow Joe to demand a rematch the following night—when his man 'would have a chance to repair the damage to his name'. If word got round, they could have a sell-out the following night. It was the kind of dodge that worked once in any town.

For the first minute that was how it went.

Jet and Terry hustled, chased, clinched twice to enrage the crowd, smacked and slapped with their practice gloves. As an exhibition it was fast, exhilarating stuff— two fit and skilful boxers, neither afraid of the other man. Enthusiastically, the crowd cheered to see 'their man' give the pro a run.

Suddenly Terry slipped inside Jet's lead and whacked an uppercut towards his head. Jet rolled away—but it stung his ear like an electric shock. His head had been nipped inside a vice. He lost vision. For two or three seconds as he guarded his head, Terry came fast and low, chopping crosses into his trunk, then aiming another uppercut at his jaw. Jet deflected it. While Terry tried to pummel his body, Jet wrapped him in a hug. Terry flicked his head up, grazing Jet's jaw. Instinctively, Jet backed away and jabbed ramrod blows at Terry's face, fists clenched as if carved from stone. The blows carried every ounce of Jet's fighting weight. Terry slipped away. He started dancing, his superior footwork keeping him out of range while he looked for openings. Jet's skull seemed awash with acid, and his eyes felt dashed with sea water. There was a blur, and Terry pounced. Jet's fist slipped past his head, letting Terry inside once again. Jet grabbed him. They wrestled. Through the shrieking crowd they heard the bell. They separated. As they moved apart, Terry flicked a parting shot at Jet's face and caught him moving away. Jet started after him across the ring. Joe Hake was in the neutral corner, and the crowd roared to see him leap between the boxers. He manhandled Jet to the corner. 'Hang on, for Christ's sake.'

Joe reached down for the wooden stool and pushed Jet on to it. Jet spat his gumshield. 'The little bastard.'

'You were meant to dive. But it was a lovely show.'

The crowd agreed. The racket they were making, they couldn't hear a word.

'He went for my head.'

'You're both in practice gloves—you won't get hurt.'

'I'll kill the little sod.'

'Yeah, I thought you was looking serious—that's why I rung the bell. It was only a two-minute round, mind, but the crowd'll never know. Ready?'

Jet glared across the ring to where Terry was being rubbed down by Lee Leonard. 'Keep the little bastard away from my head.'

'Hurt you, did he? I'll have a word when we get started. Here we go.'

Joe removed the stool, dropped it off the ring, and trotted away. Jet watched Terry, wondering if he'd remember to take the drop in this round as he had been instructed. If he didn't, Jet would have to make him.

At the bell they came out quickly. Terry even grinned. To roars from the excited crowd, Jet led orthodox, good-looking lefts while waiting for Terry to show his plan. Perhaps Lee had talked some sense into him. Perhaps he was ready to take his dive. But it didn't look like it. Terry tried to nail him with a vicious right hook, but Jet was alert now, fighting professionally. He blocked the blow, put a short right on Terry's mouth, then thumped another on to his nose. Terry back-pedalled, ducked aside, but Jet was hunting him. Terry tried to dodge, and Jet blocked him with a haymaker. Though Terry warded it, he was manoeuvred into a corner, where the crowd howled for his destruction. He covered up, tried to tempt Jet to come inside, but Jet stayed where he could use his reach. At full arm's length, he jabbed and hooked into Terry's defence. A dash for freedom brought a hook to Terry's head. He dropped to his knee. As Jet moved back, Joe began a count. But Terry jumped up and charged, trying to catch Jet off-guard. They stood chest to chest, slamming hard blows at each other's bodies. When Terry got close he tried to butt him but missed. Though Jet chopped Terry's head the full sting was dissipated by the practice gloves. The crowd was loving it, but the two men ignored their constant noise, aware only of the close pressure of each other's bodies, the smack of gloves. Again Terry used his head. Again tried an uppercut. One of his blows drew a trickle of blood from Jet's nose, but he was unaware of it. Jet was winning now—his heavier blows taking their toll. Terry was slowing, becoming desperate. When he tried a low punch, Jet was waiting. Jet twisted, took it on his thigh, saw Terry's face unguarded. In proper gloves, Jet's blow would have finished him, but Terry rocked, clung, pinioned his arms and Joe intervened.

'Break.'

He heaved at them.

'Break, I said.'

They broke, Jet watching for a parting blow. Then Joe's face obscured his view. Joe was leaning close, saying something. Jet couldn't hear above the baying crowd. He raised his arms to continue as Joe reached for his microphone: 'That's enough, ladies and gentlemen, your attention please.'

The crowd shouted for another pint of blood.

'Ladies and gentlemen, in the second round of this middleweight contest, with the contender having sustained a serious cut above one eye, the referee has stopped the fight. A brave loser, ladies and gents, but to avoid the risk of further injury, I declare the winner is Terry Sykes.'

Out in the trailer that was their dressing room Joe would not leave them on their own. He recognised the animosity between his boxers and did not want a second contest without gloves. 'Not bleedin' professional, not by a long chalk.'

Neither man would speak to him. They remained at opposite ends of the trailer—Terry washing himself at the sink and Jet changing into outdoor clothes.

'You both should've done what I bleedin' told you. Jet, you was supposed to take a count in the first round. Terry, you should've stayed down in the next. Christ, d'you think I pay my bleedin' boxers to knock seven kinds of shit out of each other? What d'you think this is, the Albert Hall? It's a game, you stupid turnips, not a grudge match. Who started this?'

No reply.

'Oh, bleedin' noble, I must say! Sticking up for each other now. Or 'ave you knocked each other soddin' speechless? You do realise we have another show tonight?'

Terry dried his face.

Joe said, 'I blame you most, Jet. You wanted to down him, so I ruled you out. Terry, you're such a git, I had to let you win. No justice, is there?'

Lee Leonard came in from outside. Joe said, 'At last, someone with a tongue in their head. How'd we get on with the 'at?'

'Pretty good,' Lee said. 'They all think you're a crook, Joe, but they're damn proud of their local boy. Couldn't give him enough.'

'There you are, see, Jet—I got 'em on your side. The silly bleeders all think I cheated you. Works every time.'

Lee emptied the hat on to the physio table, and Joe

continued talking as he gazed at the money. 'Did you hear me tell the crowd to come back tomorrow 'cos their local boy might want a return? What d'you think—are you dickheads up to it?'

No reply.

NINETEEN

Jet had not changed from his morning run. First he wanted to sweep out the ring, tidy the rig, get all of the sweaty jobs out of the way, then he'd strip off and use Joe's shower. Out in the fairground the day was warm and sunny, and from several caravans the smell of bacon and eggs drifted through the air. Gaffers were checking their stalls; ride-boys hung around the Dodgems; Stella had vanished with her friends.

When he reached the boxing booth he saw the girl from the stall opposite waving a newspaper—Collette, that was her name.

'Hi, Jet. I didn't know you were famous.'

She smiled at him, wide-mouthed, lots of sparkling white teeth. 'You're in the paper.' Her eyes were laughing.

As he strolled towards her he was struck by the way that the sun seemed to burn in her red hair. A good-looking girl.

'It's tucked away inside.—Look.'

She held the paper open, and Jet had to lean close to read across her shoulder. She smelt of freesias. *Million Pound Brother Lives In A Caravan*. Three paragraphs and a small photograph. When he had read it, he said, 'Not even my caravan.'

The smudgy picture might have been snapped at some London caravan site. Maybe it was where the journalist went for his holidays—but the text was right. The longest paragraph recapitulated the original Drive Away Millions story; another recalled how the trail had gone cold; but it was the first paragraph that did the damage. It named Jet and the fair, both accurately, and placed them there in Bude. Could have drawn a map and had done with it.

'Well, fancy that,' said Collette. 'You're thirty-one.' She grinned. 'And Stella's eight. Is that right?'

He nodded.

'You don't look thirty-one.' She was watching him.

Jet shrugged. 'I suppose you're going to ask me where the money is.'

'Oh sure, you know exactly. That's why you're just a canvas-man.'

'Hm.' He moved away.

'Don't be touchy. I know you're a boxer really—though it doesn't say that here.'

He paused. 'Can't know everything.'

'They'd have printed it if they'd known. It would be worth a paragraph.'

'That's me—a small paragraph.'

Collette laughed at him. 'What a grump. Couldn't you sleep last night?'

But his thoughts had moved elsewhere. He crossed to the boxing booth and climbed the steps, hoping that the story wouldn't complicate his life.

He had swept the ring and started tightening the canvas when Joe Hake entered through the flap. 'God, the dust, my son. You'll ruin your lungs.' He was carrying a news-paper. 'Seen this? It wasn't me who spilled the beans.'

'Sell-out edition.'

Joe came close, peered in his face. 'Can't be easy to hide from the papers.'

'Scott did. But I'm not hiding.'

'No? This is a bit of a comedown, though, isn't it?'

In the muffled silence inside the tent was a private world, a confessional. Joe asked, 'Still feeling bloody about last night?'

'It's gone now.'

'Things do.' Joe tapped the paper. 'Passing thirty, that's the pig.'

'Yeah, great article,' Jet said. 'Has all the details.'

'Thirty-one. A couple of years before you quit. Still, life ain't over yet.'

'Downhill, though.'

'It's easier downhill—no more ambition, no trying to get some place you'll never make.'

'Just a long slide into middle age. Yeah, thanks.'

Joe chuckled, glancing round his empty booth. Daylight leached through the canvas tent-sides, so that they looked mottled, like blotting paper. 'I'm sliding into *old* age. I should give this up, you know?'

'That makes two of us.'

'No, I'm too old to start something new, but you can do anything you like.—Buy the booth, for instance.'

Jet laughed hollowly.

Joe said, 'No, you're right. This game is finished—folk don't want it any more. Did you know this is the only boxing rig left in the country?'

'You're kidding.'

'Wish I was. There used to be me and Ronnie Taylor— now even he has stopped. Christ, in the old days there was any number of us. I ran three different boxing booths at once—we had lads fighting each other just for a crack inside the ring. Some'd fight the pros, some'd take on each other. They loved it. Quick clean fight, winner got a fiver. Where are they now? World's gone soft.'

'Kids seem tough enough to me.'

'Maybe they're tough enough to kick somebody, but they

won't come in a ring and fight man to man. They're not fit enough either.'

'Come on.'

'I'm serious. I ain't saying this just because you 'ad to gee last night. Christ, we've always done that. But there ain't the interest any more. Any kid who *can* fight nowadays wants to turn professional—thinks he can earn a fortune. Kids today don't want to know about a ten pound contest—they're not interested in *fifty* pound.'

'You blame them?'

'Yeah. Yes, I do. Mind you, this bleeding story in the papers could change a thing or two. If it gets a run you'll be a celebrity. We'll have to drop that "local boy makes return bid" stuff. Half the punters will come just to see *you*. I'll put you on the platform.'

'You won't.'

'How's your head?'

'Breaking up.'

'You could be a draw.'

'Nine days' wonder.'

'Nine days! We'll make a fortune.'

'*Two* days then.'

'That's still half a dozen fights. Lots of lovely 'ats.'

'No one will put money in *my* hat, Joe—'

'It won't be *your* hat, will it? They'll be paying the stick.'

'I'm not fighting punters.'

'Too bloody scared,' cut in a new voice. Standing inside the tent flap was Terry Sykes. He leered at them. Joe inhaled noisily but didn't say anything while Jet turned back to the canvas and tugged a rope.

Terry laughed. 'You can't stash your loot under there.'

Joe said, 'Shut up.'

Terry didn't: 'Gonna use the money to buy your pension?'

'I said shut up.'

'Oh, he needs you to speak up for him? I knew he was past it.'

Jet straightened up. 'Come in the ring.'

Joe took command. 'That's enough. You two behaved like prats last night, so listen: I don't care if you hate each other's guts, but when you work for me you're on the same side. Christ, all I need is you knock each other senseless.'

Terry laughed. 'He's soft in the head already.'

'You won't be told, will you?'

'Nothing personal, Mr Hake. I was just wondering why he was sweeping out the ring when he could be leading a life of Riley with his rich brother.'

—At whose house, far away, three men had watched for several careful minutes. No one else was watching. There was no protection. It was back to normal.

Ray Lyons opened his car door. Because he moved without warning, the other two were caught unawares. Craig recovered fastest—was out, had caught Ray up before Vinnie had disentangled from the rear. He still had his arm in a sling. Ray rang the bell.

Presumably Claire Heywood was no longer being hassled, because the door she opened was not on a chain. Before she could say anything, Ray slapped his hand on her chest and pushed her inside. The three men came in and closed the door.

'Where's your husband?'

'I—'

'We ain't cops, lady, we don't play by the rules.'

She had her back against the wall.

'See this vase?' Ray lifted it from the hall table, balancing it in his hand. 'You like it?'

Suddenly he rammed it towards her, smashing it beside her head. Shattered china burst against the wall, and he continued speaking—urgently, insistently, breathing in her face. 'Few inches to the side and you'd have copped it. Bust your head open. Don't fuck us about.'

She looked terrified.

'Where is he?'

Claire whimpered.

'Three of us, right? And we ain't leaving.'

Though she was aware of the other men, she couldn't tear her eyes from his coarse face.

'He phoned you yet?'

'N-no.'

'Don't lie.'

Claire gasped asthmatically. Ray reached out and grabbed the front of her dress. As his grip tightened he glanced at his hand. 'Hey, look at that.'

On Ray's hand lay a line of blood where the smashed china had cut his flesh. 'I'm bleeding. You want to *taste* it?'

Claire frowned. Ray raised his hand before her face. 'I said fucking *taste* it.'

He tried to put his hand against her mouth but she turned away. He pressed Claire's head against the wall and left a smear of his blood along her cheek. 'Why am I bleeding, lady?'

She stopped cowering away from him. Suddenly she yelled, 'How do I know where he is? I'm the last person!'

'You're waiting for him, lady.'

'What?'

'Till the fuss dies down.'

'Then I'll pack my bags and take a holiday?' She was shouting again. Vinnie and Craig were amazed at her. 'Is that what you think? I'll sell the house? Don't you know the police watch every move I make? They watch me, they tap the phone—'

'Don't give me that—'

'What would *you* do, if you were them?' Her eyes blazed. 'Think about it—yes, think—because they're the same as you. All of you—police, journalists—all of you think we had a cosy plan between husband and wife. You're so stupid—'

Ray growled but Claire did not stop. 'Yes, *stupid*, that's the word. You don't think! My husband planned it, didn't he? You know he did. Everybody knows. He planned it, arranged his passport—*didn't he*? A quick way out.'

'What are you—'

'If we'd been part of his horrible plan, we'd have gone by now—*wouldn't we*? We'd have left the day before.'

'Yeah, given the game away—'

'You stupid, stupid man!'

Ray stared at her.

'Go on, hit me, do what you like. "Give the game away"—what game? Game! The police knew he'd stolen it inside half an hour.' Fully erect she continued shouting: 'What difference would it make if we had disappeared? They already knew he was guilty—it didn't matter about us. It didn't . . .' Her face crumpled. Tears spurted from her eyes. 'It didn't . . . doesn't . . . matter about us. He's left us.'

Now she folded, began sliding down the wall, her mouth slack as if Ray had punched her. She was on her knees. The three men watched uncomfortably. Ray asked, 'Wanna get your man back?'

Sobbing, she reached into her skirt to find a hankie. Lyons glared at Craig and Vinnie. 'There's got to be something here, something in the house.'

'Like what?'

'Something the others missed.' Ray nodded at Vinnie. 'Look after *her*. Come on, you.'

Craig followed him into the immaculate sitting room. Ray said, 'Take the place apart. I'll do the bedrooms.'

'The cops done it a week ago.'

'We'll do it again.'

'They'll have gone through this with a toothcomb. There's nothing here.'

'*They* went through it, son, I did not. I wanna see for myself.'

The blond boy shrugged. 'Waste of time.'

'Do it.'

'So I cut her cushions open—make a mess of the place? Some point in that?'

Ray hesitated. 'It's where the bastard lived. I wanna get his smell.'

He walked to a cupboard, opened its door, and gazed silently at what was inside. Then he opened a drawer and ran his fingers through some table linen. He tugged at a second drawer and a tray of cutlery fell to the floor. He stared at it blankly. 'I'll do upstairs.'

When he had left the room, Craig put his hands in his pockets and sauntered back to the hall. Claire was sitting on the floor. Because Vinnie had his arm in the sling it looked as if *he* was the one hurt, as if *he* was waiting for an ambulance. Upstairs, Ray thumped around.

Craig said casually, 'You see, your husband, Mrs Heywood, he has gone seriously out of line—in fact, he has crossed right over the line. There's no hope for him, I suppose. But you and your son could be OK if you co-operate.'

When she glanced up at him her eyes were dull.

Craig continued: 'It's a lot of money, two million, so there'd be enough for us to see you right. But you'll have to tell us if he contacts you.'

'Leave me your address,' she answered bitterly.

Craig chuckled. 'Feeling better? Listen, don't try to run away or talk to the law, because they're no protection, see? No protection at all. I mean, the police didn't stop us, did they? And we're standing in your house—right here with you, nice and private, on our own. We could do anything, understand?'

They heard Ray slam a door. Craig said, 'If you act sensibly you'll be OK.'

Another thump, and Ray reappeared. Halfway down the stairs he asked, 'Where's that boy of yours?' He reached the bottom and strode up to Claire. 'The kid back at school?'

She shook her head—a tiny tremble, as if she had just woken up. 'Tommy?' She sounded as if she had been doped.

'Yeah.' Lyons bent towards her and blew stale breath in her face. 'We'll be keeping an eye on him.'

Claire showed no reaction. She had disassociated again. Ray felt frustrated. He wanted to shake the woman back to sensibility. He wanted to hit something, but he did not know what.

TWENTY

At around four o'clock kids called in at the fair on their way home from school. Mostly they wandered around sniggering at the stalls, eyeing the rides, trying slot machines in arcades. Rides were open but did little business; the Big Wheel was quarter full and on the Dodgems, ride-boys made up the numbers to add a spot of pace. The Octopus had not opened, but the Caterpillar gave longer rides. Two of the shooting galleries remained closed.

The woman with the briefcase looked out of place. She was neatly but casually dressed in soft top and skirt, and wore flat shoes. A little mud had splattered her right calf. She was a small-boned, quick-moving, attractive woman of twenty-six—the kind who didn't look as if she ought to attract attention, yet did: something pert and sexy in the way she moved. Boyish hair. Dramatic lips.

Yet at this time of afternoon in a travelling fairground the only glances which came her way were mild and cautious—because of the briefcase. Even so, when she paused to ask at the Lucky Rabbit stall opposite she was dealt with civilly. 'They don't open till after dark. You could come back then.'

'Where would I find him now?'

'Friend of his?'

'Business.' She tried a friendly smile, but it still looked like business. She added, 'It's a personal matter.'

Collette decided that the woman was too short to be a policewoman and would find him anyway. 'He's over there—see, by the Caterpillar? The tall one, with darker hair.'

Beside the ride two men were talking—or one was talking: he had a notebook, while the man with darker hair looked ready to walk away. The woman hurried over to them. 'Mr Heywood, can I have a word?'

'Another journalist?'

'Not at all.'

The man with the notebook grinned. 'She's not a journalist—you can talk to *her*. Hiya Kelly, what you doing?'

'Private matter.'

'Hm. Interesting.'

'I said private. But I'll let you finish.'

'I think we've done.' He turned to Jet and said with exaggerated courtesy, 'Thank you so much, Mr Heywood—but if you do want a chat, my number's on the card.'

He held it out, and seemed slightly surprised when Jet took the card and slipped it in his pocket. Jet looked at the waiting woman. 'D'you have a card too?'

'Afraid not.'

She glanced at the other man, who said, 'I can take a hint.' As he left, he called, 'Ring me any time, Mr Heywood. Twenty-four hours a day.'

While he drifted off between the stalls, Jet said, 'So, Miss Kelly, you're not a journalist?'

She produced a laminated photo-card. 'Education and Welfare Officer, North Devon Social Services.' She saw his shoulders slump. 'And it isn't Miss Kelly, it's Kelly Rice.'

Behind him the Caterpillar began to move.

'I've had your notes referred from Lewisham. I assume Stella is with you?'

'Stella?'

'You're still together?'

'Oh no, I'm afraid not. I dropped her off a cliff—she wouldn't eat her breakfast.'

'I need to speak with her.'

'Only her—or all the other kids in the fair?'

The Caterpillar behind him snaked its way round its oval course. She had to raise her voice: 'We like to visit every child during the season.'

'But starting with mine—who's had her notes passed down from Lewisham?'

'You're a single parent, you're on the register, you took her out of school—then disappeared. I don't want to get off on the wrong foot with you, Mr Heywood. It's for Stella's good.'

'Oh, perhaps you're going to pay her an allowance? She gets nothing now.'

Miss Rice repositioned her briefcase. 'Well, let me see. On the wages you earn here, she may well be eligible for—'

'We can manage. We're OK.'

She tried a smile. 'Would you mind if we moved from here? That ride makes me giddy.'

He turned, surprised. The rattling carriages trundled up and down on their gently hilly track. 'Maybe you'd like a ride on the Big Wheel?'

'No thanks.'

He looked her full in the face for the first time. 'Queasy stomach?'

'No, but I'm never relaxed when I'm ... It isn't easy, you know, trying to intervene between parent and child.'

'Intervene?'

'Interfere, you'd call it.'

He studied her for another moment. 'OK,' he said. 'Come and interfere with me.'

Kelly Rice did not like the caravan: the cramped space, the shared facilities, the decidedly casual state of tidiness, all encouraged her to interfere. The beds were too close to each other, there was no bath, not even a shower. They had a twin gas-ring—camping gas—but no oven, no fridge.

'We buy fresh every day.'

Stella added, 'There's plenty of food around the fair.'

At least the little girl looked healthy, Kelly thought, and her clothes were no worse than on any other travelling child. In her father's company she seemed relaxed, with none of the frightened subservience that might suggest abuse. Nor did she seem over-worldly or emotionally tied in an unhealthy way. But Kelly had read the Heywood file; she knew the suspicions already raised. There had been instances of over-closeness, of excessive cuddling, of collusion in truanting from her previous school. There had been that previous business with her mother. Now, Stella Heywood was a growing girl living alone with a single father—a casually employed, unsettled man whose only profession was as a boxer, and in whom the potential for violence could never be far. The most recent addition to his file said that his brother was a wanted criminal suspected of grand larceny and murder. Though Jet himself had not been implicated, the possibility could not be dismissed.

Kelly smiled her businesswoman's smile. 'Is Stella receiving education?'

'She will in autumn.'

'We can make provision,' Kelly said. 'Study packs, peripatetic teachers.'

'Pathetic teachers!' Stella laughed.

'No, peripatetic. It means—'

'I know. Our old music teacher used to travel from school to school.'

'In London?'

'Ladywell. She was soft.'

'Did you like the school in Ladywell?'

'It wasn't bad.'

'And did you have lots of friends?'

'No one has *lots* of friends.'

'Do you miss them?'

Stella shrugged. 'We live here now.'

'Don't you miss going to school?'

'Of course not.'

Jet said, 'Well, if you're staying—how about a cup of tea?'

'Thank you.' These interviews could be such hard work. 'I'd love one.'

Stella said, 'I'll make it.'

'No,' Jet said. 'You have a chat with Miss—er—what was it?'

'Rice.'

'That's it. The nice Miss Rice.' Her face had frozen. He added, 'Miss Kelly Rice. We're on first name terms.' He smiled and lit the gas.

Stella said, 'We need some milk—I'll get it!' and shot to the door. Kelly would have stopped her but the girl had gone. She didn't see the child pause on the top step to roll her eyes dramatically at her father. When Jet grinned, Kelly assumed he was returning her own smile.

Stella went, and Jet asked, 'You want to take my girl away?'

'Certainly not.'

'Isn't that why you're here—to make an assessment?'

His large brown eyes seemed mesmerising—a troubled,

unavoidable stare. She wondered if it was the same gaze he gave opponents in the ring.

She cleared her throat. 'Well, obviously we must check the child's environment—'

'And what d'you make of it?'

Kelly exhaled. 'We always take into account a multiplicity of—'

'But how about the caravan?'

'It's just a part of—'

'Would you say this was an unhealthy environment?'

'No, I . . . wouldn't say that.'

'You wouldn't *say* it, but would you write it in your report? Because if you're not happy about something, Miss—Kelly, would' you talk to me about it, rather than write it up for someone else?'

'I'm not unhappy.' She was being defensive, she knew. She felt the presence of the man as if he and she were in the ring and he had her in the corner, was raining blows on her.

'You're not unhappy, Miss Rice—a little girl who lives alone with a man? Who doesn't go to school? Who lives in a six-foot wide caravan—you're not unhappy? Talk to me, for Christ's sake, tell me what you really think!'

'Please don't be aggressive.'

Jet snorted, and turned back to watch the kettle. She sat in silence, hating her job.

Soon, Stella appeared with a small jug of milk. 'Oh Dad, didn't you lay the table? I'll do it—you make the tea.'

Both adults watched like scolded children while Stella laid three china cups and matching saucers. She fetched a sugar bowl, which also matched. Kelly said brightly, 'That's a pretty tea service. Have you had it long?'

'I won it on the coconuts.'

'I suppose you get lots of practice, living here.'

'It's better than school.'

'Do you help on the stalls?'

'Only the coconuts—that's how I won this.'

'You don't help in Daddy's boxing booth?'

'No fear!'

Jet poured the tea.

Stella said, 'Sorry, but we only have two chairs. We could sit on the beds.' But the adults looked so po-faced that Stella said she'd sit on the floor.

Jet and Kelly sat opposite each other at the tiny table. Kelly wondered what kind of parent Jet really was, and she guessed that he was wondering what she would report. She didn't know yet. In the little dwelling, with the smell of tea and with Stella chattering, everything seemed warm and safe. Stella seemed content, though Jet still seemed on guard against a new attack. He seemed volatile, living on the edge. Even as she drank her tea she could feel his tension. Week after week, she thought, cooped up inside this tiny caravan—would the girl be safe? Kelly could not be sure.

TWENTY-ONE

The following morning, in the gentle sun, Joe Hake stood at the edge of the fairground glaring across the fields. Approaching him was a sorry sight: Jet and Lee Leonard supporting a hobbling Terry Sykes—his arms around their shoulders, his foot lifted from the ground.

'You done him over?'

'Sprained me ankle.'

'I can see that—I'm not blind.'

Lee said, 'He's awful heavy for such a tich.'

'Take him in the trailer.' Joe followed them among the caravans. 'I thought running was good for you? Don't you get enough exercise in the ring?'

'Not in this town.'

At the trailer, Joe held the narrow door open while the two men helped Terry up the steps, inside, and on to the physio table. Inside was chilly at this time of day. Joe leant over the table and eased the leg of Terry's tracksuit along his calf. When he squeezed the ankle, Terry yelped.

'Be grateful it ain't broken.'

Jet crossed to the shower and turned it on. Behind him at the table Joe announced, 'Two bleedin' cripples I'm supporting. I'm down to one fit fighter now—bleedin' one! Christ, time was when I travelled a dozen. One! At this rate I'll be in the ring meself.'

Lee said, 'We'll be all right, Joe, I can manage.'

Joe shook his head. 'Son, you may be good . . .'

Jet, meanwhile, had stripped and stepped into the shower. He knew where this talk was leading and did not want to hear.

'Seriously,' Lee persisted. 'Tell the punters I'm the undefeated champion—make them too scared of me to fight. Then find a load of local kids who'll take each other on. People go for stuff like that.'

'Only when there's a real fight on as well.'

Jet held his head beneath the feeble shower. Perhaps he could pretend he was invisible.

Lee continued: 'I'll only have to fight two or three times a night.'

Finally Joe turned to Jet: 'Well, me old china, looks like you're on.'

Jet closed his eyes, but heard Terry from the table: 'Oh look, he's got another headache!'

Jet remained in the tepid shower, soaping beneath his arms, watching the others while they watched him. There was nothing to say.

'I know what you're thinking,' Joe Hake said. 'You're worried what'll happen. You're thinking there is always some punter who should have turned professional, and Sod's Law says he'll call for you.'

Jet was rinsing off the soap. 'Ain't he beautiful,' Terry laughed.

Joe glared at him on the table. 'Want me to massage your twisted ankle? Just shut up.'

As Jet left the shower and took a towel, Joe asked, 'Well?'

'OK, I'll have to. But don't give me any budding professionals.'

Lee had started stripping in his turn. 'Don't worry, they're easy here.'

Joe agreed. 'That's right, son, and I'll pick out the easy

numbers. I get any real fighters, I'll tell 'em they're the wrong weight.'

It was Lee's turn in the shower now, rivulets of water popping on his skin. 'You can feed them up to me.'

'You lads,' Joe scoffed. 'You don't 'arf 'ave it easy. When I started in this game—'

'Forty bouts a night,' Jet interrupted with a laugh.

'Fighting at the door,' Lee said.

'They'd pay *us* for a chance to fight—'

'Oh no,' Joe said quickly—smiling now as he strapped Terry's ankle. 'They still wanted to be paid.'

'A quid was a quid,' agreed Jet.

Lee added, 'Six rounds of drinks and change for the bus fare—'

'And you'll never believe who came in here once?'

Lee rolled his eyes. 'Not a famous fighter?'

'Billy Walker,' Jet said reverentially.

'*Johnny* Walker, more like.'

'And Henry Cooper.'

'No!'

'And Mohammed Ali.'

'Of course, he was only young then,' said Lee.

'But keen as mustard.'

'Sharp as a knife. He stepped inside this ring—'

'Did an exhibition—'

'Wouldn't take a penny—'

'Wouldn't have got one, not round here.'

Joe interrupted: 'You can laugh, but Ali did come to the fairground once—not here, mind, but at Ronnie Taylor's—'

Lee started singing: 'It seems to me—'

Jet helped him: 'That I've heard that song before!'

Joe laughed with them while insisting, 'It's still bleedin' true.'

They chuckled again, until Terry, cold and forgotten on the table, said, 'Don't mind me. I'll sort myself out.'

He swung himself off the table, tested his bandaged ankle on the floor, then hopped independently to the door.

'Mind the step,' Lee called.

'Fuck your arse.'

Lee howled with delight. 'Oh, my, my, my! Dirty mouth, dirty body. You haven't had your shower yet, duckie!'

Terry tugged the door open. 'Got a stick?'

'This ain't a hospital,' Joe said. 'I'll help you down the stair.'

As he went to help him, Lee called from the shower, 'There's room in here for two, Terry darling.' He offered the soap in his big hand.

'Stuff it up your arse.'

'Love to, darling—want to help?'

But Terry and Joe had gone. Lee grinned. 'Pity. I could have blown bubbles at him.'

Lee was in an impish mood all morning. When a second reporter appeared at the fairground, Jet would have turned him away if Lee had not butted in: 'Hey mister, you know that Jet was middleweight championship contender—fought at Lewisham Baths?'

'Baths?'

'They cover them over, like at Wembley—you've heard of Wembley Pool?'

The man looked doubtful.

'Jet fought at Wembley as well.—You getting this down?'

When the man glanced at Jet for confirmation, Lee said, 'He's a bit sensitive because he lost that one.'

The reporter smiled uncertainly at Jet: 'About your brother—'

'Don't want to talk about it.'

'I told you he was sensitive.'

'You've not heard from him, I suppose?'

Jet looked wearily at the young reporter. Lee spoke for him: 'Afraid not, my friend—not since he came and left that big bulging suitcase. That *was* your brother, wasn't it, Jet?' Lee nudged the reporter confidentially. 'He was driving this new Jaguar—very nice—but we couldn't get a proper look because it was the middle of the night.'

'OK. OK. Do you mind if I talk to Mr Heywood on his own?'

'He can be dangerous.'

Jet said, 'I am not talking to anyone. I don't know what my brother did. I just want to be left alone.'

'Sensitive, I told you.'

The reporter drew a breath. 'Can we—'

'No,' snapped Jet. 'There's nothing I want to say.'

'*I'm* available for an exclusive,' Lee offered. 'Shots of me in trunks, my rise to fame—'

Jet began to walk away. The reporter tried to follow but Lee placed a hand upon his chest. 'I'd leave it, if I were you.' His tone was light but his stance was firm. 'Though I'm still free, if you're interested.'

The thought of returning to the ring began to grow on him. He had never liked drifting along as a canvas-man, and as a boxer he would earn more. The way things were, he earned barely enough for food, and certainly couldn't afford to buy Stella clothes. Eventually she would grow tired of sweater and jeans.

And a boxer was what he was. Last winter in London, humping boxes in the warehouse, had been bad enough, but now—tidying around the ring, doing fit-ups and pull-downs at weekends, watching Lee and Terry up in the lights—was degrading, made him feel old. He could be somebody again. Already he was striding around the fairground, he was grinning at showmen who grinned back at him. And there was that auburn-haired Collette from the Lucky Rabbit booth—the girl with the open air complexion and welcoming body, the friendly one—she had caught up with him among the stalls: 'I hear you'll be fighting again—is that right?'

'For a little while.'

'Bet you're a better draw than Terry.'

'He's sprained his ankle.'

'I wish he'd sprained his wrist.'

'Oh yeah?'

'So he'd keep his hands to himself.'

'He been bothering you?'

'A bit.' She leant against Jet's arm and grinned up at him. 'Should I have told you?'

Jet shrugged.

'Would you have protected me?'

He felt her warm body against his side. 'You asking?'

'You offering?'

He laughed nervously, suddenly aware that this teasing girl was coming on to him.

She asked, 'Are you starting tonight?'

'Guess so.'

'Well, either you are or you aren't. Are you on the platform?'

'Me and Lee.'

'In your boxing kit?'

'Uh-huh.'

'Terry always hid inside his hood. You won't disappoint us all like that?'

'I've nothing to hide.'

'We'll have to see about that. Maybe I'll come in and watch you fight.'

'I wouldn't hold your breath.'

'What *should* I hold?'

Collette laughed.

'Hold my hand,' said Doris firmly.

'It'll be dark.'

'Oh, that old Mr Sun, he'll squeak in between the cracks.'

'I'll still be frightened.'

'Not if I hold your hand.'

She and Stella were sitting on the steps of the old woman's trailer, faces lifted to the morning sun. Stella wore sweater and jeans, but Mrs Diamonte was dressed for her public—brown hair lacquered high, voluminous cotton dress, chunky rings on each finger. As Doris rose heavily to her feet she released an almost visible cloud of powdery perfume.

'We'll take a peek before the punters get here.'

Cautiously, Stella rose. As they climbed the steps to the Haunted House she took a firmer grip of Doris's hand.

'Just a mo, my dove.' Doris reached inside the ticket booth to pull the heavy mains switch. The House shuddered and began to hum. As Stella stood inside the doorway she felt the wooden floor tremble beneath her feet as if it were shivering with fear. But *she* wasn't going to tremble: when the old lady walked inside the House, Stella put on a brave face. Doris had started up the stairs—wooden, uneven, disappearing into gloom. There was no banister. These rickety stairs were merely the entrance to the House, and though they looked unsound, Stella followed Doris, knowing they must be safe.

'Careful!' called Mrs Diamonte. 'That seventh step's a dodgy one—seventh from the top, seventh from the bottom, just miss it out.'

Ahead on the landing, she was already opening the flimsy door.

'After you, my dove.'

'You first.'

Doris smiled and disappeared, leaving the door to swing shut. When Stella reached the small landing, the floor tilted suddenly and propelled her towards the entrance. But she was not frightened. She pushed the door ajar and felt her way into the dark interior. Something brushed against her face. She stood absolutely still, trying to breathe steadily. Fronds were hanging from the ceiling. Doris had not lied to her—there *was* some daylight inside: a kind of cheerless half-light across the main corridor, enough to show Stella that it stretched along the back of the House. There was no sign of Doris. If she was hiding, if the horrible House was full of nasty surprises, Stella would not go on. She could still go back out through that swinging door.

'You all right, my dove?'

Doris had reappeared halfway along the corridor.

'I don't like it.'

'Come to me. I'll hold your hand.' Doris reached out to her. 'Like I promised.'

Cautiously Stella inched towards her. If the old lady tried to slip away again, Stella would turn straight round and go home.—Light flashed; there was a ghostly laugh; and in a cabinet beside her a jointed skeleton moved its hand. The shock was momentary. These surprises were only tricks, she thought—things to make her jump; not the kind of truly horrid, crawling, menacing monsters that scared her in the dark. She marched forward to grab the woman's hand.

'It's just a toy, my dove. Look, can you see down by your foot?'

There was little light, but Stella could feel the pressure pad beside her shoe. When she touched it again there was another laugh. She pressed a third time. It laughed again.

'See, you're getting used to it now.'

'Does it work by electricity?'

'Some do. That one's hydraulic—a little bellows thing.'

'What's one of those?'

'I'll tell you later when we're out.'

They walked to the end of the rear corridor, rounded a corner and almost immediately had to turn again into a thin passageway doubling back through the centre of the House. Here the gloom increased. Something slithery—something like a spider's web—hung in her way, but she brushed it aside. Doris released her hand. Stella guessed that somewhere along this passageway . . . There it was: another light flashed to show an execution block, a man kneeling, eyes staring, a blade falling, a grinding noise, a swish, the man's head toppling to the floor then rolling away. Someone cackled. The light went out, and suddenly it had become too dark to see. Stella couldn't move.

'Are you there, my dove?'

'I'm scared.'

'Don't worry, it'll be lighter round the corner.'

Doris took her hand again, led her through a door, and sure enough, the light grew better. It was still dim but less claustrophobic.

'Step to the side if you don't like water.'

Stella glanced down. A dark inlay. She edged around it.

'That works the water pistol. Quite a laugh.'

Another corner and they were in a corridor along the upstairs front. Halfway along she saw a grimy window, which let in hardly any light. Stella realised that this must be the central window visible from outside, the one between the words 'Haunted' and 'House'. It existed less for customers to look out of than for waiting spectators to see inside. Beside that window something would happen.

From outside, Stella had watched people pass it, and when they got there they often screamed.

'You first, Mrs Diamonte.'

'There's nothing here to hurt you.'

'You first.'

'We'll go together.'

Something cold and rubbery brushed Stella's face. Doris laughed, saying, 'Dead Man's Fingers.' Stella would not be scared.

Hand in hand they approached the window. In the murky light she could see that the wooden walls were painted a shabby black. She could see no tricks here, nothing hanging down. The floor seemed sound—though with its whole length lined with rubber, she couldn't tell. A surprise was about to happen. Whatever it was wouldn't matter, because it wasn't dark.

A spurt of water splashed in her face. Freezing cold. It made her gasp.—Of course, that was what she had seen from outside. People stumbled around the House laughing, and they whooped at every shock. Here, cold water made them shriek.

'Only fun, my little dove.'

Stella reached for her broad soft palm and they moved through the door to the other stairs down. There were no windows; the flight was enclosed. For safety reasons, the stairs had been lit by a weak red bulb. Feeble as it was, it emphasised the lack of light when they came out in the corridor.

Stella gasped as the ground gave way. She was in a pit several inches deep, in which the hard flooring had been replaced by a balloon of rubber, rocking like water beneath her feet. Stella clambered out.

'Here you are, my love.'

When she moved, a light clicked on beside her. Behind a little window was an illuminated skull, on whose dusty grey surface trembled a brown hispidulous spider. The light went out.

It seemed awfully dark. Stella knew that somewhere along here would be another nasty surprise—something special—perhaps the main frightening tableau of the ground floor. Doris came behind her, holding her trailing hand, encouraging Stella to walk first. Any pressure pad, any rocking panel in the floor, must be triggered by the child, or there would be no surprise; Doris had explained this and Stella understood—

Something brushed against her foot. She stopped. Something living—like a rat.

'We aren't there yet, my dove.'

Stella couldn't move. Whatever had touched her had not felt like any of the other mechanical tricks. It had touched and moved away. 'I'm frightened.'

'Right behind you.'

'I felt something.'

'Don't worry. Now, here comes another little surprise—but it can't hurt us, you know that.'

Slowly, Stella moved her toe. She could feel nothing unusual. The floor seemed solid now. She took a breath. Her only option was to continue forward, round to the next corridor, past whatever tableau lay in store, past all the other creepy things—then outside. She was nearly there. She heard a low, sinister laugh from her left. An orange light snapped on to reveal a large open coffin—a body inside—a head turning towards her—then the light snapped out.

But in that last moment of dying light Stella had seen something dark and scuttling—the rat. It was in the corridor. With them.

'I . . . saw . . .' She didn't want to name it. 'I think I saw—a mouse.'

'No, love, no chance of that.'

The evil blackness was closing in. She leant back into the comforting bulk of Mrs Diamonte. 'It was awfully big.'

'Wait a second and we'll see.'

Doris left her—she actually let go of Stella's hand and drifted back the way they had come. That low laugh again. The orange light. In the coffin the head began to turn—and along the corridor, exposed by the murky light, was a large black cat.

'Merlin!'

The light clicked out.

'I told you we didn't have no mice—not with my Merlin here.'

Stella flushed with warm relief: it was only the cat that had brushed against her feet. She felt bolder now, light-headed, as if the unsociable black tom might somehow protect her in the dark.—The dark. It was so very dark.

She called 'Merlin!' but nothing came.

She called 'Mrs Diamonte,' and the faint reply sounded far away. Suddenly her fear returned. She knew she couldn't move. When she tried to move her foot it simply would not unstick from the floor. It was as if her bones had melted and some drug seeped through her veins. She allowed her trembling knees to yield, and squatted on the floor.

Mrs Diamonte called her name. She could not reply. She heard her name again and gave a sob.

Then Doris was stumbling through the gloom. With the child crumpled on the floor, Doris almost fell over her in the dark. But she bent, took hold of her and scooped her to her commodious breast.

'There, there, my dove.'

'Where's Merlin?' Stella was surprised to find her voice back again.

'Oh, goodness knows. He's got a hundred ways in and out.'

'He frightened me. He didn't mean to.'

Doris began walking with her in her arms. 'No, he likes you, don't you mind him.'

Stella nestled into the woman's warmth. She took little notice as Doris clattered through the tableaux on the dark ground floor, as lights flickered on and off, as strange sounds screeched.

'Oh, they're simple old machines, all out of date,' Doris murmured reassuringly.

At last she pushed a door and they were out in fresh daylight. There was a final wail from a last machine. But she was free. Stella opened her eyes to sunlight in a different world.

'Yes, out of date, like poor old me. All of us show people's out of date. If we packed up and stayed at home, folks wouldn't miss us.'

'I bet they would.'

'No, it's us fair people as would miss the travelling, that's all. Sometimes I think I'd like to be free of it, but it's all I has. Same for most of us, I reckon.' Doris squinted in the bright light. 'You and your Dad, now, being gorgios—'

'We're not!'

'Half gorgios, then. Mind you, you're better off with gorgios.'

She smiled down at the dark-haired Stella, then suddenly swooped with her in her arms. 'Not as we don't want you, you pretty little thing, but us travellers, we're fading out. The truth is, my dove, that you young girls are better off with gorgios, in their safe respectable— boring world!'

TWENTY-TWO

A professional boxer for eleven years: Kelly tried to imagine it. In her work dossiers she was more used to tales of unemployment or casual labour. Few of her clients had a fixed profession, though she did have the occasional one who had been made redundant, an office manager who slept with his child, a shop assistant with a violent streak. What must it be like, she wondered, to fight for your living?

Kelly was alone in her flat, reading the Heywood file over a tepid supper. Changed from her smart business clothes into tee-shirt and jeans, she looked like an underfed teenager off her feed.

'Children And Young Persons Act 1933'. Kelly turned apathetically to section 31—criteria for care or supervision orders. The Heywoods did not match the criteria exactly, but cases rarely did: they required interpretation, a professional view. The Act established that to deliberately leave a child without adult supervision was sufficient cause for a care order. Nothing more was needed. The child's age was not material, though family circumstances were. Professionals must decide.

Kelly took a sip of coffee but it had grown cold. Jet and Stella Heywood did not fit easily with these descriptions on their file. They seemed relaxed with each other yesterday, in what on the surface seemed a healthy way. Yet the London office—a Mr Creel—had recently almost taken the little girl away. Reading between the lines, it seemed that the Heywoods had quit their London flat just in time. Had they realised? She could not tell. Now, in the caravan, their living conditions had deteriorated— had become more cramped—and the father's income was no less precarious than before. The man must be eligible for State assistance, yet had not asked for it. Some people might have seen that as commendable, but it would not be thought so in *her* department: to deliberately keep a child below the breadline was not a virtuous act.

God, what a job this was. Kelly sighed. She left the table and began to clear away. Her assessment of the Heywood case came down to this: (one) that there were no conclusive grounds to remove the child, and (two) that the relationship between father and daughter was not such as would ordinarily appear abnormal. But in the dossier were recent adverse reports and earlier accounts of physical cruelty. There was a suggestion in the file that the earlier problems were more the fault of the young girl's mother, though that seemed unlikely, Kelly thought. The mother was no longer there, and the child was still officially 'at risk'.

She would have to watch her.

Thank God *she* did not have children: such a responsibility. There was no training for parenthood, no entry qualifications, no exams to pass. It was one great gamble. For the Heywoods, presumably one could only hope for the best. The child was sweet, and below the father's exterior toughness he seemed quite decent. Good-looking too. Distinctly dishy. In the tiny caravan yesterday he had seemed relaxed but forceful—there had been so much of him. Kelly shivered. She would hate to take his child away—how would he react?

Best not to think about it.

Jet moved easily, eyes wary, staying beyond his opponent's reach. Despite Joe's original promise, the man was big—probably light heavyweight, though that was only because he needed to lose some weight. His bulk made him look powerful beside Jet, and for most of the first round Jet concentrated on staying out of reach— tiring the man and keeping away from any sucker punch. Once, when the man stood flat-footed, Jet stepped in and thumped him twice in the guts. Those blows hurt. They sapped him. Jet saw horror in the other's eyes.

But during the first interval the man regained confidence. In round two he tried to use his muscle, to come in close—and although Jet jabbed his way easily from each impending clinch, he could hear the crowd rising behind their man.—Until Jet blocked him with a cross to the nose, then followed with a blow to the cheek and a jolter to the big man's heart. As the man staggered backward, Jet followed through with a flurry of blows. At the ropes the man covered badly, leaving the whole of his rib exposed. Jet ignored the gap and dabbed instead at his opponent's arms. There was still a round to go.

Once inside the third round, Jet could sprint. He danced around the man, first opening his guard with a strong left jab, then chopping into the big man's ribs. It slowed the man, who could no longer avoid Jet's fists. A sudden left and right and he was on his backside.

Jet glided to a neutral corner. The man should be able to get up but Joe would probably decide to stop the fight. Even if the man *could* last a little longer, there was no need for him to be butchered. When Joe did stop it, the man made no protest; in the short applause as they clambered from the ring he began to smile, proud to have lasted this long with a professional. He grinned at Jet and muttered, 'Thanks mate,' and Jet, knowing the surge of friendship which often followed a fight, wrapped an arm round his shoulder and said, 'You did bloody well.'

'Yeah, didn't I?' The man was as happy as a kid at playtime. Pubs would have no trouble with him tonight.

On the outside platform, Joe Hake saw that his boxers were laughing, so he killed the mike.

'Act as if you mean business, boys. Right? And remember—you ain't world champions. These grockles can still turn up the odd surprise.'

Lee said, 'The only thing they'll turn up is their feet.'

'Some of these farmers' boys,' Joe warned, 'are built like cart-horses. You watch your step.'

'Gimme, gimme, gimme.'

Joe switched on his microphone. While he continued his patter, Jet and Lee danced around the platform as if beside a pool. Jet felt on top of the world. They were in another class. There might be some strong boyos down there on the ground, but they would not be fit, not professionally trained. Even if they had been inside a ring, it would not have been since school.

'Two famous boxers are here tonight: Lee Leonard, the Caribbean champion, and the one without the suntan is Jumping Jet Heywood—brother of the famous Scott. That's the bank robber. You've read about the Heywoods? Well, here he is. And I'll tell you this, folks—he is fighting for love, because he don't need money!'

Jet stared beyond them, preferring not to catch anybody's eye. Behind the crowd he noticed Terry Sykes chatting to Collette. Terry had his back to the booth and seemed intent on the good-looking showgirl. But suddenly she glanced across his shoulder and caught Jet's eye. She gave her big open smile and waved cheerfully at him.

It wasn't an easy scrap, but Lee put his man down in the

second round. It seemed to be a night of big opponents, and this one must have weighed fifteen stone, none of it fat. Though Lee was only a light-heavy, around one seventy pounds, he was the biggest man Joe had, and had to take all comers. In the corner, Jet told him, 'Use your ringcraft—keep out of his way—let him run out of steam—catch him in round three.' Lee nodded and ignored every word.

The way he flattened the man was awesome. And risky. He bewildered him with a barrage, uncaring that he left himself wide open. Jet remembered that Lee was only twenty-one, in his first fairground season. He and Terry had learnt through several seasons that survival came not from winning but from not getting hurt.

Lee left the ring looking less cocky than usual, leaving Jet to help his opponent out through the ropes. The man was groggy. He became entangled as he struggled through. But for Jet it seemed that the booth would always be home territory—the canvas beneath his feet, the warm floodlight glare, the noisy fevered crowd. Their unseen faces were like an evening tide—rolling in for each show, ebbing out into the night. The faces changed. The opponents changed. The only constant was the travelling fair and this close-knit family where Jet belonged.

At the end of his first evening in the ring, Jet strolled around the fair. The cold tang of sea air cutting between the trailers wrapped the smells and took them away. Stalls were closing, music had stopped, and the few remaining punters laughed and shouted at each other, reluctant to leave the muddy patch of ground. By now, most holidaymakers had disappeared to their boarding houses or to the parked caravans along the cliff, leaving only these local lads to kick around between closing stalls. They were looking for excitement and a little fun, but the burghers of Bude, like those in other towns, expected the visiting fair to close at ten; they didn't want the noise of hurdy gurdies and stale pop music to drift across their town all night.

Jet watched the last customers trickle away. He felt tired but quietly triumphant—three fights, and none of them a problem. Where Lee Leonard tried to despatch his fights too quickly, Jet went for early dominance, then played them out. Joe had told him to take no risks, and Jet had made absolutely sure that he protected his head. Out here in the chill night air he felt remarkably clear-headed; each shuttered stall and empty ride appeared sharply focused; each sound he heard was bright and distinct.

At the edge of the fair he ambled carelessly among the parked caravans, lorries and dark looming trailers. He dipped in and out of murky pools of light like a slow fish in a shallow stream. From inside the vehicles he heard murmuring voices and a few TVs. As he approached his own small caravan he could see that Stella had not yet gone to bed, because the main light inside was shining through the curtain. Once in bed she preferred to have only her nightlight, which was too weak to be visible from outside. She was probably waiting to hear about his fights.

Jet ran up the three short steps, grinning as he went into the caravan. At their tiny table, Stella sat facing the door, opposite a visitor who faced away from him—a stranger who Jet did not immediately recognise. Stella did not smile. Her face looked white, as if she might be in pain. Only when the stranger turned to greet him did Jet recognise his ex-wife.

She held up a newspaper opened at his story. 'I thought I'd never find you,' Angie said.

TWENTY-THREE

'Hello Jet, it's been a while.'

'Christ.'

She smiled, waiting for him.

'Well, Angie, how've you been?'

'I get along.' She and Jet were staring at each other, reabsorbing the person they had once shared a marriage with. The changes in Angie were subtle, not as he might have predicted: good-looking, of course, but her blonde hair was now a little longer, where he would have expected her to wear it short. She seemed slimmer than before. Leaner.

'Still boxing? Must be time to quit.'

'I have to live.'

She was wearing a pale green top and matching skirt, with a droopy collar to set it off. Green? Angie had never worn green. It looked expensive, and probably was. The handbag, though, was red, which was more typical of her. In Jet's shabby caravan, the well-dressed Angie should have looked out of place—except that she never had cared about the mess around her, so long as she herself remained immaculate.

'I never got used to you boxing. I suppose I was scared for you.'

'Scared for me?' he echoed.

'Sure I was, honey. Wasn't that part of our problem?'

Her blue eyes seemed deep and lustrous.

He stumbled towards the chair where he flopped down heavily. Stella sat opposite him across the table in silence. Angie moved behind him and rested her hands on his shoulders. He flinched. She said, 'You must be tired, of course. Are your muscles tight?'

When Angie began to stroke him, it seemed to Jet that he could feel the coolness of her strong fingers through the fabric of his top. Angie said, 'Actually, I did go in to see you fight tonight. I'd forgotten how good you look in the ring.'

Stella frowned at him, but her father seemed hypnotised by the massage. He said, 'You never used to watch.'

Angie stopped massaging and bent round to look in his face. 'I don't pretend I ever liked it. Violent. Primitive.' She chuckled throatily. 'You did fascinate me, Jet.'

Now that she had stopped working on his shoulders he found it easier to speak: 'Why are you here?'

That long slow smile that he remembered well. But she disappeared behind his back, and in a moment her strong cool fingers were on his neck, massaging the muscles beneath his skin. He shivered.

'Things haven't worked for me, Jet—why pretend? How's it been for you?'

Jet found himself staring into his daughter's eyes— dark reflections of his own. Her face was frozen.

Angie said, 'You don't realise they're the good times till they're gone.'

Jet grinned at Stella but she did not respond. There was something chilling about the way that she sat unmoving, transferring her gaze from one parent to the other, which suddenly reminded him of her cousin Tommy. He hadn't noticed that before.

Angie manipulated his neck. 'When I heard about Scott on the radio my first reaction was to rush to your old flat.'

'We'd moved.'

'I didn't go there in the end. I thought—well, that whatever I did might be misconstrued. You know, all that money? I didn't know what sort of welcome I'd get.'

Jet remained silent. His eyes were closed as she continued to massage him.

She said, 'You're very quiet, Stella.'

The little girl shrugged.

Angie stopped what she was doing and left her fingers resting between Jet's shoulder blades. He opened his eyes and smiled at his daughter. She did not smile back.

Angie whispered, 'It hasn't been easy for any of us.'

She lowered her thumbs and began to knead his vertebrae, but Jet jerked forward. 'What happened, Angie—did he throw you out?'

She moved away. There was no other chair, but she looked too restless to sit down. 'Who—Geoff? That's long dead. I wasted a lot of time searching for . . . I don't know. Nothing changes.'

She tilted her head appealingly. He muttered, 'You get older.'

She chuckled. 'Thanks, babe. Well, when you do, maybe you stop searching for what isn't there. What was it Judy Garland said in *Wizard of Oz*? "I went all that way only to find that what I was looking for was right back where I started, all the time." Something like that.'

'This isn't where you started, Angie.'

'This caravan?' She glanced around. 'No, it's pretty low, isn't it? That's not what I meant.' She shrugged, but she still looked restless. 'Aren't you going to offer me a drink?'

Stella said, 'Daddy doesn't drink any more.'

'Oh?' Angie glanced at him and laughed nervously. 'Well done.'

'Not strictly true.'

Stella said, 'We like this caravan.'

Angie gave a placatory smile. 'Do you enjoy life on the move?'

Stella nodded.

'And you, Jet? But of course, you always did.'

'I'm more comfortable when I'm travelling.'

Angie would have prowled but there was no room. 'This is small, though. I'd hoped you might have a spare bed.'

'Sorry.'

She sighed. 'I drove straight down here, you see, and it's late now. Haven't booked in anywhere.'

'It's early season. There'll be plenty of rooms.'

Angie pouted. 'It's rather late, honey, for waking land-ladies. How big is your bed?'

'Single—barely that.'

'Hey.' She came closer and touched his shoulder from the front. The one lamp inside the caravan caught the highlights in her hair. He smelled her scent. 'I didn't come to *sleep* with you, you know? Christ, we've known each other long enough to sleep in the same bed without having sex.'

He glanced at Stella as he said, 'I haven't seen you in two years.'

Angie smiled. 'And how do I look?—No, don't tell me. We'll sleep head to toe—that should be harmless.'

'No.'

Her eyes glittered. 'Come on, honey. It's way past eleven now. You know how parochial people are.'

'Offer them cash.'

She chuckled shortly. 'I have to watch my last few pennies. You know, maybe it *is* cosy in this little van. All I need is a place to lay my poor tired head. I'll just *sleep* here, nothing more.'

'Angie, my bed is like a baby's cot.'

She knelt beside him at his chair. 'Hey, honey, you've

been fighting. I keep forgetting. Aren't you tired? Want to go to bed?'

'Sure, but—'

'Any bruises? Any tender parts?'

She raised her hand on to his chest. He laid his own hand on hers. 'I'll be all right.'

'Still hard all over?—Hey, Stella, honey, why don't you run and fetch some nice warm water? Daddy needs a wash.'

'We have water here.'

Jet removed her hand. 'It's late, Angie. Time to go.'

'I see.' Slowly, Angie rose. 'I hoped things might be different.' She glanced at the small curtained window. 'God knows where I'll find to sleep. Couldn't I curl up on the floor?'

As she widened her appealing eyes, Angie looked suddenly vulnerable, even a little scared. She glanced at Stella but concentrated on Jet: 'I suppose there's no chance I could sleep in Stella's bed?'

Stella answered quickly, 'It's too small.'

Angie shivered. 'My God.'

She turned away from them, and from the floor beside the door she picked up a flimsy cotton shawl. Jet hadn't noticed it before. The shawl was so thin it looked cold before she put it on. He said, 'Look, um, maybe Stella could share with me—top to toe, like you said—and you could use her bed? Just for tonight.'

Angie turned to her daughter—who snapped, 'No, we don't want you here! You left us. You can't come back.'

'Hey.' Angie, incredibly, managed to smile. She stepped forward, dropped the shawl, and tried to cuddle her angry daughter. 'Hey, hey. I know you're upset—'

Stella broke away. 'You walked out on us. You left Daddy and went off with that Geoff—'

'Stella, darling—'

'You've only come here for the money!'

Angie protested, 'Money—what do you mean?'

'You want it.'

'No, honey. You don't have the money.'

'Go away!' cried Stella. 'Don't come back.'

Jet wrapped his arms around his struggling daughter. 'Don't, Stella—'

But she tore herself from his grasp. 'How could you? You don't love me, Daddy!'

Angie said, 'Oh, for Christ's sake!' But Jet now had taken her arm and was manoeuvring her to the door, saying, 'That's enough. You see how it is. You'll have to sleep in your car—or knock someone's door down. But leave us alone.'

Stella collected her mother's shawl and held it out to her. Angie took it without thinking. 'OK,' she said, calmness returning. 'We can talk about it tomorrow, yes? When we've all had time to sleep on it.'

She smiled at Jet and left.

TWENTY-FOUR

Kelly wondered if she was trespassing. It certainly felt like it. Picking her way between the huddle of caravans and trailers beside the fairground she felt like a burglar in the dark. A dog had growled at her and she had stopped, hesitated, had thought about returning to the car park, but had gone on. Somehow she felt that the dog would sense if she turned back; it would smell her fear.

Towards the end of the dark crescent of parked vehicles, well away from the dog, she paused again. Over her thin tee-shirt and jeans Kelly wore a shapeless but warm bomber jacket, and she huddled into it. She should not have come. Yet it was only by coming in the night she might find out.

Ten yards in front of her stood the Heywood caravan. A light shone from the little window, and behind the curtain a shadow moved. The physical presence of that tiny caravan nestling among huge trailers and mobile homes bore little resemblance to the dry description she had written earlier in her formal notes. Equally poor had been her description of the atmosphere within its shell: on her visit yesterday she had seen a strong and stable parent-child relationship in a poor but acceptable environment. Yet in the notes as she had written them the balance had shifted to emphasise the possibilities of harm; the stable relationship appeared a sham. Kelly had tried to rework her notes, to rectify the balance, but the changes had not worked. Even if she rewrote the notes completely, Kelly felt she still would not get them right; they would probably read no differently from the first—though the words might be different their meaning would seem the same. Staring at the little caravan, Kelly knew that her difficulty with the notes was because she herself was still uncertain: she didn't know if there was a problem here or not.

Suddenly the door opened from the caravan. Silhouetted against the stream of light were Jet Heywood and a blonde woman. They were coming out. With the light behind them, Kelly found it difficult to make out their faces but Jet seemed almost to be sending the woman away. On the bottom caravan step the woman turned for a final word. She had to bend her head back to look up at him, and something about the position that she assumed was as if she was pleading with him. It looked oddly touching. For a moment, Kelly wondered if they would kiss, but the woman turned abruptly and came toward her. In the darkness as she approached, Kelly saw a striking blonde woman, immaculately dressed, a lion's mane of glorious hair round an angry face. The woman swept past without a word—she actually touched her—perhaps assuming that the girl in bomber jacket and jeans must be a fairground worker.

Kelly might have spoken as she passed but could think of nothing to say. Glancing back towards the caravan she saw Jet at the top of his steps, looking down at her. He did not move. Kelly inched forward into the shaft of weak light that fell from the caravan doorway. The nearer that she got, the more Jet's features became lost in shade. He had not moved.

'I was passing by,' she said, realising immediately that it sounded inept.

'Enjoy your walk.'

'I didn't mean—'

She could hear his sigh. He leant his head inside the caravan and said to someone—Stella, she supposed—'I'll be just a moment,' then he closed the door and came down the steps. 'This is not a good time.'

'I didn't realise that you had company.'

'I don't have now.' He came close to her. 'Yes?'

Kelly did not know what to say. 'Um . . . Your friend was leaving anyway, I think?'

'Don't worry, you didn't scare her off.'

'No, I—'

'How long have you been out here?'

'I've just arrived.'

He stared at her, disbelievingly. 'Lucky you weren't eaten by the dogs.'

'Dogs?'

'They don't like prowlers.'

Kelly glanced behind her. 'Your friend—will she be safe?'

'Oh, yeah.' He paused. 'I hope the dogs will be.'

Kelly laughed shortly, hoping that this showed a softening in his attitude. 'I thought she looked quite nice.'

'Yeah? Well . . . Why have you come?'

'Oh.' Kelly shrugged helplessly.

'Snooping?'

She shook her head, but then admitted, 'I suppose you'd call it that.'

'Great.' His voice was dull. 'At least you're honest.'

'If nothing else.' She tried to inject a note of banter. 'Two woman callers late at night—what will Stella think?'

The joke bombed. 'The hell does that mean?'

'I was only—'

'Think I was having sex with her—in front of Stella?'

'Of course not—'

'But you thought I *might* have been. Christ, you people—you're the ones who are depraved.'

'I'm sorry, that wasn't what I meant.'

As she spoke, the caravan door opened again and Stella appeared above the steps. 'Dad, are you still talking to her? I want to go to bed.'

'I'm coming. She's leaving now.'

Stella peered down at them. 'Who's that?'

Kelly answered first. 'Kelly Rice—remember? I came to see you yesterday. I just popped back tonight for another word.'

Jet said, 'But she's leaving now.'

Stella was coming down the steps. 'You're the social worker.'

'Yes.'

'That's all right, then. Do you want to come in?'

'I—no, it doesn't matter now.'

In the strange half-light it seemed to Kelly that the little girl looked far older than her eight short years. Stella said, 'But you must come in if you want to.'

'Well—'

'Mrs Rice is leaving.'

Stella ignored him. 'It's *Miss* Rice, isn't it?'

'Yes.'

'Since you've come all this way—'

Jet said, 'Stella, it's far too late—'

'But Daddy, where are your manners?' The mature child brushed him aside. 'Of course the nice social worker can talk to us. We have nothing to hide.'

The little girl had more experience of the social services than Kelly had: visits had been sporadic but had stretched back across several years. Right from the first, when Angie had still been with them, Stella had known the dangers: social workers broke up families; if you

gave the wrong answer they'd scoop you up and carry
you away. They were no one's friends. It was because
Stella had learnt these lessons, first from Angie and then
from Jet, that tonight, as midnight tiredness soaked into
her, she did not behave as a small child. She offered tea
like a grown-up housewife, and when they declined, made
coffee instead. She busied herself at the two-ring burner.
Kelly was as confused now as earlier when she had read
her notes back in her room. She didn't say anything—
merely sat at the table like a customer in a small café.
But Stella did not act like a waitress; she fussed around
her silent father like—like what, Kelly wondered—like a
perfect mother in a bedtime story. Kelly wondered
whether the child saw this laying out of china as a ceremony that would bind her father to her, reclaiming him
perhaps from the woman who had been here before. Or
if not from that blonde woman, Kelly thought, perhaps
from *her*? Perhaps the child perceived every woman visitor as a rival for her father's love? No—this case was
complex enough as it was, and these were nothing more
than the bizarre fantasies one had round midnight. Stella
was just a little girl who loved her father as a daughter
should.

When she had poured Kelly's coffee, Stella asked, 'How
many sugars?'

'One.'

'I'll do it.'

The child was ministering to Kelly as to an infirm
visitor, or to an aged aunt who might leave a settlement
in her will. Stella smiled ingratiatingly and asked, 'Have
you visited the fair?'

'No, I suppose I should.'

'I help run the coconuts.'

'That sounds nice.'

Stella pulled a face—understandably, Kelly thought.

She felt a fraud here, drinking coffee in their caravan. There was nothing unhealthy to be seen. She would have liked to have found a way to switch the conversation to another subject, to behave like a genuine visitor, but she found it impossible—why else would she be here? What normal visitor turned up at midnight? Also, of course, she wanted to ask about that blonde woman. No one mentioned her, as if the woman had never been there. But Kelly remembered her posture on the caravan steps— supplicating was how it seemed. What had she been doing there? From her clothes, she was not from the fairground—she looked too smart to have even visited the fair. Had she seen Jet boxing? Could she be some kind of wealthy boxing groupie who followed the booth from town to town? Or was it only Jet she followed? Whoever the woman was—and Kelly knew she could not ask—she and Jet and Stella had been cooped together in this closed caravan. Doing what? Jet had been sensitive about the woman being there when Kelly had made her ill-judged quip, and he clearly believed that Kelly had been spying on them. Which in a way, of course . . .

She drank the last of her coffee, looked up, and realised that Stella had now left the table and was sitting exhausted on the bed. Her little act was over; she was eight years old and tired. Kelly said, 'Slip into bed, Stella. I'm going now.'

'All right.' Without another word, Stella crawled beneath her blankets and closed her eyes.

Kelly turned to Jet and whispered, 'Won't the light bother her?'

'Want to talk outside?'

'If you like.'

'What I'd like is she gets to sleep.'

Jet stood up and switched off the overhead lamp, leaving the caravan in the gentle glow of a tiny nightlight. He said, 'She doesn't like the dark.'

He and Kelly stood for a moment by the table, looking along the caravan at Stella in her bunk. Kelly whispered, 'Good night,' and Jet added, 'I'm popping outside, just for a bit.'

What Stella mumbled could have been in protest or agreement. It was like the last murmur of a patient as anaesthetic took its hold.

Outside, Kelly stumbled through an apology, but he was hardly listening. Night-time quiet had descended on the fair, stars glistened, and Jet was thinking of the times when he and Stella had crept out among darkened rides and stalls. Now, as he and Kelly paused between the trailers, someone's radio was playing softly. There was a moderate breeze, and it carried with it the sound of waves breaking on the shore.

He took her from the outlying vehicles into the empty fair itself. Shuttered stalls were damp with starlight. Loose canvas covers rippled in the breeze. She said, 'Everything is just left standing here.'

'Of course.'

'Anyone could come in.'

'Well, *you* did.'

'No, I meant . . . troublemakers.'

'You spend your days dealing with troublemakers, Miss Rice. Most people aren't like that.'

'I'm not a probation officer.'

'No?' He did not sound interested. 'What *do* you do?'

'Well, social work covers a multitude of sins.' She pulled a face. 'Office joke.'

'Social work.'

'Yes.'

'Problem families?'

'In a sense. Not always.' She knew what he was getting at, and blushed slightly in the dark. Beside them loomed the Helter Skelter, the gleaming mouth of its shute looking as if at any moment someone might come hurtling down. 'We try to help families.'

He did not respond to that. 'Been in it long?'

'Just over a year. I used to be—'

'No kids of your own?'

'Not married.'

She glanced up at him.

'Then—uh—how come you think that *you* know more than parents?'

She felt deflated. He spoke quietly, but his attitude was familiarly aggressive. Kelly had learnt by now that the more she tried to help people the more they hated back. She was not cut out for this.

He led her across to the empty Dodgems stand. Its floor was empty, all the cars huddled at one end. He said, 'I'm sorry. I suppose a lot of your . . . cases feel like that?'

'Most of them.'

He was gazing across the shiny Dodgems floor and she knew that his thoughts were barely with her. He muttered, 'Well, I'm just like everyone else.' He was staring as if out to sea. 'Anyway, now that we're out here, was there something you had to say?'

'Not really.'

'Not really?'

'Not at all.'

He continued staring across the Dodgems floor. He is not making eye contact, she thought: something is troubling him. He said, 'There was something you had to *ask* me, perhaps?'

'No, I . . . only came here for the ride.' She laughed slightly, watching him, hoping that he would smile. 'But it's too late now. The fair's closed.'

He nodded. 'I better go take a peep at Stella.' It seemed to be a question, as if he needed permission to leave.

'Of course. Then d'you think you . . . Could you walk me out to my car? I'm a bit frightened on my own.'

'Really? Yes, Stella's afraid of the dark.'

'It's a bit spooky here.'

He smiled faintly. 'You think so? Well, let's check on Stella first.'

She was fast asleep and lay sprawled on her back, hands clutching the rumpled blankets, head to one side, mouth open, snoring like a well-fed baby. Her face was framed by her black hair. In the intimacy of the caravan Kelly thought the child looked beautiful. Beside her, Jet bent forward to brush a lock of hair away from her mouth. For a moment his hand lingered on Stella's shoulder, then he eased her gently on to her side. Her snoring faltered, then stopped. As Jet moved away he bumped against Kelly's arm. She whispered, 'Sorry', and he stared at her. She felt gawky as a schoolgirl. When she withdrew to the table he muttered, 'It's very late.'

'I suppose it is.' She realised that she was blushing.

'What happens now?'

She could not answer. It was as if she was rooted to the only safe place on the floor.

He rephrased the question: 'What would you *like* to do?'

His whisper echoed like a distant sea. Kelly wasn't certain what he meant, whether he thought of her as a social worker or as a young woman late at night. She heard the echo again as he inhaled. But he didn't speak. He simply stood before her and watched her face. Oh God. She felt her stomach tighten. Eventually he stepped closer and put his large hands upon her arms. This must not happen. No. Then she was kissing him. As his tongue

thrust into her mouth Kelly was genuinely surprised—
not that he was kissing her but that she allowed him,
responded to him, had hoped that it would happen. For
how long? She did not know. Perhaps all that she was
responding to was the claustrophobic closeness of the
caravan, the sleeping child, the silent romance of the
shuttered fair—or had the need for him been there
before? When she had sat studying her case-notes, had
the hidden urge to hold him, rather than the ambiguities
of the case, drawn her to him in the night?

He broke away. As Kelly stared into his face, the air
between them seemed tangible enough to eat. She felt
hollow, incomplete. Jet's dark-framed face was grave,
intent on her, examining her almost as a doctor might
search for pain. Then he smiled and Kelly whispered,
'We'll have to be very quiet.'

His eyebrows flickered, and she nodded beyond to the
sleeping child. He repeated softly, 'Quiet? You weren't
thinking we could ... in front of Stella?'

She smiled hastily, confused.

'What was that you said earlier about bringing strange
women home?'

'No,' she said, 'I didn't mean—'

The intimacy between them was crumbling into shards.
'I'd better leave.'

Yet when she first stepped forward she felt so weak
that she could not have brushed a curtain aside. She saw
him open the caravan door, the darkness impenetrably
black, fresh air flooding in sharp and cool. As she drifted
through the doorway, her foot outside on the step, Kelly
turned for one last word. Jet Heywood nodded. There
seemed nothing she could say. She had been utterly
unprofessional. Carefully she picked her way down the
three short steps. She must not fall.

Behind her, the door closed, cutting off the one faint

stream of light. Kelly turned towards the darkened caravan and saw him standing on the steps. Just his shape
above her in the shadow.

The shadow moved. 'I'll walk you to your car.'

She should have told him no, that she could manage,
but she didn't want him to go back inside. Jet took her
arm. She shivered. Unprofessional, she repeated to
herself. Unprofessional.

'You said you were afraid of the dark.'

'Yes. Thank you.'

Now she could look along the dark line of trailers and
stall-backs to where their shapes disappeared in blackness. Large vehicles crowded the murky path. Cables and
tow bars lay on the ground.

He said, 'There are nightlights in the midway,' and he
steered her between two stalls into the body of the fair.
Main pathways were gloomily illuminated, while long
shadows lay across the stall-fronts. The rides were eerily
still.

'Did I tell you that my Stella doesn't like the dark?'

'Yes, you said.'

'Yes, earlier.'

They were like strangers struggling to make safe conversation. It seemed incredible to her that two minutes
ago they had been in each other's arms. When Kelly lifted
her head to breathe night air she became suddenly aware
of his pressure on her arm: a father's guiding hand. But
she was not a child. By now she could see quite easily
and she turned brightly to him, saying, 'Thanks for walking me—I can find my own way now.'

'I've come this far.'

His pace did not alter.

'You don't have to bother.'

'It's no bother.'

She kept her eyes ahead. Under the sparse array of

lamps the gaudy colours on the wooden stalls seemed to have had their freshness sucked away. What was left was monochrome. She said, 'I'm sorry if I said something wrong.'

'In the caravan? That was my fault. I shouldn't have kissed you.'

'No.'

When she looked at him, he smiled. 'Late at night, you know, it's natural.'

Kelly peered around at the sleeping fair. She had to change the subject. 'It looks better in the half-light. There's a kind of magic.'

'There's always magic in a fairground, even when it's crowded.'

'There's more now.'

'Dark magic.'

'It's lonely.'

He seemed surprised. 'You're lonely?'

'Not now.' She moved closer to him, though she knew she shouldn't. They were approaching the deserted Dodgems where they had been before. 'Everything seems so still, so magical—no Dodgem cars and shrieking people.'

'That's when it *was* magic—the excitement.'

'*Now* is the magic time. Look at it: the great empty floor, cars sleeping at one end, the canopy—it's magical.'

'The enchanted ballroom. Come inside.'

Jet led her on to the wide smooth Dodgem platform. At the far end, cars stood with their masts reaching at lopsided angles into the nets, and the rail around the empty floor was like a picket fence. Jet pointed to it: 'Out there is where people wait and watch the enchanted dancers, and the cars—you see?' He smiled. 'They are the Ten Cents A Dance girls waiting in their stall. They want to watch us do our exhibition dance.'

Kelly laughed nervously. 'You're not going to switch on the music?'

'We don't need it. Do you dance?'

'Well—I go to the disco.'

'Disco! This is the enchanted ballroom. Can you waltz?'

Kelly wondered if he was serious. 'I—sort of know—'

'One, two, three. One, two, three. Easy. Have you ever danced the Valeta?'

'What's that?'

'Mum and Dad used to dance it. Dad taught us.'

'He taught you to waltz?'

'Sure—the Valeta, it's a kind of waltz. Me and Scott used to do it. Dad would call out the words and Mum would join in singing the tune. It was fun.'

'I can't imagine it—two boys.'

'I'll teach you. This is the easiest waltz there is. The whole tune *is* the waltz. It's just *one*, two, three; one, two, three; *one*, two, three; one. See? Each line is the same. Anyone can do it. Ready?'

Self-consciously, Kelly glanced around her, as if beyond that picket rail there really might be people at tables, or as if the enchanted ballroom might not have been concealed in midnight gloom. But outside was silence. There was no music—only Jet whispering the tune in her ear as he held her formally for the dance. He began to move, guiding her across the wide empty floor.

'*One*, two, three; one, two, three; *one*, two, three; one.

One, two, three; one, two, three; *one*, two, three; one.

One, two, three; one, two, three; one, two, three; *o-o-one* . . .

One, two, three; one, two, three; *one, two, three; one*!'

He ended their exaggeratedly graceful waltz with a

sudden scamper through the last few steps. Kelly laughed with him. As their laughter faded, he began talking quietly in the dark and she no longer worried that someone might be watching; she was alone with him under a darkened canopy in the night. He began to whisk her around the floor a second time, and this time she joined his parody of the steps.

> '*One*, two, three; one, two, three; *one*, two, three; one.
> *One*, two, three; one, two, three; *one*, two, three; one.'

They were singing now into each other's faces:

> '*One*, two, three; one, two, three; one, two, three; o-o-one . . .
> *One*, two, three; one, two, three; *one. two, three; one!*'

'And again!' Jet cried. But this time, while she sang 'One, two, three; one, two, three,' Jet accompanied with

> '*Hum*pety, Dumpety, *sat* on a *wall*.
> *Hum*pety, Dumpety, *had* a great fall.
> *All* the king's horses and *all* the king's men
> *Could*n't put Humpty to-geth-er again.'

As they reached the final stamping steps they broke off laughing, clutching at each other. 'There's more!'

> 'I met a sweet girl at *Hamp*stead fair.
> Hand in hand we *ran* down from there.
> *Kent*ish Town, Euston, *Step*ney, Bow,
> *Is*lington, Archway—now back we go!'

He seemed lost in the dance, and she could imagine his childhood memories pouring in from the dark.

'I'm the Queen of Nanky-poo
And I don't know what to do.
The butcher's boy has eyes of blue—
He loves hanky panky too!'

This time when they finished, when they collapsed in
each other's arms, Kelly did not hear the undertone to
his laughter. She did not read what was in his eyes.
She couldn't know that Jet was suddenly swamped by
memories of other, more recent dances. When he stared
at Kelly's pert face, at her dramatic lips and pointed
chin, at her short brown hair and tiger eyes, all he saw
was the blonde remembered face of Angie, his former
wife.

TWENTY-FIVE

'In a fresh statement on the Drive Away Millions affair, police have confirmed that the missing driver, Scott Wayne Heywood, is now wanted on suspicion of murder. It has also been revealed that Mr Clifford Lyons, whose body was found in the wreckage of the burnt-out armoured van, had been shot with a single bullet through the chest. Pathologists have since confirmed that he died as a result of that wound, and not of the fire. Police at this stage have no firm idea of the whereabouts either of Heywood or of the missing money, though several lines of investigation are being actively pursued. It is ten days now since the armoured van, believed to have been carrying around two million pounds in used notes, disappeared on its journey to a south London incinerator. The van itself was discovered in a matter of hours, burnt out and empty apart from the body of Mr Lyons, but by the time it was discovered, both the money and driver had disappeared. With Mr Lyons having been shot, the hunt for Heywood became one for both robbery and murder. Yet one question remains unanswered: the puzzle for insurance analysts and journalists alike is that until the day of the robbery, Scott Heywood seemed a man of unblemished character. Before being employed as a driver he had been scrupulously vetted by his company, Force Five, who declared his record to be absolutely clean. The company described Heywood as a trusted employee who had driven a number of high-value consignments before. And though the police search is now concentrated on him, the possibility still remains that Heywood may have been a victim of this crime rather than its perpetrator. With no clues to the whereabouts of either Heywood or the money, the Drive Away Millions case remains wide open to speculation.'

Terry Sykes leans forward, switches off the radio and shakes his head. He looks eagerly around the trailer as if to share scorn and incredulity. But the trailer is empty. Terry hobbles two steps to pick up his stick, then makes his way out to the fresh air. The story stinks, it seems to him: no one can tell *him* that a man whose brother is worth two million quid bums around a fairground for Joe Hake. Christ, except for Terry's ankle, Jet would still be sweeping floors. It isn't natural. Even if Jet did not know what his brother was up to in the first place, he sure knows now. Even if he doesn't know where he is hiding he is going to stick his head up and take a look. Isn't he? Two million pound!

Terry picks his way across the mud, stabbing holes in the ground like a park attendant collecting leaves. He mutters like an old man. This stupid stick. Not bleeding fit. He lifts the back flap to the booth and scowls inside. An added penance in a way is to come here and watch them work out. Lee is up there in the ring, skipping nonchalantly as if he could maintain his unbroken rhythm for two more hours. A well-oiled glistening automaton. Of course, those darkies, Terry tells himself, can turn their brains off, can simply jog along like machines. Like when they're dancing. Something they inherited from their ancestors, from being slaves. They don't think much, have no concentration to disturb. That must be it. Everyone knows that a black brain is smaller than a white—that's a medical fact. They'd be better off as slaves.

Bloody Heywood is still trying to get fit. Look at him—poncey sweater over his tracksuit, pumping the speedball, dancing around. Makes you wonder. Yeah, when Heywood turned up last weekend, he moped about and kept his head down, stayed out of sight. Low profile, as they say. But now that he knows no one has followed him he has put his head up out of the shell. Yeah, that poor head of his—he got a crack on it, didn't he, before he came? Just about the same time that his clever brother made his move. Ain't that a wonderful coincidence?

Jet hasn't noticed him. Concentrating on the speedball, on the rhythm of his hands, Jet knows that this is what he wants for summer—to regain his fitness, to become faster, to earn some money while he can. What if he *is* getting too old—what if he'll never reach the top? He still has a couple of years. After that, he can talk to Joe more seriously about the booth—or he can join Floyd Carter's gym up in town. Work in a health club.—No, to hell with that. What he would really like, Jet decides, fists clattering against the speedball, is to travel the country-side like Joe. Must have a word with him.

Meanwhile, this summer, he can work three or four fights a night—mainly amateurs, puffed up with beer. He can handle that. Even his headaches are on the fade—give another week and they'll be gone.

Another week, another town. You don't have to live in a place to be a part of it. Take last night: estranged wife appears out of the blue, local girlfriend comes to call. Is that what Kelly wants to be? She seems to play two different roles—the social worker at first, but then later, in the enchanted ballroom—

The speedball slaps against his face. He steps back

smartly, eyes stinging, and Terry sniggers but Jet doesn't hear. He raises a glove to wipe his eye.

Bloody women, they always get you.

It is early evening, about five o'clock. Claire Heywood and young Tommy sit at their dining table, eating tea. Most families would not use their dining room for a casual supper—mother and son, just the two—but Claire likes to do things properly: prepare food in the kitchen but eat it here. When the doorbell rings, Claire puts down her butter knife and dabs her lips with the linen napkin— not a paper one, nothing vulgar. There are some women, Claire supposes, who at a time like this might let standards slip. But not her.

In the neat and narrow front hall, Claire tries to make out the blurred shape visible through the frosted glass of the front door. Not familiar. But it wouldn't be: in these painful days since Scott disappeared it is seldom friends who come to call.

'Who is it?'

A muffled voice—male, indistinct. Claire checks that the heavy bolt lies in its place.

'I didn't hear you. Who is that, please?'

'Open up.' The front door shakes as the man raps again.—Not a policeman, or he would have said. Another journalist—some wretched person like that. Although he won't be able to see her, Claire shakes her head before backing away down the hall.

A heavy hand clamps across her mouth.

While Ticky was ringing at their door, Ray Lyons had entered through the back. Then, as he let Ticky in, he kept his hand across Claire's mouth, and did not release it until the three of them were in the dining room. He warned her not to scream. But when he did remove his hand Claire's first reaction was to retch. She wiped her tainted lips against her sleeve but could not lose the taste of that man's hand, his dirt and sweat.

'Put the knife down, boy,' he said.

Claire felt separated from the things about her. Images swam as if she and the room were under water. She saw a boy—Tommy—standing beside the table pointing a bread knife at the men. The boy's face looked deathly pale. He did not move. No one moved. Everything continued in slow motion.

Claire recognised the man now.

When he spoke again, Claire was surprised to hear that his voice sounded quite calm: 'Put it down, I told you, kid.'

Tommy shook his head. His dark unblinking eyes were fixed on the tall man. Claire felt the man move beside her—she reached out but was too late. His hand whipped forward, and she clutched helplessly at him as he grabbed Tommy's wrist. With his other hand he removed the knife. His companion—a malevolent looking, dwarf-like man—scampered over and collected it, leering at her as he moved past.

The big man placed his hand against Claire's chest and shoved her away. He spoke to the boy: 'Little hero, aren't we?' He patted Tommy's hair. 'Wanna help your Mummy?'

The man's fingers tightened. Suddenly he yanked the boy's head back and smacked his face. Claire cried out, rushing to help him, but Ray blocked her. 'Any more trouble and I'll knock his block off.'

Though Claire was sobbing, her son seemed calm. Ray said, 'Now, lady, think about this: d'you want us to stay with you all night?'

His deep-set eyes glittered beneath dark glistening hair. He stooped towards her, as if unable to hear her reply. '*Do yer?*' he bellowed.

Claire could not speak. Her throat seemed to have locked open, as if she had swallowed something which had stuck. She stared at him. When she moved nearer to Tommy and pulled him against her, the boy squirmed and twisted to face the man.

'Where's your husband?'

She shook her head. Words would not come.

'You fucking bitch. I told you last time we don't piss around. I want your husband and I want him *now*!'

Ray thumped the table and a cup toppled from its saucer, spilling tea across the tablecloth. When he saw her staring at it, Ray reached over, grasped her chin, forcing her to look at him. Claire tightened her own hold on her young son.

Ray's cheekbones had peaked white. 'I should kill him, you know that? I'll kill you as well, you don't fucking speak. Your husband, lady, your fucking husband, he killed my—'

'Careful!' Ticky yelped. 'Don't tell her that.'

Ray glared at him as if wondering who he was.

'Don't give her our names,' said Ticky meaningfully.

Ray continued to stare at him, then turned to Claire: 'He thinks you'll tell the cops.'

Ray's teeth showed in what he might have thought a grin. 'No. D'you think the cops are gonna protect you? Don't hold your breath.'

Last time, Claire thought, the little man had not been with him—perhaps he was the big man's boss. Ray squeezed her chin, stared in her face. 'Tell us where your husband is and we'll go away.' He spoke softly, in short bursts, as if he might at any moment lose control.

She opened her mouth but no sound emerged. She mouthed, 'I don't know.'

He frowned.

Desperately, she shook her head.

'*Where is he?*'

Tommy tried to struggle free from her. 'Leave Mummy alone!'

'Oh.' Ray grinned savagely. He took hold of her son's arms, then told Claire, 'Let him go.'

Her eyes widened.

'*Let him go!*' Ray pulled him free.

'Don't hurt him!'

Ray tossed the boy aside and grabbed her dress. 'I thought you couldn't speak? OK, Ticky, deal with the boy.'

Ticky had already grabbed him. He was angry at Ray's use of his name, but Ray didn't notice.

Ray said, 'Now, lady, this is the last time I ask you nicely.'

'I don't know! He just vanished—I don't know where he's gone.'

'He's been in touch with you.'

'He hasn't.'

'I *know* he has.' They stared at each other, looking for clues in the other's face. 'He phoned you, didn't he?'

'No.'

Claire was more concerned about the little man who had put his arms around young Tommy. He seemed to be nuzzling Tommy's hair.

Ray said, 'OK, I tried, but you want it hard. Open your bag, Ticky.'

Ticky raised his head. 'All right, *Ray.*' He emphasised the name, then he dragged the boy to where his sports bag lay beside the door. With one arm around the boy's chest, Ticky stooped to unzip the bag. Ray kept tight hold on Claire. Ticky brought out a large lemonade bottle filled with pinkish liquid, and asked, 'We're going through with it?'

'We have a choice?' Ray jerked Claire as he spoke to her: 'Know what's in his bottle?'

She shook her head, eyes full of tears.

'Petrol. He's gonna pour it on your boy.'

'No!'

She started forward, but was unable to shake Ray's grip.

'Open the bottle. We ain't got all night.'

Claire kicked behind her at his shins—and for a single moment thought she had struggled free. He let go one arm. Before he hit her. The blow landed where Claire's shoulder joined her neck. She crumpled. The pain was terrible and she was about to vomit. On her knees at the big man's side, Claire tried to prevent herself from passing out. Someone said something. Her head was full of noise. She saw the little man wave his bottle over Tommy's head.

Ray said, 'Last chance.'

'No, please.' Half sobbing, half gagging, Claire tried to scramble to her feet. Ray held her down with one huge hand.

'Please!'

Ray slapped her cheek. 'Gonna tell us?'

'I—can't.'

'Soak the boy.'

Ticky inverted the bottle and slurped its contents over the struggling Tommy. A smell of petrol filled the room and the air shimmered with vapour. Like a grinning troll, Ticky shook his bottle. Holding Tommy by the hair, he stood well back from him, well away from the splashing fuel, and Tommy cried. When the bottle was empty Ticky tossed it away and stood with the sodden child suspended from his fist. Ticky's other hand dipped into his pocket and emerged with a cigarette lighter. Like a third-rate conjuror at a children's party, he waved the silver lighter before his audience.

Ray said, 'Light him up.'

Ticky queried: 'Is that all right, then, Mrs H? You won't tell us where Scott is?'

Claire became hysterical. Ray shook her. 'Your boy will burn like a roman candle.'

'Please!'

'Where's your husband?'

'I don't know!'

'That's it.'

Claire saw Ticky raise his hand and flick his lighter to produce a motionless yellow flame. Tommy stopped struggling. Ray slipped his hand around her mouth. She could not scream but tried to bite him.

Ticky killed the lighter and gazed at her with a puzzled expression. 'Did you say something, ma'am—did you want to talk?'

Though Ray's hand had loosened, she could not reply. She thought that surely the two men must see now that she had nothing to tell them, but Ticky just shrugged and relit the lighter. Claire shuddered. As the flame emerged, a sudden gush of bile erupted from her stomach. Ray pulled his hand away and Claire fell forward, vomiting on the carpet. Frantically she crawled across the porridge-like mess to save her son—but Ticky had doused the flame again, had let Tommy go. The boy rushed to his mother. He collapsed and hugged her on the reeking carpet. Petrol and vomit.

Ticky said, 'Remember now, you've no protection. We can come and get you any time.'

Ray strode past him to the door. He had lost interest. Ticky bobbed around like a helpful neighbour: 'As soon as we've gone, I think you'd better change his clothes—give him a nice warm bath, then put all his dirty clothes in the washing machine. OK?'

Ray said, 'Why bother? Might as well burn them. They should go well.'

Jet is in the ring, delivering a barrage. He wants to catch the boy early so he is left weakened but still standing, and then carry him to the next round. He is heavy, has started eagerly. Each time the boy hears the crowd he remembers that his friends are watching, and he wonders why he cannot connect. To him, this blazing white light has become merciless.

In its bleak glare the boy already stands flat on his feet, lumbering forward and trying haymakers. Jet steps inside and hugs him, to allow a rest. But the boy rears, swings his head, and Jet steps backwards and jabs his midriff as he leaves. The boy looks puzzled. His eyes have crossed. For the remainder of round one, Jet feints, pretends to hit him, spins it out.

The boy needs his half minute between the rounds. He sips water, feels the towel cool on his face. At the bell, he sees his friends down in the crowd, laughing, cheering, encouraging him on. As he moves into the ring he is inexperienced enough to wave to them, but Jet waits, knowing that he can clip him any time and put him down. When the boy does arrive Jet puts two straight lefts into his face. From the ringside those jabs look nothing, just orthodox deliveries, but Jet's arm is a rod of iron. All his weight is along that arm.

The boy is wavering. His gloves swipe the air. Jet puts a hard one below his heart and the boy shudders. He takes an uppercut to the jaw. Almost finished, semiconscious, the boy lurches against the ropes. Jet follows. He won't mark him—his friends are here. He won't shame the kid now he's gone. Jet glances briefly towards Joe and he doesn't see the last desperate fling. It explodes against his head. In a white-hot flash of blinding pain Jet thinks that his skull has cracked apart. A surge of red rushes through a breach. Jet staggers but keeps his guard, takes the next blow on his gloves, drops on his knee. In his ears a giant roars. It might be the crowd. The noise is changing, has become a single sustained scream. The note softens, becomes background, a wind howling along a pipe. Jet hears, 'Six!'

He tries to focus.

'Seven.'

Joe's voice reverberates. Jet unbends.

'Eight.'

Joe presses hard on his shoulder, and it takes a moment for Jet to realise that Joe does not want him to stand up.

'Nine.'

Jet scrambles to his feet. He puts his guard up, demonstrating that he can continue, but Joe has smothered him, is embracing him, is declaring to the crowd: 'The fight's over. In the second round the referee has stopped the fight. A victory for the challenger, folks. Give the local boy a big hand.'

Suddenly a robe appears. As it is draped around Jet's shoulders another wave of pain washes through his head. He stumbles, but Joe has hold of him. Lee is there as well. His dark face hangs before Jet's eyes before Joe tells him, 'Look after the other boy.'

Now the pain bears down fully. Jet's eyes are balls of stone. Strangely, it seems that the air temperature is falling. Perhaps the people milling around have caused a draught. He has left the ring now, and all these people are in his way, are touching him. Joe Hake pushes Jet through the crowd, holding him erect as if he loves him and is protective before other men.

The pain has permeated every part of him. Its continuous grinding presence is squeezing from all sides. His throat aches as if corroded.

In the trailer, the stale air seems filled with a curious rustling. Joe talks but Jet doesn't listen to him—only to the rustling inside his head. Across the trailer beside the shower he sees the boy putting on his clothes while Lee Leonard stands beside him holding his gloves. The boy looks across at Jet and asks, 'All right then, mate? Feeling better now?'

Jet inclines his head. He cannot nod. He hears Joe telling him to get on the table.

'No.'

'What's up?'

'I can't.'

Jet feels that the moment he tilts his head back to lie down he will spill the liquid inside his skull.

'Stay on the stool, then.'

Joe raises his finger before Jet's face and performs the concussion test. Both Lee and the boy stand watching silently.

The door opens. Terry Sykes scuttles in with the collection hat and grins delightedly at Jet. 'He caught you good and proper, no mistake.'

'Cut it out,' Joe snaps. 'Right, son.'—This to the boy. 'You had a nice evening. You came up trumps. But you don't think I'm going to give you fifty pound, do you?'

The boy looks wary.

'You don't really think you're on for fifty pound?'

The boy thrusts his jaw out. 'Yeah.'

'Well, you're right!' Joe slaps his shoulder. 'Honest Joe Hake, they call me. People think I'll cheat 'em. But no.

You go straight outside and tell your mates you got gen-u-ine prize money. Fifty pound you earned tonight.'

'And the 'at,' says Terry Sykes.

'Yes, and the 'at. How much 'as the brave boy earned?'

Terry frowns. 'At least a tenner, I should think.'

'There you go—ten quid on fifty.' Joe counts notes in front of him. 'Five and ten—fifteen—and ten and five—my God, this *is* your lucky night. Fancy a game of cards, son, before you go?'

'No fear.'

'Away you go then.'

As Terry bundles him through the door, Joe says, 'I thought he'd stay all night. You'll be all right in a minute, Jet.'

'Right.'

'I had to stop it. You know, your 'ead.'

'Right.'

'And don't you worry about that fifty quid.'

'Right.'

'Just don't make it a habit.'

'Right.'

Outside on the platform the cold breeze slaps across their faces. Despite his throbbing head, Jet hopes that the fresh air will pull him round. He and Lee jog around the platform, throwing punches, scowling at the people down below. Joe switches off his microphone and stands with his back to the crowd while he speaks.

'There's a hundred punters down there, caught the smell of blood. Once in a while, see, it does no harm to let one win. Word gets round. Now, everyone thinks they can have a share in it—like their team has scored a point. Every bleeder down there fancies he can take you—either of you. Feeling better, son?'

'I'll do.'

'You can rest a couple of sets.'

When Joe clicks the mike back on, the crowd becomes instantly vociferous, jeering at the boxers—who ignore them, bobbing and weaving, flicking punches. Jet's pain has become localised above his ear. He hears his name called, hears a taunt about the fight. Laughter trickles from the ground. Joe whips it up.

'You want to fight him? Yes, come on. It's a great show in here tonight. Want to try your luck? You there! You look a strong lad—wanna have a go? How about fighting that boy next to you? I'll give five pound to the winner of you two. Guaranteed. Come along, lads, we'll pair you off, put you in the ring, see what you're made of. I've got the gloves; you got the talent. Ha, ha. Three short rounds, each a tiny minute and a half, a full minute's rest between each round—a piece of cake. Every winner gets five pound—the loser gets a damn good hiding. Ha, ha. Do you want a fiver? Come up and fight for it. Remember, you don't have to fight one of my champions, just take each other and win five pound. I've cut the rounds to a minute and a half—no time at all. Queensberry rules and no one gets hurt. Who wants a fiver? Yes, that's one of these bits of paper. Here they are: a fistful of fivers, and I am giving them away. Am I mad? I think I am.'

Joe has run his booth for more than twenty years. It is second nature for him to spot the likeliest faces from those staring back at him—the eager ones, the tough boys and bully walkers. He can spot which ones will fight for a fiver. He can spot their mates as they egg them on. Joe watches, sees who they encourage, then he points to the lad and lets him know he has seen him. Beckons him on to stage.

'Here are your lads—give 'em a great big hand! Who else down there wants a share of glory? Who else wants money for fighting? Come in pairs or on your own, bring

your friends—if you've got any—and I'll give the winner
a five-pound note. Yes, ladies and gentlemen, these are
local boys—come and see them fight. This is real boxing
tonight—live, before your very eyes.'

Terry Sykes stands in the dark behind the crowd, cap
on head, stick in hand, and he grins at the girl on the
Lucky Rabbit stall. 'Bleedin' amateurs. It'll be like the
pub car park on Saturday night.'

'Better for everyone if they fight down here.'

'Public service.' He grins again. If he can't box he can
use his time. And this is *her* slack time too, because
while Joe hustles, the nearby stalls stand idle, unable to
compete against his microphone. Terry smiles again. 'Run
this stall all on your own, do you?'

She looks behind her. 'Can't see anyone else.'

'All yours, then, is it? Not your husband's?'

She gives him the fish eye, so he presses on: 'Ain't you
got an old man?'

'Do I look the type for older men?'

'You know what I mean.'

'Oh, yes, don't worry, I know. The stall belongs to my
Dad. We've several bits of side stuff.'

'Nice. Sleep in the same trailer, do you?'

'Isn't it time you went for entry money?'

'Joe's not finished yet.'

'You should feel these muscles, ladies and gentlemen!
They would terrify you. They terrify *me*! Ha, ha. What's
your name, lad? Speak up—the girls can't hear you. Yes,
folks, this is where the champions all began in the old
days—young men like these coming into a boxing booth.
They became champions. And today, for just two pound
you'll get the finest value on any fairground.'

When Jet re-enters the booth, the glaring light hits him
and seems to press him down. As the nausea rises, he

pushes back out through the incoming crowd into fresh air, and stands outside on the walkway, mouth open, sucking in the night. He hears a girl ask, 'Are you feeling sick?'

'I'll be all right.'

He darts away from her between the stalls, and in the shadows he begins to vomit. His stomach heaves, his throat strains, and he spits a thin sour liquid on to the ground. When he continues to heave, nothing comes. His throat is hot.

The girl's hand rests on his arm, and when she speaks she places her other hand on his brow. 'Let it come. Don't try to fight it. Try breathing normally.'

But what he makes is a horrible sound. Part of him wants to be left alone so that he can crumple into a corner and hug the anguish to his chest. Part of him wants the girl to stay. He knows that it is the auburn-haired girl from the Lucky Rabbit stall.

'That's better now, long steady breaths. Take it in and hold it. Wait. Let it out slowly. Breathe in and hold it. That's very good.—Oops.'

She holds him tight as he throws up. It seems that the more disgusting Jet becomes the closer she draws near. But he is detached from what is happening; instead of shivering on his knees he is an abstract spirit hovering above in the dark.

She says, 'You're nearly done. Can't be much more left.'

He mumbles but makes no sense.

'Wait a minute,' Collette says.

Jet feels a quietness settling on to him. He feels the girl wrapped against his shoulders like a cloak against the cold. Though he may not retch again, the sharp pain piercing his skull cannot be eased. He thinks, absurdly, of aspirin—but it would not be strong enough. And if he could swallow some they would not stay down.

'Take it easy.'

'I'm all right.'

When he stands, the girl remains against his side, saying, 'I'll help you back to your caravan.'

'No, I—' Jet shakes his head, but then has to pause again to let the wave of pain subside. 'God, I stink.'

'Not as bad as the hot dog stall. Vinegar and onions.'

'Don't.'

'I bet the thought of it makes you feel sick.'

'Nothing left.'

This time he doesn't shake his head, but moves it slowly from side to side as if performing a Chinese exercise at dawn. 'I've got to get back to work.'

'Don't make me laugh.'

'Not fighting. I have to second.'

'What you have to do is lie down.'

'No, it's . . . passing now. Must've been something I ate.'

'Don't kid me. I heard about the knock-out.'

As they emerge on to the midway, Collette holds on to him like a nurse.

Jet says, 'I really am OK.'

There is no crowd in front of the boxing booth now, no one on stage, and the single string of lamps rocks in the breeze. Over the loudspeakers they can hear crowd noise from inside. The canvas booth looks like a badly wrapped parcel bulging at the seams.

'Don't go in, Jet.'

He disentangles her fingers and approaches the booth. Then he turns to look at her properly: pale face beneath auburn hair, dark eyes locked on to his. She does not move. Jet takes a sudden breath, but turns again to go inside.

Late in the gruelling evening, after another first round

knock-out, Joe rounded on Lee: 'What the hell was that about? You tried to tear his face off.'

Lee was using his teeth to untie his glove lace. 'He was bigger than me, Joe.'

'Bigger—so what? It was what he called you, wasn't it?'

'The man called me something? What was that?'

'Listen, son, you got to get used to this racist shit—especially here. Half these country boys ain't never seen a black man before.'

'What you mean is they don't like to see a black man whip a white man. But when they do, they'll come back to see me beaten. Bigger crowds. You should be grateful, Joe.'

Joe paused, studying him. 'You won't learn, will you?'

'I *am* learning. Hey, this is one summer of my life. After this I won't be back, because I am not spending the next ten years fighting fairs. In a couple of years' time I'm going for the title.'

Joe snorted.

'You just watch me, uncle Joe. I am not here to pass the time, and I am not slogging away at this till I end up licking my wounds in a miserable trailer—' Lee stopped as he caught Jet's eye. 'Hey, I'm sorry, man, you know?'

'I know.'

Joe exhaled and shook his head. 'What a night. The thing is, Lee, I can't let you keep beating 'em up.' Joe turned. 'And as for you, Jet—Christ, I can't put anyone in with you. That bloody head of yours.'

'I'm all right.'

'You're all wrong. One punch—that's all he landed. If I put you up again you could get slaughtered.'

'I'll be all right.'

'Will you stop saying that?' Joe pointed at him. 'Perhaps you don't care if you get killed—but I could lose me licence!' Joe grinned. 'What a poxy pair. We're closing for tonight.'

Lee grinned back. 'Big deal. It's nearly ten o'clock.'

Jet winked at him. 'Why don't you fetch Terry? He could challenge them to a stick fight.'

'Oh, that's ripe, that's really ripe. Roll up, you ladies and gentlemen, come and see two cripples and a psychopath. Am I mad? They'll think I am.'

The crowd did not want to leave the fair. The weather had stayed mild, and in the slightly damp darkness they lingered beside the booths while they closed. Here and there, people pleaded for a final turn. Showmen shrugged and took their cash.

Jet dawdled on the midway with the fresh air cool on his face. Though the pain had subsided he remembered Joe Hake's words: if I put you up again you could get killed. Exaggerating. The old man had been angry because of Lee—seeing the boy tear into his opponent, taunting him, grinding punches into his face. But boxing had never been the sport of gentlemen.

Tentatively, Jet touched that soft part above his ear. Even a gentle press made him wince. Must be some bruise. He was still pressing at it, testing it, as he approached the caravan—and he wasn't aware of someone waiting in the dark until she said, 'I was beginning to think you weren't coming home.'

It took him a second or two: she could have been any punter girl out late.

'Oh, yeah, Miss . . .'

'Miss! Kelly, if you *please*.' She smiled at him. She wore a raincoat tonight, belted tightly round her waist, and it emphasised her slenderness.

He produced a smile. 'Thought you were telling me off about not coming home. Sounded like the social worker.'

'Like a wife maybe.'

'What do social workers say?'

She held his eyes and smiled. 'This one says that she's off duty now, sir.'

'Sir?'

'Well, you called me Miss.'

'OK. I'll have to pop inside to Stella.'

'Yes, she's still awake.'

Jet frowned.

Kelly said, 'It was cold out here. I could have been waiting for hours.'

'She asked you in?'

'I knocked.' Though she smiled again Kelly knew what he was thinking—that she was still the social worker.

'I'll just pop in,' he said.

'I'll wait.'

Stella's eyes were unblinking—dark and fathomless, unchildlike eyes. Around her bed it was black with shadow and in the glow of the flickering nightlight the caravan walls quivered as in a tent.

She asked, 'Did you see that social worker?'

'She's outside. Don't worry—she didn't come back again to check on us.'

'Oh, is it just a social call?' Stella had rehearsed this line. 'Is she still waiting?'

'Mhm. What did you two talk about?'

'Nothing much.'

He touched the girl's black hair. 'How come I ask a question and you don't answer?'

'Ask a silly question.' She grinned impishly.

'Another crack like that and I'll blow your light out. Now, go off to sleep and I'll see you later.'

'Are you going out with her?'

'We have to talk about something.'

'What sort of something?' She was suddenly alert.

'Nothing serious. Just . . .'

'Just a little walk in the moonlight?' Her eyes were huge again.

'No, no. It's cloudy—you can't see the moon.'

'Liar,' she whispered.

Jet smiled, then went to the cupboard and took out a bottle of aspirin. He swallowed some without water. As he replaced the lid he glanced back at Stella, who said, 'I don't trust that social worker, Dad. She asked a lot of questions.'

'You said it was nothing much.'

'Well . . .'

'She was just making conversation, I expect.'

Stella sat up. He said, 'Do you want me to stay till you're asleep?'

'I shan't be asleep for ages.'

'Then I'll wait for ages.'

'Why'd you take those pills?'

'Headache.'

She watched him. 'Are you OK, Dad?'

'Hm. All right.'

Stella lay down, slowly. 'You'd better go if she's outside waiting.'

'There's no hurry.'

'Oh, go on.'

Though the fair was still not dead, most shutters had been erected, some lamps were out, and the sideways were beginning to mottle with shade. There was no music.

Kelly held Jet's hand. He and she looked like any other couple with nowhere to go. He was silent at her side because the headache had not gone away. It was a dull background ache—nothing serious, he thought, nothing that aspirins would not cure.

She said, 'You'll only be here a couple more days.'

'Uh-huh.'

'I brought my car if you'd like a ride.'

'Uh-huh.'

'We can go somewhere quieter.'

She was half a pace ahead, almost pulling him along. Glancing down at her short cropped hair, quite mannish above the raincoat collar, he wondered why she had come. He had made no overtures to her. But he lengthened his stride, released her hand, and put his arm around her slim shoulders. Against his side she seemed small and fragile, lost inside her bulky coat like a present waiting to be unwrapped. He squeezed her and she laughed.

But he did not laugh with her. From the corner of his eye he had seen Collette loitering by her stall. He wanted to say something but she disappeared. This was one of those nights when nothing he did seemed to turn out right.

The van with London plates snaked through Bude's outlying streets—quiet, respectable and dark. Every third house seemed to be Bed and Breakfast. In the centre of the little town stood an open common like a village green, with red brick houses arranged around its sides, its far end open to the sea. But he wasn't interested in the sea. Ahead to his left were the unmistakable lights of the travelling fair—strings of bulbs and messy strips of neon, but even as he watched, the lights on the Big Wheel suddenly extinguished. Without its dominating presence, the remaining lamps looked feeble against the dark. They threw up a dull orange pall. At the exit car park he saw the last aimless people come straggling through. The fair was almost empty, which was good. In a nearby side street he stopped, turned the engine off, and listened to the metal carcass of the vehicle creaking as it cooled. He had driven with the heater turned up high, and for a while the warm fug lingered with him inside, and the windows filmed across with mist. It would be a while yet before he felt cold.

Kelly drove Jet less than a mile before turning along a hardened track leading to the clifftop. At times she drove so slowly that he could have walked beside the car and not been left behind. Stones clunked against the chassis underneath. Finally, when she stopped, she heaved sharply on the handbrake as if afraid the car might run away. But it was level here; she had only snatched at the brake through nervousness.

She smiled at him. Jet sat with the window open, his head framed against the clarity of the night sky, as dispassionate as a driving instructor. Had she passed the test?

'This is nice,' he said, and Kelly relaxed. 'I can smell the sea.'

'You can hear it—listen.'

From the black emptiness outside came the suppressed breathing of the sea, and it seemed to grow in volume till it filled the car. Kelly knew that what she was doing was foolish—but who would ever hear of it? He would be gone next week. She reached across the gear lever and took his hand. When Jet kissed her, it seemed both exploratory and familiar, as if at some earlier time they had been lovers and he was reminding himself of how she felt. Oh, she had been so lonely. She sank against the seat back.

When he kissed her again she moved his hand on to her breast. Her other hand was behind his head. Their tongues probed and intertwined, and she felt his hand slip inside her raincoat.

For Jet, the cramped closeness inside the car did not

excite him as it should—he felt confined. He moved his head. She asked, 'What's wrong?'

'Came up for air.'

She stroked his cheek, and he lay his lips against her palm. She smelt of dark red roses. As he opened the window she said, 'We could get in the back, and we'd have more room.'

From opposite sides they left the car like strangers. She was opening the rear door when he said, 'Look at the sea.'

They were a few yards from the edge of the cliff. The ground did not fall suddenly away, merely tilted and became steeper. The way it ran away was in some ways more dangerous than a sudden fall—more inviting. When he took her by the hand Kelly thought for a moment that they might run down the grassy slope, but he led her gently, walking to the point where the pitch grew steeper and they seemed suspended above the sea. She snuggled into his side. Out on the surface of the dark water were grey-white streaks of lazy foam. A few small lights quivered on the waves. Jet gazed at the unrewarding view as if one of those bobbing lights might send a signal.

'Did you want to walk?' she asked hesitantly.

'No.'

She squeezed his hand.

Jet was reviving in the salt sea air. He felt comforted by its glistening blackness, the shining sea and a falling sky. His head was clearer now—perhaps from fresh air, or the aspirins, or from the unhurrying passage of time. Everything passed eventually. When he looked at the tiny stars light-years above him he did not feel awed or insignificant, merely aware of himself on the clifftop, with the wind breathing in his face, and with a girl standing by his side. He said, 'We are the only people here.'

He felt her lean against him and place her far hand on

to his chest. She had moved in front of him and was staring into his face. She had night magic in her eyes, and did not speak.

This time when Jet kissed her, she seemed to taste of night itself—not of this salty outdoor breeze but of an intimately shared bed. He undid her coat, wrapped his arms inside and placed his hands on the warm fabric of her shirt. Her raincoat was a loose changing bag inside which they pulled at each other's clothes. When he touched the skin above her rib she gasped beside his ear. She whispered, 'Come back to the car.'

They staggered up towards it, stumbling in each other's way as if tied together in a three-legged race. She fell laughing against her small car, and said, 'Let's snuggle up in the back.'

'Not enough room.'

'We'll make room.'

'No.'

He pressed her against the side of the car and undid the remaining buttons of her shirt. While he reached behind to unfasten her bra, Kelly rolled his sweater up over his chest, her eyes glinting as she stroked his skin. Their flesh touched. Jet had one hand on her breasts while his other tangled in her red cropped hair. She laughed in her throat and leant her head back. Jet swooped on her with his kiss. In the cool night air her skin was warm. He began tugging at her skirt, the material bunching between her thigh and the raincoat against the car. As he bundled the skirt around her hips Kelly slid her hand down between their bodies to cup the hardness in his pants. She rubbed him, felt the size of him. His fingers were inside her panties. He eased the elastic away, met the curls of her pubic hair, then pressed his fingers softly into her wetness. 'Oh yes,' she sighed. 'That's good.'

She allowed herself to be supported by the metalwork

of the car as his fingers probed her, as his other hand played with her exposed breasts. She squeezed him and asked, 'Where's the zip?'

'This is a tracksuit.'

She could hardly move now because of the pleasure gushing between her legs—but then she shuddered, locked her fingers into his waistband and tugged his soft trousers down. She seized him. She used both her hands to stroke him and he arched his back. She said, 'Oh my darling,' and pushed her hips against him, holding him flat against her belly. They kissed, and then with surprising sureness Jet pulled her panties down and she stepped out of them. Instantly, she dropped to her knees to help him kick free of his heavy tracksuit trousers, then she clasped him and took him in her mouth.

'No.'

But she had closed her lips on it, her tongue lapping the tip as she sucked him in. Jet's fingers tightened in her short hair, but then he pulled away from her with a movement so sudden that she stumbled forward. But his hands were on her elbows and he lifted her up.

Leaning back against the car, Kelly felt his warm hardness above her navel. 'You're too tall for me,' she laughed.

'Turn round.'

Jet moved her body so she faced away from him, and he pushed her long raincoat aside. Oh God, she thought, where is he going to—

Then she knew. Jet used his knee to spread her naked legs, then pushed the top of her body forwards. Lying away from him across the engine casing—still warm, she noticed—she felt him slide into her from behind. He worked himself in cautiously, as if unsure whether she was ready, but by now Kelly was so loose and aching that he could have stabbed her with a spear and she would have let him in. She engulfed him. Sprawling across the engine, her hands flat against lukewarm metal, she sighed at every stroke. Behind and above her, Jet gazed at Kelly's short cropped hair above the boyish coat. Detached and in sweet control, he pumped anonymously from behind and stared beyond to the dark wide sea.

Late night, beyond midnight, thin clouds scudding across pale stars. Caravans creaking in the wind. Beneath a trailer he hears a dog. It growls, sticks out its snout, keeps one eye open as he returns. As Jet approaches his caravan, the little nightlight is too dim to shine through the curtain, and the caravan seems as dark and restful as all the others. Near the end of the line of slumbering trailers it squats on its patch of muddy grass. Its base is submerged in starless shadow.

Jet creeps quietly up the three metal steps, opens the door and glides inside. She is not asleep. As he closes the door he feels ashamed. 'I didn't mean to wake you.'

'I'm already awake.'

'I'm sorry I was so long.'

'Has she gone?'

Jet takes a breath. 'Yes, she's gone.'

'No one's outside?'

He moves towards her bed and rests his hand on it. He can feel the rigid body beneath the blankets. 'Were you frightened?'

'There's someone here.'

A chair scrapes as Jet turns round. In the dim shadow by their little table, a man is rising. It is his brother Scott.

TWENTY-SEVEN

The most surprising thing was the look of him. When Scott stepped forward from the shadow, Jet saw that his brother's hair was shorter, lightened. It seemed patchy, as if he had used a bleach which hadn't worked. His normally regular dark hair now wilted in a crew-cut, and his face was thinner, pale, in need of sunlight.

'Not in Bermuda?'

'Haven't made it yet.' Scott grinned in the treacly half-light like an actor at first rehearsal.

'Those the finest clothes money can buy?'

Scott wore a padded windcheater and dark pants: unremarkable clothes.

'I had a spree in C&A. Paid with cash.' The rueful grin again. He added, 'The money doesn't seem to be marked in any way. I keep spending it—no one reacts.'

'Should they?'

'No, it's just money. A little old and worn—but it's been well loved.'

'No one saw you coming here?'

Scott shrugged. 'Everyone thinks I'm dead or . . . in Bermuda, like you say.'

'Have you really got that two million?'

'Yeah. But it won't change my life.'

Jet smiled. 'I suppose you need somewhere to hide.'

'Here? Yeah, this'd be good. I could hide beneath the bed.'

Stella giggled. Jet glanced round at her: 'You're not tired, Stella?'

'Not now.' She was sitting up in the narrow bed with her knees tucked to her chin.

Scott said, 'I've already found myself a place. It'll do.'

'Where?'

Scott's eyes wandered. 'At first I stayed in a small hotel, but I didn't like it. Then a Bed & Breakfast—that was worse: too intimate. Tiny dining room, people chatting over breakfast—where've you come from, are you alone?' Scott paused, chewing his lip. 'I slept a couple of nights in the van, but that was dangerous. I looked like a vagrant, you know? No fixed abode.'

'We know the feeling.'

'Didn't want to draw attention to myself.'

'Is this the same van you stole in London?'

'The Force Five?' Scott was about to chuckle, but his face clouded. 'No, that one burnt out.'

Jet moved to collect the kettle. 'We heard.' He kept his tone neutral as he asked, 'What exactly happened?'

Scott sighed heavily. 'Mind if I sit down?' He did so.

Jet glanced at Stella again, whose eyes were wide.

'This is the first time I've talked about it. May not be easy.'

Jet lit the gas.

'Well, the robbery went like clockwork, as you might have heard. Force Five had a contract to take old banknotes to the incinerator. We were security vetted, turned inside out.'

'Somebody blundered.'

'It was a couple of years ago, you see. I'd hardly joined. Once we'd passed the test, the bank must've thought that was it, you know, nothing would change?' Scott shook his head. 'Banks don't know what money means.'

Jet moved the kettle on the flame. 'Did you dream up the snatch yourself?'

'I was approached.'

'Who by?'

Scott glanced at him. 'You wouldn't want to know.'

'Do I know him?' No reaction. Jet spooned coffee grains into cups.

'Well, anyway . . .' Scott faded out. He was frowning at his fingernails, as if he was wondering if they were another thing he should have disguised.

Jet prompted: 'Well, anyway?'

'Anyway. We decided we ought to do it.'

Scott sighed. Light hair did not suit him—he looked several years older than he had only two short weeks before. 'My part was to drive the van as usual and keep calling in by radio. As usual.' He stared at the kettle as it began to sing. 'There was a yard I had to drive to, where this guy was waiting.'

'Which guy?'

'Oh, it was . . . Cliff Lyons. You know the name?'

'Who doesn't—now?'

Scott watched the kettle. Couldn't take his eyes off it.

Jet asked, 'Was he your partner?'

Scott looked up. 'One of the gang.'

'You were in a gang?'

'Sure.' Scott grimaced as if he had found something unpleasant between his teeth. 'I'm not going to tell you who they are.'

'Did you run out on them?'

Scott looked surprised. 'How d'you know that?'

'Why else would you be here? I mean, you *are* on your own, aren't you?'

'Oh, I'm on my own all right.'

The kettle boiled and Jet lifted it from the ring. 'Like a tea, Stella?'

'Please.'

Jet dropped a teabag in her mug and added water. Then he poured two coffees. While Jet was stirring, Scott said, 'Cliff Lyons was waiting with the lorry—the idea being that he'd sit in the yard with the ramp down, and I'd drive the van up and straight inside.'

'A covered lorry?'

'Of course. Removal truck.'

Jet handed Scott a coffee.

'We'd slip the van inside, close the back and drive away. The cops would start looking for a Force Five van, while we were chuntering off in our big lorry among the traffic.'

'But it didn't go like that.' Jet gave Stella her mug of tea.

'Not exactly. The truck was waiting all right, and I drove inside it. That all went just as it should.'

Stella had both hands around the mug as if to warm them. Jet smiled down at her.

'Lyons is waiting inside the truck and tries to shoot me.'

Stella gasped. Jet steadied her mug of tea. He watched his daughter as Scott continued: 'Bastard tells me he's going to do it. He *tells* me. What would you do?'

Jet stared into Stella's dark eyes. 'What *did* you do?'

'I said I had a question—just one question.'

'And?' Jet stayed with Stella.

'I said, "My question is—" and grabbed the gun.'

'He let you?'

'Don't be daft. But he was close, and well, he always had too much lip. He was . . . over-excited is the word. He'd been waiting since—oh, I don't know how long he'd been waiting, but he just seized up. He meant to kill me.'

There was silence in the caravan. Scott chuckled. 'And *you're* supposed to be the fighter.'

'Family trait.'

'Anyway, we fought, and I managed to pull the gun away from him, and . . . Then it was his turn to get scared, you see? He started pleading with me. A mistake.'

'Mistake?'

'Yeah, he ought to have tried to get the gun.' Scott's eyes were bleak. 'Though I'd have shot him anyway.'

Jet glanced at Stella. 'D'you want that tea?'

'I'm still drinking it. What happened next, uncle Scott?'

Scott sighed. 'Oh, I did as we'd planned—drove the truck away. Cliff had been meant to drive it, but, well, I left him where he was, in the back of the lorry beside the van. Then I found somewhere—it's difficult, you know, to find somewhere lonely—and I took the money out, rolled the van down out of the truck . . . No, wait, I put him inside first, that's right.'

Scott paused as he remembered it. Stella asked, 'Was he still dead?'

'Oh yeah, they don't wake up.'

'I didn't mean that.' Stella was embarrassed. 'I meant, was he really dead the first time?'

Scott's face was expressionless. He looked a stranger now. 'Yeah, he was dead all right. Anyway, I put him in the van and set light to it. Watched it burn. Then I drove the truck to Basingstoke.'

'Why there?'

'Why not? Unlikely sort of place.'

'It said on the news you dressed him in your uniform.'

'Oh yeah, that's right, I did that first. Thought it might put the coppers off the track—for a bit, you know? And I needed his clothes, you see—I couldn't keep prancing around in my uniform.'

'You didn't have some with you?'

'No, I'd left them with—Well, anyway, like I said, I drove the removal truck to Basingstoke and bought a second-hand van—for cash, of course, ha, ha. Got a good

price, actually. Then I dumped the truck in a lorry park.
So . . . that's how I got the van.'

No one said anything for a while. Stella sipped her tea.
Jet returned to the small table for his coffee, saying, 'I
don't want to be involved in this, Scott.'

'I just need a favour.'

Jet sat opposite him at the table. 'This was murder,
Scott. Armed robbery.'

'Wasn't meant to be. I was just the driver.'

'You still murdered him.'

'Self-defence.'

Jet shook his head. It was late and he was tired. 'Two
million quid and you're sitting in my caravan. Was it
worth it?'

'It will be—but I need your help. I'll pay you, Jet.'

'Don't say that.'

His brother dropped his head. 'You're the only one I
can turn to.'

Jet did not reply but Stella spoke behind him: 'He's
your brother, Dad. If we don't help him he might get
caught.'

Neither man responded to her. Then Scott said, 'Put
up a blind for me.'

'What does that mean?'

'The cops are wondering where I am—right? England
or abroad. If you could pop across the Channel on a day
trip—'

'A day trip!'

'Yeah, you'd be back by tea time. Take a ferry out from
Plymouth—or fly from Exeter, I don't mind. Send Claire
a postcard. Then come straight back.'

'What d'you think—she'll give it to the police?'

'It'll be intercepted.'

Jet snorted. 'Christ, Scott, what have you been
reading?'

'Get alive, man! Yes, intercepted. D'you think the police have given up on me? Of course they read my mail.'

'I see. You want me to send the cops a postcard?'

'No, make it a letter—they'll steam it open anyway. A letter would look better—more authentic.'

'Steam it open? The local bobby down at the station boils up a kettle—'

'A postcard, then, make it easy for them—'

'You're round the twist.'

'Seriously. They'll see the postcard, believe me. They're *waiting* for me to get in touch with Claire—'

'What *about* Claire? Is she waiting—what's the plan?'

'Oh, it seemed so simple.'

Scott swallowed some coffee, but Jet pressed him: 'What about her?'

Scott sighed. 'I'm leaving her. That was the plan.'

'Was?'

'It still is.' Scott could not meet his brother's eye.

'Then she'll appreciate a postcard.'

'Ah, shit, I mean, I know that this looks bad—'

'That's right.'

'But it's bad for me as well, you know? I hadn't realised how lonely I would feel. Empty. Pointless. Everything is so bloody pointless.'

'Money can't buy you everything?'

'Too right.'

'You thought it would? Grow up, Scott—you were better off driving the van.'

'I was dead when I did that—numb from my goolies up. But now, I only have to get past this waiting stage—'

'And what about Claire and Tommy? They're desperate.'

'Oh, they'll get over it. Christ, me and Claire—it was over anyway. Jesus. All this money and I'm still pinned down. I can't do anything. The cops are watching every port and airport, and I'm stuck.'

'But you think *I'll* be able to breeze out of the country without a care?'

'No one's looking for *you*.'

'Really?'

'They're office boys. They do not think. You'll walk past some plonker with a card in front of him, or some fancy computer screen, and he'll have a whole *list* of wanted names—ex-IRA men, Arab terrorists, Scott Heywood, Henry Scott—'

'And he'll see *Jet* Heywood wander past, and—'

'So what? How many Heywoods d'you think leave the country *every day*? No one will notice you.'

'Yeah, if I'm lucky.'

'You will be. And even if you're not—there's no law to stop you going on holiday. You can do anything you want.—And I'll pay you, remember.'

'I told you not to say that.'

'Be realistic. I've got all this money—'

'I don't want to hear about it. I am not interested in your money.'

'As the actress said. Look, you're my brother, Jet. I know you're not after the sodding money, but don't turn down a gift horse. It's money—you know that stuff? You don't even have to wait for it. Do the job and I'll pay you straight away—here, in English money, in bloody England. How much d'you want? Just name it.'

'You live in a fantasy world, you know?'

'Fantasy! I've got two million pounds in my little room—genuine, spendable bank notes. I had to kill a man, I'm on the run, and you tell me I'm living in a fantasy! For Christ's sake, Jet, help me.'

Jet smiled. 'I can't mosey off to France—I've got a job to do.'

'Fuck the job. Listen—get this inside your head—I'll pay you *regardless* of if it works. Send the postcard and

I'll give you—what?—a hundred thousand pounds?—for nothing, one day's work. Not even work, for Christ's sake, a nice day out.'

Jet was shaking his head again, as if he admired the salesman's patter but would not buy the goods. Scott tried to close the sale: 'One hundred thousand pounds, Jet—immediately—whatever happens. Because if I get away, it's worth it, I won't notice the money's gone. But if I don't get away . . . if they catch me, well, I'll lose the bloody lot—everything except your hundred bloody grand. It would keep me cheerful to know we made something out of this. I mean, during my fifteen years in prison I might not laugh or sing happy songs, but I'd feel a damn sight better knowing they didn't get every penny back. I *want* you to have the money.'

Jet had run out of answers. Only stubbornness made him shake his head.

Scott said, 'I'm your brother, aren't I? You can't let me go inside.'

'That's below the belt.'

Scott reached across the table and touched his arm. 'How much longer are you going to fight in fairgrounds?'

Behind him, Stella coughed. Jet looked round. She sat in her bed stifling a second cough in her hand. 'I didn't mean anything. I only coughed, Dad.'

He smiled. 'Well, what do you think—shall we quit—give up the fairground?'

Stella drew a breath. 'I . . . I heard about that fight tonight.'

Jet glanced aside. Scott caught his eye.

'Doris told me, Dad. She said I shouldn't say anything.'

Scott asked, 'What's this?'

Jet whispered, 'Nothing. Well . . . OK, maybe earlier, could be someone was trying to tell me something.' He stared at the little table.

Scott asked, 'And?'

Jet exhaled. 'I'll give you an answer tomorrow. Will that be all right?'

'This is tomorrow.'

'You know what I mean.'

'I'm counting on you, Jet.'

Jet, Lee and Terry were cleaning out the booth. Now that Jet was not the canvas-man, their habit was to do it early, sweaty from their run, so that when they had had a shower and changed their clothes they need not be dirty again all day. Though Terry had not come running with them, he could walk freely now and no longer limped. He was tightening guy-ropes. Lee picked rubbish off the floor while Jet swept the ring.

Joe Hake appeared. 'Visitors, Jet, at your caravan.'

Jet went as he was—tracksuit and muddy shoes, lines of sweat upon his face. Approaching the caravan, he could see no one waiting for him outside so he climbed the steps, pushed open the door.

'Hello, Daddy.—Here he is.' Something false in Stella's tone.

Waiting with her inside the caravan were Kelly and a balding, portly man in a cheap suit. He smiled ingratiatingly. 'Good morning, sir. Alan Meaburn. Not inconvenient, I hope? We'd like a little informal chat, if you don't mind.'

'How little?'

'It won't take long.'

Stella said, 'I offered a cup of tea but they wouldn't have one.'

Jet stared coldly at the visitors. 'Is this a check-up?'

Kelly said, 'Oh, no—' but Meaburn raised a silencing

hand: 'Nothing to worry about, sir, I'm sure. I was admiring your caravan—though perhaps it does seem rather small.'

'I didn't build it.'

'No, quite, quite. A pity! I suppose a caravan like this is all right for an occasional weekend, but well . . . How long do you intend to dwell in it?'

'Is there a time limit?'

Meaburn sighed. 'Don't you find it a little small?'

'For what?'

'It's cosy,' Stella said. 'We only sleep here, so it's just a bedroom, really. I like it here.' She shone a Shirley Temple smile.

Meaburn smiled back at her, acting too. 'And of course, Stella, you wouldn't mind missing school?'

'Oh, we have classes here,' Stella said. 'All the children get together for reading and arithmetic.'

'How often?'

Stella fluttered her eyelashes and tried to hide the brittleness in her voice. 'We know it isn't a proper school, but we're only away for summertime—one term. We make up for it in winter.'

'Dear me! You miss an entire term of schooling—'

Kelly interrupted. 'Fairground children everywhere—'

'What we have to consider, Miss Rice, is the *combination* of disadvantages, isn't it? Cramped living conditions, no privacy, no education.' He met Jet's eye. 'A single parent.'

'Want me to get married?'

'Oh, you know what people say, Mr Heywood, *ordinary* people—people who don't wander around in caravans.'

Kelly protested: 'This is a fairground, Alan. It's another lifestyle—'

'Romantic, isn't it? Medieval. Of course, some people would say it means smelly caravans in the mud, kids running wild. Ha, ha. They'd ask what kind of upbringing is that for a little child?' He chuckled pointlessly.

No one responded. Meaburn glanced amiably at the caravan interior, and said, 'There is a view, of course, that children are best raised inside the four walls of a decent home, with a mother and father, properly married. What d'you say to that?'

Jet put his hands in his pockets to reduce the risk of thumping Meaburn. But the man couldn't stop: 'I suppose it does seem a bit old-fashioned, but I see the results of broken families every day—they form my casebook.' He tutted sympathetically. 'And here we have a child at risk—'

'What risk?'

Meaburn hesitated. 'Absolutely, take your point. Still, poor housing for a start.—If you can call this housing—'

'We're travellers.'

'Yes, yes, quite right. Mind you, some people would call you parasites, I dare say?'

Jet glared at him. 'I work for my living. I don't draw a penny from the state. You do, though—you draw all your wages—'

Kelly stepped between them as Stella said, 'You could send us a teacher here. In some towns they do.'

Meaburn glanced down at her. 'If only. I wish I could—really. But in Devon we don't have a grant for that, you see? Can you read and write?'

'Of course. Lend me your notebook and I'll show you.'

'That sounds a bit cheeky to me, miss.'

Jet placed a hand on Meaburn's chest. 'I've had enough of this.'

Meaburn backed against the table. 'No call for violence, sir, don't get upset. Your daughter needs to maintain her studies. Then when she joins a regular school in winter, she'll not be left behind.'

Jet's fingers tightened on Meaburn's shirtfront. 'She can read, write and add up. She can handle money. She can cook. She can fit a power line to a dynamo and lay it straight. She can cleat the canvas to a sidestall and rig up lamps.'

'I can drive a Scammel,' Stella said.

Jet looked at her. 'When did you learn that?'

'Well, I can a bit. Duke showed me.'

Meaburn tried to squirm from Jet's grasp. 'I don't see what—'

'The point is—' Jet released him. 'She is learning skills that she can use—that she'll need when she grows up. She can learn academic stuff in wintertime.'

'Laying power lines, ' Meaburn muttered.

Stella said, 'When I grow up I'll have an Octopus.'

He frowned at her.

'Or a Caterpillar.'

Kelly explained that these were fairground rides.

'Because when I grow up there may not be any Octo-puses left. You see, to make an Octopus work, you mount it on the centre truck of an army searchlight carrier—and to make it spin round, you use the Gardner that drove the searchlight. But no one's making searchlights any more, so when I grow up I may *have* to have a Caterpillar.'

All three adults stared at her. Meaburn coughed. 'I see. Well, we'll discuss your case in committee.' He looked meaningfully at Jet. 'We will be writing to you.'

Jet nodded. 'Just as well we can read.'

Meaburn summoned Kelly to follow, but as he left the caravan she hung back and whispered, 'I'm sorry—he's a career man from Benefits. I'll talk to him then come back.'

'Don't.'

Kelly frowned.

'Don't come back.'

Kelly seemed to age before their eyes, then she turned and followed her boss outside. The Heywoods waited till they had gone. 'I never did like that lady,' Stella said.

Ticky knew that the safest time would be lunchtime. Waiting in the street outside the school he watched the kids jostle each other in the playground, saw half the children tumble out through the gates heading for the shops or a quick run home. Because Tommy did not come out, Ticky could not speak to him. He watched the boy wandering in the playground, hands in pockets, scuffing his shoes. Poor little blighter, Ticky thought—doesn't fancy running home to his gloomy house and depressed mother, and has no money for local shops. There won't be much money in the Heywood house now, with Daddy not bringing wages home.

Ticky timed his walk beside the railings. When the fat boy came out through the gate he noticed Ticky but looked away. He scuttled down the street and didn't look behind. But he knew, all right. He was one of the solitary ones, like Tommy, and though he kept his head firmly to the front he sensed Ticky close behind. Ticky knew from the way that the boy hunched his shoulders and walked more hastily than usual. But once Ticky had followed him across the street there was no point in either of them pretending. At the far kerb the boy hesitated, but Ticky did not speak, and the boy continued round the corner into the alley leading to the baker's shop.

'Not in the mood for me today, my little Treasure?'

'Sod off.'

Ticky held his arm. They were the only people in the alleyway. 'Now that's not very nice.'

'I'm busy.'

'I've got a job for you.'

'I can't.'

Ticky pressed him gently against the wall and smiled directly into his face. He was an inch taller than the fat boy and was exhilarated by the rare sense of dominance. 'Don't make me angry, Treasure.'

The boy squirmed.

'You know a lad called Tommy Heywood?'

'I might.' The boy raised his head, looked slyly back at him.

'Bring him over here.'

The boy sneered. 'Tommy don't know where his Dad is, Tick. Everyone's asking him all the time.'

'Including grown-ups?'

'I dunno. I expect the teachers have—and the cops, of course.'

'I want a word with him.'

The boy snorted, then he frowned. 'D'you *know* Tommy Heywood, then? I mean, have you . . .?'

'What?'

They stared at each other. The boy said, 'If he don't know you, he won't come.'

'You're bigger than he is.'

'I can't drag him out the playground.'

'Tell him I've brought a message from his Dad.'

The boy shook his head uncertainly. Ticky said, 'But don't tell him what my name is.'

'It'll cost a fiver.'

'If you want paying, you have to earn it, my little Treasure.'

When the two boys walked into the alley Ticky was waiting behind the wall. He grabbed the smaller boy and told the fat one he could scram. Tommy stood white-faced and rigid in the lonely alleyway.

'Remember me, old son? Don't try to run away.'

Ticky leered at him, letting his bad breath flutter

across Tommy's face. 'Last time we met, you tried to get stroppy with me—and you nearly died, didn't you? D'you remember the other man—the big nasty one—told me to soak you in petrol and set you alight? Well, I didn't, did I? Because I'm not cruel like he is—he's a bastard, isn't he? He still wants to kill you, actually, Tommy—yes, that's your name, I remember—and the thing is, Tommy, the thing is that if you don't want that nasty man to burn you, and if you don't want him to hurt that nice Mummy of yours as well, you better be nice to me. He could hurt your Mummy—d'you know what men do to ladies to hurt them, Tommy? No? Well, never mind. I'll tell you a secret, would you like that? It's about your Dad—Scott, his name is, I know him too—your Dad is wanted by the cops. But I can help him. Yes I can. It's what I do—I help people like your Dad to escape the law. And if I help your dad to get away, then you can be with him again. You'd like that, wouldn't you? Live happily, lots of money, and all that. But the thing is—Tommy—that I can't help your Dad if I can't *talk* to him. So when you see your Dad, which you will do soon, you'll have to tell me, is that understood?'

Tommy jerked his arm, but Ticky kept his hold.

'Don't try to get away—there's nowhere you can run, we'll always find you. We've been inside your house twice already, haven't we?'

Tommy frowned.

'Yes, twice—didn't Mummy tell you? You ask her. No, on second thoughts, don't tell her we had this chat—let it be a secret between us. Will that be OK? D'you like secrets? Yes, of course you do. You see, it's safer for you, Tommy, if we meet out here. We can have a chat and you won't get hurt—not out here, in the open air. Because what you *don't* want, Tommy, is for us to come into your house again. You don't want to see that nasty man.'

Ticky sucked his teeth.

'He wants to burn you—oh yes, he does. He likes it. Remember how he made me pour the petrol on you—remember how it smelt? All I had to do was strike a match, and you was roasted. You don't want that. But remember, Tommy, we can find you anywhere—you could be tucked up in your bed and we would find you. I'd like to find you in your bed—I bet you look sweet in it. Yes? What d'you think about when you're in bed? Do you touch yourself—I mean, down here, down between your legs? No, don't struggle, because I know you do. Every little boy likes to touch himself down here—it's natural, it's nice. Every boy likes to touch his willy, even if he doesn't want to talk about it. See? We're all the same. Do your friends talk about it, Tommy, how to make it hard? I bet they do.'

Ticky raised his hand to the boy's pale cheek, then stroked it softly. 'Anyway, just remember that I'm your friend. I'm your Daddy's friend too, Tommy, are you listening? I shall let you go now, because I'm always nice to you. Aren't I? Yes, I'm nice. And I am going to see you every day so we can have a chat. It'll be nice, just you and me. We might play some games too, if you like. But you mustn't tell anybody what I've said. Because if you tell anyone, you know what'll happen? Do you? Yes, the nasty man—he'll burn you. And the cops will catch your father—yes, they will. They're really angry with him. And if they catch him, he'll be dead, because the cops will hang him. You don't want that. You don't want to be the reason your Dad gets hung. But you keep our secret and it'll all be fine. And Tommy, here's a bar of chocolate, to show I can be nice. I'll be your friend, is that all right?'

TWENTY-NINE

A long evening. Nine o'clock, it seemed interminable. Three boxers on the platform looking sullen, jaded—only Joe in buoyant mood. He had urged them earlier to pose more threateningly, to work up the crowd while he drew them in. Terry's ankle no longer pained him, Jet's head had remained clear, but both men were only on the stage for show. They couldn't risk a fight. Lee was fit, but even he couldn't fight each session. So Joe was setting up a boxing carnival, taking all-comers and having them fight a series of scraps against each other instead of against his boys. He was plucking youngsters from the crowd.

'There's a boy coming up and he wants to box. Who wants to fight him—put him down? Three rounds by Queensberry rules—the winner gets a five-pound note. Yes, that's a five-pound note for every winner. Come on lads, you would fight for free. Here's another—I mean you, son, come on up. Yes, you're the one, don't you be bashful. What's your name?'

He was assembling a short line of awkward boys. They stood on the platform beneath the bead of lights, rough clothes unkempt in the harsh white glare.

'There's a lad on the outside wants to have a go. I can see you! Come on, young man, pick one of these. Up you come now. Yes, come on, come on—we know you want to. Hurry up, my son, don't you want five pounds?' Joe pointed elsewhere in the crowd. 'You, son, done any boxing? Does anybody know?'

A knot of teenagers shouted that their friend could fight and they pushed him forward. He came red-faced. Joe urged the others: 'That's six up here now, and each fight will cost me a five-pound note. Three tremendous scraps. Shall we start the show? No! I will not allow it, I want one more. That's right—when I invite you inside my booth I promise you the finest show in any fairground and I insist you get full value. Another couple. Another two. Where can I find a couple of mates? Step up here, lads, show what you're made of—you'll go away better mates than when you came in. Come along, my boys, don't let us down. I will definitely give you a five-pound note. Yes, here it is. Who wants it? I am giving cash away. Am I mad? I think I am.'

But they wouldn't come. Joe had committed himself to supply four fights.

'I know what you're thinking—I'm not paying enough! Do you want more money? You want a tenner? Here's what you do: challenge any one of my professional boxers and you could win a ten-pound note. Stay three rounds and the tenner's yours. But listen: put him down and you scoop the jackpot—that's fifty pound—I said fifty—if you knock him out. Are you up to that? Who wants my money? Here we go, then—I'll make it even better: see this boxer?' He raised Lee's arm. 'D'you see how small he is—see how thin? Go on, Lee, show the folks how weak you are.'

Lee dropped to his knees, cavorted round the stage.

'Fifty pound. Who'll take my money? This man's a bleeding pushover.'

'A bleeding nigger,' someone called. 'Can't even walk straight.'

Several people laughed. Lee stood up. He couldn't see

where the taunt had come from but he beckoned to the crowd. Joe restrained him. 'Who's the lad out there all mouth and trousers? Who's the one thinks he can beat my boy? Ladies and gentlemen, I give you Mr Lee Leonard, light heavyweight championship contender of the West Indies. Who wants to take him on?'

No takers. The boxers could see now who it was had shouted, but the man was small. Joe appealed again: 'Don't let us all get cold up here. We want a fighter. Right then, here's my final offer, and this *is* an offer—any man, any man who'll take Lee Leonard on—just take him on, you don't have to last three rounds—will earn a tenner. Step in the ring with him and the tenner's yours.'

Joe could sense he was losing the crowd. One of the young boys already on the platform was leaning out, laughing at some girls.

'Who's that down there, son—is she your girlfriend? Your sister? And is that her friend? Are they with you and this lad here? That's lovely. Right girls, here's an offer: if the boys can do it, why can't you? Who says that girls aren't as good as boys? So my girls, it's a five-pound note if you'll fight each other! Yes, I'm serious. I am not mad, I just think I am. A five-pound note—all right, then, a *ten*-pound note—split between you. Yes? What do *you* think, ladies and gentlemen, shall we ask these lovely young girls to put on some gloves? What did you say, folks—I didn't hear you! All together now, ladies and gentlemen, do you want these girls to give us a show?'

It was the fight everybody wanted. The packed crowd watched the boys blitz through tigerish scraps—they cheered the blood, laughed when they fell—but they were waiting for that pair of game young girls. Both wore shirts and jeans. They had taken off their coats and sweaters, left shoes with Joe, slipped their hands into enormous gloves—and when they climbed up on to the stained canvas ring the crowd cheered as if the girls were opposing champions. Ribaldry was lost in thunderous noise. Joe took it seriously, and so did they. Each came out in an orthodox stance, gloves high, small face pinched in the stark light. The redheaded girl seemed more aggressive. She prowled for a few seconds, then rushed her blonde opponent. But the blonde was fast. She skipped deftly aside and clipped the other girl rushing by. The redhead turned but was caught again with a jab to the head. The crowd shrieked with joy. Already the girls had slipped into classic roles of fight-maker and counter-puncher. They fought keenly, neither holding back. A feminine instinct kept their blows face-high. The fight looked crisp, brighter than earlier from clumping boys. Noise was deafening. But in the second minute the strain began to tell; the girls moved heavily on their heels. The redhead pushed forward again and the blonde thumped her in the chest. So the redhead grabbed her, tried to maul. To hell with boxing.

Joe shouted, 'Break!'

It was a foreign language. The girls clasped each other, trying to grip with the large leather gloves. The redhead butted. The blonde jerked her knee. Then they both tried to knee each other, wrestling, arms entwined, heads pressed against the other's shoulder, hopping awkwardly with one knee poised. Joe muscled in, pushed the girls apart, called 'Break' again to no avail. They stuck together like human magnets. They didn't need the screaming crowd—they were clamped together, hopping, staggering. When Joe tried to separate them the girls fell down. The crowd laughed. Joe laughed with them. The girls leapt up, saw him laughing, and with four gloves flailing they ran Joe down.

Between shows, Jet slipped out of the trailer and joined the throng on the brightly lit midway. He wore a track-suit, and his dark hair, cut short now he was boxing, clung to his head. He reached the coconuts but she wasn't there. He cursed himself. He knew that in the evenings he was leaving Stella too much alone—there were nights when the first time he saw her was when he returned to their caravan and found her in bed. It wasn't right; she was safe among show people but shouldn't be so much on her own.

He checked with Doris but she wasn't there.

The Haunted House was near the fairground centre. Jet paused a moment by its lurid frontage before plunging down a sideway towards his home. Once there, he was struck again by the smallness of his caravan, squeezed between two trailers like a child between adults. He went inside.

Stella and Scott sat at the table. From their expressions Jet felt that he had interrupted something. Stella looked rapt, as if Scott had been telling a story, while Scott's mouth stayed open as if he had stopped mid-word.

Stella asked, 'Did you want a coffee?'

'Wondered how you were.'

'I'm fine. Are *you* all right?'

'Yeah, I'm not boxing tonight—just on show.'

'Uncle's come to keep me company.'

Jet glanced at him—still not used to Scott's bleached crew-cut and tired face. Scott said, 'Bad penny—always turns up.'

'I forgot—you wanted a decision.'

'Well, when you're ready.'

'We'll talk later.' He was aware of Scott staring at him, trying to read whether Jet would do the trip to France. 'I'm still working—there's another show.'

'Oh.' Scott watched him. 'Can I wait?'

'Of course.'

'Safe as anywhere,' Scott said with a nervous laugh.

'It may be better you stay inside. The crowd seems uneasy tonight.'

Five minutes later, Jet felt their smouldering anger rise like a heat haze from the ground. He wondered why. He was on the open-air platform with Lee and Terry for the last set, and the crowd seemed mutinous, like a mob at closing time locked outside the pub. They were shouting back at Joe Hake's patter. He was asking kids to fight but they wouldn't come. Watching the shuffling crowd, Jet recognised faces from the previous night. He saw a shaven-headed white ox that Lee had ripped apart. Was it only a day ago? It seemed a fortnight. Yet it was only last night—Thursday—that Jet had had his head whacked, that Lee had humiliated that ox. A single day. And afterwards, Jet remembered, the social worker had been waiting, had driven him to the windswept cliff. Yes. Jet scoured the crowd again, but she was not there. Well, she wouldn't be—though she might come later, despite what he'd said this morning when she came visiting with her boss. Perhaps she wanted to continue—to arrive last thing at night, go for a drive. It didn't matter; the fair would soon move on. And although he had told her not to come back, perhaps she would follow like a roadie's groupie around the West Country as they roamed. His gaze softened. At the back, behind the crowd, he spotted Collette from the Lucky Rabbit stall. She raised a hand, gave a little smile, and he grinned across at her, wondering why he had ever bothered with the boyish Kelly when sweet Collette was at the fair.

Joe changed his patter: 'Here we go then, ladies and gentlemen, we have a challenger! Make way for the big man before he treads on your feet.'

He was certainly big: sixteen stone of dull aggression, brown matted hair—and he came from that knot of buddies the ox had with him. Jet spoke in Leonard's ear: 'They found a local Tarzan.'

'To teach me a lesson?'

'That's what they hope.'

Lee watched the man climb up on stage. 'That's Bluto, man. I'll eat my spinach.'

Joe was welcoming the challenger: 'Here's a fine figure of a man, but can he win my fifty pound? Look at our challenger, ladies and gentlemen, feast your eyes on him. Hercules, I promise you—a man mountain straight from Dartmoor. I ask you, folks, to compare these men. Lee Leonard the Black Bomber—light heavyweight champion of the West Indies—weighs in at one seventy pounds. And your challenger—he's a local man—what's your name, my friend?'

'Call me Ringo,' the Mountain muttered. He had a London accent.

'Ringo!' Joe laughed into his mike.

The man pushed him. 'You think that's funny?'

Joe stumbled but continued his patter: 'Well, this is Ringo, folks—a local man from deepest Devon. But will the local challenger defeat my Bomber? What do you think, ladies and gents? Here is my Lee Leonard, one seventy pounds, and here is Mr Ringo—yes, that's his name—Mr Ringo weighing—let's see now, let's take a look at him, I've done it all me life—yes, Ringo must weigh two twenty-five. Well, how about it, ladies and gentlemen, is Lee gonna be a giant killer? Will I lose my fifty pound? There's only one way you can find out: step inside that little doorway and for just two pound—that's right, I said two pound—which is nothing, it will buy you nothing—except *here*, except *tonight*, when that trifling payment, ladies and gentlemen, will buy you the finest heavyweight boxing contest you will see for many years. And it's live, my friends, this fight will happen before your very eyes. It is a privilege. I should put the price up. I should charge a tenner. But I won't. I will not charge you ten pound. No. I will not charge you five. No. Nor four. Nor three. No. Tonight, ladies and gentlemen, you can see the heavy-weight contest of a lifetime for the paltry sum of just two pounds!'

He was heavy but he was light. Man Mountain Ringo skipped out of his corner like a man who had definitely fought before. He wore tee-shirt and jeans, and the buckle to his jeans lay like a shield across his midriff. His canvas boots looked as if he had worn them specifically to come in the ring. He reached the centre and released two vicious hooks, but Lee swayed away from them. Lee was on his mettle, elusive and out of range. He watched the Mountain's fists.

Lee moved effortlessly about the ring, making Ringo chase. He knew that many challengers who came out blazing soon burnt out like paper fires. Ringo would want to use his weight. Twice he seemed to trap Lee in a corner but each time, Lee stung him on the head and slipped away. Electric eel. In those first minutes of the opening round, Ringo might tire or land a punch. Lee looked for a chance to slow him down.

What the crowd saw was their hero making the run-ning. It didn't matter that most of the spectators hadn't heard of him before—against the fairground professional he was their man. Every move he made drew joyous noise. Every haymaker got a roar. Ringo's punches looked fearsome. Only once did he leave himself exposed, and Lee was on him in an instant with a flurry of punches, short and hard. Ringo grabbed at him. Lee slipped away.

On Ringo's face was a pinkish blotch, but it would not trouble him. He chased again.

Someone threw a coin and it struck Lee's cheek—sharp, high, making him glance sideways. It was enough. Ringo crashed in, grabbed Lee by the arms and head-butted him. Though Lee jerked away, it cracked near his eye.

'Break!'

They took no notice. Lee squirmed from Ringo's grasp, jabbing as he went. Ringo followed. Joe didn't call 'Break' again, because the crowd was enjoying what they saw. He only needed to keep out of the way. Ringo hustled after Lee but ran into jabs of steel. Lee back-pedalled. Ringo lunged and Lee jabbed his face. Ringo was angry but he was not hurt.

—Until he took a ramrod on the nose. He was jolted. The crowd knew it. Lee nipped in with fists like pistons. Ringo clutched at him, pulled him close. Lee tucked his head against Ringo's shoulder and leant close to restrict his moves.

'Break!'

Lee wouldn't. Nor would Ringo.

'I said Break!'

Ringo relaxed his grip slightly and Lee stepped back. Ringo swung at him. As Lee stepped inside, Ringo man-handled him against the ropes.

'Stand back!' Joe yelled. The crowd yelled louder.

'Break!'

Ringo forced Lee against the ropes but Lee trapped his arms. They heaved at each other. Terry rang the bell.

They did not stop.

Terry rang the bell again. Joe shouted, tried to push between them—but they were mauling each other, trying to land a punch. The crowd screamed. As Jet and Terry scrambled into the ring, Lee and Ringo continued wrestling. Joe tried to separate them, Jet and Terry helped force the men apart. As they hauled Ringo towards his corner they saw that another man had climbed in the ring, ready to fight. Terry went for him, and the man scrambled smartly back out through the ropes.

The two boxers were now in their corners. Joe, Jet and Terry confronted Ringo, but the big man sneered at what they said. In the opposite corner, Lee sat alone. A trickle of blood ran down his cheek.

There was a one-minute interval.

At the start of the second the pace was cautious. The men prowled, looking for their chance while the crowd sang at them. Lee was edging closer. When he shot a sudden left, Ringo swayed aside and defended properly, holding back from Lee, taunting him to try again. Lee circled, flicking jabs, as if on a cord that Ringo held. The crowd grew restless and wanted action. Halfway through the round, someone threw a bottle into the ring. It hit the deck, quivered, then rolled drunkenly across the canvas.

Joe stopped the fight. As he turned to the sullen crowd, Lee kicked the bottle out of the ring, watching Ringo while he did so. Joe clicked his mike: 'If someone wants a fight they can put the gloves on.'

The crowd jeered.

'Now, ladies and gents, let's have some order. You want to see this fight? Of course you do. So behave yourselves.'

Someone yelled, 'You daft old gypsy! Stick one on 'im, Ringo!'

The crowd laughed.

'Box on.'

Lee was fastest. He skipped in quickly, arms deceptively loose as he flicked cutting blows. Ringo covered up. The crowd howled. Lee stayed close to him, hammering rapid stinging punches which Ringo absorbed on his broad arms. He looked frustrated, a goaded bull. He threw himself at Lee, ignoring the barrage, crashing through by weight alone. Lee clipped his head and stopped him short. For a moment, Ringo paused. But Lee was on to him again, hustling and confusing him. Lee came too close. Ringo's arms snapped about him in a wrestler's grip. The two men grappled and ignored Joe's 'Break!'. Ringo bored savagely with his head, tried to use his knee, struggled to twist his man around.

Joe shouted, 'Break! Stand back!' to no avail. The crowd bayed, enjoying what it saw. Ringo tried to wrestle Lee to the deck, and both men slithered to their knees. Then Lee was free of him, was on his feet as Ringo clambered up. For just one moment Ringo left his head exposed, but Lee waited. He would fight him clean. Once Ringo was up, Joe tried to check him but was overwhelmed. Ringo charged—into Lee's right hook. A combination rattled his head. As Ringo raised his tired arms, Lee sunk a fist deep in his belly. Ringo's eyes opened, his mouth gaped. He stood solid as a tree while Lee chopped into him—body punch, uppercut and then a hook. The big tree swayed.

Joe forced himself between them, using his back to hold Lee off. He peered into Ringo's face. When he turned to Lee, the boy was dancing, gloves poised to finish the job. Joe took his arm, but when he tried to raise it the crowd screamed, 'No!' Ringo was still on his feet.

The crowd saw Joe reach for his mike but they would not let him end the contest. They howled at him. By now, Ringo had had longer than a standing count. He raised his gloves again and shambled towards Lee. Joe stood in front of him, but the Man Mountain was an avalanche and swept him aside. Joe nodded at Terry to ring the bell.

Who knows if Ringo ever heard it? He lurched forward, thrashing at Lee—who parried, backed off and thumped him on the jaw. Ringo stood his ground but would not go down. Lee swung at his midriff. Ringo creaked, tilted, shifted on his base. Crowd noise faded.

There was a moment during which neither boxer made a move. When Joe nipped forward, Lee, staring curiously at Ringo as if unsure what to do, crashed a right hook against the big man's head. Ringo shivered, a tremor rippling to his feet. His knees buckled and he slithered to the floor.

There was one pulse-beat of sickened silence. Then a lone voice, male, cracking at the edge, called, 'Bastard hit him after the bell.' The crowd erupted.

Jet and Terry slipped inside the ropes. Their movements could have been rehearsed. The four men—Joe and his three powerful boxers—stood each at the midpoint of a rope, facing the crowd as it screamed invective. Behind them, motionless on the canvas, lay the fallen Ringo. He would have to wait.

THIRTY

Stella was asleep. When Jet bent over her he did not kiss her in case she woke. He turned his head to look at Scott seated at the table. Almost the entire length of the tiny caravan lay between them, as if Scott and Stella had stayed deliberately apart, and Jet again felt he had interrupted some communication between them. But it wasn't possible: Stella was asleep.

Scott said, 'She got bored with me.' He was playing Patience with his own well-used pack of cards. He looked bored himself, not interested enough to cheat.

Jet sat down with him and Scott placed a card. 'Finished working now?'

'Yeah.'

'Much fun?'

Jet shook his head.

'No. It doesn't look like it.'

Jet said, 'We had a man took on Lee Leonard. A big man. He got hurt.'

'Leonard?'

'No, the other one. Had to get a doctor. That's why I'm late.'

Scott placed another card. 'Do you enjoy this? Hurting people—getting hurt yourself?'

'That isn't why we do it.'

Scott chuckled. 'Still no way to live. What're you going to do?'

Jet sighed. 'I'll see the season out. Then . . . I might go in with Joe—'

'No, that isn't what I meant. What are you going to do about the postcard, the trip to France?'

'Ah.'

'Be there and back by tea time. Then I'll disappear.' Scott kept an eye on him. 'I'll stay out of the way, I won't hang around. Then in a week or so, when they've got the postcard, I'll slip across to Ireland, fly out from there. They'll have stopped looking, see?'

'You reckon?'

'They've got other things to do. You hardly hear the story on the radio now—I'm not news any more. But don't worry, I'll pay you before I disappear.'

'I'm not doing it.'

'Don't be daft. A hundred thousand—it'll change your life.'

'I don't want the money.'

'For Christ's sake! You don't have to *do* anything—a day out is all. Has boxing mashed your brain?'

'Count me out.'

'I'm your brother. If you don't want the money, do it for me.'

'What do *you* want with the money, Scott—are you going to give some to Claire and Tommy?'

Scott looked away. 'Yeah, of course. Actually, I already did—because I was thinking about paying *you*. I put some in a parcel and posted it to Dad.' He put down his cards. 'How much d'you think was right? I've got so much that it's kind of meaningless, you know?'

'Don't you want to see your son again?'

Scott stared at his unfinished game. 'Sure, one day.'

'You just walked out on them as if they didn't exist.'

'It's too late for that. I've got my own life I want to live.

Listen, I did not steal this money just to live the same old life abroad. I want to do something—enjoy myself.'

'Without your family.'

'I'll send them more money—lots of it—when I get a chance. They'll have a few thousand anyway—Monday's post. It's something, isn't it? Christ, Jet, you've been through this—you and Angie—you know how couples fall apart.'

'That was different.'

Scott snorted. Jet said, 'When we broke, everyone expected it. Everyone except me. But you and Claire weren't like us. You didn't have arguments all the time. Have you found a girl?'

'No.'

'Then why?'

'Nothing dramatic, nothing at all. That's the point, Jet, we had nothing at all. We just shared a house.'

They wouldn't look at each other, as if it was their own relationship which had petered out. The two brothers sat in the softly lit caravan, staring into shadows. It was late, the fair had closed, but occasional crowd noise came from outside. Shouts and jeers.

Scott said, 'She won't miss me. She never had me— well, not recently. But once she's got the money she can start again. I tell you, there's thousands of couples— millions—would give their eye teeth for a chance like that. I mean, think of it, Jet! Wipe the whole slate clean. Three wishes time. Start your whole damn life again. Fantastic. One day, she and I, we might meet someplace abroad, by accident, and she'll admit that I acted for the best.'

Jet's thoughts seemed elsewhere. He was not listening to Scott. 'What's all that noise?'

Outside, the shouting had grown more insistent. There

were other noises. Jet jumped up, went to the door and opened it.

A surge of crowd noise. A roar. Shouts. Jet turned. 'Look after Stella. Keep the door shut!' He disappeared.

It was on the midway. As Jet ran between two trailers he could see action in the light. He heard the call of 'Sticks!'

Once he was on the midway Jet joined a knot of burly fairground men. He had a stick thrust into his hand—a metal tent peg, a metre long.

'Sticks!'

He and the showmen were outnumbered by the mob— about forty men, tough, young, here for a fight. They stood swaying, jeering, singing what sounded like football chants. They looked truculent and prepared, and at their heart Jet recognised the ox-man with his shaven head. He heard the crowd's chant consolidate, become one word: 'Ringo-o. Ringo-o.' They were edging forward.

'Sticks!'

Fairground men were still appearing from the shadows. Where there had been fifteen, there now were twenty. Several more to come.

'Ri-ingo-o.'

The mob began to realise they should not have waited. Ride boys and canvas-men were still emerging from the dark. Two dozen now. Anyone in the crowd who had his eyes open could see that the fairground men held sticks, were pressed together in a unit, were moving forward.

The mob splintered. A group in the centre surged forward and the edges broke away. The centre charged at the men with sticks but broke like a wave on a harbour wall. Two men fell. The showmen moved forward like a drilled platoon, and before them the youths started backing off, pretending that they weren't fleeing. As the showmen advanced, the youths shouted, scurried and flung clods of mud.

Retreating along the midway, the mob suddenly scattered between the stalls, hammering the woodwork as they ran. They were being chased to the dark perimeter where the trailers stood. Where women and children waited. Several had pans of scalding water. One or two held kitchen knives. A kid with a three-foot spike nipped low and fast, swinging his stave at the strangers' knees.

Now they began to run in earnest, pounding the trailers as they passed. A window shattered. But these were the acts of a retreating army, as showmen chased them from the fair.

It was a one-sided contest, with the town boys scattered and disorganised. Those who had left the lighted walkways ran into groups of women between the stalls, no less ferocious than their men. The townies ran like frightened cats. Till the fairground entrance. There, as if to block it, appeared a tractor. While retreating youths flooded past it, the large tractor accelerated through the entrance, churning mud on the sodden midway. On board were four men with wooden poles—larger than the staves the showmen used—and the four townies struck out at any attempt to board. The tractor rammed a Chip'n'Hot Stuff stall. Then it reversed to try again. By now the battle to board it had grown furious. Several townies came back to help, while those on board lashed out with their sticks. By now canvas-men were all about, some climbing on. One grabbed the heavy steering wheel and the tractor turned, almost missed the stall, but caught the corner. The glancing blow crumpled the front support, and the wooden booth sagged like a dismantled tent. The tractor teemed with fighting men. It headed drunkenly for the exit, bumping into stalls, missing men by inches as they stumbled from its wheels.

In the confused mêleé in the tractor's wake the canvas-men regrouped. This was a skirmish without uniforms, and only showmen knew who was on which side. They cracked at the floundering townies, chased them out like sheep. Jet was in the thick of it. He saw Lee Leonard grab a man from the mud and toss him away like a sack of grain. He hit the ground and crawled away.

Showmen were gathering at the entrance, hitting stragglers as they scuttled through. Out in the car park Jet saw the ox-man standing on the tractor to rally his troops, but they were losing heart. Some drifted away. Some shuffled in the dark.

Lee grabbed Jet's arm. 'Bad scene, man.'

'If we don't chase them they'll be here all night.'

'No, they're ready for their beds. Listen, were you still in your caravan when they had a go at it?'

'What?' Jet stared into Lee's dark eyes.

'No? You better take a look at it, 'cos we're through here.'

But Jet was running back to his caravan. He shot along the midway, past fairground families checking damage, and slipped behind the stalls to the heavy trailers. It was quieter, darker, though every trailer showed an inside light. He slowed. At first glance his caravan seemed as he had left it, but as he drew closer he saw the broken window. Sprayed in paint above it were the words '*Boxer Here*'. Something about the crudity of the lettering made the caravan look as if it had been jolted out of line. But he didn't stop to think about it. The door was unlocked. No one was inside.

The stillness inside the caravan was unreal, as if the cramped interior had been preserved as a museum exhibit. He went to Stella's empty bed and put his hand beneath the blankets. It felt cold. He stared about him as if she could be there.

Scott's playing cards lay abandoned on the table. Jet stared at them, but they were only cards; they didn't tell him anything; they held no message. When he looked about the caravan for a note his shoes crunched on broken glass.

From outside he heard the sound of police sirens, more than one. Late as usual.

He went out on to the steps and peered into the semi-darkness. The sirens stopped mid-bray. Though there were still a few isolated shouts in the night, he guessed that most of the crowd would have disappeared. Everything seemed a long way away.

In the dark pathway between the trailers he saw two people run across a gap and slip inside a vehicle. He saw another man, perhaps the Duke, walking in the shadows. Jet called, 'Stella!'

No one replied.

She must be with Scott—of course, she had to be. The disturbance would have frightened both of them—Stella, because she was a child, Scott because he was a wanted man.

Who had broken the window? Jet turned to read the two stark words, '*Boxer Here*'. Who had painted that? He imagined a splinter group from the crowd running through the dark to the one caravan marked out for them. He saw them smash the window. He saw them burst inside. Was that what had happened?

No, it surely could not have been like that.

Behind him, he pushed the door to but did not lock it— Stella might not have taken her key. Through the semi-darkness he walked to the back of the fair, as far away as he could get from the police in the car park at the front, and he called Stella's name again. He stared into the dark behind the fairground. There was no one there. Suddenly he turned and began to search methodically among the dimly lit booths. Though police were talking to people at the front entrance, most of the fairground people kept away. As did he. He asked anyone he saw in the walkways if they had seen his child.

Inexorably, he came towards the front. He paused. No one among that remaining small crowd would have noticed Stella, and Jet wanted to stay away from the police. He wandered back towards the Haunted House. Though the House itself was now dark and closed, there was a light from the wagon beside it where Doris lived. He knocked at her door and it opened straight away.

Doris was clad in a red dressing gown which almost touched the floor. 'Hello, my love. Thought you was the law. You come on in.'

Once they were inside the amber-lit interior, Doris unwrapped the front of her huge red dressing gown to reveal that beneath it she was fully dressed. 'Just for show, my love. I'd have tweaked them that I'd been in bed.'

'Police won't come here.'

'Why not? Them coppers likes to wake us up.'

'Have you seen Stella?'

Doris laughed. 'You haven't lost my little dove, have you?' She saw his face. 'Something wrong?'

'Someone attacked my caravan. She was in it.'

'Who could've done such an awful thing?'

'I thought she'd be safe.'

'Oh Jet, no one would take the child! She must've run off. Bet your life she's hiding somewhere.'

'That's why I came to you—'

'She'll come back, my love. You've made me feel quite peculiar. We better have a drink.'

'No, I—'

'Have a glass of rum. Do you good. I'm going to.'

From a small cupboard in the pine-clad wall she produced a bottle of dark Navy. The glasses were out on display, together with the sparkling china and silver ornaments. Her home was as crammed and fussy as a Victorian parlour, and it was hard to remember that they were in a three-ton truck. Doris poured rum generously, like Victorian wine. 'Rum for your tum, that's what they say. Settles you down.'

The heat inside the wagon was beginning to get to him, and without asking he sank into a chair. Doris thrust the glass into his hand and smiled down at him. 'Bottoms up, my love.' She drank. 'My Harry used to like a glass of rum. Used to say—well, you know.'

'No?' Jet closed his eyes.

'You're far too young.'

Jet snorted. Fumes of rum had filled his nose.

'Well, whisky makes you frisky, and brandy makes you randy—but it's a glass of rum as makes you come.' Doris laughed.

'I hope you're not trying to seduce me, Doris.'

'We'll see about that! You don't drink beer, do you, Jet?'

'Why—does it make you queer?'

'No good to no one. Gin keeps you thin, stout brings it out.'

'Sherry?'

'Makes you merry, you know that. But a girl who drinks port is a girl who soon gets caught.'

'Doris, where d'you think Stella would go to hide?'

'Well.' Doris put down her glass. 'If she was in trouble, the first person she'd run to is you. Bet money on that.'

'Suppose she couldn't find me?'

'Hm. I suppose she'd come to me.'

'That's what I thought.'

'Now listen, my love, don't you go getting gloomy on me. No one is going to harm that dear little girl. I wish she was *my* daughter, and that's a fact. It'd be nice to have a child again.'

Doris raised her glass to the light and the facets sparkled. She said, 'At first, when my Harry died and Marianne was gone, I used to hire a young lad to help me on the rig. But it never worked out. Those boys, they'd always try to take advantage. There was one—he used to sneak his girlfriends inside my Haunted House—well, you can imagine. He'd get the girl frightened, and my, my, my.'

'I must go, Doris. Though it's cosy and warm in here.'

'Not just the rum, you know.' She watched him stand. 'These wagons is better than houses—they keep you warmer. Now, don't you worry—I bet your Stella is back in the caravan now, wondering where you've got to. So you give her a great big kiss from me.'

'When I find her.'

She wasn't in the caravan; she wasn't with Duke; no one had seen her. By this time, a single police car was parked across the entrance to the fair with three men beside it, arguing wearily. Another group was clearing up the Chip'n'Hot Stuff stall, and inside the fairground a few rough repairs were being made. As Jet passed the darkened Dodgems, one of the ride-boys asked if he'd found his daughter.

'I was going to ask *you* that.'

'She'll be around. Probably wondering where you are.'

It was possible. She wasn't in any of the obvious places, so Jet continued to the boxing booth. Like the other stalls it was not illuminated, and although he knew she couldn't be inside he approached the entrance. He heard his name. In the deep shadow beside the small stall opposite were Collette and Terry.

'Still not found her?' Collette asked.

Jet shook his head. 'I thought she might have come here.'

'No,' said Terry with a grin. 'Me and Joe came back to guard it. I've been here ever since.'

'I'll still take a look.'

'Don't you believe me?'

'She might be inside.' Jet climbed on to the platform.

'I was giving Collette a hand. They done her stall.'

Jet faced them from the stage. 'Much damage?'

'Nothing I can't manage,' Collette said. 'On my own.'

Terry shrugged.

Jet moved the flap and went inside. It was totally dark. When he found the switch the interior shuddered with sudden light. He shielded his eyes. 'Stella! Stella, are you in here?'

Nothing. Footsteps behind. Terry said, 'I told you.'

Jet nodded. He felt tired. 'Did they attack here too?'

'Tried to. It was only kids.' Terry wandered past him.

In the glaring light the booth looked tawdry, its walls streaked with shadow, the ropes sagging round the ring.

'I'll check in the trailer.'

'Joe'll be in there.'

Collette had followed them into the booth, and she touched Jet's arm. 'She isn't here.'

'All the same—'

'I'd have seen her.'

'Yeah, and I would,' agreed Terry. 'I've not been away.'

Jet looked at him. 'No?'

'What's up?' Joe Hake appeared from the other doorway. 'Hi, Joe.'

'What you doing—you know what time it is?' Joe wore a coat above pyjamas. Collette said, 'He can't find Stella. She's not with you?'

'Me? No. She'll be at someone's trailer.' He glared at Jet. 'You do know whose fault this is, don't you? That fucking Leonard—excuse my French. They were looking for him.'

Jet said, 'I know.'

'Too much to prove, that boy. He ain't the fairground type.'

'He's black for starters,' Terry said.

'Give it up. That's what made him do it—people shouting up at him, calling names.'

'Should be used to it,' laughed Terry. 'It's not as if he's only just *turned* black.'

No one else laughed.

Jet said, 'Someone marked my caravan.'

Terry turned. 'What, marked it out, you mean?' He grinned.

'Good guess.' Jet stared thoughtfully at him. 'But of course, you've been here all the time.'

'Yeah. What you saying?' Terry bobbed his head evasively as if in the ring.

'No, it couldn't have been you, Terry. Whoever painted it knew how to spell.'

'You accusing me, or what? I've been here—ask Collette.'

She shrugged disinterestedly. 'I don't know.'

'I been helping you clear up.'

'Did I ask you to?'

'Wasn't I?'

'Yes.'

Jet asked, 'Where were you before the fight?'

'What fight?'

'The yobbos, idiot, before the mob came in.'

'You saying I invited them?'

'And where were you straight *after* they came in, when the trouble started?'

'Before or after? Make up your mind.'

'After—when it started—'

'Oh, *after*, not before—'

Jet pointed. 'Don't get funny with me! You painted that on my wall.'

'Don't fucking point at me.'

'You did it, didn't you?'

'Stop it!' Joe's roar filled the empty booth. 'Terry, you get over here. Jet, don't you bloody move. Christ, as if I ain't got enough bleedin' trouble.'

Terry cheerfully obeyed. Joe sent him to the trailer. 'Jet, I think you need some sleep. We all do.'

They stared at each other without animosity. 'So your daughter's missing? You better look for her.'

Jet nodded, and Collette came close. 'I'll help,' she said.

He didn't speak till they were outside. Then he said, 'You better carry on and fix your stall.'

'It's fixed. That Terry, I couldn't get rid of him. Said he wanted to walk me home.'

'I bet.'

'So I'd be safe! Some hope.' She glanced at him. 'Did he write something on your caravan?'

'I expect so.'

'He's a burke. God, it's cold. I hope Stella isn't . . .'

'What?'

'Out in it.'

She took his hand and squeezed it before she spoke: 'She'll be all right. Townies don't like show people, but this had nothing to do with her. They wouldn't hurt a child.'

Jet grunted.

'Let me help you look.'

He hesitated, then said, 'Thanks. OK, we'll do a circuit of the fair—you go that way, I'll go this.'

If Collette had meant that the two of them should look together she didn't say so.

Somehow, once they had parted, the night seemed

colder and more dark. Hardly anyone was about. A chill dampness was in from the sea. When Jet eventually arrived at his caravan, even from a distance it looked forlorn. Inside, the air was cold. The broken window shone against the black night sky like shattered ice. He fetched a dustpan and began to sweep glass splinters from the floor. They had scattered everywhere, and he would be finding them for weeks. Each time he found another he would remember the night that Stella disappeared.

He heard a step.

Collette was in the doorway. She said, 'She'll be all right, I'm sure.'

He continued sweeping. She said, 'With all that fighting, no one would have noticed her slip away.'

'Maybe.'

'She'll be in one of the trailers.'

'Someone would have told me.'

Collette knew that that was true. After a moment she suggested she make some coffee.

'I don't need it; I won't sleep.—You're probably right, she'll be OK.'

He smiled wearily. He had made too much of this: obviously Stella was with her uncle Scott. Collette shifted in the doorway: 'Jet, you can't just sit alone and wait.'

'No?'

'Let me sit with you.'

He forced a smile. 'No. Please. I'm better on my own.'

She stared at him, and he looked away. Then she said, 'Well, some other time, perhaps.'

'Some other time.'

THIRTY-ONE

When daylight finally thinned the darkness, Jet was almost asleep in his chair. He had spent the night trying not to worry: Stella must be with Scott and by now would be sleeping soundly. To her this would have been an adventure. But thinking of Scott reminded Jet of the decision he had to make. France. He didn't want to think about it. If he refused to make the trip, Scott would continue to badger him. Jet was his only hope, he'd say. Scott was fixated at the best of times, and this was hardly that. He would hang around the caravan, pestering Jet to go. Neither brother would shift his ground. Scott *couldn't* shift his. He would appeal to Jet as his brother, saying he was his one way out, and Jet would become increasingly uncomfortable until eventually he sent Scott away. But he knew that he couldn't do that—send his brother off to fend for himself alone. On the other hand he did not want to get involved with the money. Scott carried the air of a doomed venture with him like an ill-fitting coat, and Jet knew that if he allowed himself to become involved he would be sucked into his brother's failed enterprise. Enterprise! Robbery and murder. He must not become embroiled in that. The best thing for him to do was to tell Scott right away, to repeat that he would not go to France and that was that. Though, of course, Scott would simply stay with them in the caravan, sitting at their table like a ghost who would not quit.

Maybe he'd persuade Stella to wheedle at Jet. Maybe even now he was persuading her of his case—telling her, ask your Daddy, get him to do this little thing for me. She wouldn't understand—she'd see that her uncle was deep in trouble and that her father refused to do the simplest thing. She knew about Scott and the robbery, but being a kid she would think it exciting, nothing more. Tonight, perhaps Scott had shown her some of the stolen money, using it to bind her to his gang—just you and me and Daddy, was what he'd say.

To see the money would make it real. Jet didn't want Stella infected by it—neither did he want to see a note of it himself. He did not want to believe that Scott could have done the robbery, that he had killed a man, that he had left his family, just like that. All Jet wanted was to stay here with the fair and to bury himself in its world. Inside his caravan in the corner of the fairground, he was away from that exterior world—from townies and their burdensome possessions—from stolen money and the law. His brother's fantasy of a life abroad, luxuriating in the sun, had no reality for Jet—he neither believed in it nor wanted it. He just wanted to stay where he was. Show people had become his family; tonight had made that clear—their unity against the townies, and the way that, despite the fracas, they had found time to tell each other about the missing Stella and had shown him that they wanted to help. Travelling people bonded, had more empathy with each other than outsiders knew.

It was time for breakfast. He had sat in the chair so long his joints had stiffened like mortised wood. In the town outside, people would be getting ready for work—no, this was Saturday. Even so. But if he listened carefully he could hear the drone of their outside world—a faint traffic noise, of course, but also an underlying thrum that was the combined sound of people waking, talking to each

other, turning on their radios and starting cars. That
pattern, all those people doing much the same, was what
his brother must have wanted to leave behind. Perhaps
Scott would enjoy the fairground, with its unhurried
mornings.

Someone knocked on the door. Jet eased to his feet.

Waiting on the steps were Kelly Rice and that boss of
hers—Meaburn, that was his name—wearing the same
cheap suit as yesterday, with his lifeless hair freshly
combed. Kelly was in her raincoat, her hair too short to
have been combed.

'Mr Heywood?' asked Meaburn, with a nervous chuckle.
'Remember us?'

Jet didn't bother to answer. When he looked at Kelly
she looked away.

Meaburn asked, 'May we come in, sir?'

'What for?'

'It might be better.'

'I prefer outside.'

'It's a little more private inside, Mr Heywood. We'd like
a word with Stella, if that's all right.'

'She's out.'

'These little girls—they get up to anything! Yes, they
do. Now, as you know, she hasn't been attending school.'

'It's Saturday. We've been through that.'

'Quite right. I understand. But we are just a touch
concerned about—'

'Go away.'

'You really must let us—'

'Go.'

'Mr Heywood, we don't want to upset the child—'

Jet had turned to go back inside. Kelly said, 'Your window's broken.'

'I know.' He closed the door on them.

Though Jet had fixed cardboard across the shattered

window, Meaburn's voice could still be heard: 'There are people in my office who might say this wasn't a suitable upbringing for a child. They might indeed. So we have to speak to you, Mr Heywood.'

'Go away!'

Meaburn pounded at the door. When Jet pushed it open, Meaburn scuttled down the steps. He cowered when Jet followed, but Jet made no attempt to touch him.

'No way you'll see my daughter. Go back to your office and do something useful.'

Meaburn glanced at Kelly. 'We must insist—'

'You want me to hit you? Is that the only way you'll leave?'

Kelly said quickly, 'Jet, don't make us call the police. We have to speak to Stella. There's no choice.'

'What d'you mean, no choice?'

'It's too late now.' She was pleading but he would not soften.

'Any talking we can do out here.'

Meaburn bristled. 'One might almost believe you were hiding your daughter from us.'

'No.'

But Jet knew that they would not leave. Other people had emerged to watch. One asked, 'Hey mister, did you drive here?'

Meaburn's eyes flickered. For some reason he would not look round. 'I think that must be our affair.'

'You better check your car's all right.'

Meaburn glanced at the man.

'Be only sensible, I'd say.'

A young boy laughed and Meaburn sighed. He returned his gaze to Jet. 'Mr Heywood, I must insist that you give us access—now—to your daughter Stella. I must warn you—'

A pebble landed near his feet. He turned on the boy

who had thrown it, but a man moved instantly between them. The boy peeped out from behind the man's legs: 'You from the Social?'

Meaburn turned away. The boy said, 'Let's have a game of football in the car park.' He laughed and ran away.

'Is that where your car is?' Jet asked.

'I—I won't have this. Are you threatening me, Mr Heywood?'

'Me?'

Other showmen were arriving. Meaburn held his ground. 'We demand to see your child.'

One or two people glanced at each other, knowing that Stella had disappeared. Someone muttered, 'Bloody cheek,' and a woman who Jet hardly recognised walked up and tapped Meaburn on the chest: 'Why d'youse pick on travelling people? Why us? We looks after our kids— we're with them all the time. *We* don't send them off all day out of sight.'

'And in the evenings,' someone added, 'our kids are with us. We know where our kids are every moment—not like townies.'

Meaburn was growing redder under attack. Kelly tried to calm things: 'Please believe that we're here to help. We're on your side—'

'*Out*side's where you belong!'

Kelly tried again: 'We realise that travellers are a valid minority in a multicultural—'

But Meaburn had had enough. 'You people don't deserve help! You disobey rules, you don't pay taxes, you drive filthy vehicles from town to town—'

'We're not pikeys!'

'You make too much noise, you're dirty, your kids are uncontrolled—'

'And they take your car apart,' Jet added.

Meaburn screamed at him: 'You stand there, condoning vandalism. You encouraged that boy!'

Kelly tried to restrain him. 'Mr Heywood's only trying to warn us. He has not refused access before—he has been helpful, and I'm sure he will be again.' She glanced at Jet but he was looking beyond her. 'He's a loving father.'

Jet had moved. In a curiously shambling gait he shouldered through the group of people as if unsure whether to walk or run. Further along the sideway was his missing daughter, walking stiffly—almost warily. Perhaps she was walking in that odd fashion because of the crowd outside her caravan, or perhaps because of the person at her side. The woman beside her could hold both Stella and Jet in check. It was her mother Angie.

To see them look at her warmed Angie's heart. It was the second splinter of warmth that morning and she was grateful for it. She had been cold in bed, cold when she had dressed in the frugal boarding house, cold at breakfast, cold in the car, cold as she sat outside the fairground rehearsing her lines. She hadn't liked those lines; they sounded false—and if she could not believe in the lines herself, why should Jet? It was a rotten script. Yet it was then, while she sat in the freezing car, that she had had her first flash of warmth, a glimpse of sun on a foggy day. As if Fortune itself had lent a hand, her daughter Stella had been delivered—literally delivered—outside her door.

Angie had remained in the car, letting the child stroll through the fairground entrance, in among the stalls. She had had to wait till Scott drove away. She recognised him, of course, despite his lightened hair—yet the mild shock of seeing him there so unexpectedly seemed to jam her thoughts. For those few jolting seconds she was indecisive.

Should she stay in the car and follow him? She decided

not: in films someone might follow a criminal to his lair, but not in real life. Scott would see her following. In films, people rarely noticed the car behind, but in the quiet streets of Bude—and especially as Scott arrived wherever it was he was hiding, as he slowed and parked, ever cautious—he would see the car behind. But she had been tempted. Here was the man himself. Two million pounds. No. Even if she did manage to discover Scott's hideout, it would be a temporary resting place—the money would not be there. And in any case, then what? Angie could hardly threaten that unless he paid her she would betray his whereabouts—that sort of thing again only worked in films. Her threat would have no weight. And if she told the police the money would be gone.

Besides, before she could carry out her threat, Scott would disappear. She couldn't stop him. She could do nothing on her own. But in that fairground car park, in those few seconds when she had seen his face, Angie had made her choice. Given longer, she might have switched on her car and followed him, but she doubted it. Her original plan remained sound—and was strengthened now by seeing the child. As she had guessed, Scott had come running to his big brother—and in fact, those two brothers had come so close to each other that Stella could move freely between them. Yes, as Angie had suspected, Jet and Stella were the best route to Scott.

'Hello, Jet. Who are all these people?'

Angie enjoyed the moment. She held her blonde head high. Though she had not expected an audience she appreciated the way everybody turned to face her.

Stella left her side, but instead of rushing to Jet she walked to him, meeting her father in an awkward embrace, barely touching. As if to ward him off, she held her teddy night-gown case in front of her, tight against her chest. Jet placed his hand on her head but kept his eyes on Angie.

'Something happened?' Angie asked.

A balding, dull-looking man in a suit drifted towards them. 'Good morning, Stella. Do you remember me?'

'You're the social worker,' Stella said.

Of course he was; Angie did not need the man identified, she knew the type. He said, 'That's right, Stella. We've come to talk with you. Can we go inside?'

'What's this about?' Angie asked. She was not going to be left outside.

'And who are you?'

'Where I come from, mister, a gentleman introduces himself to a lady.'

Someone chuckled.

The man hovered over Stella as if afraid that she might run. 'I'm afraid this is none of your business, madam. We have work to do.'

'I *beg* your pardon?'

The man ignored her, squinting at the small crowd around him like an inept school teacher in an unruly class. 'Would you all please return to your caravans? Please. This is a family matter, I'm afraid.'

'I'm her mother,' Angie said.

She enjoyed that. The portly guy paused, his mouth slack, dead as a bloater on a slab. His sidekick—some redhead with an urchin cut—looked as if she was about to sneeze.

'I've come back,' Angie explained.

She couldn't tell which of them looked the more depressed. Angie gave the redhead a speculative look, which was not returned. The man clicked into life. 'You can't all be living in this caravan.'

'People do.'

The redhead spoke: 'But there are only two beds.'

'That's all we need.'

Angie grinned fetchingly at Jet but he would not respond. Here she was, come back to help them, and all he and Stella could do was clutch at each other. They looked like an ad for the Widowers and Orphans Fund. His face seemed pale, and Stella held her teddy-case in her hands as tight as if it held her dowry.

The redhead again: 'Are you telling us you slept the night here?'

'Has it spoilt your fun?'

A beauty, which struck the little redhead right where she lived. Angie said, 'I have enjoyed our chat, but we must be getting along. Come on, Stella.'

She was moving past the social workers when the roly poly man tried again: 'Wait a minute. Excuse me. How do we know that you're this man's wife? You could be anyone.'

'This man's wife? One way of putting it. Stella, honey, tell the feller who I am.'

There was a tiny pause before the child admitted, 'She's my mother.'

'Are you sure?' the man demanded.

'What d'you mean, sure? Think she doesn't know her own mother? Tell him, honey.'

The child was silent.

'Oh, she's jealous,' said Angie lightly. 'You know how girls can be.' She gave the redhead a triumphant smile. 'But if you'll excuse us, we have some catching up to do.'

It seemed extraordinary that this had ever been her family. She had been *married* to this man. He was not a stranger, of course—she recognised every feature, every mannerism, as she might recognise items in a long-lost closet of old clothes. He was still good-looking—distinctly so, since he was fit—but he did not attract her. Not really.

He would be easy enough to go to bed with, but it would mean no more to her than slipping into that old set of clothes.

She sat on his bed inside the caravan while he and Stella made coffee. Little Stella had grown older—but although it was mildly interesting to see how her daughter had developed, Angie felt no maternal tug at the heartstrings, however *that* might feel. Stella looked a sweet kid but the world was full of them. And since Stella obviously loved her father—Angie could tell from the way the child stayed close to him—there was no need for her to feel guilty. Jet and Stella were happier this way. They should be grateful: without Angie around, they had made themselves a cosy little home.

Which was what it was. Look at him: thirty years old and in a caravan. How different it had once seemed! When she had married Jet he had seemed bound for fortune—success of some kind, at any rate. Gottfleisch used to say that Jet could be British champion; he talked of future world title fights. Everything about Jet in those days had been full of promise—promise of success. And Angie liked successful men. What was wrong with that?

What was wrong, Angie thought wryly, was that she never did pick successful types. Fast starters but poor finishers—like herself, perhaps. Hardly out of school she became engaged to the son of a local club owner, but he ended up in jail. Marriage called off. Before his sentence was even decided she had met Abraham—beautiful speaker, beautiful body, said he worked in films—and she had fallen for it. Yes, the corniest of lines but she was only nineteen then, so it didn't hurt *too* much. Then came the City type. He had told her—maybe he believed—that he hankered for kinky sex, mutual exploration and supreme fulfilment, but it turned out all he really wanted was young flesh. He had a wife. He went back to her. And after that came Jet, rising fast in boxing, set for the top. So she married him.

Their early days were wonderful. Money almost flowed. Before the ceremony she had let herself become pregnant. 'I'm not pressurising you,' she had said, 'but I want your baby whatever happens.' Resist that.

He didn't. And if he had? If he'd left her pregnant? One in three kids are bastards anyway.

After four years the marriage had started mouldering. Jet lost two crucial fights, Gottfleisch withdrew support, money melting like slush in spring. Angie found herself stuck in a little flat, looking after a kid who suddenly seemed as tiresome and restricting as every other brat, and life closed in on her. Her life was one third through. The next third could look like this—raising kids in dreary surroundings on a fitful income. That would be two thirds and nothing done. The last third wouldn't matter anyway.

Angie had always believed that people who got anywhere in this world were separated from the herd by the way that they did not put up with things. Angie would not either. She couldn't. It was not her fault. She did once try to explain to Jet that it wasn't him that she had grown tired of, it was how they lived. But he wouldn't listen—talked of families and responsibility. Eventually Angie had pointed out that since he seemed unable to support her, it was her responsibility to support herself.

Heigh-ho.

Now here the pillock was, living proof. In direct contact with two million pounds—two million pounds!—yet living squalidly in a caravan. She shook her head. A residual softness for the man stopped her from feeling too contemptuous—Jet was what he was and that was that.

Stella placed a coffee in Angie's hands. The mug was warm, comforting—making Angie suddenly realise how cold it was in the caravan. It was cold everywhere today.

She stood up, wrapping both hands around the mug to draw some warmth from it. She saw Stella waiting in front of her and did not know what to say.

'How long has the window been broken?'

'Someone threw a stone through it last night.'

They continued to stare at each other till Stella asked, 'Have you come back to stay with us, Mummy?'

Angie chuckled nervously. 'Daddy and I haven't talked about that yet. I had to get rid of those social workers. But I miss you, sure.'

When she glanced at Jet she found him staring at her, also clutching a mug of coffee. He said, 'Thanks anyway.'

She said, 'They'll be back.'

'Doesn't matter. The fair leaves tomorrow.'

'Oh, it's Saturday. I forgot.'

They smiled at each other, on common ground. She said, 'Travelling is what you like, isn't it? I suppose I'm the same—can't stay still.'

'I noticed.'

'Where'd it get us? Here we are, both on our uppers—in a caravan, for God's sake!' She flashed her old familiar grin. 'Once upon a time we did pretty well, though. Remember?'

'Hm.'

'Oh, come on, Jet, those were the good times.'

She emphasised her line with a step towards him, but Stella intervened: 'They weren't good times—you made Daddy cry!'

Jet reacted sharply: 'Stella, that's enough.'

'Well, it's true. We don't want her back.'

He lunged at her. Angie thought he was going to hit her but Stella never moved. Jet's powerful hands wrapped around his daughter's head and he pulled her close to him.

Angie whispered, 'That's an awful thing to say. I'm your mother. You're my only child.'

'I hate you.' Stella nestled against Jet's chest.

Angie took a careful breath. 'Sometimes hate and love can seem the same—have you ever noticed that? Like hot and cold. If you're in a dark place and touch a piece of ice you could think you've burnt yourself. Hot and cold can feel the same. They both burn.'

Stella gazed blankly at her.

'I don't hate you, Stella. A mother cannot hate her child—it isn't physically possible. But I do understand how you feel, and I want to put it behind us, and start again.' A brave smile.

'No.'

Jet said, 'Angie, don't do this.'

'I'm her mother.'

Jet was softening. She had to concentrate on Stella. 'Honey, I know you're hurt and angry. You see, deep down, Stella, you're afraid to release your love.—No, I've been there, honey, I understand. I really do.'

Angie squatted in front of them, her face level with her daughter's. 'Sometimes it's best to have a damn good cuddle and cry everything out. What d'you say?'

Stella's eyes were wide but Jet spoke first: 'You're talking rubbish, Angie. Go away.'

It was like a slap. 'A mother can't forget her child—'

'You did!' shrieked Stella. 'You did, you did.'

Slowly, Angie stood up. Soft and conciliatory was a mistake; it left her disadvantaged. But she gazed sympathetically at Jet. 'What did those social workers want?'

He mumbled, 'Nothing.'

'I suppose they don't approve of this environment.'

'That's their affair.'

'Look around you, Jet. Of course they don't. You're a

traveller, a single parent. Christ, even the window's broken. Couldn't you—'

'It only happened last night.'

They studied each other.

'Yes, you told me.'

Idly, she wondered whether to reveal that she had spotted his brother in the car park, but she knew she shouldn't yet. 'Those social workers, they'll hound you.'

'We finish here tonight.'

'And when you arrive at the next town they'll be waiting, won't they? You do realise the only reason they left today was because I was here?'

'So?'

'Perhaps you need me, honey.'

If Jet had been vulnerable earlier, he was not now. He had rebuilt his defences. 'Leave us alone, Angie. Just go away.'

She dropped her mild demeanour like a discarded scarf. The glance she gave around the interior was as scathing as any social worker's might be. She was well out of this. She could not live this way. Jet and Stella had sunk like sediment and would never share his brother's wealth. The Heywoods were like castaways on separate islands: Jet and Stella on a birdlimed rock; Scott—quiet Scott—marooned with treasure he could not spend. And she? In choppy water between coral reefs.

THIRTY-TWO

'People eventually give up chasing,' Doris told her. 'Half us here are running from something—no, that's not true, not the real show people. I mean those who join us, like your Dad.'

She gave an easygoing grin. In the Diamonte caravan she and Stella were drinking tea. Though Crown Derby gleamed from the pine-clad walls, Doris and Stella drank from lurid pink china given away as prizes. The cat slept on Doris's lap.

'What matters to my way of thinking is how people behaves *now*, when they're with *us*,' Doris explained.

'But suppose someone once did something horrible—if he was a murderer?'

Doris offered a piece of biscuit to the sleeping cat. 'There's murdering and killing, my little dove. One person might kill by accident, while someone else don't kill no one, but is really nasty all the time. He might be ten times as bad.'

'But killing is the worst thing you can do.'

'You think so, Stella love? Oh, look at Merlin, he's eaten every scrap of my biscuit! You naughty cat.'

'You gave it to him.'

Doris raised a painted eyebrow. 'Did I? Fancy. Now I've forgotten where I was. Yes, what about those boys who beat up old ladies, just to steal a half-empty purse? And those bullies who pick on children many a day? And those men who can't have a drink without poggering someone afterwards?'

'And spies and traitors—they're really bad.'

'I don't think there's many of *them*.' Doris tickled the cat as it stretched its neck. 'Oh, there's people out there—and I hope you never meet a single one of them—there's people who has rottenness in their bones. And the way I look at it, my dove, is that if you've done something wrong but you are sorry, and if you really try to make up for it, why, I think you deserve a chance, whatever you've done. Isn't that right, my Merlin—eh, my dove?' The cat closed its eyes. 'But if you're one of them miserable scoundrels who keeps on doing mean-hearted things, well, I think you're worse than a once-off murderer any day.'

'Worse than a man who kills someone and steals a million pounds?'

'Look: a nasty person who sticks to mean and petty crime—he gets petty punishments, don't he? So he never stops. But a decent person who makes just one mistake—they throws the book at him. They puts him in jail for years and years, and when eventually he comes out people say, oh, he did a serious crime, we can't have him round here—and he's finished, see? Meanwhile that other one is still as bad as he ever was, but he's getting away with it. So what me and Merlin says is, yes, it is important what you done, but it's what you're doing now that really counts. See? And I'll tell you another thing: my tea's gone cold, and it's high time you poured me another one.'

When Doris reached across to stroke the girl's dark hair, the cat jumped down from her lap. Stella poured two cups of tea.

'I've heard townies say we're *all* a bunch of crooks.'

'Only because we're different, my little dove. Anything that's different, it scares the townies.'

Merlin placed his front paws on Stella's lap, and she

raised her hands to let him jump up. The child spoke carefully. 'On the other side of the world there are people we've never met, and there are millions of children who never go to school at all and who don't live in a proper house, but they're still people, aren't they, like us?'

'Of course they is.' Doris sat back in her comfortable chair. 'People do live in the funniest places. You take Merlin—I reckon if he couldn't live here with me, he'd be just as happy next door in the Haunted House. Second home to him, it is. But me now, I couldn't live in a "proper house" as you call it, no, I couldn't.'

'I didn't mean—'

'I know, my dove. But if I lived in a house, I'd be lonely—never seeing who's next door, never speaking to no one. Like living in a box, you see, and frightened to come out.'

'Dad and I lived in a flat before we came here. It wasn't bad.'

'I couldn't do it. I'll tell you this, I would never sleep upstairs. No, it's not natural, stuck up there.'

Stella laughed. 'Oh, Doris—'

'No, I've known travellers go into houses and they died of it. My old great Nan, why she—' Doris dabbed her eye. 'Well, my Nan, you see, was too old to travel—or so they said—and they put her in one of they council houses on some estate. She tried it for just one night but couldn't be doing with it. So next day she went into the front room and pitched her tent right on the carpet. "These houses is all right," she says, "except they got these terrible walls. These walls, they fence you in." Well, she slept like that, on the carpet in her tent, a whole fortnight, night after night, until the end.'

'Oh, Doris.'

'It wouldn't work.'

'Did she die there?'

'Die? Why, she went back on the road, lived another

dozen years. Her and me, we're Romanies, you see, and they calls us Romanies because we roam. Of course, most of the fairground folk here now aren't Romanies—no, they're not. Just travellers. Nothing wrong with that. No. And with any luck, my dove, when you grows up, you'll be a traveller too. Would you like that?'

Stella tickled the sleeping cat. 'It's what I really want to do.'

Gottfleisch transferred the doughnut to his other hand while he answered the telephone. Beneath his vast red dressing gown he was naked, rolls of fat beneath the cloth. Craig, roped to the bed, wore leather vest and *lederhosen*. He lay on his belly with head turned sideways on the pillow.

Gottfleisch said, 'Yes?' into the receiver then nothing more. Craig closed his eyes.

'I *might* pay for the information. That depends. I'd want to hear it first.'

Craig shifted his body on the satin sheets. He was quite comfortable, despite the ropes.

'It *is* Scott we're talking about, and not Jet? Hm. Yes, I'd pay.'

Gottfleisch sniffed at the doughnut, then put it down.

'No, not until we laid our hands on him.' Gottfleisch smiled as if talking face to face. 'You will have to trust me, I'm afraid. But I keep my word, as you surely know. So let me see . . . I could go as far as ten thousand.' He licked his fingers. 'More? You're a greedy girl. No, not in advance.'

Craig had opened his eyes. Gottfleisch gazed at him absently. The blond boy listened.

'Of course I trust you. In any case, if you double-crossed me I'd have you killed. But to business: I presume he's on the move? Exactly. So there isn't time to pay you in advance. Ah, Angela, my darling child, let me offer you a special deal. The moment I have Scott Heywood back, I shall give you . . . twenty thousand pounds. That's twice what the information is worth, of course.'

He paused, then chuckled at something Angie said. Haggling over money was familiar ground to him, and he dropped his free hand to Craig's white leg and stroked the golden hairs along the calf. Craig shivered.

'What? Oh, Angela, my darling, Angela, please!' Gottfleisch purred mock disapproval. 'Ten percent of what, precisely? Gross! Where do you learn these awful words? You mean net, dear girl, after expenses—and five percent, not ten.'

He listened, smiling faintly, his plump hand at the crevice behind Craig's knee.

'I don't know. Nobody knows *exactly* how much was in the van. Ah, the newspapers, my dear! Don't believe a word. Besides, by the time I've fenced the money it'll be worth only half. All of this takes time.'

He began to tickle the inside of Craig's pale thigh.

'I am offering twenty thousand on account, made up later to five percent of the net. No, no, *you* listen, my darling girl: you don't have anyone else to turn to.— Nonsense, and you know you can rely on me. Payment guaranteed. Darling—darling, listen to me: anyone else would simply shoot you, they'd not pay up. Have you thought of that?'

Gottfleisch let his broad fingers slide beneath the hem of Craig's *lederhosen*.

'The truth is, Angela darling, that you have no bargaining power at all—but I'm a generous man. Renowned for it. Twenty thousand down and five percent of what we make.—In advance? Darling, how can I—all right, I'll tell you what: five thousand down, fifteen on delivery. Yes?

No, five, I said, not ten. Oh, ten, if you insist. I'll have it delivered—where are you, by the way?'

Gottfleisch's gentle fingers made Craig gasp.

'That's a little vague, darling, isn't it, if I'm to pay you in advance? Where should we bring the money?'

He listened, grunted, and replaced the receiver. 'I can't bear people who will not trust me. However, if Angela is in Cornwall, she is with her ex-husband. In which case, Scott must be there as well. Of course, if we find him first, I don't need to pay her, do I?'

Craig muttered, 'Women!'

Gottfleisch gripped his *lederhosen* and pulled them down. 'Who needs them, eh, dear boy?'

The man hit the deck hard, groaned, rolled over. He would not get up. Tight-lipped, Joe glared at Lee as he began the count. Lee had his hands down, was skipping on the spot. He looked bored, detached, as if these fights had no more to teach him.

Terry muttered, 'Round one again.'

'Won't listen.'

Jet held the dripping sponge as he waited to leap into the ring. Crowd reaction was mixed. Though they liked a knock-out they preferred a longer show.

Terry said, 'Joe'll give him the push.'

'You fit?'

'Yeah, I'll fight Monday. You?'

Jet didn't answer. The moment Joe arrived at Ten, Jet clambered under the ropes and ran to revive the groggy loser. He slapped the sodden sponge on the man's face and lifted his head gently from the floor. 'Sniff this.'

Smelling salts did the trick as usual, making the man yelp and jerk away. Joe began his spiel: 'In the first round of this heavyweight contest, the defending champion wins by a knock-out. So let's hear a big hand for our gallant loser. That's the way. I thank you, folks. You've been a fine crowd tonight, and on your way out be sure to show your appreciation for this gallant boy. Put your nobbins in the hat. Give him some coins. Give him a pound. Here is a boy risked everything tonight, gave us a show. He did not win his money, but you can make it up to him. Show your appreciation, ladies and gents, in the customary way—put something in the loser's hat. Was he worth a pound? I think he was.'

The gallant loser stumbled to his feet, staring after the departing crowd. No one lingered. Somewhere out there would be his friends who had watched him lose. Jet said, 'We'll take you round the back.'

'What for?' The man stared bitterly at the thinning crowd.

'Get you dressed. Patch up your face.'

'Face?' The man raised his gloved hand and touched his skin.

'You'll be all right.'

Jet led him to the side and helped him through the ropes. He wondered about Terry's forecast; if Joe did replace Lee he might not stop there. All three would be reviewed—which was why Terry would be fit on Monday, whatever happened. But Jet knew that he himself was no reserve. That coshing had done more than raise a bump. Maybe his skull was cracked. Whether it was or not, he couldn't fight again—not for some time. He'd have to talk to Joe.

It was dark and damp; there was a cold wind from the sea; yet as it was Saturday night the fair thronged with people. The Big Wheel turned. The Wheel of Fortune span. At the Dodgems stand, the cars bulged with passengers and people queued for rides. Girls screamed on the Octopus and Swirl, while their men practised on shooting galleries or lost their money in arcades. Garishly lit barkers on joints and hooplas were warmed by trade. At the Lucky Rabbit stall, Collette laughed. At the Haunted House, Doris sat in her booth. At Duke's coconut shy, he was alone.

Jet had asked Stella to go home early.

Ray Lyons and Ticky arrived at nine. First they located the boxing booth to check that Jet was there, then they asked stall-holders where they could find his caravan. But it didn't get them far. Ticky said, 'They won't blab to strangers.'

'1 could make 'em.'

Ray looked hard and dangerous. On the way down he had driven too fast, glaring through the windscreen, cursing each delay. Ticky had cowered in the passenger seat, and he still looked like a frightened weasel inside his woollen overcoat.

'Don't make a fuss, Ray.'

'Why not?'

'Draw attention. We can find it on our own.'

Ray wasn't listening. Clad in a lightweight windcheater he seemed impervious to the cold, and he stared at the passers-by as if there might be someone he would recognise. He sneered at the shooting gallery and sneered at Ticky: 'Find it on our own. The caravan won't have his name on it, will it?'

Ticky tugged gently at his arm. 'We can have a look.'

'You think it'll have red and gold letters—here lives the great Marvo?' But he followed the little man between the stalls towards the trailers that lay behind. 'Could be any one of 'em.'

'I don't think so. Big ones will be for permanents.'

Ticky seemed to know what he was doing. He approached a likely caravan wedged between two trucks and tried to peep inside. He was too small, like a kid in a grown-up's overcoat. Impatiently, Ray climbed the three steps to try the door.

'Ray, careful!'

The door was locked. As Ray peered through the caravan window Ticky stayed in the darker shadows some yards away. Ray sniffed. 'Fuck knows. Let's try another.'

Ticky felt sick. Fairground noise continued around them and the line of vehicles was suffused with secondary light. He felt exposed. 'We'll just walk along, OK?'

Ray barged past him and strode down the line of vehicles. Perhaps he *wanted* someone to challenge him. Ticky glanced to his side between the trailers to check what lay beyond in case he had to run.

Ray said, 'That looks favourite.'

The small caravan ahead had a light behind its curtain. Ticky had registered that it was occupied before he noticed the painted words which Ray had seen: *'Boxer Here'*.

'Well, well.'

Nervousness made Ticky hang back, but Ray marched forward to try the door. It wasn't locked. Ray walked in. As Ticky darted forward he heard the child inside: 'Who are you—what do you want?'

'We're police,' said Ray unconvincingly.

'Go away!'

As Ticky came in through the door, Ray's huge body blocked her from his view. He was saying, 'Yeah, police. Got some questions for yer.'

'Go away!'

'That's enough of that.'

Stella tried to scream but Ray was too close. He slammed a hand across her mouth and put his other hand behind her head. She could not move from him.

'You behave yourself, little girl. We've seen your Dad.'

She shook her head.

'Oh yes we have. He's in the boxing booth, ain't he? Right. Well, your Daddy's answering questions now—helping with enquiries.'

Ray leered at Ticky above her head. 'Where's your uncle Scott?'

She shook her head again.

'Don't tell me you don't know, girl. I'll knock your block off.'

Ticky squirmed between them. His overcoat smelt of fish. 'Be gentle. She's only small and delicate. Let *me* handle her.'

Ray didn't know about Ticky's predilections. Ticky pressed close to her, his heavy overcoat against her cotton dress. He said, 'Now, dear, we're police officers, and your Daddy's in some trouble. You could be too. In a moment, this—officer—will take his hand away from your mouth—OK? You can tell us what you know—OK? Because you mustn't be naughty to a policeman, must you?'

Ticky gestured for Ray to remove his hand but Ray ignored him: 'If she yells again—'

'She won't.'

Ticky manoeuvred his face where she could see it and he smiled at her. She was pale and wide-eyed, and in her cotton dress and cardigan she seemed to Ticky young and vulnerable. Her dark hair curled as if it had been permed. 'You're a nice girl, aren't you? You won't let me down.'

Reluctantly, Ray removed his hand. She did not scream. Ray stepped back but Ticky stayed. Stella stared at them. From outside came shrieks of laughter and distorted music. Ticky placed his hands softly on Stella's arms. 'That's better, isn't it? Eh? Cat got your tongue?'

She looked tense and didn't breathe. Ticky said, 'Let's you and me keep Daddy out of trouble. You don't want him to go to prison, do you?'

She did not reply. He touched her cheek. 'Do you?'

'You're not police.'

'Yes, we are, dear,' Ticky crooned.

'Where's your ID?'

Ticky let his hand slide down her face until it rested on her shoulder. Inside the gaping sleeve of his overcoat she could see his grubby shirt-cuff. He smelt fetid. 'Don't you love your Daddy?'

Out in the fairground people still shrieked with joy. Pop tunes churned into one melody. She said, 'He's coming back.'

'Who is?'

'My Dad'll be here any moment.'

'No, he won't—'

'And he'll smash you up. He's a boxer.'

'We know your Dad.'

Ticky smiled. His false teeth gleamed, and he massaged her shoulder while he spoke: 'You and I have got to help him, haven't we?'

'You're not police.'

'Too fucking right,' Ray snapped. But Ticky held him off, staring intently at the little girl. 'I won't let that man hurt you. Don't worry, I'm your friend.'

Stella seemed about to cry. Ticky said, 'Please tell me, dear, then he won't hurt you.' He had stopped massaging her shoulder. Now his fingers stroked her neck. 'Come on, Stella, you can trust me. That's right, we know your name.'

He smiled coquettishly and ran his finger down the buttons of her cardigan. She backed away. Ray said, 'For fuck's sake.'

Ticky excluded him again. Proximity to the little girl had quelled his fear. He was aware of nothing other than the girl. 'Come and sit here on my knee. I'll look after you.'

'No!'

'Come on.'

'I won't.'

Ray snarled, 'That's enough of that.'

But when Ray moved, Ticky scooped her in his arms. He sat heavily on her bed and clasped the struggling girl on his knee. His coat had flopped open, and he pulled her head inside it against his filthy sweaty shirt.

'What is this?' asked Ray suspiciously.

'Leave me alone with her. She'll talk to me.'

'I'll make her talk.'

'No.' Ticky nuzzled Stella's hair. 'You'll tell me, darling, won't you—if that horrid man goes away?'

Stella had become inert. Ticky whispered, 'Stella, remember, we've already got your Dad.' She wouldn't look at him. 'You're the only one can save him.' She shook her head. 'Don't you want to?'

She asked, 'How?'

In the trailer behind the boxing booth Joe Hake was laying down the law to his three men. 'You think you have a choice in this? You don't. I can pull punters from the crowd, I can make 'em fight each other, but what they really want is a display. It's what they pay for.'

Lee Leonard shrugged. 'I've given a display—every night.'

'Display? You half murder them.'

'What d'you want, Joe? I've got to slow them down.'

'*Slow* them? Oh, forget it, you're not my problem—just *one* of them—but you two, what am I paying you for?'

Terry said, 'I'm ready. I know I done my foot in, but I'm ready now.'

'Tonight?'

'Well, I'd rather Monday, you know, but—'

'Get changed. You're on. How about you, Jet?'

'I can't.'

'Your head?'

'Yeah.'

'You should see a doctor.'

'I did.'

Joe drew a breath then let it out. He smiled encouragingly: 'It can't *still* be bad.'

'It's *my* head.'

Terry filled the pause. 'Well, I'm ready, like I told you. Just don't start me off with someone good!'

'You want one of them spunky girls?'

'I wish! But listen—I could fight Jet again. No, seriously, I could gee for him. I ain't fought since Tuesday—they've all forgot. Yeah, I could come up from the crowd—'

Joe said, 'It's a thought.'

'I'm not fighting.'

'No one will remember who he is, Jet, you know that. It's a different crowd every night.'

Terry punched Jet on the arm. 'All right, then, Sport?'

Jet replied to Joe: 'I'm not doing this.'

Terry said, 'I'll be careful.'

'No.'

'You're bigger than me, Jet—I can hardly reach up to your head.'

'No.'

Joe grinned. 'Definitely no?'

'No.'

Terry laughed. Lee stretched his arms. 'Well, I'm ready, Joe. I'll take anybody.'

Joe said, 'That's the trouble.'

Stella was led into the car park between the two men. No one saw her. Ticky's brainwave: he had slipped out to buy a rubber face mask, and they led her away disguised as Snow White. She walked stiffly, each little hand clas-

ped in one of theirs. Because Ray towered above her she
had to reach up to him, but Ticky was only a couple of
inches taller, like an older brother. He was swathed in
his trailing overcoat while Stella shivered in the cold, still
wearing only a cardigan over the cotton dress. Behind the
mask, Ticky's rolled-up handkerchief was stuffed inside
her mouth and she was breathing through her nose. The
wad of material hurt her mouth, and the smell of rubber
brought tears to her eyes. She could hardly see through
the jagged eye-holes of the Snow White mask.

Ticky had insisted that they lead her through the fairground, saying they would be less conspicuous in the
crowd. But no one recognised the girl; she looked like a
kiddy with two uncles.

In the car park they stopped suddenly beside a car.
Stella scolded herself for not catching its registration
number—it might have been useful later, to tell Daddy
or the real police. If she ever spoke to them.

She and Ticky climbed in the back. Despite the rubbery
smell of the face mask she detected a new smell of stale
tobacco—and the little man smelt of fish.

The car shuddered into life. The little man lolled beside
her in the back seat with his overcoat open, his arm
around her shoulders. She jabbed an elbow in his side,
and made him gasp. 'You watch yourself, girlie. Do what
you're told.'

Ray said, 'And you keep your hands to yourself.'

But as the car moved away Ticky left his arm around
her and squeezed. She jabbed him back. Ray snarled, 'For
Christ's sake!' and Ticky removed his arm.

'I was going to take her mask off. That's all.'

'Leave it on.'

In an odd way, Stella felt protected, wearing it. But
behind the rubber her face felt hot, and with her mouth
full of wadding she could hardly breathe. The man's hand

was now loitering near her knee. She didn't know which of the two men was the more threatening. She wished Daddy was here.

Saturday night punters had filled the booth, and were roaring for their man. There was not a single paying customer who did not want to see the pro beaten. They felt humiliated, angry. Word had spread that Joe's men cheated, used weights in their gloves, that they head-butted and hit low. His boxers were not real boxers but were gypsies, tinkers, crooks on the run. Perhaps tonight would be the night that their lad did something. This one, for instance—he might be a little smaller than the pro but he seemed to know what he was about.

'This one', the local favourite, was Jet Heywood and he had Lee Leonard on the ropes. Third minute of the first round, fists flying fast, Jet pressed him, wouldn't let him slide. Joe dodged beside them. To the crowd he seemed anxious for his man, but he held his palm face down, telling Terry not to ring the bell. The crowd bellowed hate. Lee had been trying to cover up but he now swung sideways on the ropes, turning slightly to let his outside arm drop down. The crowd realised. They screamed but it was too late. Suddenly Lee struck, hit low, buried his fist in the challenger's shorts. Jet crumpled. He sunk to his knees, turned imploringly to Joe, left himself unguarded. Lee saw his head and swung for it. Incredibly, he missed. A sitting target but he missed. Joe moved between them. Lee tried to barge past him as Terry rattled on the bell. Lee didn't seem to hear it but kept tussling with the referee, trying to get past him, back at his man. Terry leapt in to help Joe lead him to his corner. When they finally hauled him away, Lee shook his fist at the crowd.

—Who were making so much noise already they could

shout no louder. Several coins landed in the ring. Lee had to step in from his corner to escape clasping hands.

Joe approached the hurt-looking Jet in the opposite corner and peered carefully into his face. He stood back and shook his head vigorously to show that in his opinion Jet should not carry on. The crowd erupted. Joe shrugged, leant forward, and squinted anxiously in Jet's eyes. 'They hate 'im, don't they?'

'Never fails.'

'All right?'

'Hardly touched me.'

'Could be an asset to the business, but . . .'

'Ambitious.'

'Too young. Shame, really.'

Joe stepped back, still frowning, while Jet mimed eagerness to go on. The crowd noisily agreed. Joe capitulated: 'Seconds out! Second round.'

Lee rushed across as if to finish it but walked straight into Jet's left arm. He recoiled. When Jet pursued him, Lee skipped away, pointing and cursing loudly. His gumshield blurred the words. Joe waved his finger as the crowd seethed. Lee tried an Ali shuffle, circling, teasing, but it didn't work. Each time he darted forward Jet seemed to catch him. To improve the sound, the boxers were slapping with the inside of their gloves. Practice ones, of course. Most of Lee's blows landed on Jet's arms; a few to the body, none to the head.

Lee nipped forward into a clinch. He trapped Jet's arm inside his own, took a half step back to let the crowd see what he was doing, then thumped two loud slaps against Jet's ribs. For some reason the referee did not notice that Lee was cheating, and the crowd had to yell out that Lee was holding as he continued to thump his trapped opponent. Had any pro been in the audience he would have wondered why Lee did not go for the other's head—

except that any pro in the audience would have had this fight sussed.

Jet flashed an uppercut and broke free. Lee jumped away and Jet pursued him—too eagerly. Lee feinted a left and stepped forward with a right cross. That blow could have felled an ape—except that Lee's arm was limp, and though the blow seemed to meet Jet's jaw it actually landed on his chest. Jet staggered as Lee pressed forward. But Jet wasn't beaten. A howl of relief came from the crowd as they saw their hero retaliate. A scrap ensued. Now the Black Bomber seemed shocked, confused, unable to put the White Hope down. Suddenly Lee was running from the fight and Jet was chasing him. Lee couldn't get away. He looked in trouble, started covering up. Jet's blows rained in, the slap of leather lost in the crowd's frantic noise. Lee couldn't shake him. He swung a desperate back-hander but it missed, leaving himself wide open. Jet caught him with a left-right combination, and Lee froze. For one instant he swayed on his feet. The crowd howled. Jet rammed a left jab to the Bomber's stomach, then a decapitating right to his jaw.

There was a mass orgasm of exhilaration.

Lee crash-landed on his back, twitched and lay strangely still. Joe dropped to his knee, forgetting the count while he patted the Bomber's face. Looking worried, Joe stood up to begin the count. At four the crowd joined in. At seven Joe stopped to wave Jet away. Eight, nine and ten were sung aloud. Joe looked again at the recumbent Lee, then with apparent reluctance raised Jet's hand. The crowd cheered. Jet could have been world champion.

By now Terry was in the ring, tending the fallen Bomber. Lee had his eyes open but he did not move, waiting till Jet glanced in his direction. When he did so,

Lee winked at him. Jet turned to grin broadly at the crowd.

Once the car had arrived at the boarding house Ray climbed out, leaving Stella and Ticky waiting in the back. She felt less safe without Ray. So that she could direct them to the house, her mask and gag had been removed— but she felt almost naked now without them. She sat rigid in her seat, watching the little man at her side as he in turn watched Ray through the windscreen. Stella glanced at the street outside. Dark. No one out of doors.

When Ray walked up to the boarding house, Stella felt a movement from the nasty man. He had slid his arm around her again. Suddenly he wrapped his hand around her mouth. He placed his other hand on her knee.

She started struggling. When she tried to bite the hand on her mouth he moved his other hand to pin her down. 'Shut up,' he hissed. 'I wasn't doing anything. You keep still and I won't hurt you.'

She stopped struggling and tried to read his eyes. 'We'll make a bargain, dear,' he said. 'You be good and I'll be good. All right?'

She remained motionless, and he repeated, 'All right?'

Stella nodded. Ticky kept one hand lightly across her mouth and used his other to wind down the window. Ray was talking to somebody at the boarding house. They could not see who. Ray's voice could be faintly heard: 'Mr Scott, I think it was. I mean, he's my brother's friend. I think his name is Scott.'

A woman's voice, inaudible.

Ray said, 'I only know the bloke by sight. Quite tall, dark hair.'

'I don't think so,' the woman said. She moved forward, and Stella recognised her from last night. 'It must be another house.'

'No, it's definitely here. He pointed it out to me.'

'Here?'

'He's got a London accent, like me. You might have seen him with a little girl.'

'Girl?'

Stella willed the woman to remember.

'Yeah, about eight years old, with the same dark hair.'

'Well . . .' The landlady looked askance at Ray.

'Her name's Stella,' he said.

'Oh, Stella. Yes. Do you know her?'

'Yeah, pretty kid. Dark curly hair.'

'Not with a Mr Scott. There was Mr Woodman, but he left this morning.'

'Woodman—that could be it.'

'Woodman doesn't sound like Scott.'

'Left this morning? Yeah, Scott Woodman, that's it.'

'*Stanley Woodman*, I'm afraid. You've got the wrong man.'

'No, that's him.'

'Mr Woodman didn't have dark hair.'

'Well, I'd like to see him.'

'I told you, he left this morning. Will that be all?'

'It's urgent.'

'But he's gone.'

'I wanna see his room.'

'Will you kindly remove your foot? Mr Woodman left with his daughter this morning.'

'Daughter?'

'Stella. I thought you—Oh, good night, please go away.'

'Wait a minute. I'm sorry, missis, but Stella ain't his daughter. This is serious, see?'

'Look, whoever you are, you don't know the gentleman's name or even what he looks like. Mr Woodman is a respectable man who came to collect his daughter from school.'

'What school?'

'I have no idea. Will you kindly leave?'

'This Woodman—'

'Is someone else. He paid cash and left. Goodnight.'

'With his daughter, you say?'

'Good night.'

The woman stayed on her step to make sure that the man did leave. Some kind of detective perhaps. Though wouldn't he have said so? She watched him walk to a nearby car and climb in the driving seat. There seemed to be somebody in the back, though she couldn't—yes, there was somebody, perhaps a boy, he was leaning sideways. As the car drove off she made a note of its number.

Always a sensible precaution. She would write it down.

The car turned a couple of corners before it stopped. Ticky prodded Stella to sit up. Ray left the engine running and said, 'You little bitch.'

Stella blinked at him.

'Think it's clever, dragging us out here?'

She didn't answer. Ticky said, 'This was the right place, Ray—'

'Shut up.'

'The woman said so.'

'I said shut up.'

Ticky sighed. 'It's not the girl's fault if Woody's gone.'

'If you don't shut up I'll reach down your throat, pull out your tonsils. Yeah, Heywood was there. So was the girl. She was with him when he checked out.'

'Well, then.'

'So she knew he'd gone, you stupid pervert.'

Ticky paled. Ray continued: 'Now listen, girlie, I am not a patient man. Where's your uncle Scott?'

Stella mumbled, 'I don't know.'

'You were with him—right? When he checked out?'

She nodded.

'Where'd he take you then?'

She swallowed. 'Back to the fair.'

'Oh, fucking clever. You *knew* he wasn't out here. Brought us on a goosechase.'

She began to cry.

'I'll give you something to cry about.'

He raised his hand, but it was Ticky who reached her first. He grabbed her and pulled her head against his chest. She found herself inside his enormous overcoat again, by his dirty shirt. He said, 'Leave her—let me try.'

Stella tensed. Ticky lowered his mouth to her ear. 'Come to Ticky. I'll be your friend.'

She heard the big man shift suddenly in the front seat, but nothing happened. Ticky said, 'We must find your uncle, Stella. We don't want *you*.' She felt his hand stroking her hair. 'We don't want your Daddy neither—just your uncle. Now, I bet you're fond of uncle, but he's been naughty, Stella—the coppers want him. So do we. And we won't hurt him half as much as the police will—in fact, we'll help him. But we've got to get to him before the police do.'

He lifted her face and held it close to his own. His breath smelt terrible. 'Let's go and find him, eh? Then we'll take you home.'

They both sensed Ray leaning towards them. Quickly, Ticky said, 'I bet Daddy's worried about you, right? Shall we take you home?'

Ray leant across the back of his seat. 'You gonna tell us?'

'I—I can't.'

'You fucking mean?'

'I—I don't know—'

'You *do*! Where did he go?'

When she didn't answer, Ticky murmured, 'You'll have to tell us, Stella, or we'll punish you.'

'We'll punish her, all right. A roman candle.'

Every few seconds, Stella peered outside. The street was black and empty. Trapped in the car with two frightening men, she wanted to scream—to anyone—but there was no one there. Ray glared at her, and Ticky stroked her hair.

Ray turned away and put the car in gear. As they glided forwards, he said, 'Maybe she knows, maybe she don't. But I bet her Dad does.'

The landlady was speaking on the phone: 'It may be nothing but it seemed so odd. The man was obviously chasing my Mr Woodman. Yes. And that's another thing: he didn't call him Woodman, he called him 'Mr Scott'. Yes, I know, but—what? Yes, Scott, that's right. Then he said it might be Scott Woodman. He didn't know him, don't you see? I—what did *who* look like—Mr Woodman? Well, quite pleasant. No, I realise that. Let me see. Tall— quite tall—well-built—no, not fat. Um, gingery colour, I suppose, quite short. No. No, but do you know, the man who came for him thought the same thing—tried to insist, in fact—that he must have dark hair. But he didn't. What? Well, yes, I suppose so, but men don't do that, do they? Yes, I suppose he could have dyed it. Anyway, sergeant, I have the man's car number, I wrote it down. No, the one who called for him. Mr Scott's? You mean Woodman—yes, he had a *van*. Well, of course, I'll have the number in my book. Could you wait a moment?'

Collette touched his arm, then moved away. At first, as she continued putting up the covers, Jet stood distracted. Then he began to help. Silently they raised the wooden shutters to close her stall, lamp bulbs extinguished, each blank panel making the next appear forlorn. Above and below the plain boards ran the coloured lettering, *Lucky Rabbit Stall—Everybody Wins*, but without lighting the words looked flat. All the other stalls were closed or closing. No music played. Last stragglers wandered through the walkways in a lingering smell of fried onions.

When they had secured the last shutter Collette said, 'This is getting to be a habit.'

Jet tried to smile.

She said, 'Last night, I mean—wasn't she with her mother?'

'No.'

'Well, that's what I heard. She could be with her again.'

'No.'

'Hey, Jet.' Collette drifted closer. 'Every kid has a mother, you know. You can't pretend she doesn't exist. I suppose she must want Stella back?'

'I don't think so.'

'Then there isn't a problem.'

He couldn't think of anything safe to say. Collette was still close—he was aware of that—and pressing him. She asked, 'How about Stella—does she want to see her mother? It would be natural.'

'No, it isn't that. I'd better go.'

'Jet, you have to let people help you.'

He tried a reassuring smile which didn't come off. 'Oh, she'll turn up in the morning, like she did today.'

'She'd better not be late—we pull down at dawn.'

'Well . . .' Jet shrugged.

She paused. 'You're not quitting the fair?'

'No.'

'You had me worried.—I mean *wondering*, you had me wondering.'

He smiled at her. 'Look, I need to make a phone call, so . . .'

'I could use a walk, if it isn't private. I can wait outside.'

The midway was now almost deserted. They walked along it without touching. Jet said, 'You see, I had this trouble with some social workers, and I thought, well—'

'That they've taken her away?'

'They threatened to.'

'Then you'd better not tell them she's gone missing.'

'You see, I—I know somebody there. You said I should let people help.'

'Not social workers.'

They walked in silence till they reached the phone booth. At the door he said, 'If I just talk to her, she'll have to tell me. And if she doesn't—well, Stella can't be with them.'

Collette nodded. When Jet went inside the phone booth she walked a few yards away. She didn't want to hear. He had said, 'She. If I just talk to her'. Yet he had seemed awkward, as if holding something back. She. Of course, there were plenty of female social workers, but perhaps Jet really meant his wife. Who else would he phone at this time of night? Collette hunched her shoulders against the chill.

Jet emerged. 'I only got her answering machine—must be an office number.'

'D'you have another?'

He shook his head. 'Try to let people help, you get a machine.'

Collette said, 'Makes you feel lonelier than you did before.'

The car park was empty when Ray drove in, the fair sleeping, stalls and trailers lumps in the dark. When he switched off the engine he demanded the gag.

Ticky said, 'I'll do it.'

Ray watched him ferret in his overcoat pocket and pull out the handkerchief as if it were a trophy. Ticky said, 'It's easier for me 'cos I'm in the back.'

When he leant towards her the foul smell of his breath made Stella recoil. Quick as a snake he rammed the wad hard against her lips, and though she tried to keep her mouth shut some of the material slipped between her teeth. As she felt his scrabbling fingers she kept her teeth clamped shut. A flicker of annoyance flashed across his features. He kept his revolting face close to hers, and the stench from his mouth was like the bottom of a month-old dustbin. 'You mustn't try to stop me, Stella.'

His dirty thumbs pushed against her teeth. He was whispering: 'Open your mouth. Let me slip it in.'

She shook her head. His thumbs continued to press the gag into place and his fingers lay sticky on her cheeks. He was being gentle. 'Relax, I won't hurt you. Just squeeze it in and you'll be all right.'

She would not give way. He changed position, letting his hands crawl across her face—one pushing the gag, the other pinching her nose. She couldn't breathe, she began to struggle, but the little man had put his knee against her body and was leaning on her, pressing her against the car door. His open coat dropped round her like a tent. She wanted to scream but she would not open her mouth. Her lungs were bursting. Her throat heaved. Tears stabbed at her eyes.

When her mouth finally had to open, he crammed the gag into place. She squirmed on the seat. Ticky released her nose and she exhaled sharply, painfully, trying to breathe around the ball of cloth inside her mouth. But she could only snort awkwardly through her nose.

'There, there. That wasn't so bad.'

He remained astride her, sitting back now as if playing a game. He stroked her face. Instead of rolling off her he stooped forward to kiss her forehead. She heard Ray: 'Leave the little tyke alone.'

Ticky obeyed. Only when he slumped heavily beside her did Stella allow her eyes to briefly close. Her mouth was full of cotton.

Ray said, 'You'll enjoy the next bit.'

She glanced at him, startled, but he was sneering at Ticky: 'Right up your street.'

Ticky moaned.

Ray said, 'Syphon some petrol into the bottle.—Hey!' He smiled. 'Pity all the cars have gone—you'll have to use our own.'

Ticky looked as if he wanted to protest but Ray snarled, 'Go on.'

She saw the little man's sorrowful glance, and when he turned away she hoped for just a moment that he might disobey. But he didn't. All that happened was that, instead of opening the door straight away, Ticky rolled down the window, leant through and opened it from outside. He climbed out, and a cold draught of air whipped in. Stella grabbed at her own door handle but nothing budged.

'Child lock,' said Ray. He had turned to face her. 'You don't want to go out there, girl. Be out of the frying pan into the fire.'

As they approached his caravan Jet and Collette were silent. She was wondering if he would invite her in, but he seemed hardly aware of her. He had decided that Stella must be with Scott again; she couldn't be with the social workers—they would have left a note. Or an invoice. And she was not with Angie, because she would never go with her. So Stella had to be with Scott. He had probably come back to try again to persuade his brother to go to France. But why had she gone off with Scott? She had not even taken her teddy night-gown case. It was still on her bed, beneath her pillow. She had left suddenly, taking nothing with her.

The fair was silent, the damp night closed in on it like a shroud. From occasional trailers a light glimmered, but by now most people were asleep. Jet had left a nightlight in their caravan, a lamp in the window to draw Stella home.

Collette said, 'Perhaps she's back now.'

'I doubt it.'

Collette swallowed. 'If she's not here at daybreak, we can help you try to—'

'It doesn't matter. Thanks.'

She frowned at him. They had reached the caravan. He said, 'You were right earlier.—About us not staying with the fair. We're not coming on.'

He looked cold in the moist darkness, and she felt his chill. 'Oh, that's . . . Why not?'

'No way to bring up a kid.'

'She's happy here.'

Collette moved her hands awkwardly, wanting to touch him. 'Stella loves the fairground. She told me.'

'There are other reasons.'

He shuffled his feet on the cold ground as if waiting for her to go. She said, 'Isn't there anything we can do to help?'

He smiled, but was looking beyond her as if he still hoped to see Stella appear from the dark. 'We're better on our own.'

'Nobody is.'

She reached out to touch his arm but he jerked it from her. 'You've an early start, Collette. Better get some sleep.'

'And you?'

'Don't worry about me and Stella. We'll be all right.'

When Ticky climbed back into the car he first put the flagon of petrol down on the floor, then he changed his mind and put it into the pocket of his overcoat. The smell came with him. While syphoning fuel from the car he must have spilt some, but at least the oily smell helped mask his own odours.

Ray said, 'Wait here till I come back.'

'Right.'

'If I've got him with me, pull her out and move away from the car.'

'Yeah, like you said.'

Ray sighed. 'Don't get sarky with me, sunshine—I've worked with idiots before. And *wait* before you pour the juice on her.'

'So he sees it. I know.'

Ray turned away to remove the keys. 'I'll be what— three minutes? Maybe more, if there's someone with him.'

'The place looks quiet.'

'Yeah.' Ray glanced at him once as he opened the door. 'Don't do nothing stupid.'

'Such as what?'

Ray grimaced as he climbed out. Dirty little pervert.

He knew what Ticky wanted to do to the girl. The runt was small, but not that small, surely? It'd be like trying to ram it inside a beer bottle. Still, there were plenty like Ticky—little toads who had not grown up. It made him sick. Left to Ray, he'd hang nonces by their balls to dry in the air. Might even do that on the long drive home; it could break the journey.

But for now he had to find Jet Heywood. Probably at his caravan.

At least Ray had left the window open, because Ticky closed his immediately to stop the draught. Stella didn't mind the draught—to be trapped in a closed car with smelly Ticky would be disgusting. It could make her faint. Stella had read about ladies fainting. It sounded interesting, although she didn't know anyone who had ever fainted, and *she* certainly wouldn't—not with this man sitting by her side. With the cotton gag crammed in her mouth she was breathing through her nose, and that increased her sense of smell. Petrol and BO. He leant against her. 'You're such a pretty little thing. Don't you like that nasty gag?'

Stella shook her head.

'If I take it out, will your uncle Ticky get a kiss?'

She tried to squirm away but he drew her close inside his overcoat. She could hear his heart now—a floppy sound. It disgusted her.

Ticky murmured in her ear: 'I could look after you, Stella, and protect you from that Ray—because he is horrible.' Ticky chuckled. 'Not like me.'

She screwed her eyes shut, as if that might somehow blot out his smell. But it didn't. She felt as if she was trapped inside the folded wings of a giant bat, stifled, unable to move. Then the coat shifted and Ticky's fluttering hand ran down her body.

'Such a sweet one.'

When his hand dropped to her leg it rested warm and quivering on her thigh. Through her cotton dress she felt his sweat. Suddenly his damp hand began crawling along her leg. She grabbed at him, trying to lift his hand away, but his clammy fingers slid between her thighs and squeezed the flesh. She clenched, she tugged at him, trying in vain to shout through the gag. She used one hand to haul at him and with the other tried to tug the gag from her mouth. But he quickly yanked her hand away and forced her against the car seat.

'That's better. You'll enjoy it now. It'll be our little secret. No one will know.'

Though she was pulling at his intruding hand he had worked it higher between her thighs. She pushed her own hand in his way. He was still pinning her against the seat and he spoke across her muffled screams: 'Ssh, you'll like it. Everyone likes it, you'll soon see.'

Then he pulled his hand out from between her legs, grasped her blocking hand and tugged it free. He tried to force his knee between her unprotected thighs, pushing down on her, hurting, driving her legs apart. He held both her hands against the seat back and tried to kiss her swollen mouth. She threshed violently to avoid him. He laughed. When he swooped again, her head caught his cheek. He drew back.

'You little tiger. I'll have you now.'

He pulled one of Stella's hands down to the thick bunched cloth of his trousers. 'There now, touch it. This your first time?'

He held her hand there and stared in her face. 'See what it feels like? Go on, it's nice.'

She didn't move. Tentatively, he released her hand. 'Go on, squeeze it, I won't mind.'

Still she did not move. Ticky placed his free hand on

Stella's thigh at the place where his knee had forced her legs apart. 'That's the way, ' he said.

She seemed to relent. Raising her face as if to study Ticky for the first time, Stella relaxed, sighed, sank back—then slammed forward with her head. She cracked his nose. He screamed. As he sprang back she struggled free. He clutched her cardigan but she struck again. He recoiled in pain, and in that moment she was released. She jabbed for his eyes. Fingers like pencils. He screamed again. She wriggled between the front uprights and clambered across the front squab for the door. She felt him grab at her but the seat backs were in his way. As he tried to follow her she punched his nose. Her fist was small but his nose already flamed in agony. Involuntarily, he jerked away from her, jamming his head between the seats.

Stella pushed the door open, tumbled out and began to run.

At the far side of the car park, beyond the fence, Stella saw a policeman at the roadside checking cars. She hesitated, thought of running to him, but rushed the other way to the fair. Cops and social workers could not be trusted. They locked you up.

When Ticky stumbled out of the car he saw Stella running. He didn't see the cop, didn't see her hesitate; he only saw that she had pulled out the gag and thrown it away.

As she ran through the fair the stalls were wrapped in darkness. Behind them, trailers lay out of sight. It would be safer there, but darker, and she was frightened of the dark. Here on the midway was dark enough.

She heard Ticky running behind her—saw his overcoat flapping like a soldier's cape. She would have screamed but he was too close to her. There wasn't time—he was only yards away. Could she out-sprint him? Like goblin and fairy the two small figures ran between the fairground stalls. He was even closer. She could hear him pant. She too was panting—could not have screamed now if she had wanted—could only run, run, run between the shuttered booths. He would catch her soon—they were still too far from Daddy's caravan. She turned beside a stall, darted behind, shot across a pathway. Ahead of her stood the Diamonte trailer—but it was wrapped in darkness, all closed up. With Ticky hard on her heels, Stella dashed away from it, into the open doorway of the Haunted House.

THIRTY-FOUR

Ray Lyons knew the way. Silently he glided between the trailers on the far side. There were few lights, although someone's TV was playing a late-night film. Cautiously he approached Jet's caravan: with his daughter missing there was no telling what he might have done, who he might have told. Who he might have with him.

Ray waited by the next-door trailer, watching, listening for a warning sound. If he had been the waiting kind he would have stood there longer.

Tucked inside his windcheater was a .38 single-action Mauser—an uncomplicated machine, the kind he liked. Taking the revolver in his hand, Ray drifted to the caravan and placed his foot on the bottom step. The perforated metal did not creak. He moved to the second step. Before mounting the last one, Ray squinted at the door handle. There was nothing to show whether the door was locked, and Ray didn't know enough about Jet to make a guess. Some people would lock a door, some would not. Timid people, bashful types, always locked their doors, but Jet was a professional fighter. If that meant anything. Ray frowned at the handle and chewed his lip. If he grabbed at it but the door was locked he would give the game away, but if the door was unlocked he'd get inside. It was a risk.

There hadn't been a sound from inside or from anywhere close to him here outside. The breeze blew and something somewhere rattled on a wire, but there were no human noises. He stood on the last step and tapped on the door. From inside he heard Jet's voice. Placing his lips close to the crack, Ray said softly, 'Open up.'

'Who's that?'

'We found your daughter.'

Ray heard a chair scrape, a shuffled movement, saw the door handle begin to move—it had not been locked. But Jet didn't open it. 'Who are you?'

Ray shouldered the door and barged inside. Jet might have hit him but he saw the gun. Couldn't miss it—it was in his face. Ray watched him register the reality of it, saw him take his eyes off the gun to stare at *him*, waited till the slow punk recognised who he was. Then Ray asked, 'How's your head?'

Jet looked tired but he was still dressed. 'Have you got my daughter?'

Ray nodded. His next glance told him Jet was not alone. Ray started. That was when Jet might have jumped him—except for the pistol, which never flinched. Ray cursed his carelessness—as if it mattered. Jet's companion had no gun, and was the man that Ray was looking for. Scott Heywood.

The blackness was so intense she could have touched it— could have taken hold of it, as the heavy darkness had taken her. All her terror flooded back. A sour taste rose in her throat. Stella knew that she must not let the weakness paralyse her and deliver her to Ticky. She started to climb the wooden stairs. Which one was squishy? The seventh—she remembered that. When she reached the sixth she raised a foot tentatively in the darkness to reach beyond to the stair above. But she overstepped, felt a nothingness, stumbled forward and scraped her shin. Because she couldn't see, she used her hands to find her bearings. When she heaved herself on to the eighth step she clunked the seventh with her shoe. She paused, heard herself breathing.

Below, in the dim entrance-way she saw a movement. Ticky whispered, 'Stella?'

Motionless above him, the girl made out his shape. He would be peering up at her, feeling the surfaces. Though he must know that she was inside, he could not be certain whether the rickety stairs were the only route. He was listening. She tried not to breathe. Once he started after her she would have to move. Perhaps he would wait there . . .

Her eyes were becoming accustomed to the blackness. He appeared more clearly. Still waiting inside the entrance, the faint light from outside helped make him visible, but when he looked up he looked only into darkness. Stella tried to remember the layout of this fiendish sideshow. Last time, the electricity had been on, there had been a little daylight, there had been Doris. Now she had to concentrate—what was the layout? First, at the top of the stairs, the rocking floormat: when she stepped on the mat the floor would tilt as if it had given way. That whole landing was a trap, but it was unavoidable.

Below, Ticky moved. He tried the steps. He didn't know what lay ahead—a regular flight or not—so he moved heavily, feeling with his hands and making some noise. At each sound she inched away from him, climbing higher towards the top. He seemed unsure that she was there.

'Stella?'

He called it softly, questioningly. Stella stopped. She could hardly see him. Already, he was high enough on the stairs to have moved beyond the faint light from the entrance. She could no longer tell how fast he was climbing. She moved up another step. How much further was it to the top?

A thump. She heard Ticky curse the seventh step.

As he recovered, she reached the landing. The whole of this was dangerous, and yet—carefully she inched round the edge of the unstable floor, her back against the wall. There was a border around the loose section, and if she could stay on it . . .

Ticky was clambering higher. Faster.

Beside her was the door. If she pushed it open she would be inside. She had to remember about those corridors—three running parallel: one to the other side, along the back; then the central one; then the third away again along the front. No short cuts.

'I can hear you, Stella.'

She was absolutely still. No, he hadn't heard her—he was tricking. As he came closer up the stairs she could hear his breathing. Why wasn't *he* afraid of the dark? The dark. The smothering inky blackness was about to terrify her again. A whimper fluttered in her chest. In an attempt to stifle it, she bit her lower lip and screwed both eyes shut.

Ridiculous. She could see nothing anyway. Ticky bumped against the wall, closer to the top. Now she knew that she couldn't wait. She pushed the door and it made a creak.

'So that's where you are.'

She found herself in a darker void. Something slimy brushed against her face. She scuttled past. Beneath her foot the hydraulic pad set off its ghostly laugh, and she gasped aloud. Though she had heard it before, it now seemed louder. Different. As if . . .

Ticky came through the door. 'Are you frightened, Angel?'

Squatting on the floor she told herself that he might not see her, just as she could not see him. They both waited in the dark, listening for a sound. But Stella couldn't wait, not again. As she stood up, her shoe squeaked on the floor and he said, 'I heard that.'

She ran away.

Ticky had kept his hand on the door behind him. He had no fear of darkness but he knew that the inside of this dark interior would be a maze. Since the luscious child lived at the fair she must know her way around it— probably played in the House every day. Had probably lured him here deliberately. What was best to do? If he plunged inside after her he would soon be lost. Should he wait outside? No, she might stay in there all night.

Ticky eased back through the door, and the landing floor tilted beneath his feet.—Again, but it still caught him. When he lurched against the side, the bottle in his overcoat thumped the wooden wall. He cursed, felt to check that the thing hadn't broken, then ran down the flight of dodgy stairs, stumbling on the seventh, and emerged where he had first come in. This was the entrance. The exit was over there, also at the front. There were only two doors. Nothing at the back, he was sure of that. But he dared not wait for her. She would not come out.

Beside him at the entrance was the ticket cubicle— empty, naturally, and open to the air. Ticky peeped behind the counter and saw a black 30-amp fuse box, the handle down. The dark fairground was everywhere deserted. Dead of night. What would happen, he wondered, if he pulled the lever—would the House light up and help him find her? Or would there be music, waking everyone up? No, not at a Haunted House. No music. But there might be light. He needed light to find her.

Ticky reached down and pulled the switch.

As the internal lamps flickered into life the dim blues and

reds seemed unnaturally bright. Beside Stella's fingers glowed that stupid skull. But now that she was able to see she ran quickly along the gloomy corridor, its backlit panels showing her the way. She had to run; she knew who had switched on these lights. She knew why he had done it. At the end of the corridor, Stella swept aside the curtain of lacy spiders' webs, turned the corner—into a tableau. In front of her a desperate man jerked, his hand reached up, and with a rusty scrape the guillotine blade shuddered down. His head dropped, rolled to its basket, and the lights went out.

At first, when Ticky had turned the power on, nothing seemed to respond. Then across the front of the House, neon tubes flickered into lurid life. Ticky stared at them, then slammed the switch back down. The House returned to darkness. For a few seconds he heard a residual throbbing from its ventilation, then that stopped as well. Ticky moved inside the entrance. Not a bright idea. Another few seconds and he would have had fairground staff out of their caravans—but as it was, with just that one short burst . . .

He didn't linger. He had no time to wait for curious neighbours, and no time to play hide and seek with a stupid girl. He had to get hold of her quickly. By now, Ray Lyons should be marching her father back to the car park. Ticky ran up the stairs.

To hell with its tricks and traps—they couldn't hurt him. He stumbled again on the seventh step, lost his footing a third time at the top, but this time he plunged straight through the door in to the upstairs passageways. Spiders' webs and dangling leaves were no impediment. The ghostly cackle and hydraulic updraughts could be ignored. But it was truly dark. On the stairs had been a faint glimmer from below, but he was now in an unlit passageway. Not a spark of light. Not a sound. Ticky paused, strained his ears—caught a noise from behind the wall. Stella. She must have turned at the end of this into another corridor. He began to run. In this rear corridor, with the power off, the various devices did not work. Nothing would bar his way except the end of the passageway. He reached it sooner than he expected, crashed into the end wall, felt round the thin partition and entered the central corridor. It seemed even darker, if that was possible. He paused. The girl had been in here, might be here still, unless she had found some side alcove to hide in. And if she had, he might run straight past—if he couldn't see. He needed light.

He felt in a pocket for his box of matches, but before opening the carton he sniffed his fingers for any trace of petrol. Nothing there. Earlier he had spilt some on his coat, but it must have evaporated. So there was nothing to worry about. Ticky struck a match.

'People said you was dead,' Ray said calmly. 'Very soon you will be.'

He relaxed against the caravan door, though he did not look relaxed. Both brothers were silent under his gun and did not move. 'Got the money here?'

The punk boxer answered, 'Take a look.'

Ray pointed the gun at him. 'I got news for you, son—you're disposable. Keep your mouth shut.'

Jet shrugged. 'Shoot us, you'll never find the money.'

'I can afford to shoot one of you.'

He kept his gun on Jet but stared at the silent Scott—the bastard who had killed his brother. He would not survive the night. Scott knew where the money was, and he would spill it before he died—change his will, as it were, make Ray his heir. Up to now, all Scott had done was sit at the table as if his thoughts were elsewhere.

While Ray had waited outside, Scott had not spoken. He had not spoken since Ray came in. Ray said, 'OK, Woody, let me lay it out: show us where the money is, you walk away. You won't be rich but you won't be dead either.' He paused. 'Don't tell us, and you will be.'

It was quite a long speech by Ray's standards and though he was pleased with it, Scott still did not react. Jet said, 'Tell "us"—who's us?'

Ray's eyes flickered across him. 'We're the ones who've got your daughter.'

Stella found herself against a door—but which one was it—did it have the trick step or the water jet? She eased it open and knelt quickly to feel along the rubber floor. Level. This must be the water jet. As she crept through on hands and knees, water squirted above her head. She stood up and turned carefully into the final front corridor. Here it was not absolutely dark. Halfway along was the only window in the House—though it let in little light. She paused. Wasn't there a trick beside that window? There must be, though she couldn't remember which trick it was. It probably wouldn't work without electricity.

What was that?

She heard the ghost laugh again. Ticky must have set it off. Then she heard him crashing along the central corridor, not bothering what was in his way. She began to run. Sponge fingers brushed her face—then the floor tilted and she toppled against the window.

In the dark walkway below, two men were walking. They glanced up at the Haunted House and she recognised them. She put her face against the murky window—it wasn't glass—some kind of plastic—and knocked, but they didn't hear. Should she call? No. Ticky was blundering nearer. She mustn't let him know where she was.

Two men knock on Doris's door, and her voice answers them from bed.
—Had she been at the House?
—No.
—Had the lights been on?
—No.
—They weren't on now.
—That was all right then, wasn't it?

'I tell you what,' Ray declares. 'You both know where the money is, so if I shoot one of you I can still find out.' He points the gun at Jet. 'What d'you think?'
'We're not talking.'
'Then you better come and see your daughter—say good-bye to her.'

Ticky hears the girl stumbling down the stairs. As he rounds the corner from the middle corridor, a squirt of water wets his face. He wipes his eye and as if by doing so, finds that he can see. Halfway along this front corridor is a dirty window, and its dim light shows the way. He dashes forward, trips by the window, curses and runs on. When he leaves the corridor he treads in something soft—a water pit, two inches deep. Very funny, ha, ha, ha. Putting his hands out to feel the walls, Ticky runs downstairs. Now it has become dark again—darker than before. When he reaches the bottom it is like the darkest, deepest hole in the world. He can't find the door in to the ground floor. He will have to strike another match.

It is a tricky one, Ray knows—he could shoot the wrong man first. Better play another card.

'You know something?' he asks Jet. 'Your little daughter's *burning* for you to talk. Didn't I tell you? We poured petrol on her.'

Jet is watching him. Even his brother lifts his head. Ray smiles. 'I'd get sensible, if I was you. And I wouldn't try nothing. 'Cos if you die, who'll save your daughter?'

On the ground floor are two wide sections. The tricks and tableaux here are more elaborate, though for the moment, each is unlit and silent. Stella tries to remember the ground floor layout—a Victorian graveyard, a witch's feast, a body on a table, the vampire bats. All of these lie invisible in the dark and will form a maze of obstacles to bar her way. But they also provide hiding places—such as the crevice in which she now squats, absolutely still.

First she hears, then worse, she *sees* the little man. He has lit a match to creep inside. He holds it above his head, and it illuminates both his face and the grotesque furniture he stands beside. The match goes out.

She can hear Ticky working his way along. For the next few steps he won't need a match, but by the time he reaches her, he'll probably have struck the next. In this crowded chamber Ticky will work his way methodically, match after match. It won't be enough that she stays silent, she must be completely out of sight. The crevice that conceals her is behind a mechanical tableau—lifeless, without power—a baby tumbling from its pram. The pram itself is large, unwieldy, and Stella hides in the dust-filled gap behind. She huddles into it, trying to make herself disappear.

A sudden movement. Something stirring in the dark, something brushing against her legs. It begins to purr. After one heart-stopping moment she realises that it is the black cat Merlin. She drops her hand down, tries to shush it, but another sound comes now—Ticky's voice.

'Oh, there you are.'

Ray can hear it too—the faint sound of police sirens coming their way. More than one. He frowns—sees Woody smirking—so he has to say something. 'Coincidence.'

'Don't bet on it.'

This is Jet. He isn't smirking—he stands facing Ray, leaning towards him. Balanced. He has had too much time. Usually Ray doesn't go in for talking—just smacks 'em early, gets it done. As one of the sirens starts winding down, Ray cocks his pistol.

'You will never know.'

He hears a chair scrape. It's the muted Scott. He leaps at Ray as he fires, and the two men crash to the floor. Ray grips his .38 and fires again.

Now the boxer is down there with them, has his knee against Ray's face. One of the bastards is pulling at his gun. Ray tussles. His vision clears. Jet Heywood is kneeling on him, holding his arm, pounding his face. Ray punches back. Jet hits him again. Ray slams his free hand against Jet's face and pushes upward. His left arm is inside Jet's to deflect his blows. Ray heaves. Jet shifts. A sudden movement releases him, and Ray rolls upright, smacking his gun hand towards Jet's head. Though it hits his neck, the man still wilts. But as Ray tries to roll away, both the Heywoods are lying across him. Ray has the gun and he swings it at Jet.

Who uppercuts him. Ray slumps back heavily against the bed.

Like a Halloween lantern, Ticky looms above the child. He grins eagerly in the matchlight.

'Hello, my angel.'

He reaches down to her and she cowers away. He snatches her arm. The flame flickers. Its last trembling light shows that beyond the mechanical pram Stella has nowhere to go. She is trapped in a box, and when blackness returns, Ticky knows that he can relax and take his time. He strikes another and drops the carton. As the light flares, Stella tries to wriggle further behind the pram, but there is no room. Ticky stretches for her, leans against the pram, clutches her shoulder. She will not budge. He pulls harder, but the wretched pram blocks his way. He tries again.

He says, 'You're a real tease.'

Ticky worms himself even closer. There is little room. He is panting, sweating, unaware of how much he smells. He leans against her.

'This is nice.'

As the match dies he watches her face. In its spluttering light they are crouched beside the pram like antique dolls—she kneeling, he stooped above. Darkness again.

The only sound is Ticky's breathing.—Except . . . There is another sound, from outside: sirens, faint in the distance—police sirens. Ticky pauses. No, there must have been an accident somewhere. They're not coming here. He can forget about outside. Concentrate on the girl. Though he cannot see her, he puts out his hand to feel her curly hair, her soft trembling face. He fondles her cardigan.

'We could have a lovely time.'

In a moment he will let his hand drop to her lap, but for now in the darkness he wants only to stroke her tender young face. Silk-soft. It makes him ache. His need for the girl is not sordid. People don't understand. His adoration of her—yes, adoration—isn't sick but pure. Purer than the dirty fantasies of lovesick boys. Ticky's fingers trace her jawline.

'Stop it. Go away.'

Ticky slowly exhales. He reaches into the pocket of his

trailing overcoat, and then remembers—fumbles on the floor for the rattling matchbox. When he picks it up his fingers shake, as if he were himself a child. Carefully, he strikes one. Light flares. The black cat jumps. A blur of blackness—sharp thorn needles in his face. He leaps up—jolts the pram—a lever clicks—the pram tips. Ticky crashes over, falls awkwardly, and in the flickering light he sees a baby leaping at him. *A baby*? Sudden dampness. Ticky gasps. As the burning match flutters downward he realises that in his overcoat pocket the petrol bottle has shattered.

The match drops in his lap.

Jet cannot staunch the blood. His brother's chest melts into red. Though Jet has pulled a sheet from the bed, though he has pressed it against the wound, Scott's blood oozes through the linen.

If Scott is bleeding he cannot be dead.

Jet leans to his brother's face, speaks to him, tries to detect a sign of breath. He wants to shake him, wake him up.

In the chill silence, he is barely aware that the sirens have stopped. Perhaps they have gone on to somewhere else.

Beside his brother on the floor the other man is stirring. Jet knows that he should deal with him, but he hasn't the energy. He watches Scott. Did his head move? Did his position change? He ought to replace the soiled sheet, sodden with blood, but it has become part of his brother's flesh.

The other man recovers. In dream-like slow motion he reaches for the pistol lying on the floor. He doesn't get to it. Before his fingers can touch the handle Jet has kicked it aside, thumped him on the jaw. But it is a weary blow—on the big man it acts merely as a tonic. He grabs

Jet's legs to bring him down. Jet tries to hold on to him but the man slithers to the door and stumbles outside.

At the bottom step Jet catches up with him. They fall in the mud. The man is big but is no match for the boxer. Jet pins him to the ground. Someone shouts. They both ignore it. Each wants revenge for his brother's death. Jet clasps his fingers round Ray's neck, will strangle him, take life for life—

Someone is hauling at his arm. Shouting in his face. Lee Leonard is shouting. Shouting what?

'Get off him, man—you're killing him!'

'My brother—he killed—'

Jet's words make no sense.

'Get away from him.'

But Jet will not release Ray Lyons. Still pinning the big man to the muddy ground, Jet punches, misses, is pulled to his feet, cannot free himself from Lee's embrace.

'Jet! Stop it, man. Look over there.'

Jet concentrates on Ray. The man is rolling across the ground, trying to rise, heavy on his knees. The man is bleeding, filthy—but alive. Jet struggles. Lee grips him tight. Ray kneels in the mud, staring at the small crowd gathered before them. Fairground workers cluster in the darkness. In front of these are four policemen. Each kneels on his knee. Each holds a gun. Each aims at Jet.

'Put your hands up.'

Another policeman emerges from the crowd. Though he wears uniform he carries no gun. He repeats his words.

Jet stares. Lee nudges him. Jet raises his hands.

'And you,' the policeman says.

After a slight pause, Lee lifts his own hands. Ray Lyons starts to crawl away. When the policeman shouts again, Ray glances back.

'Yes, you.'

Ray waits on hands and knees, assessing the gaps between the trailers.

'Over here, sir, please. Come out of the way.' He is addressing Ray as an innocent, caught by the villains.

There is a stirring in the small crowd. Something has distracted them. Shouting in the distance. People move. Jet hears, 'Fire!' Distant shouting. 'Fire!' once again.

Lee is watching the policemen kneeling with their guns, and whispers, 'Don't tell the buggers to fire!'

As the crowd begins to break away, Jet and Lee remain where they are, their hands raised. From behind the trailers they see a flickering glow, hear crackling flames. More shouting. One of the crouched policemen glances round. Everyone can smell the smoke now. Above trailer roofs, the orange glow is flecked with red. A sudden fountain of sparks spurts into the air.

From the dissolving crowd, through the four kneeling policemen, a dark-haired child runs across damp grass. 'Daddy!' she calls and Jet drops his hands.

THIRTY-FIVE

The man found inside the Haunted House was called Mark Tickell. His burns were third degree and the hospital thought it unlikely he would live. Ray Lyons was in custody, Scott Heywood dead. The police had spent an extraordinary amount of time with Scott Heywood's van, parked outside the fair. They had cleared other cars from the street and evacuated twenty houses. Though the child had told them the money was inside the van, they could not discount the possibility of a boobytrap. They ordered a detector robot from the military base at Plymouth.

In the first grey light of dawn the little machine trundled down the street, raised a crane-like proboscis and sniffed the van. Like a starling deciding whether to peck a crust, the robot pottered cautiously around the vehicle. Occasionally it leant forward to tap with its long beak.

Inside the fairground, showmen began the pull-down. They had had little sleep. Jet Heywood took Stella with him to help strike the boxing booth. He felt empty, as mechanical in his actions as that robot in the street. After two hours of questioning in the small hours, the police had conceded that Jet had little to tell them—was not involved, they said. Though he felt a damn sight more involved than they were.

Once the booth was dismantled and on its lorry, he and Stella walked to the charred carcass of the Haunted

House, where Doris stood gazing at its remains. 'I'll have to leave it here,' she said. 'Like it's been cremated.'

'The local council won't be pleased.'

'No choice, my love. Insurance, you see. They'll have to inspect it—satisfy themselves that it's a write-off.'

'Not much doubt.'

He stared dully at the blackened bones of it. He felt he had a hangover coming, but it hadn't started yet.

Doris smiled at Stella. 'And how are *you*, my dove?'

'I'm sorry about the fire, Mrs Diamonte.'

'It wasn't *your* fault, my dove, were it? Anyway, I'll make a pretty packet on the insurance, I shouldn't wonder. At least they can't say I burnt it down myself!'

Jet asked, 'Will you buy another?'

'No, take the cash, I think.'

'Will you give up travelling?'

'Da-ad!'

Doris smiled. 'Never. I might turn me hand to doing the Hokibens, 'cos I'm a dab hand at fortune-telling, you know.'

'Should've told me before. Could have saved me a lot of grief.'

When they reached their caravan, they found Collette inside washing the floor. 'I'm afraid you've lost your carpet.'

Jet seemed embarrassed. 'You shouldn't be doing this.'

'The police left it in such a mess. It's not right you have to clear it up.'

She was not explicit about the kind of mess the police had left, or what it was that had ruined his small carpet. 'Anyway, I've done it now. All clean.'

She smiled, and the three of them stood awkwardly, as if inspecting her work. 'Your friend Terry offered to help but I told him to sod off. Anything you need?'

'Just sleep. But thanks. Thanks a lot.'

'Well, we've been through that,' she said. 'How are you, Stella, love?'

'All right, thanks. Can I keep that book for a few more days?'

'Sure. Give it me in Brixham.'

Collette glanced at him, then left the caravan. Jet frowned at Stella: 'What book?'

'Oh, she lends me books. She has a box full.'

Jet nodded, studying his daughter, his mind numb. Time passed. He didn't know how long. When he went to the doorway and gazed across the fairground, Collette had disappeared. The Big Wheel was down, and beyond the trailers lay an open space. Nearby, from beneath someone's caravan, came Merlin, the Diamonte cat. Stella had not explained about the cat—there were some things she would not discuss—and Jet saw it simply as a cat. He admired the way it wandered unconcernedly through the collapsing fairground. A free spirit. Jet knew that this might be the last time he would see the fair, but he didn't want to think about it. This had been his home.

Back inside the caravan, sitting at their little table, he smiled at his daughter—who asked, 'Isn't it time we hitched up to be off?'

Jet took a breath. 'I was thinking we'd let them go without us.'

'Why?' She asked it quietly.

'This is no life for a little—for you, Stella. I'm out working all the time, not a proper father.'

He made eye contact, but she did not react. He said, 'I'm too old to box—and, well, Terry's fit now, so I'll earn even less. I don't even get a nobbins, sweeping floors. Maybe we'll go back to London. I could talk to Floyd Carter—he's got a gym.'

'Did you talk to Joe?'

'Not yet.'

'I thought you said you might take over from him?'

'He doesn't want to retire.'

'He does.'

'I can't afford it.'

'Yes, you can.'

He walked over and sat beside her on the bed. Inside the caravan it was as quiet and intimate as at dead of night. He took her hand. 'Little girls believe their daddies can do anything. I wish they could. But your Daddy can't fight any more.'

She was silent for several moments. 'What would you *like* to do?'

'Like?'

'Yes, like. You keep saying what you can't do, but what would you *like* to do—if you could do anything?'

He chuckled. 'Anything!'

Stella squeezed his hand.

Jet said, 'I'd like to stay with the fair, of course, but . . . there are the two of us.'

'I like it here.'

'Me too. Still—'

He tried to rise but she would not release him. 'Wait, Dad. Can you keep a secret?'

She looked so serious that it made him laugh. He pulled her close to him and continued to laugh as if she had cracked a priceless joke. It was a release. He needed it.

Stella had taken out her teddy night-gown case. 'When Uncle Scott made the parcel of money to send to Auntie—'

She stopped. Jet was staring at it as if he had suddenly realised. Stella unzipped the back and removed the night-dress, neatly folded. Then she took a plastic bag containing a small pack of well-used banknotes. 'He gave me ten of these bags,' she said. 'Twenty thousand pounds—in case something happened.'

Jet sat very still. She said, 'We don't have to give it back.'

'Why not?'

'They don't know it's missing. No one knows how much was inside the van—not after he'd had it for so long. That's what he said.'

'Christ.' Jet shook his head.

'He tried to give me more, but I wouldn't take it.'

'Why not?'

'Because Teddy would have been too fat.'

The sun shone weakly on his face and he looked up at it, aware for the first time that it was shining. He hadn't noticed it, just as he hadn't noticed the pull-down taking place around him. Already he was thinking like a capitalist: if he put the whole twenty thousand up to buy Joe's boxing booth, he'd have no money left for them to live on. He and Stella would have to stay in the caravan, and she would never have new clothes. The money belonged to Stella anyway, if it belonged to anyone. It wasn't right for him to "invest" it on the child's behalf.

Whether twenty thousand would be enough to buy the boxing booth he didn't know, but maybe Joe would let him buy into a partnership for half of it. Perhaps he could invest ten thousand and work alongside Joe for a couple more years while the old man gradually withdrew. That would make better sense for both of them.

If he kept the money.

Jet was outside, alone in what had been the midway. All the stalls were down, mostly loaded onto trailers, and the muddy field looked like the aftermath of a battle—a sense of weary quiet and moving on. There was a smell of breakfast before they hit the road.

He couldn't keep the cash.

On balance, Scott had probably been right when he

told Stella no one would miss the money, and since the cops had already scoured through Jet's caravan, they would not be back.—Though they had been looking for blood, not for missing money. If he became suddenly flush again, they might notice that.

He'd have to give it back.

Jet turned at the exit to the car park and looked at the the disassembled fair. The soft morning light had lain a kind of peace over the site, as if the shrunken booths had snuggled under their blankets and gone back to sleep. He continued thinking about the money. If he put ten thousand into the business and matched that ten with another ten—borrowed, say, from someone pound for pound, the booth as collateral—and if he kept ten thousand back to supplement his wages, that should be enough to keep him going for another year and a half. And after that? Jet chuckled—it would make a change to think beyond the next *day* and a half. Strange how a few thousand pounds could change the way he looked at life. Maybe it began to explain the change that had occurred in Scott. Though it had done *him* no good.

Jet shivered slightly, though the morning was not cold. Acquisition of money brought an odd maturity. It was like that day when he was a kid, the first time he had ever sipped a taste of beer—he'd expected the first forbidden mouthful to reveal a new and exciting experience, but it had tasted sour and flat. He'd been disappointed.

Pausing beside the phone kiosk, Jet watched a long lorry snaking from the fairground. How would the police react, he wondered, to his confessing he had another twenty grand? Would they applaud his honesty or think he was a fool? Would the bank decide he deserved a small reward?

As he lifted the receiver to make the call, the thought struck him that it was the bank, in fact, that he should be phoning—to ask them whether, in the circumstances, they might lend him a few thousand pounds. It was a perfectly sound business proposition: he would put ten thousand in with Joe, plus however much more he borrowed to make his stake more reasonable, and keep a few thousand back to look after Stella through the coming year. With his sudden wealth, then, the first thing he had to do was to borrow more.

Still, money always attracted money, as he had found in the days when he had had plenty of it. With twenty thousand of his own now he should be good for a few thousand more—if he asked the right person.

He keyed in the number.

The showman's lorry trundling noisily past the phone kiosk made it hard for him to hear. He pressed the receiver close against his cheek and said, 'My name's Jet Heywood. Can I speak to Mr Gottfleisch?'

He wondered if Gottfleisch would remember him.